— BOOK 1 —

TARAN EMPIRE SAGA

EMPIRE REBORN

A K DUBOFF

Published by Dawnrunner Press
Cover by Robert Rajszczak

ISBN-10: 1954344198
ISBN-13: 978-1954344198
Copyright Registration Number: TXu002248345

0 9 8 7 6 5 4 3

Produced in the United States of America

TABLE OF CONTENTS

THE CADICLE UNIVERSE

Tarans are the predominant race in the Cadicle Universe; humans are a Taran genetic offshoot. Most of the Taran sphere falls within the purview of the Taran Empire, governed from the planet Tararia by a council of High Dynasty families. Earth is one of several rogue colonies on the outskirts of the Empire, separated so long ago that they have forgotten their Taran ancestry.

The Tararian Guard is the primary military force for the Taran Empire. Its counterpart, the Tararian Selective Service, includes a specialty branch with Agents gifted in telekinetic and telepathic abilities. The TSS is headquartered at a base inside Earth's moon, and its iconic Agents are known in Earth lore as the mysterious 'men in black'.

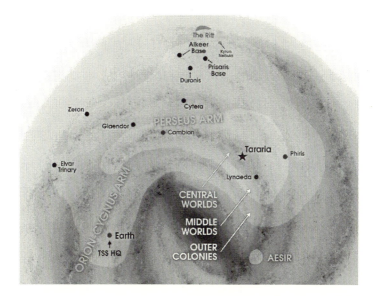

CHAPTER 1

JASON SIETINEN SPED through the training course in his fighter with practiced precision, using the neural link to operate the spacecraft as an extension of himself. He couldn't help grinning as the G-forces pressed him against the cushioned, ergonomic seat; the sophisticated environmental systems dampened the true force from the maneuvers but left just enough sensation for him to connect with the craft. He relished the heaviness of his limbs as he took in the dazzling starscape around him.

Stars, I've missed this! Volunteering as a space combat instructor had been a stroke of genius to get him flying again without shirking his growing leadership responsibilities.

With an exhilarated tingle in his chest, like he always got from a good flight, he looped the craft back around to his students who'd been observing the demonstration run.

Jason was about to address the young pilots when a cold chill suddenly ran through him. His vision narrowed and the jovial chatter on the comms faded to the background as a presence intruded at the edge of his consciousness.

He froze, palms sweating and pulse racing, despite his training. He'd experienced the same foreboding sensation only once, years before, though he'd never been sure if it had been real—a prophesy or a waking nightmare. *No, we beat them. They're gone. This can't be right.*

The darkness pressed against his mind, closing in around him. Such immense power, sinister and all-consuming. Memories of past visions rushed back and merged with his present perception. His surroundings melted away, leaving only his heartbeat pounding in his ears and ragged breath. He was alone in the void, trapped by the crushing force. Something was coming…

And then it vanished.

Jason drew a deep breath of the crisp, oxygen-rich air to steady himself. His mouth was dry and skin itched. He made a conscious effort to slow his racing pulse. *What in the stars was that?*

His students were still joking with each other on the comms, oblivious to what he'd felt. He wanted to tell himself it was just a bizarre manifestation of stress, but he'd learned to trust his instincts more than that.

"CACI," he privately addressed the onboard AI, "are you picking up any unusual readings?"

"Nominal," the synthetic female voice replied. Sensor data scrolled across the head-up display on the windshield, casting a soft red and blue glow inside the cockpit.

He reviewed the information on the HUD, seeing nothing of note. "What about any recently filed incident reports?"

"Specify parameters."

Truthfully, Jason didn't know what he was asking. He glanced at his waiting students. If there wasn't immediate danger in the vicinity, then anything else could wait. This was his students' first venture into real fighters, and he wanted it to be a good experience for them.

"Disregard." He tried to suppress the uneasy feeling and return his attention to the lesson at hand. "So, *that's* how it's done. Easy, right?" Jason said in a more upbeat tone than he felt, bringing his fighter alongside the row of ten waiting vessels.

"This is nothing like the sims," muttered Bret Hamlin, one of the Initiates. It was unclear if he'd meant to broadcast the sentiment on an open channel, but Jason wasn't about to let it slip by.

"In fact, it's *exactly* like the flight simulators. Though it might not look it while you're parked out here watching me do all the work, give yourself a chance to get a feel for the controls. You'll be surprised." The sleek fighters, styled with tapered wings and rear fins suited for both spaceflight and in-atmosphere combat, were an ideal practice craft to help the pilots hone their skills.

"I think it's pretty spot on so far," Alisha Delroe chimed in, always the suck-up. Her teacher-crush had been obvious to Jason from day one, but he'd made a point to not encourage her.

"Sampsen, you're up. Just a maneuvering run, no targets. Don't be a showoff," Jason instructed.

Thankfully, Wes Sampsen did as he was told. His flight lines were loose and his reactions slow, but it was a decent initial run. Jason would rather see a student be too cautious out of the gate than try to act like a hotshot. Confidence could be built; breaking down cockiness was a lot harder.

"Nice work," Jason complimented the pilot trainee. "Delroe, go for it."

"*Aye*, sir," Alisha acknowledged with far more sultriness

than was warranted.

Jason's stomach lurched. With his athletic build, chestnut hair, and striking bioluminescent teal eyes, he was used to getting that kind of attention, but it still made him uncomfortable. While his popularity had been well and good growing up on Earth, now that he was an active participant in the galaxy-spanning Taran Empire, he could never be sure if it was *him* or his family name that people were interested in. The Sietinen Dynasty was tantamount to royalty, but Jason couldn't care less about their wealth and influence—that was his twin sister's domain. She played princess while he got to be the consummate soldier and leave the politicking to the people who actually cared.

Alisha broke her fighter from the lineup and entered the training course.

"Watch your lines," Jason called to Alisha over the comms as she cut a little too close to one of the buoys that defined the flight lanes.

The course was designed to help students get comfortable maneuvering out in the black versus inside flight simulators. Only time in a genuine spacecraft revealed the psychological impact of facing an immense expanse where the nearest celestial body was a distant speck.

"Easy, Delroe!" Jason warned again as Alisha made another dangerous turn.

Young trainees like her were all too common—trying to prove they were the next superstar. The Tararian Selective Service's training program was effective at reining in those reckless impulses, but it took years to mold someone into a TSS Agent who would be valuable to society. Early on, emerging telekinetic and telepathic abilities had a way of getting in teenagers' heads. They felt invincible. Jason knew, in retrospect, he'd suffered from the same affliction at their age. Now, at twenty-six and a graduated Agent, he had sufficient life experience to recognize when others were acting stupid even when he didn't always make the wisest decisions himself.

Alisha still hadn't throttled down. She cut another turn too tightly, barely maintaining control of her craft. Jason's heart rate accelerated as he watched her start to drift.

"That's enough, Delroe." He reached out telekinetically to slow her craft, an electric tingle running over his skin with the use of his Gifts. Not every Agent would be able to halt a racing fighter, but it was as easy as closing a door for Jason.

"Sir, I—" she started to protest as he dragged her fighter away from the course.

"Bring it in," he ordered Alisha in a firm tone, releasing the craft back to her control. "I told you to take it easy. We're not trying to set any records today."

Her comm cut out at the start of an aggravated sigh.

There's one in every group. Jason shook his head. Not everyone was a natural, as much as they wanted to be. It sucked, but that was life.

The students began chatting amongst themselves about what had happened. When he noticed the comments were about taking it slow and getting a feel for their craft, he let the discussion continue while he called up the next student.

The remaining trainees each completed a practice run. A few would need more hands-on coaching, but he was confident he could make decent pilots out of every one of them.

"All right, time to head back," he told the group when the last trainee had finished. His stomach was still knotted from the bizarre vision, and he was eager to get home to process the experience.

Jason activated the automated navigation control for a

group jump from the training course in the void between Jupiter and Saturn back to TSS Headquarters. The pre-programmed protocol allowed close proximity subspace transit to the space dock on the far side of Earth's moon, out of sight from prying eyes. With the recent rise in space traffic during Earth's mid-21st century, it was becoming more difficult to keep the base's presence secret, even with stealth shielding. Though it wasn't Jason's direct concern, he knew that a TSS team worked around the clock to keep the Taran Empire's existence hidden, through various technological, political, and private intervention means. A waste of resources, as far as he was concerned.

Blue-green light swirled around his vessel as the spatial distortion generated by the jump drive allowed the craft to slip into subspace. The hop to Headquarters was so short that he was only fully immersed in the ethereal light for the blink of an eye. As his fighter dropped back into normal space, the distortion dissipated like fog on a warm morning.

Before him was the impressive TSS spaceport, fixed via a gravity anchor to the far side of the moon from Earth. From a distance, the glow of the station's illuminated branches would merely be a faint point of light in the dark. But, up close, the dome-roofed concourses and central hub of the sprawling structure were an impressive sight to behold. Windows between the sculptured metal framework shone with a pearlescent finish, reflecting the onboard lights of the approaching ships. His heart swelled each time he saw it— originally, from the excitement of stepping into a futuristic society relative to Earth, where he'd spent the first sixteen years of his life; now, it was the welcome sight of home.

The team docked near the station's core on a short concourse dedicated to berthing the fighters used for training.

Jason shut down his own craft and then watched the remote feed of each student going through the power-down process to make sure it was safe to disembark. All reports came up blue for 'good'.

"Great work today." Jason removed his flight helmet and got out from his craft.

His students met him on the broad concourse next to one of the curved windows overlooking the moon below. They formed a semicircle around him; their light-blue flight suits, indicating their Initiate rank, contrasted his Agent black.

"So, having now been out in the real thing, how does it compare to the sims?" he asked.

A cacophony of simultaneous replies ranged from "Amazing!" to "Terrifying".

He smiled at them. "Looking forward to getting back out there?"

"Stars, yes!" they said practically in unison.

"Good. I want to clean up a couple of techniques before we go out again, but I think we can target another flight next week."

There were grins all around.

Jason escorted them to an automated transport shuttle leading to the surface port at the bottom of a crater. The three-pronged port converged in a semi-circular lobby with a bank of elevators along the curved back wall. It was the singular way to get into the secure underground base.

They filed into an elevator car, and the doors slid closed; a pulsing white light gave the only indication of downward movement as the elevator descended toward the eleven-ringed base positioned within a containment shell deep inside the moon.

The elevator stopped at Level 2, the section dedicated to

the Primus Division, the classification for the most powerful Agents and promising trainees. Different floors within the ring held a mixture of student housing, Agent quarters, common areas, and offices. It was a fully functioning city, filled with the best and brightest. Most days, Jason couldn't imagine being anywhere else.

"See you in class. Have a good afternoon." He was anxious to get to his quarters so he could reflect on the strange experience with the dark presence. *Is it worth saying something to Dad?*

"Sir, may I have a minute?" Alisha asked from behind him before he'd gone two steps.

Jason schooled his expression before turning to face her. "Of course." He tucked his flight helmet under his arm.

Alisha's helmet dangled from its chin strap in one hand while her other arm crossed over her stomach. The brows above her large, taupe eyes were drawn together with frustration she couldn't quite mask. At nineteen and in the Initiate stage of the TSS Agent training protocol, she was caught between newcomer and higher-skilled Junior Agent. It was a particularly frustrating time for students while they waited for the full extent of their Gifts to emerge. Jason's own telepathic and telekinetic abilities had developed quickly, but he'd watched many of his friends play the agonizing waiting game as their peers started to pass them by.

She waited for the other students to get beyond earshot down the hallway before continuing. "I wanted to ask about earlier. What, exactly, did I do wrong, sir?"

He raised an eyebrow. "You can't tell me?"

She frowned. "I was trying to be efficient with my trajectory. Look one target ahead."

"You were cutting within meters of the buoys. It wasn't

safe."

"I knew I had the clearance."

"You were in an unfamiliar craft," he reminded her.

"Sir, you said yourself that they handle just like the simulators. I've logged hundreds of hours in those."

She had him there. He took a measured breath. "I'll grant you that. However, there's a difference between efficiency and being needlessly reckless. Generally speaking, you *never* have to get that close, even if you have the skill to do so. You have to find the balance between what will accomplish your objective and making sure you and your craft get home intact."

Alisha nodded and looked down. "I understand. I'm sorry, sir."

She still seemed annoyed, but Jason appreciated her willingness to concede. He bent his head to catch her gaze. "Next time when I say to take it easy, don't keep pushing it, okay?"

"Yes, sir."

Jason gave her a supportive smile. "You have the fundamentals down. I'm looking forward to seeing what you can do."

Her face lit up. "Thank you, sir."

Jason resumed the walk to his quarters. With soft copper and deep red hues complementing the wood paneling and gray carpet, the residential halls felt like a cozy home rather than a military installation. After ten years with the TSS, living in the underground base seemed as normal as his childhood on Earth. He did miss being able to go into the countryside—and the rain, oddly—but his assignments to various planets offered a suitable substitute.

He was almost to his door when he spotted Gil, one of his former roommates and fellow Primus Elite, heading his way.

"Hey, what's up?" Jason asked.

Gil rubbed the edge of his overcoat between his thumb and forefinger, a nervous tick Jason had observed many times over the years. "What do you know about the attack?"

Jason's thoughts flashed to the dark presence he'd sensed during the flight lesson. "What happened?"

"I was hoping you knew. All I heard was a ship went missing, and they just found a lone survivor."

That didn't sound related to his recent experience. "Who'd you hear that from?"

"A friend out on remote assignment," Gil replied with a shrug. "I thought your parents may have said something."

Jason sighed inwardly. "Contrary to popular belief, I rarely get information before anyone else."

Gil cracked a smile. "Sure, downplay it all you want."

Jason waved him away with his flight helmet; having his parents occupy the two top TSS leadership positions of High Commander and Lead Agent had made for a challenging dynamic at times. "I need to change. I'll let you know if I get any details."

His friend started to walk away. "Oh, and are we still on for the match?"

"Shit, is that tonight?" The video game tournament had slipped his mind. He knew it was silly that they still indulged in such an unproductive diversion, but it had become a tradition.

"Dude, you can't cancel again." Gil's shoulders slumped.

Jason ran through the mental list of everything that would be delayed by attending the game. Despite the sizable disruption, his friend's pleading eyes got the better of him. "All right, I'll be there at 19:00."

Gil's face lit up with a grin. "Prepare to be slaughtered."

"That's all the trash-talk you can manage? You don't stand a chance."

"I haven't even gotten warmed up." Gil held his arms wide in challenge while he strolled away backward.

Jason shook his head as he placed his palm on the biometric lock to his door.

He'd been in the same quarters since graduating to Agent five years prior. The warm shades decorating the corridors carried into the living area, simply furnished to be both efficient and stylish—like most elements within the TSS.

Jason passed through the sliding door into the bedroom and tossed his helmet onto the double bed. He changed out of the flight suit and donned the tailored black TSS Agent uniform that was his standard attire. The t-shirt, slacks, and boots would fit with almost any outfit, but the knee-length overcoat with its narrow lapels and tapered waist gave the uniform its iconic look. Until recently, tinted glasses would have been a mandatory accessory—to hide the bioluminescent irises of those with Gifts. However, recent legislation to legalize the civilian use of those abilities had allowed the TSS and its Agents to become more accepted in society, no longer needing to downplay their differences to set others at ease.

A quick check of his message inbox confirmed that there was no mention of an attack or any other crisis. Still, as a precaution, he decided it would be better to disclose his experience than not. Since his father was often in meetings as part of his TSS High Commander responsibilities, Jason opted for a text message: >>I sensed something odd during the flight lesson. It reminded me of my vision from the nexus. We should talk when you get a chance.<<

With an uneasy knot still in his stomach, Jason settled onto the plush couch in the living area to review some of his students' written assignments. He was just getting into it when his handheld chirped.

He checked it immediately, hoping it was a response from his father. However, a text message from Tiff illuminated on the matte surface of the palm-sized device. >>What are you up to tonight?<<

Jason knew from experience that it was a thinly veiled booty call. He slid open the handheld, which activated its smooth screen, and typed back, >>Stupid amounts of work, and Gil roped me into gaming.<<

>>Booo! I was hoping to unwind. It's been a bomaxed day.<<

>>Same here, but can't tonight. I'll block out tomorrow evening.<<

>>Ugh, fine, see you then at the usual time,<< she agreed. >>Gil's lucky I actually like him, or I might not be so accommodating.<<

>>Your infinite understanding will be noted for future generations to admire.<<

>>I'm the best. Don't you forget it!<<

Jason smiled. >>Never would.<< He paused. >>Hey, you didn't hear anything about an attack on a ship, did you?<<

>>Yeah, actually,<< Tiff replied. >>There's been some chatter this afternoon. A team based at Prisaris is handling it, I think. Why?<<

His brows furrowed. >>No reason. Just heard about it from Gil, and I wondered if there was more to it.<<

Truthfully, though, anything happening near the Rift set him on edge. The tear in the fabric of reality was too powerful to be taken lightly, especially given its history from the war and the conflict that followed. In the last five years, everything had seemed under control.

Jason took a steadying breath, not wanting to jump to conclusions without having more information. His father would know if there was reason for concern. Until then, plotting how to win the game tournament would be a welcome distraction.

CHAPTER 2

IT WASN'T OFTEN that TSS High Commander Wil Sietinen found himself perplexed, but this particular set of information defied explanation. He had been studying the report from the Prisaris base for the better part of the evening and was no closer to understanding the strange incident.

"Wil, come to bed." His wife, Saera, was standing in the doorway to their bedroom. Based on the scowl twisting her beautiful features, she wasn't pleased that he'd brought work home to their quarters—not that she hadn't done the same on numerous occasions in her capacity as TSS Lead Agent.

Wil leaned back on the couch with a sigh but didn't close the report. "It doesn't make any sense."

"You can deal with it later."

"I'm not so sure," he replied with a frown. "This salvage ship attack is too bizarre to be a coincidence, given the proximity to the Rift." Ever since the end of the Bakzen War thirty years prior, the Rift had been on his mind. The Rift itself was a unique realm between conventional reality and subspace, but an enduring spatial tear had been formed within it when a planet was destroyed in a massive telekinetic assault. Despite the TSS' attempts to heal the wound, a sliver of it had remained—and was slowly growing again. He and others had been keeping an eye on it from afar, hoping nothing more would come of it. *I should have known better.*

Wil gestured to the report on the viewscreen and waited for Saera to get the gist of the contents.

"This can't be right," she murmured.

"I can't find any evidence of it being falsified. In the event it *is* genuine…"

"Stars…" She sunk down onto the couch next to him.

"We can't take any risks with the Rift. We need to be ready to respond if this situation develops."

"Do you think this has anything to do with what Jason alluded to in his message?"

If it does, we're in more danger than I can imagine. He shrugged. "This attack happened days ago."

Saera smoothed her hand over her auburn hair. "Have you spoken with him yet?"

"No, I wanted to finish going through this first, since I'd rather keep the conversation rooted in observable facts." Wil knew firsthand how visions gleaned from the spatial anomaly known as 'the nexus' were cryptic and difficult to interpret. Years ago, when his son had visited the nexus in a rite to read the energy patterns of the universe, those visions had seemed related to a revolution within the Taran Empire, which had already come to pass. However, that had only been the most convenient interpretation; other possibilities were far more terrifying.

Wil stared at the impossible report on his viewscreen. "I've always feared that what Jason saw was actually about another impending threat. He must be wondering the same thing, or he wouldn't have brought it up now."

Saera groaned. "Because things can never be easy for us."

"Hey, we had a few years without a galactic-scale disaster to worry about."

"Not funny." She continued reviewing the frustratingly sparse information—so far, only a transcript of an interview and a single image.

"Have you evaluated scan data from the area?" she asked.

"I was just about to."

Saera leaned forward, fully engaged. "Then let's figure this out."

— — —

"We have a problem."

The telepathic warning intruded into Jason's mind, snapping him awake. Beyond his father's mental presence, his bedroom was quiet and dark. Jason rolled onto his back and threaded his fingers through his hair, trying to shake off the haze of sleep. He'd only made it into bed an hour prior, after having quite the heated game competition with Gil. *"Can't it wait until morning?"*

"It's about the Rift."

Adrenaline surged through Jason. He bolted upright, his heart pounding. *"Is it related to that attack?"*

"Yes, a salvage hauler was destroyed."

"By what?"

"We're not sure," his father replied.

Jason's mind raced as an uneasy tingle crept up the back of his neck. *I'd hoped I was just being paranoid.*

The sector around the Rift had been unoccupied for decades. Salvage ships had been instructed to stay clear of the area, though it wasn't a surprise that at least one had gone in search of valuable scraps left over from the Bakzen War. Perhaps a rival had attacked the ship, but he suspected that his father wouldn't have woken him in the middle of the night if the explanation were that straightforward.

"Meet in my office," his father instructed. *"The threat may have come* through *the Rift."*

Jason's chest constricted. He threw back the bedsheets. *"I'm on my way."*

He hurriedly dressed and grabbed his handheld from the charging pad on his nightstand. *Shit, we don't need another conflict.* He slid the device into the inner breast pocket of his black overcoat and jogged to the door.

The hallways in TSS Headquarters were all but abandoned in the wee hours of the morning. Sconces lining the paneled walls were dimmed to half-brightness for the night, giving Jason the opportunity to let his senses adjust to wakefulness. As much as he and the other Agents in the TSS liked to believe that the organization's charter was now driven by academic excellence, alerts like this in the middle of the night were a reminder that their duty was to protect the Taran people, first and foremost. There would always be new threats to vanquish, and they needed to be ready for anything. Their skills were too unique for anyone to take their place.

He took the central lift to Level 1—the administrative center for TSS Headquarters—and hurried to the High Commander's office down one of the four primary corridors radiating from the dark-tiled central lobby. For most, getting called to the office would either be a great honor or a sign of impending punishment for a major indiscretion. For Jason, being the son of High Commander Wil Sietinen, a veritable living legend, it was a place for a casual family get-together as much as anything else. Tonight, however, was definitely not a social call.

One half of the wooden double-doors to the office stood open. Jason's father, mother, and three other senior Agents were waiting inside. All were dressed in Agent black, though many weren't in their full uniform. The buzz of energy in the air was palpable, with so many of the most powerful Gifted soldiers gathered in one place. Jason's skin tingled from the thrill of being in their presence—the extraordinary potential waiting to be unleashed. It wasn't like that being around all Agents, but the close bonds between this group elevated them; they were more than the sum of their parts.

After Jason entered, his father telekinetically closed the door with a wave of his hand.

"What do we know?" Jason asked.

"Not enough. I've already been over the situation with everyone here, and we've agreed you're the right person to bring in—especially considering that message you sent me." The cerulean glow from his father's bioluminescent irises stood out across the room in the dim light, the vibrant blue contrasting the shade of chestnut hair he'd passed down to Jason and his twin sister.

"It was almost like a flashback of my vision from the nexus. But it's never resurfaced like that before."

"A darkness on the horizon." His father exchanged a significant glance with the others.

"Yeah." Jason slowly closed the distance to the Agents gathered around the desk. He'd gotten used to his parents holding the foremost leadership roles in the TSS, with their longtime friends occupying positions as Division Heads. The inner circle, responsible for the safety of the Taran Empire. Jason had had to earn his place as a trusted Agent among them, regardless of his pedigree. He took the position seriously, and he knew there were few circumstances that would necessitate an urgent meeting like this. He braced for the worst.

"It's too soon to say definitively if your experience is connected to the salvage hauler attack," his father continued. "What we *have* been able to establish is that the ship shouldn't have been out where it was."

"And there were no other ships in the area, which makes it more complicated." His mother, Saera Alexri, was uncharacteristically solemn, with a tightness around her jade eyes, also casting a natural glow to evidence her advanced Gifts. In her role as Lead Agent, she'd always maintained grace and levity, even when faced with dire situations. For her to look this concerned set Jason even more on edge.

"No clues?" Jason asked. "I heard something about a survivor."

"Yes, there is one," his father replied. He leaned against his desk, crossing his toned arms. "And his story would seem far-fetched if he hadn't also delivered proof."

"A merchant ship picked up his escape pod from the salvage hauler *Andvari*," explained Michael Andres, the current head of TSS Operations and a trainer for the Primus Elite Division in which Jason had studied. He was one of Jason's parents' oldest friends, and his position as their next-in-line leader in the TSS had been secured through his loyal service in the war and the transition years that followed. "The response was initially handled by the Tararian Guard, but they've admitted they're out of their depth on this matter."

"For only the second time ever, to my recollection," Wil quipped.

Ian Mandren and Ethan Samlier—the Division Leads for the Sacon and Trion Agent classes, respectively—smirked at the comment. They never missed an opportunity to play up the TSS' rivalry with the Guard.

Appreciative his father was trying to ease the tension, Jason cracked a smile. He'd been the Agent assigned to respond to that previous call for help, and it had been deeply satisfying to watch the Guard soldiers gawk at his open use of telekinesis.

Michael didn't seem to share their amusement. No surprise there; he was always focused and serious when there was a task at hand. Still, when Michael worried, everyone worried. And right now, he looked more terrified than Jason had ever seen him.

"There's more data, but this image is most illustrative." Michael activated the holoprojector integrated into the High Commander's desk, displaying a three-dimensional rendering of…

Jason squinted at the image as he tried to figure out what it was.

The tangle of looping lines had no clear point of origin, snaking across the image and fading into the expanse beyond. A dense knot at the center appeared to be gripping something. Upon closer inspection, Jason was able to make out the form of a vessel.

"Holy shit! Is that the salvage ship?"

The realization gave a new sense of scale to the image. The vessel had to be at least two or three hundred meters in length, which meant the ethereal tentacle-like web around it stretched for kilometers in every direction.

"What is this?" Jason asked, almost breathless. *This isn't anything like what I saw in my vision.*

"That's what we need to figure out," Saera replied. "The image was captured under unusual circumstances. For simplicity's sake, it's a transdimensional snapshot—showing a structure that extends beyond what we know as spacetime reality."

"It's foking massive. I've never seen anything like it." Michael shook his head. Jason always wondered how Michael had been able to adopt the curses used by native-born Tarans rather than those he'd grown up with on Earth. Maybe with the benefit of time, it'd rub off on him, too.

Right now, though, Jason was finding it difficult to choose the right words in any language. He looked around incredulously at the solemn faces in the room. "A transdimensional space kraken? This is a joke, right?"

His parents and Michael grunted, having spent enough time on Earth to get the reference, while the two other Agents' brows furrowed slightly.

"I wish it was a hoax," his father said. "Believe me, when this landed on my desk this afternoon, I wanted to disregard it. But I've been over everything, and the image is genuine. I just wish I knew *how*."

Jason nodded. This wasn't the time for jests, even though that was his preferred coping mechanism. He was a trusted member of his parents' advisory circle, and he needed to demonstrate that he held that status because of competency rather than an expectation of birthright. The Sietinens were under enough scrutiny, as it was, for filling influential roles generation after generation.

"What are the next steps?" he asked.

"A conversation with the survivor. Preliminary reports indicate that he suffered some kind of telepathic assault from the… entity." His father looked at him. "That's why I asked you here, Jason. I'd like you to perform a telepathic evaluation and see if you can find anything others missed."

"Sure," Jason agreed, though he had no idea yet what that

might entail.

"Transportation arrangements are already underway," his mother said. "You can leave as soon as you're ready."

He nodded. "Anything in particular you'd like me to ask about?"

"I need to know if this is connected to what happened with the Gatekeepers a few months ago," his father stated. "If it is, and your vision…" He faded out.

"I understand." Jason didn't need further explanation. The attack may be a declaration of war.

CHAPTER 3

AS A RULE, Raena Sietinen didn't conduct business before breakfast—a fact her assistant, Jovan, seemed keen to ignore. "Whatever you have to say, I don't want to hear it until I've finished my coffee."

"But, my lady, it's—" Jovan insisted, a flush coming through his dark complexion.

"Nope."

"What's going on?" Ryan Dainetris, her husband, asked from deeper within their palatial bedroom suite. He approached the door, his black hair still damp from a shower, with a pastry in hand. His gaze landed on the very agitated assistant. "Oh. Good luck getting her to talk now." He took a bite of the croissant.

"A ship was destroyed," Jovan blurted out.

That caught Raena's attention. "Where?" She snatched the tablet from Jovan's quivering hands.

"Near the Rift."

"Shit," she whispered, reverting to the curses from her youth spent on Earth.

Ryan rushed to look over her shoulder, his luminescent gray eyes narrowed with concern. "What happened?"

"This doesn't say. Only that the incident involved a salvage crew—the starship *Andvari*. There was just one survivor."

"Stars..." He skimmed through the cryptic report. "Attack or accident?"

"I only know what's in the document," Jovan replied. "My lady, your father would like to speak with you. This report came directly from him when he couldn't reach you this morning."

"I'll follow up," Raena acknowledged. "Thank you."

"I'll be standing by." Her assistant bowed as Raena closed the door.

Ryan headed toward the viewscreen integrated into the wall. "I'll start a vidcall."

"No, I'm sticking to 'coffee first'," Raena stated. She flipped her chestnut hair behind her shoulder with one hand and took a sip from her mug. Running an interstellar civilization required dealing with a never-ending series of crises, and she'd learned that taking a few moments for herself and husband helped her keep a level head when it mattered. "Dad can wait fifteen minutes. If it was *that* urgent, he'd have astral projected to pester me."

Ryan hesitated. "I always forget how easy that is for you."

"Him and Jason, maybe. I'm out of practice."

Ryan shook his head. "If you say so. Shall we?" He motioned toward their breakfast table on the terrace overlooking the sea.

Raena followed him outside, trying to suppress her concerns about the destroyed ship. Since Dainetris Galactic Enterprises, the corporate arm of her husband's recently revived Dynasty, manufactured the starship involved in the incident—as well as the majority of *all* new starships in the Empire—it could be a public relations nightmare if the ship's destruction was somehow determined to be DGE's fault. However, if her father was tipping her off, that meant the Tararian Selective Service had taken notice, suggesting that something bigger was in play. After all, the TSS High Commander didn't send cryptic reports on a whim, parental relation or not.

"It's probably a one-off," Ryan said, sensing her mood.

"No, everything was going too well. There was bound to be a major issue."

Ryan eased into his usual seat at the table. "I suppose settling into a normal routine would be too much for us to ask."

She sat down across from him, smiling slightly. "I did try to warn you about my family."

"Like we had a genuine choice about any of this." He reached over the table and took her hand. "Not that I'd change anything—well, not with us, anyway."

Raena gave his hand a squeeze, then released it so she could cradle her coffee mug in both palms. "I've accepted that drama is a way of life for us. That's why I defend these moments."

"And I love you for it."

She leaned back and took a deep breath of the salty sea air rising from the vast ocean between the First and Third Regions of Tararia, the core planet of the Taran Empire. The terrace overlooked the northeastern coastline of the estate, four stories above the manicured grounds. Though picturesque, Raena hadn't completely shaken her memories of the isle's dark history when it had served as headquarters for the corrupt Priesthood, only overthrown five years before. Moving there to the newly renamed Morningstar Isle had been an intentional political move, but on days like this when bad news set the tone, she couldn't help wondering if the place was cursed.

"You're still thinking about it," Ryan said telepathically.

"Resorting to mind-reading now, are we?" she jested back. While she could have easily closed off her thoughts, she'd vowed to never keep secrets from her husband. He knew her better than anyone—even her twin brother, Jason.

"If there really is an issue," Ryan continued aloud, "your parents will handle it."

She nodded. "They always do."

"Stars, the last time they took on a big project, they overthrew the Priesthood and got us a castle to live in!"

Raena almost lost a mouthful of sweetened coffee through her nose. Somehow, he always knew just what to say to keep her thoughts from going too dark.

She admired Ryan from across the table—not just his handsome features, but the depth of his generous spirit. Like her, he hadn't found out about his royal lineage until near-adulthood, and they'd grown into their roles together. Spending their childhoods as regular civilians had granted them a perspective that none of the other High Dynasty leaders possessed.

"Don't hold your breath for another castle," Raena said, taking a cautious sip of coffee now that her chuckling had subsided. "We're finally making headway redecorating this place and I don't want to start over. Besides, the TSS can't benefit us again or we'll have a riot on our hands."

"Obviously, I'm joking." Ryan took the last bite of his buttery pastry and dusted the powdered sugar off his hands.

"I know. But even so, we walk a fine linc."

"Public approval ratings are high. People don't seem to care."

"That can shift at any moment. As it is, having members of

the Sietinen Dynasty holding the top spots in the TSS is a potential conflict of interest with political and military forces. All it would take is a spark to blow it into a big issue."

Ryan tilted his head, casting her a look he'd perfected that told her she was starting down a needlessly worrisome path.

Raena took a long drink from her mug. "And *this* is why I don't get into business before breakfast," she muttered.

"My love, let the TSS worry about the Rift. Your parents and brother can handle it."

"Yeah." She looked out at the ocean. *It could have been me.*

She'd had every bit of the Gifted talents as her brother, perhaps even more. Though she'd technically graduated from the TSS academy thanks to some rule-bending by her parents, she wasn't an Agent and could never be, because it would conflict with her political position. When she was honest with herself, there was a touch of resentment there.

It felt unfair to have had to set aside that part of herself. Her paternal grandparents had done the same, but they'd already had full careers in the TSS to explore their Gifts. Conversely, her formal telekinesis and telepathy training had been cut short at the age of only seventeen, when Raena had 'taken one for the team' and gone to study on Tararia. There, she'd apprenticed to become the perfect combination of politician and businessperson, poised to take over the Sietinen Dynasty and the family enterprise, SiNavTech. She couldn't help wonder what she might have accomplished if she'd gone down the other path.

They finished breakfast in relative silence, content to simply be in each other's company. When the meal was complete, and all requisite coffee had been consumed, it was time to find out how serious an issue they were facing.

Leaving Ryan to his own business, Raena took the short

trek down the hall to her cozy secondary office. Since she made it a point to keep work away from their private residential suite, it offered a convenient place to go for urgent meetings. While her primary workspace on the other side of the sprawling estate was designed to impress visitors, this one was sparsely furnished for productivity, with the desk arranged so she could look out to her right through the window and feel like she was flying above the waves.

She settled into the padded swivel-chair behind the desk and opened up a secure vidcall over instantaneous subspace relay to her father, following the contact instructions in his message.

The viewscreen embedded in the wall behind the three visitor chairs resolved into the image of her father in his office. It hardly seemed like he'd aged since her childhood, still appearing youthful despite being in his fifties. His commanding presence, however, was the true representation—not just of age, but of the wisdom of someone who'd lived through devastation and would do anything to prevent future tragedy. He didn't talk about it much, but Raena knew the war had changed him. But he was her dad, and she couldn't imagine him being any other way.

"Hi," she greeted. "I got your message."

"Thanks for getting back to me quickly. I'm sorry to disrupt your morning routine." Even though TSS Headquarters was on the other side of the galaxy, the time aligned with Raena's since the former Priesthood's island served as the standardized clock across the disparate Taran worlds.

She smiled. "I'm fed and caffeinated, so I'm ready for anything. Now, what about this ship?"

Her father folded his hands on his desktop. "We'll know

more soon, but I wanted you to be prepared in case it's what I fear. Something may be coming through the tear in the Rift."

Now that *I wasn't expecting.* She pursed her lips and took a calming breath through her nose. "I see."

He gave a solemn nod. "Worse, it may be connected to that incident a few months ago."

"Oh." She had no doubt which he meant. A knife drove into her heart with the reminder. Several planets in the Outer Colonies had been assaulted, displacing millions, and costing the lives of too many others. "I thought that was some sort of terraforming system run amuck. What does that have to do with a salvage ship?"

"There was more to it than what the TSS shared with the High Council at the time," he revealed.

Her eyes narrowed slightly. "What happened to transparency?"

"Information that has no actionability can cause more harm than good. It was a calculated omission."

"And it's relevant now because…?"

Her father took a deep breath and looked through the screen, giving the impression that he'd rehearsed what he was about to say. "The tech that destroyed those planets was actually alien in origin, and the beings behind that attack are not the only race out there."

Raena's eyes widened; that was new information.

"The technology is ancient. It's a remnant from a time when there was a galactic war between Tarans and two other powerful races—a fight on a scale that makes the Bakzen conflict look like child's play. That history must have been lost to modern Tarans during one of the Revolutions, like so much else."

An ancient war no one remembers? She swallowed.

"The crux of all this is that some Tarans found and used some of this old tech—a Gate-travel device, of sorts. When the alien creators found out we were using the devices, they weaponized the tech against us. They attacked our worlds by opening Gates and then used those portals to deploy some kind of accelerated process for bio-optimization, with climate and topographical transformations akin to how we would prepare a planet for colonization. Except, doing so on an inhabited world…"

Raena looked down and nodded, her stomach twisted by the horror of it all. "How did you figure all this out?"

"Because when the TSS intervened, we spoke briefly with representatives of the alien race."

"Wait, you spoke to them? Actual *aliens*, Dad! What were they like?"

He smiled at her excitement, but the tension remained around his eyes and in his shoulders. "I wish I could give you a definitive answer, but I can't. We only interacted with some sort of hybrid, genetically engineered to look Taran. I don't know what their true form is. They call themselves the 'Gatekeepers'."

"How fitting."

"They claim to want nothing to do with Tarans now, and only wanted their tech back. We gave them the Gate devices and they went on their way. We'd thought that was the end of it."

"Clearly, it wasn't, given what happened to the *Andvari*."

"No, I don't believe that was their doing."

"So who, or what, was behind it?"

"That's why I wanted to speak with you." He hesitated. "The Gatekeepers told us something else, which we omitted from the official High Council debrief. They issued a warning:

we violated a treaty, and that the 'others' wouldn't be so forgiving."

"In what way?"

"As in, would come to destroy us."

Raena almost laughed at the sheer audacity of the statement. "That has to just be posturing, right? They can't. I mean, Tarans inhabit planets spanning a quarter of this galaxy!"

"The distance is immense, yes, but we're only talking about fifteen-hundred worlds or so. With the right weapon, in actuality, that's not a lot of ground to cover."

Raena's stomach turned over. "Okay, but *why* would they do that?"

"For us violating the treaty—whatever it is. A treaty that we didn't even know about until the Gatekeepers told us." He shook his head. "I've been looking for months, Raena. I can't find the original copy in any of the digital archives, not even with the Aesir. From what I've been able to piece together, there was a truce struck between Tarans, the Gatekeepers, and the other race involved in the ancient war. References to the agreement have given us the gist, but the actual verbiage is lost, as far as I can tell. So, I can't tell you *how* we violated the treaty, because I don't even have a copy of the rules."

Raena bit down on her lower lip while she listened. "Dad, I don't know what to say," she murmured, truly at a loss for words. *Ancient, powerful aliens may be coming to destroy us?*

"So," he continued, "we were told months ago that another race was coming for us. But, without anything to substantiate the claim, we've been waiting and watching. Unfortunately, the attack on the *Andvari* is now the first evidence that the threat might be real."

"What about the attack makes you think that? And how do

you know it has anything to do with the Rift?" she asked.

"Proximity and timing, which means it's still speculation."

She could tell he was holding something back. "Why are you telling *me* rather than the High Council?"

He took a slow breath. "Because of what Jason saw in the nexus. Though your own vision wasn't related to his, you've looked into the nexus like he did. Like I did. You understand how the visions don't make any sense until suddenly they do. No one on the High Council has been through that experience."

She nodded, her stomach knotting further as she recalled the mind-bending rite she'd performed during her first meeting with the insular branch of Tarans known as the Aesir.

"That's how I know you'll believe it, without me needing to explain, when I tell you that we were wrong about our interpretation of what Jason saw in the nexus. It actually had nothing to do with the Priesthood or the Aesir. We now believe it's about what's on the horizon."

Her remaining calm evaporated.

She trusted visions gleaned from the nexus, even though she didn't fully understand the anomaly. When she'd visited the nexus, a premonition about her life with Ryan on Morningstar Isle had altered the course of her life, just as her father and brother had been guided by their own personal truths.

Over the years, she had spoken with her brother at length about his vision of a dark power spreading from the Rift. Her family had been convinced this prescience was about the Priesthood—a representation of how the Priests intended to harness the Rift's power to ascend beyond their physical forms and seize control of everything in the galaxy. So, when her family had helped dismantle the Priesthood, they had taken comfort in the knowledge that their actions had stopped the symbolic darkness.

Now, the realization that this whole time there'd been another threat brewing called into question so much she'd held as certainty. A group of people within the Empire—she could deal with that. But the Rift, the tear in reality filled with untold power? That was another matter entirely. Anything coming through the spatial anomaly was bound to be formidable in a way not even the TSS may be prepared to address.

"We don't know anything for certain," her father reiterated. "I've sent Jason to interview the survivor of the attack, to learn what he can about what we may be facing."

Raena sincerely hoped that he was wrong about all of it. Revisiting an ancient feud with an advanced alien race wasn't in her five-point plan for the year.

"All right, and if the attack *is* connected to this broken treaty and Jason's vision?" she asked.

"Then we might be going up against an enemy we can barely see, let alone have any way to fight."

"How do you mean?"

He looked off-screen for a moment. "I'd rather not get into the specifics until I hear from Jason. I've already said more than I should."

She nodded reluctantly. "Thanks, Dad. I appreciate the heads up."

She knew he wouldn't have shared the information if she wasn't his daughter. Still, there were times she wished she didn't need to navigate the political nuances between the TSS and Taran government—that she could just be a nobody living with her parents in her childhood home on Earth again. Everything had been a lot simpler back then.

"I know this information is worrying, but I didn't want you

to be caught off-guard."

"Yeah, thanks. You know how I'm good at compartmentalizing."

"Which is why I knew you could handle it. How are you doing otherwise?" he asked. There was no mistaking that it was a question from her father, not the TSS High Commander.

Raena tried to quiet the thoughts swirling in her head. "Things are pretty good. Ryan and I have been busy getting the new DGE shipyards up and running. We also started a new scholarship program for technical studies that'll feed into a job placement initiative."

"That's a great idea. And I heard the ship leasing program got rolled out."

"Yeah, we're still working out the kinks with that one. It sounds straightforward enough to hand a wanna-be captain a starship and guaranteed cargo transport contracts, but we've had issues with some of the dealers."

He smiled. "I heard that, too."

"I guess everyone would run a galactic corporation if it was easy, right?"

"Very true. I think you're handling everything brilliantly, from what I've seen."

"We're trying, at least."

Her father nodded. "Well, it's good to see you. I wish this call had been under better circumstances. It's been too long since we've spent time together."

She smiled at him. "It has. You should come visit the island. I think you'll be impressed with the transformation."

"I look forward to seeing it. We'll schedule a trip after this situation is resolved."

"I'd like that."

He looked away from the camera again then back at her.

"I'll let you return to your day. Give our best to Ryan. Love you."

"Love you, too."

When the call ended, the viewscreen briefly changed to the SiNavTech logo before automatically turning off.

Raena slouched in her seat. *Everything always comes back to the Rift.*

Even though it had been years since she'd visited it, she could still feel the pull of its power like she was there— intoxicating, addictive. The way it heightened abilities was both a blessing and a curse to Agents and others with Gifts; they could be stronger there, but too much time spent in its exotic depths made being in normal space feel empty. She didn't want to imagine what kind of entity might permanently dwell in such a place of pure, unmitigated power.

She reached out telepathically to Ryan on the other side of the estate. *"An invasion might be coming. We need to be ready."*

CHAPTER 4

UNDER THE BEST conditions, Jason found it difficult to sleep on a spacecraft while traveling through subspace. After seeing the image of the leviathan wrapped around the *Andvari*, there was no way he could nap.

He stared through the side viewport as the mesmerizing blue-green light of subspace swirled around the ship like flames in a campfire. *How much is out there that we don't know about?*

Since learning about the Taran Empire, he'd believed that the civilization had things pretty well figured out. After all, they had mastered gravity manipulation, spatial jumps, and planet bio-optimization. But the prospect that there was another race out there that dwarfed them in both scope and ability was beyond terrifying.

Following the emergency meeting with his parents in the wee hours of the morning, he'd quickly packed a travel bag and then hopped on a TSS transport ship to the other side of the galaxy. The fact that Tarans possessed technology capable of traveling such a vast distance in a matter of hours still astounded him, even after all of these years—a feat he'd loved in books and movies as a kid but that seemed like an impossible reality. Of all the things that had become available to him upon being inducted into the Taran Empire after his childhood on Earth, subspace travel was among the most thrilling.

Since sleep was out of the question and real-time communications were impossible during a subspace jump, he spent the duration of the five-hour journey reviewing all available information related to the attack on the *Andvari*. The events seemed routine enough at first, but it quickly devolved into a bizarre account of a seemingly haunted ship and crazed crewmembers. Given the outlandish claims, it made sense that his father wanted a firsthand reading of the key witness. Unfortunately, it appeared that the witness had, in fact, been unconscious for most of the alleged events. Jason tried to force back the sinking feeling that the trip might be a fruitless exercise.

When the transport ship reached its exit navigation beacon, time seemed to elongate for a moment during the transition back into normal space. Stars began peeking through the blue-green sea of light, and then the ethereal fog dissipated, leaving only an inky starscape.

"Five minutes until docking," the pilot announced over the comm.

Jason sighed. No doubt, the day was going to turn into a shitshow; he could feel it. Better to get personal business out of the way so it wouldn't be a distraction later.

He pulled out his handheld and initiated a vidcall to Tiff. It was still earlier than when she usually got up, but he couldn't wait around until after breakfast.

The screen resolved into a video of her face. She rubbed her copper eyes with one hand and rolled over, showing her dark-brown hair fanned out over pillows.

"Woke up thinking about me?" she asked with a smirk.

"More like didn't go to bed."

"That rough a night, huh? You look like shite!"

"Yeah, good morning to you, too. Tiff, I'm really sorry, but I might not be around tonight."

"Canceling again?"

"I just arrived at Prisaris. I took a transport out here in the middle of the night."

Her eyes went wide. "Fok, is this about that attack?"

"Yeah, it might be complicated. I'll know more soon."

"Shite, okay. I can't argue with that excuse. Sorry for being bitchy."

"I would have wondered if I'd called the right person if your first words were anything else."

She raised her nose with feigned superiority. "If nothing else, I'm consistent."

"And much more reliable than me, these days."

"When are you going to be home?"

"I'm not sure. Could be this afternoon. Or maybe a couple of days." He really hoped an extended stay wouldn't be necessary, but he couldn't rule out any possibility.

"Okay, well, let's get together when you're back."

"Of course."

She nodded. "Good luck, Jace. I hope it's not anything too serious."

"Me too. Talk soon." He ended the call.

As the transport ship positioned for docking, the Prisaris base came into view outside. Originally a shipyard, the facility's most prominent attribute was still its sprawling spacedocks. Since the TSS had limited production needs during peacetime, the docks were now barren skeletons, glowing slightly in the icy white lights mounted along their lengths. The few ships present were docked around the central hub, which the TSS had transformed from civilian administrative offices into a functional base with medical facilities, an investigative unit, and even a complement of TSS Militia soldiers.

Publicly, the TSS' combat-focused operations had been scaled down over the past thirty years, since the end of the Bakzen War. Now, the Tararian Guard—the TSS' counterpart—was the go-to for conventional military engagements; the Guard's peacekeeping division, the Enforcers, handled most civil disputes. By contrast, TSS Agents with their rare Gifts, served the role of specialists to call in for novel situations requiring a more calculated approach. Though mediation and negotiation were always an Agent's first choice, would-be troublemakers had a tendency to surrender when they saw their companions flung across the room by an invisible telekinetic force.

Facilities like the Prisaris base were remnants of the older TSS from wartime. While Jason admired the recent move toward academia, he was steadfast in his opinion that the TSS served a vital role in the Empire and needed to keep its combat skills sharp. It was one of the leading reasons he liked being a flight instructor—to help shape a new generation of TSS officers who could be equally skilled in offense, defense, and diplomacy. New threats like this situation in the Rift emphasized how critical it was that they not let their guard down.

Once docked, Jason sent a quick note to his father: >>I've arrived. Heading to the interview now.<<

A response came right away. >>Don't do any kind of astral projection near the Rift until we know what we're dealing with.<<

An oddly specific order, but one Jason was inclined to agree was for the best. The last thing he wanted to do was figure out how to counter an attack while his consciousness was detached from his physical self. >>Understood.<<

On that ominous note, Jason went to wait by the access hatch. As soon as it swung open with a hiss, he saw an Agent with bronze skin and black hair pacing at the base of the transparent, arched gangway leading to the station.

When the Agent noticed the hatch open, he stopped in place and went rigid with his arms at his sides. Even from meters away, Jason could sense his nerves. However, it was unclear if it was from meeting one of the TSS' highest-ranked Agents or due to the situation.

With the hopes of setting the man at ease, Jason gave him an affable smile as he approached. "Hello," he greeted as soon as he was an appropriate distance away.

"Agent Sietinen, it's a pleasure to meet you, sir." The other Agent extended his right hand, palm up, in formal greeting.

"Jason is fine." He returned the traditional gesture.

"I'm Agent Trevor Jenson. It's a relief you're here. Everyone is pretty shaken up."

"Happy to assist." Jason made a high-level telepathic assessment of the other man, judging his abilities to rate mid-range, likely placing him in the Sacon Division.

The Agent met Jason's gaze, giving a subtle telepathic acknowledgement of the probe. "The senior Primus Agent, Hylsaen, who commands the base happens to be dealing with another field assignment right now, of all the bomaxed timing."

"Isn't that how it always goes?"

Trevor sighed. "It's normally nice and quiet out here. An easy patrol assignment. None of us were expecting it to turn into the front lines again."

Jason shook his head. "Let's not get ahead of ourselves."

"Sorry." He flushed slightly. "It's just… you must have seen the image?"

"I have. But we can't forget we're TSS Agents. There isn't anything we can't handle."

Trevor brightened a small measure. "Yes, sir."

"Well, I'd rather know sooner than later how screwed we are. Shall we get to it?"

"Right, yes. The witness is being held in Medical."

"Lead the way." Jason motioned him forward.

The interior of the Prisaris station was significantly more utilitarian than TSS Headquarters, lacking the wood accents and warm painted tones that made the other base so inviting. Instead, the corridors were lined in brushed stainless steel with occasional accents in black, gray, or dark blue. Though stark, it complemented the starscape visible through the ample viewports along the exterior bulkheads.

"None of the Agents here have been able to get through to the guy," Trevor said as they walked. "I feel awful for him. What he must have been through…"

Jason couldn't imagine losing his friends in the horrific ways detailed in the report, let alone family. The members of the crew had been tormented through telepathic visions and ultimately been driven mad, with fatal implications. They'd been picked off one by one, by their own hands and the alien entity, until the ship had been destroyed. Finding out about his loved one's fates, it was no wonder the lone survivor was messed up.

"I'll see what I can do," Jason said. The code of ethics for TSS Agents was specific about the use of telepathy in interview situations. Violations of the mind were a serious concern. In general, high-level gleanings were acceptable, but deeper dives required justification. Depending on what Jason found, he might be forced to take information the survivor wasn't willing—or able—to give freely.

As they approached the door labeled as the entry to Medical, Trevor said, "He's in one of the isolation rooms through here."

Jason paused just out of sensor range from the automated door controls. "I reviewed the reports on my way over, but I'd like to hear your impressions before I go in there. Any anecdotal observations?"

The young officer shifted on his feet. "He's not entirely coherent, as you'll notice right away. The moments of lucidity seem to be tied to his mother. The Guard escorts who dropped him off also mentioned that he was talking about her when he first woke up."

Jason nodded. "I imagine they were close, living and working together."

"Yes, and with the destruction of the ship and the death of his mother, he's lost everything."

"Every action is magnified when you work with loved ones," Jason said. *I know a thing or two about that.*

"Yeah, so, he's still processing that loss, and is also messed up from whatever that telepathic assault was that knocked him out in the first place."

"Has he seen the information that he was carrying with him?"

The other Agent looked down. "Sadly, that's what… well, forgive the phrasing, but that's what broke him. He was dazed before that, kind of muttering to himself. We had him look at it, to see if he could tell us any more, and he just… It was difficult to watch, sir."

"All right, so thoughts of his mother level him out, and the attack sends his thoughts into chaos," Jason summarized.

"Based on my limited interactions with him, yes."

Jason began plotting his approach to the upcoming conversation. "Thank you, Trevor. I appreciate your insights."

"Gladly."

"Okay, time to get some answers." Jason walked through the doors into Medical.

Compared to the dim hallway, the bright, white surfaces within nearly blinded him. He blinked to force his eyes to adjust as he took in the infirmary. Six beds stood perpendicular to the back wall, with a lab area behind a glass wall to the right, and two smaller rooms with opaque walls to the left.

A middle-aged woman dressed in white turned to face them, looking over Jason from head to foot. She had no aura of abilities, marking her as a doctor from the Militia division rather than one of the Agents who'd honed their Gifts for medical pursuits. Her brows raised with surprise upon seeing him. "Are you here to interview my patient?"

Jason noted she didn't add an honorific, despite him being dressed in Agent black. He didn't care, but it was clear that she viewed the infirmary as her domain. "I am. And to potentially escort him back to TSS Headquarters for further evaluation, should I deem it necessary."

"We'll see about that."

He didn't want to pull rank unless it actually became an issue, so he let it go. "My understanding is his greatest injuries are to his mind. That is one of my specialties."

"This is Jason Sietinen," Trevor quietly hissed.

Recognition passed across the doctor's face, followed by a pink flush. "Of course, forgive me. I'll leave you to your evaluation." She took a step back to allow Jason free access to the isolation room's entry door.

Jason sensed the man inside before he saw him—radiating pain, confusion, and a projection of scattered thoughts. Without any concerted effort of telepathic gleaning, Jason was struck by the raw grief in the man; he was lost and alone.

I can't treat this like an interrogation. He needs a friend. With that approach in mind, Jason activated the door controls.

As the door slid open, the young man inside didn't so much as glance to see who was entering. He was younger than Jason had expected, maybe not even out of his teens. His blond-highlighted brown hair was mussed from too long without a proper shower, and the scent of stale sweat in the room confirmed it. The young man's gray-blue eyes were cast downward at the seam between the floor and wall opposite the bed on which he sat. The only other furniture was a small table in the corner with an accompanying chair.

"Hi, Darin," Jason greeted. "I'm sure you don't feel much like talking, but I'd like to see what I can do to help."

"There's not a foking thing you can do." Though the retort was barely above a whisper, the acidity of the tone had the presence of a shout.

Jason approached slowly, trying to balance his expression between friendly and sympathetic. "I can't bring back your family and friends, but I am in a unique position to help heal your mind."

"My brain isn't the problem." Darin pulled in on himself more. "That thing is out there. Don't you understand? It's coming for us!"

The panic in Darin's tone turned Jason's stomach. "You're safe here."

"No one is safe. Not from it. From *them*."

That kind of talk must be what the other interviewers had

taken to be a sign of a psychological break. However, there was clarity and resolution to the statements—not the disconnected nonsense that Jason had half-expected to hear, based on Trevor's warning.

"Who?" Jason ventured.

Darin laughed gruffly and wrapped his arms around himself, shaking his head. "It's everything."

"What do you mean?"

"It's everything. We're nothing. I might not remember what it showed me, but I know *that*. None of you have a foking *clue*."

No, I really don't. He suspected the 'it' the young man referenced was the entity in the photo, but he was uncertain of the deeper meaning behind the words. Regardless, he couldn't shake the feeling that Darin was speaking with profound insight rather than madness.

Regardless, it was time for a change in tactics. *Bring it back to his mother. His grounding.* Jason took a slow breath. "I know you've been through a lot. I promise I'm here to help."

"What makes you think you can do anything? The Guard was utterly useless."

"The TSS is different," Jason said with a slight smile. "Your mother was in the Guard, right? Did she ever talk about us?"

Darin softened. "Only her opinion that all of you Agents are a bunch of entitled pricks."

Jason managed to keep his expression neutral; rarely had he heard such disrespectful sentiments. Perhaps the TSS had lost some of its illustrious mystique in recent years. "Everyone's entitled to their opinion."

Darin shrugged. "I haven't seen anything yet to change my mind."

"The other Agents you've spoken to don't have my level of

ability."

"Mind-reading is mind-reading, isn't it?"

"There's quite a bit more to it than that." Jason hadn't been trained in the most nuanced aspects of psychology, but he was skilled in telepathy. Just as with physical-focused telekinetic feats, the general principle was that the stronger a person's abilities, the more they could do.

However, his innate strength meant he needed to be careful when interacting with others. Merely being in the presence of someone with his Gifts was enough to overwhelm those in a compromised state. He'd experienced that firsthand during the Awakening of his own abilities, being near his father and the other Primus Elites. They'd needed to keep shields around themselves to avoid inadvertently harming him until he learned how to guard himself; the enhanced environmental sensitivity made those with Gifts so powerful, but it was also enough to break someone's mind if they didn't know how to filter the inputs. Though Darin didn't have the same sensitivity as someone newly Awakened, his volatile emotional state made him vulnerable in other ways.

"Are you willing to talk?" Jason asked. Regardless of Darin's answer, he'd need to use telepathy to delve deeper. Nonetheless, having a conversation about the topic at hand would speed the process along.

Darin scoffed. "Do I have a choice?"

"You're not under arrest, so yes, of course."

Darin took a few seconds to respond. "You're not the first guy they sent in, which means either you're higher up, or they're hoping that someone close to my age will soften me up. If it's the latter, should have thought to send a pretty girl."

"Would that help?" Jason tilted his head, amused by the suggestion but not letting it show.

Darin shrugged. "I mean, it never hurts. I've been stuck on a ship for a long time."

"I'm afraid I'm not in a position to bring in anyone else right now, but I'd like to get you back to your life as soon as possible."

"Fine. Let's get on with it."

Jason grabbed the chair from the small desk in the corner and sat across from Darin. He began initiating a loose telepathic link, getting a feel for how much resistance he might meet.

Typically, when entering someone's mind, a telepath would first encounter a layer of outward thoughts, usually characterized as one's internal voice—the consciously controlled projection. These outward-facing thoughts could be faked, quite convincingly if the person was well-trained. Below that was a visceral level of thought and memory, with readily accessible knowledge; truth was often found in this part of the mind. In most cases, TSS Agents only went as deep as this second layer in order to verify information. However, some occasions required an intensive examination of the innermost mind, going into the subject's long-term memory and subconscious; the information garnered at that level was sometimes more than a person knew themselves, where forgotten details were buried or where fragments remained if others had tried to erase a memory.

Jason suspected that he'd been sent on the mission to verify that Darin's memories were genuine. It was unclear what someone might have to gain from faking an alien attack, but stranger things had happened.

He leaned forward in his chair and looked Darin in his eyes. "What was your role on the ship?"

"Pilot and labor. My mom is—was—the captain. I was

supposed to take over the *Andvari* from her, keep up with the salvage jobs after she retired."

Good, keep it on his mother. Jason took the opening. "Working with family can be a double-edged sword. Did you get along well?"

"Yeah. I mean, we had our moments sometimes. But things were good. What does that have to do with anything?" The bite was back in his tone.

"I ask because you were awfully far out for a salvage operation. Was that a mutual decision?"

Darin's face darkened. "You think it's our foking fault we got our crew killed?"

"That's not what I said or meant." His heart was heavy for the young man, feeling his hurt from the loss through the telepathic link. *I don't know that I'd handle it any better if I lost my family.*

When Darin didn't say anything else, Jason continued, "All I want to know is why you decided to venture from the usual salvage grounds."

"Quotas to meet. Lots of good stuff gets swooped up in the Kryon Nebula. We had a lead on valuable scrap from the war that would keep us in business."

The TSS had suspected as much, but it was still odd a singular ship would venture so far beyond the normal transit routes. "Who gave you that lead?" Jason asked.

"We always worked through Renfield, a salvage op headquartered on Duronis."

"How long did you have that business relationship?"

"I think my mom had worked with them for… I dunno, a decade." This time, at the mention of his mother, he winced.

"Do you know if Renfield is part of some larger organization?"

"How should I know? I just flew the bomaxed ship! I never should have gone along with the plan to go after scrap in the nebula."

"When did things start getting strange?" Jason questioned.

"I went to investigate a shipwreck, and I was knocked out while on board."

"And you have no memory of the subsequent events that took place on your ship?"

"I was unconscious. So, no."

Jason studied him. He couldn't blame the guy for being in the wrong place at the wrong time, but Darin was definitely holding something back. Only minutes before, he was going on about how the entity was 'everything'. The mood swings and shifts in lucidity were proving to be a challenge, after all. However, the interview was never intended to be only question and answer, so Jason prepared to delve into the man's inner mind.

"Tell me everything about what led up to when you were rendered unconscious." As Jason asked the question, he also slipped past the outer layers of Darin's mind.

The young man's surface thoughts shifted to the moment. In Jason's mind's eye, he experienced the events from Darin's vantage, feeling the pressure of his EVA suit and the anxiety of exploring the unknown as he ventured aboard an old warship for salvage. The memory of exhilaration flooded through Jason as Darin had zoomed through the old ship's corridors, much like the thrill Jason experienced while flying.

This man Jason saw on the inside reminded him much of himself—confident, capable, playful. None of that was evident in Darin now. The light was gone from his eyes and Jason could feel his emotions were on a short fuse, coiled so tight he could go from apathetic to intense, bitter anger in a flash. Though

Jason hadn't yet witnessed that swing, he was aware of the potential and knew he needed to tread carefully.

"We were scoping out a salvage target," Darin explained. "I went in to investigate with Jameel. I've done tons of EVAs, but I felt a little off from the beginning with this one. Headache, dizzy. But that could be from anything, you know? I didn't want to miss out on the action, so I stuck with it and started scoping out the ship. After a while, I started feeling worse. I was trying to head back to the *Andvari* when my memory goes blank. Next thing I remember, I'm waking up in the escape pod."

Jason continued to explore the sensory memory, playing it slowly in his mind moment-by-moment as Darin explored the ship wreckage. He'd been pushing off the bulkheads to propel himself down the corridors, looking for high-value scrap. Aside from Darin's physical discomfort from the odd headache, there was nothing remarkable about the event at first. Then, without warning, there was a bright flash followed by unconsciousness.

There has to be more to it. Jason dove deeper, isolating the moments leading up to the flash.

Except, when he tried to delve into the memory, he hit a wall. It was likely the same block the other interrogating Agents had come up against and been unable to bypass. Strange, considering that Darin didn't have abilities of his own. Usually, those without Gifts could only manage rudimentary mental guards. But this... The barrier shielding the memory had no discernable weakness. To anyone less skilled, it would be as if the sectioned off area didn't even exist.

"*Let me see,*" Jason coaxed in Darin's mind. When there was no telepathic response, Jason said aloud, "Keep thinking about that moment. Share it with me."

The mental wall remained, but its edges became more defined. Jason picked a spot and began chipping away at it, using more force than he had expected to need when he'd walked into the interview. Darin gave no indication of being in discomfort, so Jason forged ahead until there was enough of a crack in the wall to look inside.

Unlike Darin's spoken testimony that he didn't remember anything, there was a vivid memory of the encounter locked inside the vault. Now, when Jason played through the event again, there was definitely something there right before the light. A glimmer—almost like a tendril reaching out toward him. He couldn't see it, exactly, but the intensity of it seemed to make the air vibrate. The tendril extended to his forehead, and at the moment it touched him, he was frozen. It scoured his mind in one rapid wave, offering none of the deference and respect those with Gifts tried to show those they read. It was looking to gather information, and it didn't care what it did to Darin in the process.

The Everything. Jason felt the immensity of it through Darin. Awe, fear, wonder, terror. The entity had known him in his entirety in the span of an instant. While it had been too much for Darin to consciously register, it was seared into his deepest sensory memory.

What was immediately evident to Jason's trained senses was that the being didn't exist in any recognizable corporeal form. Its presence extended from somewhere unseen, in the way he sensed the immense energy of the Rift, even from afar. It made sense, given the reports from the *Andvari* and the transdimensional image of the form he'd flippantly called a 'space kraken' during the briefing. Now, he got the distinct impression that what was captured in that image didn't reflect the being's full extent. It was unlike anything he'd heard of, or even imagined. The stuff of far-fetched stories he'd read as a kid about Old Ones or ancient god-like entities.

Jason's gut wrenched. It was real. The incident, Darin's memories. No tampering; only confirmation of alien contact. It wasn't what he'd hoped to report back to Headquarters.

What in the stars are we going to do? He was careful to keep the thought to himself, maintaining a thin veil between his consciousness and the shared experience with Darin.

As he probed the memories, he found it increasingly difficult to maintain a tranquil demeanor. But, he needed to— not only as a point of professionalism, but because Darin was a scared young man who'd had his life ripped from him. It wasn't fair to put him through any more grief, even if that meant downplaying the magnitude of his own experiences.

Unfortunately, the *Andvari*'s encounter was likely just the beginning. Jason couldn't tell that to Darin. Instead, he needed to do something good to help balance out the tragedy. Maybe he could help the man move on with his life, however much was left of it to live.

"I can ease your pain," Jason said in his mind. It wasn't an official part of his assignment, but he felt it was the moral thing to do, under the circumstances.

"How?" Darin's response wasn't words so much as a cloud of skepticism in his scattered mind.

"By helping you remember the good and taking the sting out of the loss."

Darin shook his head and sniffed. "I'm sick of feeling this way," he said aloud.

"You don't have to anymore. Let me help. It's the least I can do."

"Okay."

Jason looked into his eyes. "Relax," he spoke

simultaneously out loud and in his mind.

Though he'd used the required techniques only on a couple of occasions, Jason understood the principles well enough. The basic process was to share the emotional burden of the memories—to take them in, filter, and feed them back. It was a mind-meld, of sorts. They'd practiced it as Junior Agents as a tool to cope with combat trauma. Not everyone could do it; the act took a great deal of raw telepathic ability as well as emotional fortitude. But when done successfully, the patient could get immediate relief with lasting results.

With Darin's mind open and ready, Jason began the treatment. It wouldn't be helpful in the long-term for Jason to bury the young man's pain entirely, but he could help take the edge off of it. Carefully, he skimmed through Darin's memories and pulled forward the fond memories of his mother and lost friends. With each memory brought to the forefront, the pain of the recent loss pushed back a little. As he pressed on, the horror of the loss lost its sharp edge, and instead Darin's thoughts first went to the best moments of his times with his loved ones. The loss still left a hollow place in his heart, but it no longer was the initial, overwhelming feature of those relationships.

Jason worked through the layers of memory with Darin until his sense of tragic loss had diminished to a manageable state. When Jason finished, he retreated from Darin's mind, maintaining a light touch to assess the other man's state. He felt emotionally drained by it, but he would recover quickly. The benefit to the other man was well worth the temporary discomfort.

Darin remained on the bed, still and silent. After several seconds, he finally met Jason's gaze. "It feels… different."

"I've tried to help you remember what made your

relationships special."

"Yeah, I…" Darin faded out, his gaze going distant. A slight smile touched his lips. "I needed that reminder."

"The way someone leaves us shouldn't dictate how we think about them," Jason said. "Just because they're gone, the relationship doesn't end. Their influence on your life will always remain."

They sat in silence for several seconds.

"What happens now?" Darin asked at last.

"We have what we need from you for now. We'll do what we can to help you find a way forward. As far as I'm concerned, you're free to go."

He looked down. "Thinking about that feels more doable now."

"I'm glad to hear it."

"Have you ever lost someone? The way you were talking earlier seemed heartfelt."

"I haven't in the way you did, but we've been through some things as a family—enough that I've thought about how I'd react if I did lose someone. My military training has instilled the perspective that there's always a way forward, even when the future seems too dismal to face."

Darin nodded. "It must be nice, being a part of something bigger like that."

"It is. The TSS is my extended family."

"I guess I'll need to find my own place to belong like that."

"I hope you do."

"Thank you for…" he shrugged, "whatever you want to call it. Helping me. I didn't realize how much this whole mess had blinded me."

"We all need a little help sometimes."

"Yeah." Darin swallowed hard and dropped his gaze.

Jason stood up. "Don't let this loss define you. You still have a lot of life to live."

Darin nodded slowly. "I wish I knew where to go from here. My entire life was on the *Andvari*."

"There are lots of opportunities out there. DGE is hiring like crazy."

"I'd always thought about joining the Guard."

"Lots of good people do."

"But that's not where you see the real action, is it?"

Jason shrugged. "I'm no doubt biased on the matter, but I'd direct someone toward the TSS instead any day."

Darin perked up a little. "Are you recruiting?"

"The Militia division is always looking for dedicated people." He paused. "I could put in a good word to get your application fast-tracked, if that would help."

"You'd do that for me?"

If Darin was just some random kid on the street, Jason couldn't stake his reputation on a recommendation. But he'd seen inside Darin's mind, and he knew his heart was in the right place. He couldn't think of a better place for Darin to find a new family than within the TSS. "I'd be happy to."

The young man grinned. "I don't know how to thank you."

"No need. Show it by becoming the best TSS officer you can be."

"Yes, sir!"

Jason smiled. "Thank you for your cooperation. Take care, Darin. And good luck."

As soon as Jason exited the room, Trevor came to attention.

"How did it go?"

Jason wanted to explain to the other Agent exactly how unprepared for a fight they were if this alien was as powerful as it seemed, but there were too many classified details to even hint at the true stakes. Instead, he simply gave a resolute nod. "I got what I needed."

CHAPTER 5

SOME PEOPLE WERE never content. The more time Lexi Karis spent with Oren, she became convinced that he'd find a reason to be upset, no matter his circumstances. Unfortunately, as he was her boss and mentor, she had to nod and smile rather than call him on his curmudgeon-y ways.

"Yeah, it's terrible," she half-heartedly agreed to his latest grumbling, as she had done at least a dozen times in the last ten minutes. She tucked a length of her dark-brown hair behind her ear and kept her attention on her tablet. Going through the motions of faking interest had become tedious months ago, and it was becoming increasingly more difficult to mask her frustration.

Oren was going on about the new tax on interplanetary shipping for non-essential items, or some such. She'd half-tuned him out in the interest of maintaining her sanity so she could live to fight another day; besides, she should be focusing on the inventory she was taking of the new production supplies. When he shook his head and scoffed again, it was clear that she had made the right call.

With another overly dramatic groan, Oren threw his lanky arms up in the air. "Whatever! It's pickup time, anyway." He took a brisk pace toward the storeroom's exit.

Lexi set her tablet on a workbench and jogged to catch up to him. *All right, I guess inventory can wait.*

She sensed that they were gearing up for something, but no one had shared the plan with her yet. The 'pickups' had increased in frequency, and the items she was inventorying had become more varied. At first, it had been plasheet stock for printing posters, then medical supplies, then vests that she was pretty sure were body armor. Some of the most recent crates she hadn't been allowed to see inside, which was a first.

The entire situation was proving to be much more serious than she'd anticipated when she set out to find her missing friend, Melisa. At first, Lexi had figured that Melisa had been drawn into the Sovereign Peoples Alliance's pitch about joining with like-minded people who wanted a change for the better in the Outer Colonies. Lexi could see the appeal, since they'd made it sound like there'd be… well, *action.* Instead, everything she'd seen thus far amounted to a lot of griping, standing around, and picking up items from the port. Moreover, Lexi had thus far found no explanation for how her friend had vanished without a trace shortly after arriving on Duronis.

Supply pickups always happened at the same rear exit of the local port on Duronis, where one of the shipping dock workers would meet them and pass off whatever cargo was on order for the day. The shipments had been weekly up until a month ago, but now it was almost every day. Lexi had come close to asking Oren about the Big Plan several times and had considered getting answers through other means, but she could never quite get up her nerve. Melisa had been open with her Gifts, and she'd disappeared, so Lexi had taken a more reserved approach. She needed answers, not to find herself pulled into something underground, never to be heard from again. There was no one who'd come looking for her if she vanished, too.

Oren maintained a quick pace from the facility to the street until there was too much pedestrian traffic to travel unhindered. Duron City was a proper metropolis befitting the Central Planets—a rarity in the Outer Colonies, which were often little more than glorified farming or mining communities. Her own homeworld of Cytera had been much the same way, not that she had been old enough yet at the time she left to appreciate that fact.

Lexi broke into a light jog to keep up with Oren's long, swift stride as the foot-traffic lightened again when they turned onto a side street. The darker alley was a stark contrast to the broad, pristine walkways along the main transit corridors, lined with storefronts catering to trades and essential services rather than the flashy retail establishments found along the main mall.

They hadn't come this way for a while; Oren made a point to vary the route each day. No matter the route, at least part of the trek was bound to go through a crowd. The pickups always corresponded with the commonly used end-time for the day shift in the city, placing their walk at the peak of the evening commute. Hundreds of thousands of people flooded to the maglev train system servicing the city and surrounding communities, resulting in large eddies of people around each of the transit stops. Lexi assumed that the pickups were handled at that time *because of*, rather than in spite of, the traffic. A person was much less likely to stand out in a sea than alone. That knowledge did little to quell her concerns about what plan was afoot.

As they neared the shipping port, Oren slowed his pace slightly and looked over at Lexi. "You know the routine by now."

"I do," she acknowledged.

"Do you think you could handle it on your own?"

She hoped he wasn't *trying* to be patronizing. A small child could manage to walk a kilometer to a known destination. "Yes. As long as I had a hovercart to transport the larger, heavier items, of course." To her pleasant surprise, there hadn't been even a hint of exasperation in her tone.

"Good. Beginning tomorrow, this will be your responsibility. We'd also like to expand your role in other ways."

"How so?"

He looked around, seemingly suspicious of everyone on the street. "First, I'd like to know if you're ready to take on more."

"I've been eager to," she replied. She was a grown woman well into her twenties, and they'd had her running around like an intern still in secondary school. The inventorying was the only task that seemed to have a measure of serious responsibility, but even most of that was simple counting and categorizing.

"I know some of your tasks have been… tedious. But with what we're trying to do, we need to be sure our organization has people we can trust."

"I understand."

"Excellent. We'll talk about the specifics soon." Oren nodded to the port they were rapidly approaching. "Take the lead today."

"You've got it." She forced a smile to shine through.

She couldn't say that she was excited about moving up in the organization, but it would further her chance to get answers; that was the only thing that mattered. Still, her gut clenched every time she needed to fake enthusiasm about the Sovereign Peoples Alliance's 'work'. Ultimately, though, Lexi didn't care how the Alliance intended to make its vision for the Outer Colonies a reality. The only reason she had joined the organization was because it was the sole lead she had for finding Melisa, her one true friend in the universe.

Last Lexi had heard, Melisa was excited about a new opportunity with the Alliance; then nothing. After running into dead ends with every other avenue of investigation, Lexi had finally joined the Alliance herself and begun a long-game to gain their trust. Having now worked with them for nearly four months, it had become clear that climbing the ranks was the only way she would find out what the Alliance was working on behind the scenes—and how Melisa might be involved.

With a renewed sense of purpose, Lexi led the way to the back exit of the port. Litter overflowed from dumpsters and collected in the nooks of grimy pavement, giving the alley a foul stench of rotten produce. Breathing shallowly through her mouth, she hurried to the door and pounded three times with a slow-fast-fast rhythm to signal to their contact inside. While not the most elegant or secure communication method, it was effective.

After ten seconds, the smooth door swung outward on its groaning hinges. Niko peered out, his dark eyes scanning the area to make sure there was no one else around.

"We're here for the pickup," Lexi stated. Her own blue eyes met his gaze.

He gave her a smile that he probably thought was charming but came off as predatory. "Always a pleasure to see you, Lexi, but I don't have anything for you today."

Her brows knitted. "We were expecting something."

"It's not just you. No deliveries came through today," the dock worker explained. "Everything is locked down."

"What for?"

"Ship got attacked in an adjacent sector. The TSS and Guard are still investigating, last I heard."

"You have to be foking kidding me!" Oren exclaimed. "Locking down the ports for that? As if we don't have enough regulations to deal with as it is."

Lexi had to admit that suspending all traffic did seem like an extreme measure for a single ship.

Niko nodded. "I know, can you believe this shite? I guess it's all they can do to maintain order. People would freak if the word got out."

"Word about what?" Lexi questioned.

"What supposedly happened out there. Rumor has it that the survivor told quite a story to the crew who picked him up."

Oren squinted with interest. "Oh, yeah?"

"Ghosts walking the ship and other shite."

"Don't tell me people actually believe that!" Oren laughed.

Niko shrugged. "That's not what got them all worked up. No, there's apparently some sort of invisible monster that's behind the whole deal."

He raised an eyebrow. "Sounds like tales told to children to get them to behave."

"Maybe. The Guard does seem to always treat us that way."

While Lexi was curious about the alleged attack, she didn't much like lingering in the filthy alleyway behind the port. "If everything is shut down, then where is our shipment?"

Niko's eyes shifted to the side. "Didn't make it off the cargo hauler, what with the port being shut down."

He's lying. Lexi schooled her face to impassive calm. Her ability to read people certainly wasn't something she wanted to advertise to Oren. She'd spent too long building his trust and working the connection to risk befalling the same fate as Melisa, should he find out the truth about her Gifts.

Instead, she decided to steer the conversation in a direction where Niko might expose his own lie. "What's the purpose of locking down the ports all the way over here?" she asked.

Niko shrugged. "Limiting transit traffic, I suppose. They might think the attack was by terrorists." He raised his red eyebrows at Oren.

"So, the ports are shut down and cargo isn't getting offloaded," Lexi reiterated.

"Yes. How many times do I need to tell you?"

"Then why are you here at work?" She tilted her head questioningly to drive home the incongruity of it all.

Niko made a flustered grunt at the back of his throat. "For security."

"Or you're taking this singular opportunity to stick your nose where it doesn't belong." She didn't want to call him out directly, but the frantic thoughts skittering on the surface of his mind screamed that he was up to something even shadier than these literal backdoor dealings. The man had been pestering them for months about the shipments, but the tight timing of the handoffs was intentional to minimize the likelihood of him having time to peek inside. This alleged 'port closure' was a great excuse to buy a full night to browse to his heart's content. It was a flimsy cover, but the man wasn't sharp enough to realize the faults in his plan.

Oren, being craftier than the other man, picked up on Lexi's line of questioning. "Are you *sure* our shipment didn't make it off the freighter before this shutdown?" He reached into his back waistband. "Would you like to check before I go in to inspect the storeroom myself?"

Niko gave a noncommittal shrug. "You know, things don't always go smoothly once the Enforcers get involved."

"No, which is why we go to such lengths to keep them out of it. An anonymous tip would really put a damper on your extracurricular dealings." Oren kept his hand behind his back. Though it wasn't visible from her vantage, Lexi was familiar with the pulse handgun he kept on him at all times. She'd never seen him fire it, but it'd been drawn on several occasions to make a point.

"Same goes for you," Niko replied. "What *is* it you're working on, anyway?"

"Your generous cut is exactly why you don't get to ask those questions. We have a nice arrangement here, don't we, Niko? You get a little extra for that guy of yours who likes the finer things, and we don't need to deal with the trouble of the Enforcers. I'd hate to have to end that arrangement."

"It's been two years. Perhaps it's time we revisit the terms."

That was news to Lexi. *Two years?* So, Oren and his people had been at it since well before she got involved. *What's happened to all of the shipments?*

The warehouse where she handled the inventorying was spacious, but it didn't have the capacity to handle the volume of deliveries over that length of time. She knew things must go *somewhere* after she'd processed them, but she still didn't know where. The realization that it had been going on for so long made her that much more curious.

Oren remained focused on the present—particularly Niko's sudden lack of cooperation. Her boss' face had turned a vibrant shade of red, and his arm twitched behind his back. "The terms stand, Niko. If you don't want to take another look around your storeroom for our delivery, then I'll have to come poke around myself."

Can we even get in there without raising alarms? Lexi had never been inside, so she had no idea how shipments were handled through the port. For all she knew, there could be armed guards right inside the door. Either Oren knew something she didn't, or he was being reckless. Or maybe he was just bluffing.

Niko stood motionless outside the back door, his eyes locked with Oren's. After several tense seconds, he let out an exasperated sigh. "I'll take a look." He disappeared inside.

Lexi breathed a quiet sigh of relief. The last thing she wanted was to find herself in the middle of a pissing-match-turned-firefight.

Within a minute, Niko returned carrying a rectangular shipping case. Based on his bearing, it had some heft to it, though he held it from its handle with one arm. It wasn't like the normal parcels they received, so Lexi could see why he'd been more interested in delving into this one. She recognized the case's outer material as being a shell designed to be impervious to standard scans. One would need access to military tech to get a good look inside—not something available to a dockworker while on the clock, but someone with black market connections could likely get access afterhours.

"Sorry, must have misplaced this," he muttered.

Need to give him credit for trying, Lexi thought to herself, though she was embarrassed for Niko about his poor execution of the plan. Still, she couldn't blame him for wanting a look inside. She was certainly eager to see for herself. At least that was one perk of doing inventory; she didn't know what most of the stuff was *for*, but at least she got to see the individual components most of the time.

Oren took the case from Niko. "Just don't let it happen again, and all is forgiven."

"Yeah, well, don't be late next time."

Lexi bit back a retort that they were right on time. It wasn't worth it, especially not since she would need to deal with the man one-on-one going forward. "We appreciate you sticking around to get us this even with the rest of the port closed," she told him instead.

Niko smiled with that unnervingly hostile grin of his. "Any time. Looking forward to tomorrow, assuming things have opened back up."

She gave him a noncommittal nod and wave as she turned to follow Oren from the alley. Only once they were back on the well-lit main streets out from the shadow of buildings did she begin to relax. Niko might be a problem for her going to the pickups alone, but she'd have to find a solution.

"Nice job spotting his ruse back there, Lex," Oren said as they walked.

"Just doing my job."

"Well, we're leaving this part of the operation in good hands." He smiled.

She eyed the hard case dangling from his right hand. "Something special today?"

"Very."

What a vague and unhelpful response. Obviously, they couldn't talk about details on the open streets, but she'd hoped for a little hint about what might be inside. Oh, well. They'd be back to the office soon enough.

The central office was far more than an administrative center, also serving as a warehouse, living quarters, and training center for new members of the Sovereign Peoples Alliance. Aside from the pickups at the port, Lexi could never leave the building and would still have everything she needed.

The main downside with the place was that it was barebones. The bunks were made out of either unfinished wood or plain metal, depending on which dormitory, and the furnishings in the kitchen, dining area, and workstations were equally unadorned and constructed from salvaged materials. Other items were almost always second-hand, so most plates had chips and blankets were often stained. Even so, it was cozy and functional. Honestly, it was better than a lot of places she'd been during her childhood.

When she and Oren arrived at the office, they stopped by the storeroom to place the case in a locked storage cabinet to which Lexi didn't have access; Oren still made no commentary about what was inside. They then continued on together to the rec room, as was the tradition after the pickup, marking the end of the workday. Several other compatriots were already lounging around on the rec room's couches, watching the evening news broadcast.

"How has the galaxy fared today?" Oren asked the group as he eased onto the arm of a worn, padded couch.

"Business as usual," Shena replied. The brusque brunette was a couple of years older than Lexi and had the detached attitude of someone who'd had a rough life but didn't want anyone to know it. Though she wasn't easily ruffled, Lexi had witnessed the woman snap at the strangest things. There was no doubt trauma there, not that Lexi expected to ever find out what had transpired.

Oren frowned at the viewscreen mounted to the back wall. "So, nothing about an attack?"

"What attack?" Josh craned his neck to look at them over the back of his chair. His blond brows almost disappeared into his creased forehead at the odd angle.

"Some ship got itself blown up in the adjacent sector." Oren shared what little else they'd learned from Niko at the port.

"Well, fok! Ain't that an interesting twist." Josh returned his attention to the screen.

"Strange it wasn't mentioned on the news," Shena commented.

"Of course not," Oren grunted. "Once the TSS got involved, they shut the reporting down."

Josh sighed. "When is the media going to learn to stand up for themselves?"

"What are they supposed to do? The TSS High Commander is so entrenched with the High Dynasties, no one dares break the line." Shena waved her hand dismissively.

Oren extended his lithe arms. "That's precisely the problem! They like to think that things are better since the Priesthood was ousted, but we only traded in our old overlords for new ones. At least before, they admitted they were in charge."

"I don't think the High Council has made any claims trying to downplay their position," Lexi countered.

"They don't have to," Oren said. "Just look at all their 'of the people' posturing. Trying to play up a childhood among the commoners. Right, like that makes a difference!"

Lexi didn't want to argue the point, but she happened to think it made *quite* a difference in a person's life outlook. Privately, she had a lot of respect for what the Sietinen Dynasty, in particular, had done with its position of influence. Before their interventions, keeping her Gifts a secret would have been mandatory for the sake of her life; now it was her own choice to make about how much she shared about herself with others, and she could do so without fear. At least in most circles. There was a reason she didn't broadcast her abilities within the Alliance.

"More than half of the High Dynasties have had, or currently have, someone who's trained with the TSS," Josh pointed out. "They're in bed with each other—quite literally, in some cases."

Shena scoffed. "All those 'Gifted' are freaks."

And that's *why I keep my bomaxed mouth shut.* This time, though, Lexi couldn't let the comment slide. "Don't say that."

The other woman rolled her eyes. "Don't tell me you're one of those sympathizers?"

"I just don't think it's right to categorize and judge someone based on the way they were born."

"I guess you *would* feel that way with your family from Cytera." Leave it to Shena to drive home her point with a personal attack.

"I told you not to talk about them!" Lexi snapped.

Oren held up his hands. "Don't be so bomaxed twitchy! It's not like you're on foking trial. Shite, Lex."

She forced herself to calm down. Cytera was the only topic that could set her off without warning—a fact she'd made abundantly clear to Oren when they started working together. *One* topic that was off-limits. After what had been done to her family by the leaders of the world, the sick bastards, it didn't seem like too much to ask.

"I told you not to bring it up," she said through gritted teeth.

"Yeah, whatever you say." Shena gave her a patronizing salute with one finger.

Lexi bit back a venomous response that would only make things worse. She couldn't explain *why* it was so upsetting without drawing unwanted attention.

Oren scuffed his heel on the polished concrete floor. "Cytera is a perfect example of what happens when we allow the influence of the corrupt Central Worlds to rule us. The Taran government has been experimenting on us unsuspecting citizens for centuries. You really think they're going to stop now?"

He probably meant well, but Lexi knew for a fact that he didn't understand what had happened on her homeworld or why. And he *certainly* didn't understand what it meant for her personally. With all her Gifts, the one she wished she had but didn't was the ability to melt into a wall and get away from awkward conversations.

"That was the Priesthood's doing, though," Josh said. "That's why the High Council stopped them."

Oren raised an eyebrow. "A convenient story, isn't it?"

"You don't believe them?"

"Since when do highborn do anything for the little people? Different names, different leaders, but same old shite."

Lexi could understand where Oren was coming from, but she'd allowed herself to hope that this time things would be different. The restoration of Dainetris, the Sietinen heiress being raised on Earth; it really *was* different with this generation of leaders. The new initiatives, while far from perfect, were a step in the right direction to allow civilians a chance to improve their lives.

"I can't argue that there are problems, but I think it's important to give credit where it's due," she said after considering her words for a few moments.

"Yeah, we've had worse leaders, you're right about that. The problem is, it only takes a couple of generations for those in charge to forget why they ever wanted to do anything that wasn't in their own self-interest. We need to change the entire system to set ourselves up for the future. It's not just about how things are in the present."

"I guess," she admitted.

Oren looked over the mundane news reports for several moments. "Lexi, come with me." He abruptly stood and headed toward the stairwell.

Shena and Josh gave Lexi a passing glance as she walked by, but they were already reabsorbed in the news broadcast.

What now? Lexi groaned inwardly. She should have kept her mouth shut like a smart person. For all the grief she gave Shena over her random outbursts, Lexi knew she was just as bad. When it came to discussion of Cytera and people with abilities, she had difficulty keeping her feelings in check.

It was one thing to have been forced from her homeworld, but it was quite another to know that her family had been manipulated for hundreds of years and then cast aside like worthless garbage. No outsiders knew the brutality of the world. She'd been the lucky one to get out alive. Life on the planet seemed prosperous on the surface, but the price of that seemingly happy existence had been paid in blood. She'd even had to have her irises surgically altered to remove their bioluminescent glow. Those with Gifts were a commodity at the center of the commerce. It sickened her what had transpired and that she'd been a pawn in the game.

Lexi took deep, calming breaths as she followed Oren toward the stairs. Blowing up now would be such a waste of the efforts that had gotten her this far.

At the stairwell, Oren descended one story to the level housing his office and other administrative functions. Lexi had found it strange that he'd elected a place in the basement rather than a room on one of the higher floors with a view of the city, but she supposed some people liked it cool and dark while they worked. He didn't enter the office itself but rather walked a ways down the hall before he stopped and turned to address her.

"You'd better not be having second thoughts about joining this movement. You gave me your word."

At the time she'd made her vows to support the Alliance, Lexi hadn't even known what she was signing up for. She hadn't cared; it was an 'in', and she would have taken it no matter what. In the time since, the Sovereign Peoples Alliance had done their best to shape her thinking—mostly by keeping her isolated and limiting what she was told. Now, she didn't think leaving was a genuine option. She lived with them, relied on them, had planned with them. To step away would make her a traitor to the cause, if she could even find anywhere to go.

"I'm committed. You know I am," she said. *They've made sure of it.*

For an organization pushing an agenda of giving people freedom, they had a whole lot of rules and controls over the members. If she thought about it too long, she started to feel like it was a cult. Perhaps it was, in some ways. Passionate people working toward a common cause.

"We have important work to do. I see your enthusiasm, but you must direct that fire toward productive ends."

"I know."

"It's challenging to see the universe as it is—those harsh, dark truths. The people we bring in are those who've been touched by that badness and know how important it is to stand up for a brighter future."

"That's why I joined you."

"It is one thing to join for yourself, but it is another to join because you want to be part of a movement."

Lexi wasn't sure what he meant or what was the

appropriate reply. "I'm here for the cause."

His eyes narrowed slightly. "Sometimes I wonder if you want revenge."

Of course I do! But Oren shouldn't know about that. She'd been so careful to keep the specifics about her past hidden. Others knew that she was born on Cytera, but that was the extent of the truth; everything else was a carefully fabricated narrative to paint her as an idealistic youth who'd had a rough go of it. Well, the core of that story was partially true, but few of the other details mirrored her actual experience.

She put on her sweetest smile. "Revenge? For what?"

"The atrocities the Central Planets have committed against these fringe worlds for generation after generation. Once your eyes are opened to the real state of things, a person can't help but get angry."

Lexi relaxed; if Oren knew anything about her real past, this wasn't him tipping his hand. "That frustration must be guided toward productive ends, like you said."

Oren looked her over, nodding slowly. "I've spoken with the others, and they agree that you can be an asset as we embark on the next stage of our mission."

A tingle of excitement ran up her spine. "I welcome the challenge. What does this next stage entail?"

"Fighting for independence, of course."

Lexi held back an eye-roll. "But *tactically*. What's the plan?"

"I said you were moving up in the ranks, kid. You don't have a seat at the table."

She should walk away; she knew it. Any organization that was being *that* cagey about its objectives and methods was certainly up to no good. But her fears for her future were omnipresent, and she couldn't abandon Melisa. *Where would*

I go if I left? Who would I have? Her parents were dead. She'd burned bridges with all of the friends that counted. Even her sister was unlikely to take her call after how they'd left things. Without any money to her name now, she'd be forced to rely on petty crime just to keep a roof over her head. Her Gifts made that easy, but it ripped away part of her soul every time she stole or swindled. Besides, now that she was finally making progress with infiltrating the Alliance, she felt compelled to stay the course.

"I just want to know how I can best serve the mission." She hated herself for saying it. Oren and his compatriots were planning something bad, and here she was going along as an accomplice.

"All will become clear soon." He smiled pensively. "Let me show you something."

CHAPTER 6

THE RETURN FLIGHT to TSS Headquarters gave Jason time to process the meeting with Darin and think about what the alien contact meant for the TSS going forward. While the touch with the being in Darin's memory hadn't been particularly sinister, it had solidified for Jason that the being, and its kind, were what he had seen in his nexus vision. Something immense was coming.

He stifled a yawn while descending the central elevator into the heart of Headquarters. It had been a long day, and it wasn't over yet.

Echoes from Darin's broken mind still swirled at the edge of Jason's consciousness—the downside to using telepathy to dive deep. The images stuck around. Some telepaths couldn't take it and were sucked in, blurring the boundary where the subject's memories ended and their own began. Though Jason had never felt at risk in that way, he still kept a little of everyone he read with him. In time, the memories would fade and become unrecognizable in the background. But for now, he may as well have been on the *Andvari* himself.

Jason checked the time on his handheld. He still had twenty minutes before the scheduled meeting with his parents to debrief about what he'd learned.

Following the upcoming debrief, the rest of his schedule was looking fairly clear, so he wanted to stay true to his promise to get together with Tiff. He pulled up his text thread with her and sent a message. >>Hey, just got home.<<

>>Oh, hey!<< she wrote back right away. >>How did it go?<<

>>That's for a longer conversation.<<

This time, there was a several second delay. >>Okay. Are you free tonight, then?<<

>>I was hoping you hadn't already made other plans. I could really use a night away from all this.<<

>>Yeah, of course. I'd also like to talk about something.<<

>>Sure. You know I'm always happy to lend an ear.<<

"Jason!" a voice called from behind him.

He slipped his handheld into his pocket and turned to see Gil approaching from the Primus Agent offices in the administrative wing, where he was headed himself. "Hi, Gil."

"Is it true?" his friend asked, barely above a whisper.

"We're still looking into the details," Jason said. It was technically true, and he couldn't share the full extent of what was going on until his father decided to make a formal announcement.

Gil paled. "Shite, that bad?" He shook his head. "When I saw that the incident with the *Andvari* had suddenly become classified—"

"I wish I could talk about it, but I can't," Jason cut in. "We're taking care of it."

"Right, yeah." He swallowed. "Uh, welcome home."

"Game night next week, maybe?" Jason suggested, hoping

to soften the blow of not being able to share the specifics of his most recent assignment.

"Sure, that'd be great." Gil nodded to him and then resumed his walk down the hall.

Since there wasn't enough time to go to his quarters before the meeting, Jason decided to head to the High Commander's office early.

As he passed by the Lead Agent's office, he noticed the glass walls were set to full transparency—normally tinted opaque with the environmental controls. His mother waved to him from behind the desk inside. She grabbed her handheld from the desktop and jogged across her office to meet him.

"Well?" she asked.

"It's genuine."

She took a slow breath. "Okay."

Together, they walked the rest of the way to the High Commander's office at the end of the hall.

Saera opened the door without knocking and Jason followed her inside. Pacing next to the wooden desk, his father was finishing up a voice call.

"Right. Yes. I'll keep you apprised. Talk soon." Wil terminated the communication and sighed. "I hear you don't bring good news."

"Afraid not." Jason closed the door.

Wil took a seat behind the desk and gestured for them to sit in the visitor chairs across from him. "I was surprised to see you recommended Darin for the Militia Division."

"The poor kid lost everything on the *Andvari*. He needs direction and a community."

"We do try to make the TSS feel like a family," his mother replied. "I hope he can find that with us."

His father nodded his agreement but remained focused on

the more pressing issue. "Do you feel confident in what you got from his mind?"

"Yes," Jason confirmed. "It took a little digging, but I got through the block. I'd never seen anything quite like it."

"So, the being is telepathic?" Saera asked.

"It's a lot more than that."

His father had his full attention on him. "How so?"

"What we could see in that image was only part of it. This entity looks massive, but it's just a temporary manifestation. I don't think it has any kind of set physical form. I believe it's from a higher dimension and that it is, indeed, using the tear in the Rift as a gateway to spacetime."

"Worst-case scenario, then," Wil stated flatly.

"It's looking that way."

"What an odd way to make first contact—attacking a random civilian ship," Saera commented.

"I don't think that's what it was." Jason sat up straighter. "On the way back, I mulled it over and reread part of the initial findings report. I have a hypothesis. Rather than an attack, I believe it was an experiment."

His parents exchanged glances. "Go on," his father prompted.

"Going through Darin's memories and, more or less, experiencing the contact firsthand made it clear that the being was curious. It wanted to learn about our Taran form. It basically scanned him, but it wasn't particularly careful in how it went about it, and it shocked Darin's system enough to put him in a coma.

"Then, there's what happened to the ship," Jason continued. "People started seeing things. Seemed like the ship was haunted. But I don't think the crew was going crazy—not in the least. I think the entity was testing them. It used the info it got from Darin to design various scenarios, and the *Andvari*'s crew was its lab rats."

Wil's brows drew together. "I could see that. But to what end?"

"I haven't a clue." Jason shook his head. "All I know is that the entity looked at Darin as a tool to be used until he was no longer helpful. It was only a flash, but that's not a feeling I'll forget anytime soon."

Wil folded his hands on the desktop. "All right, let's say this *wasn't* an attack but some sort of... scouting mission. What would it have learned?"

"That's the problem." Jason swallowed hard. "I think the crew probably pissed it off."

"By destroying the ship," Saera murmured, having put the pieces together for herself.

"Yep. Let's assume it came through the Rift to scout out what Tarans are up to—possibly in response to what went on with the Gatekeepers, and the *Andvari* became the ambassadors for our race. Upon first contact, one person passed out, another threw themselves out an airlock, and the others gave their lives defending their ship. And in their final moments, they sent comatose Darin in an escape pod with all the information they had before turning their ship into a bomb with the express purpose of hurting the thing that had been terrorizing them. And maybe they succeeded; we can't be sure what happened after the escape pod was sent, only what their intentions were and that the *Andvari* did eventually explode. In any case, we know what happens when a plaything tries to hurt us."

"Your curiosity turns to hate, and you discard it," Wil said.

"Or destroy it," Saera added.

Jason looked between them and nodded. "Right. Now, we

may never know if this scout *was* coming here to figure out how best to wipe us out—as the Gatekeepers said the 'others' would—or if it may have been looking to extend a peace offering. But I can imagine what kind of impression it left with."

"Assuming it even 'went' anywhere." Wil groaned softly. "A higher-dimensional being could… We have no way to guess what kind of abilities it might possess. Fok, it could be listening to us right now and we'd never know."

"Well, it *did* single out Darin and the *Andvari*. That wouldn't have been necessary if it were that omniscient," Jason pointed out.

"True. I guess that is a bit of good news." Nothing about Wil's expression indicated he received any solace from the observation.

"There might still be an opportunity for diplomacy," Saera said. "We'll reexamine the existing information from this new perspective and see what else we can learn."

"I hope so." Jason looked down. "I don't know how we'd defend ourselves against something like this. Whatever we're facing, I feel confident now that it's the darkness from my vision."

"We'll find a solution," his mother assured him.

More than he'd ever wanted anything, he hoped she was right.

—   —   —

Wil took in Jason's account of the interrogation at the Prisaris base, growing increasingly concerned with each new detail. The written reports hadn't done the situation justice.

What the fok are we going up against? He tried to keep his expression neutral as his fatherly instinct kicked in to shield his son from additional worry; he needed a response plan before he raised the alarm. "Anything else?"

Jason shook his head. "Nothing that seems relevant. I'll let you know if anything else comes to mind later."

Wil nodded. "Well, at least now we have confirmation and can plan accordingly."

"I'll be standing by," Jason said as he rose from his seat.

"Thanks, Jason. Good work out there."

His son inclined his head and left Wil and Saera alone in the office.

"I've just gotta say it…" Saera slumped back in her chair, "this sucks."

He couldn't help chuckling. "It is less than ideal."

She straightened. "But we'll find a solution, because we've fought too long and hard for our children to not be safe."

Wil nodded. "I will never stop fighting to give them the best possible future." He always put his children first. The future of the Empire was *their* future, and it shaped every decision he made as a leader.

When it had come time for him and Saera to start a family, they'd made the difficult decision to keep the twins in the dark about the Taran Empire—to preserve their innocence for as long as possible. Between the messy politics on Tararia under the Priesthood's rule and the aftermath of the Bakzen War, there was too much baggage to dump on young children. Wil knew firsthand what it was like to grow up in TSS Headquarters with parents serving dual roles as Agents and dynastic scions; he'd never had a chance to just be a kid. So, he'd done everything he could to give his children a proper childhood unburdened by galactic-scale responsibilities.

Once the twins' Gifts emerged at the age of sixteen, they

had learned the truth about their birthright. Though they were justifiably upset about the deception at first, in the years since, they'd come to understand why information had been kept from them. Wil had no regrets. He was proud of the young adults his children had become, and he credited their compassion and open-mindedness to having lived among people from all walks of life.

Now, all of them would be put to the test with this new transdimensional menace. Wil knew he couldn't protect his children from everything, but he would always shield them as best he could. At present, that meant figuring out a way to make contact with the aliens.

He stood, feeling the need to pace while he worked through the new information. "We can't go into an engagement blind."

"Find a way to see the alien the way the *Andvari* did, you mean?"

"Yes, but a still image won't do it. We need to replicate those conditions in real-time."

"That's a tall order. From what the data showed, they nearly destroyed their own ship in the process."

"They were a group of moderately trained civilians. Our engineering team is the best."

"Should probably get them on it sooner than later."

"Consider it done." He paused and took a heavy breath. "We also need to know the terms of that treaty between the three races—what, exactly, we did to violate it. Not to mention, it would be helpful to know more about the circumstances surrounding that ancient conflict; there must be a reason the three races decided to strike a deal rather than battle it out to the end."

"It seems the Gatekeepers were most upset about the use of their Gate tech, so I'd wager it had something to do with that."

"I was thinking the same thing. But is it related to one race using the technology of another? Or traveling through the Gate to the Gatekeeper's world? Or the technology itself? Are our forces equally matched? Each of those variables changes the conversation a little. *Something* sparked the Gatekeepers to reveal themselves to us now and then prompted these other beings to send a scout—assuming Jason's hypothesis pans out."

"I suppose it isn't a viable option to just *ask* the Gatekeepers?"

Wil shook his head. "You saw what they were willing to do to us. That's not a line of communication I'm ready to reopen." The Gatekeepers had intentionally unleashed tech on populated worlds, transforming the biome of planets in a matter of hours. Millions had died, and the Gatekeepers hadn't shown any remorse. Not since the Bakzen War had Wil witnessed that level of disregard for life, and he had every intention of steering clear of the aliens.

Saera frowned. "I'm not sure where that leaves us. We can't just wait around twiddling our thumbs until these transdimensional beings decide to attack!"

"Never. We prepare for all contingencies. It's the TSS way."

"Even so, narrowing it down a *little* would be helpful."

"There is one possible way to get a more definitive answer about the treaty," Wil mused.

"How? You've already spoken to the Aesir. They don't have anything in their records."

The Aesir had been Wil's go-to information source about past events, since they were former members of the Priesthood and had taken a copy of the organization's collective knowledge when they split from the rest of the Taran Empire one thousand years prior. However, they were a private people, so getting a straight answer was often difficult. "The Aesir aren't the sole keepers of historical information."

His wife raised an eyebrow quizzically.

"The Priesthood's island," he explained. "They had vast records in the underground vaults. It's possible we missed something in the raid. If this ancient war was such a big deal, I'd expect the Priesthood to have gathered any available information about it."

She frowned. "The references you saw in the Aesir's records indicated that it was potentially tens or hundreds of thousands of years ago. That predates the formation of the Priesthood."

"However, they fancied themselves the official recordkeepers for Tarans. *Someone* would have made a copy of something as important as a galactic treaty, and the Priesthood would almost certainly have acquired that documentation when they came into power."

Saera started to perk up. "And if it wasn't a digital record, then the Aesir wouldn't have had a copy of it to take with them when they branched off, so it wouldn't be in their archives now."

"Exactly."

Saera nodded thoughtfully. "That is an interesting angle."

"I'll add, Raena invited us to visit the island. Apparently, the renovations are going quite well."

"I suppose it would be appropriate for us to find a suitable location for a parents' guest suite somewhere out-of-the-way… say, in a neglected basement?" She straightened in her chair.

Wil smiled. "A former records room, perhaps?"

"I like the way you think."

CHAPTER 7

LEXI'S HEART RACED as she followed Oren down the hallway to the lone door at a dead end. The door was always kept locked, as far as Lexi knew. Exactly once, she'd gotten up the courage to try the handle and found it immobile. Casual questions to others had confirmed that there was an air of mystery about where it might lead.

Unlike the biometric locks that controlled most access points, Oren produced a physical key from his pants pocket to open the door. There was a heavy metal clang as the deadbolt disengaged. He pushed the door open, causing it to let out an ominous creak and burst of musty air that smelled faintly of wet soil.

"Where are we going?" Lexi asked.

Oren stepped through the opening without a reply.

In a depressing realization, it occurred to Lexi that no one would come looking for her if she never returned from the basement. She could be walking into a death trap right now and there wasn't a soul outside the Alliance that would notice if she disappeared.

The thought was sobering, but it also put into perspective that she had nothing to lose by following Oren inside. *I'm already in this deep. What does it matter?*

The door was atop a flight of stairs flanked by old brick walls that curved into an arched ceiling. That kind of stonework wasn't seen in the newer parts of the city, though Lexi recognized the reddish bricks as similar to those found in the foundations of older buildings in the Historic District. They were formed from the clay harvested locally and had made for an abundant construction material for early colonists. Once the interplanetary shipping routes were established, the material had fallen out of style in favor of metal, glass, and stones from offworld to denote Duronis' burgeoning prosperity. The bricks' presence here must mean they were headed into one of the old structures upon which the Alliance's office had been constructed.

Lighting in the hallway was dim and had a somewhat yellow cast. The circular fixtures installed at two-meter intervals along the ceiling had been attached to the outside of the stones rather than being inset like most lights found throughout the planet's structures.

Two stories down, the switch-backed stairwell opened into a broad tunnel. A different set of lights activated to reveal that the tunnel was lined with marked crates arranged on storage racks. The rows upon rows of crates stretched as far as Lexi could see down the tunnel, disappearing into the distant shadows and beyond the curvature of the span. It answered the niggling question at the back of her mind about what happened to all of the items after she had completed the inventorying, but far, far more questions now surfaced. Even when accounting for two years' worth of deliveries, there were more materials than she or her predecessor would have processed on their own, based on the standard shipment size. However, that detail paled compared to the other aspects of the cache.

"What is this place?" she asked more inelegantly than she'd intended.

"Our stores," Oren replied.

"Right. But, like, did you build this storeroom, or…?" The ancient stone bracing in the tunnel made it clear that it had been there for a while, but she wanted to extract as much information as possible while she had him in a forthcoming mood.

He shook his head. "It's part of the old transit network. Few even remember there used to be a subway in this city."

"Nice." She peered at the nearby crates. The numbering scheme wasn't what she used for processing everything in the workshop on the surface.

"Yes, the materials are sorted after they leave your care," Oren answered her unspoken question. "You will soon have a much better understanding of the operation."

"Is this all of the stores?"

"It is one facility of many. The old transit network works quite well for getting between some of the locations."

Lexi's heart pounded in her chest. The scale of the operation was massive compared to what she'd pictured.

How many other people are doing my same job in other offices? Everything suddenly seemed much more real. It would appear the actual work was about to begin. *Maybe once I connect with other people, I can find out where Melisa was transferred.*

"We have been diligent in our preparations," Oren said. "Our allies are patient and have been biding their time. This new event presents the opportunity we've been waiting for."

"What?"

"The attack. It's the perfect opening."

Lexi looked down the sea of crates, not quite seeing how the things were connected. "You were saying earlier that this whole mess with the ship attack is getting blown out of proportion."

Oren nodded. "Oh, I do believe it is. But it honestly doesn't matter if the threat is real or not. The key thing is the Guard and TSS are distracted."

"An opportunity to create disruption when they least expect it," Lexi realized. *And an opportunity for me to learn what the Alliance is really up to.*

— — —

Raena frowned at the news coverage of a rally on Duronis. Generally, she didn't watch live broadcasts, but Jovan had brought this one to her attention.

"What am I missing?" she asked her assistant.

There'd been plenty of public demonstrations during her five years in the leadership spotlight—no surprise, considering that her induction into office corresponded with the Priesthood's removal from power. Changing leaders after millennia tended to get people riled up. This particular gathering didn't strike her as being any different than those.

"Look at the signs in the background." Javon zoomed in on the upper right of the holographic projection, focusing on a poster affixed to the side of a building.

The rectangular sign read: 'Independence is Freedom. Freedom is Power.'

Its sentiment wasn't anything new. Half of the Outer Colonies wanted to be more closely integrated with the Middle and Central Worlds; the other half wished they could be free from Tararian rule. Which planets had which perspective varied from year-to-year as they went through their own local and planetary government leaders. Invariably, the remote worlds always realized that they were better off with the opportunities and resources afforded by an ongoing connection to the core planets. For a world to cut ties with the rest of the Empire was to condemn its people to a bleak future.

So, while the poster's call for independence leading to power made for a nice slogan, Raena knew it was a hollow aspiration. However, the note handwritten in red ink drew her attention: 'Sietinen: High Council. TSS. What's next?'

She frowned. Complaints about the government in general were one thing, but rarely were specific leaders called out. And last she'd heard, Sietinen had one of the best reputations among the High Dynasties.

"Do you know what prompted this?" Raena asked Jovan.

"The posters began popping up this morning in cities all across Duronis. It seems highly coordinated."

"That planet name came up recently. Wasn't that also where the *Andvari*'s salvage contract originated?"

"Yes, my lady."

Her chest tightened. "It can't be a coincidence that this campaign launched so soon after news of the attack became public."

He bowed his head. "It seemed prudent to bring it to your attention immediately."

"Thank you, Jovan."

There were worse ways to start the day, but Raena didn't like the direction in which the week was trending. First an attack, then civil unrest calling out her family, specifically. It didn't bode well for what was to come, especially with her parents' spontaneous visit.

>>More fun times,<< Raena wrote to Ryan on her handheld and linked to the relevant video clip.

It didn't take long to get a response. >>I'm sure it will blow over, like it always does. Though the optics aren't great with the timing of your parents' visit.<<

>>Should I tell them not to come?<< Raena was painfully aware of how it looked every time she got together with her parents. A High Dynasty heiress meeting with the TSS High Commander and Lead Agent in private. She hated that such thoughts even came to mind, but it was the reality of the situation. Politics and military were *supposed* to be kept siloed in the interest of checks and balances, but they were inexorably entwined with her family.

>>No, they wouldn't have asked to come if it wasn't important.<< Ryan's word echoed his statements when Raena had broached the topic of her parents' visit.

Raena had received the request with only a day's notice. It was very unlike them. Her father, in particular, was deliberate in his actions, so there was a reason for coming besides catching up with his daughter and son-in-law.

Raena massaged her left temple with her fingertips. >>Okay, I'll see you at dinner.<<

There was nothing she could do at the moment regarding the disruption on Duronis or how it would look to have her parents arrive and provide a perfect photo op to prove the protesters' point. Trying to hide the meeting wouldn't look good, either. So, she set about her remaining tasks for the day and tried to suppress the feeling of imminent doom welling in her chest.

By dinnertime, the sting of the earlier news had faded to the background, replaced by excitement to see her parents. It had been almost two years since their last visit to Morningstar

Isle, though Raena had seen them elsewhere in the interim. She looked forward to showing them how the place formerly used as a beacon of oppression had been turned into a loving home. Granted, the interior renovations weren't complete, but the energy of the place had shifted. She knew they'd appreciate it more than most visitors.

She went to meet Ryan on the west terrace next to the garden, where they often met for lunch or had dinner whenever they wanted to be outside. It was located between their two work areas, so it had become a convenient place to meet up without wasting time trekking across the entire estate.

Ryan was hunched over the table when she arrived, absorbed with reading something on his handheld.

"Hey," she greeted telepathically when he didn't look up.

He set the device down. "This day, I swear," he muttered, shaking his head.

"What's wrong?"

"Just got a report of another starship dealer who was inflating lease terms. I understand why people in the Outer Colonies think we're trying to gouge them—all the people in the middle want to increase their cut rather than deliver on the promises we've made."

"Everything is too big." Raena rubbed his back before sitting next to him. "It's like playing a massive game of telephone across the galaxy. The message gets diluted by the time it filters down."

"What?"

"Never mind." She forgot, sometimes, Ryan had played different childhood games while growing up on Tararia than those she had played on Earth. "My point is, we need to find a way to more directly interface with our people."

"Even so, will they believe what we say?"

"If there's follow-through, yes. The issue isn't the idea behind these new initiatives, but that they're not being executed in the way we envisioned."

"It's the bomaxed Lower Dynasties! Everything is a political power-grab game to them. Like that shite that went down with Arvonen and the Gate research that got us all in this mess. Ridiculous."

"I know." Raena took his hand. "You're doing great, Ryan."

"The fact that business is good is secondary. I still feel like we could do more to create job opportunities and help make things more affordable so people can get ahead in life."

"That will always be a challenge for us. We both grew up without the comforts of wealth and power being givens in our lives, so we think about those who are living paycheck-to-paycheck. No one else in the High Dynasties will ever appreciate that perspective. It's why it's so important we stay the course and lead by example."

"Right, and we've made a good start. But reducing transit fees and opening up new shipyards is just scratching the surface."

"These things take time."

"I know. Still, it's frustrating. I got handed all of this wealth by birthright, yet it's all tied up in DGE, and I can't do what I'd like to help families improve their circumstances."

"The harsh truth is we can't help everyone personally. However, these little price cuts, new jobs, and scholarships will reap long-term benefits."

"Your grandparents are on board, but the other High Dynasties need to rethink their businesses, too."

"Once they see what good work you're doing, I'm sure they'll follow suit. With all the colonization expansion going on, DGE is primed to shine."

"And I have every intention to do the Dainetris name proud. The Dynasty is here to stay this time," he said, resolute.

The whole mess with Dainetris' temporary fall from power two centuries prior turned Raena's stomach. The Priesthood had ruined Ryan's ancestors when they spoke out against the organization's misconduct, so it was no wonder people nowadays didn't trust leaders to act in the public's best interest. Even once files detailing the Priesthood's millennia of corruption had been released, too many people were still skeptical about the High Council's intentions. 'Doing the right thing' wasn't a sufficient motive, apparently. *But we're not like the Priesthood.*

Raena and her husband had truly tried to live by 'doing the right thing' as their mantra. She'd been handed so much power at a young age, and though she hadn't wanted any of it, she couldn't turn away when others were counting on her. The power distance between rulers and their people had become so great that they needed someone like her who hadn't lived like royalty for her whole life. She could help heal the divide.

With that mindset, every one of her business decisions, political moves, and personal relationships needed to pass an ethical test designed to favor the public good. Outsiders could be as skeptical as they wanted, but Raena had made it her life's mission to be the kind of leader people *wanted* to have, not just the one they were stuck with. That's why it stung so much to see the posters suggesting she was part of a devious plot fueled by greed or megalomania. *I'll prove to them I'm not in this for myself. Every day I can try to be a better person.*

Food arrived, breaking Raena from her ruminations. The hot turkey and cheese sandwich was one of her favorites, so at least the day had that going for it.

"So, my parents will arrive tomorrow," she said after

finishing the first quarter of her meal. The gooey cheese oozing from between the bread didn't make for the most delicate eating experience, but the chef had never failed to deliver after Raena had a heart-to-heart with him about the merits of carbs and cheese. Comfort food was called that for a reason, after all.

Ryan swallowed a bite of his own sandwich with a more restrained portion of fillings. "I'm curious to learn what prompted the visit."

"Me too. It'll be strange having them here. The last time we were all together on the island, it still had so much of the Priesthood in the space."

"All the more reason to make new memories."

"Yeah, I know. It sucks that there's this other stuff going on. It would be nice to just have family time. I think my grandparents are planning to come over, too."

"Speaking of which, should I invite my mom?" Ryan asked.

"That's a great idea! It would also help with the optics—a proper family gathering that isn't restricted to TSS special guests."

Ryan raised an eyebrow. "Not everything is about how things look on the news, you know."

She took a mental step back. "Sorry. What I meant to say was, it would be lovely to see her."

"I don't know if she'll go for it. It still freaks her out to be around High Dynasty types."

"Well, *you're* one of those now."

"I guess so, but it's different with immediate family."

"Then the answer to making her comfortable is to nurture a closer relationship with us," Raena said. "If she can think of you purely as her son, without the external factors, then that's how she can think about me and my family, too; let us be *people* rather than figureheads."

"That's easier said than done."

It had taken a while for even Ryan to build a sociable relationship with his mother as an adult, after growing up away from her as a Ward—essentially foster care, as Raena understood the arrangement. All the Priesthood's doing, to keep an eye on Ryan once he'd been discovered as a lost scion of the allegedly extinct Dainetris bloodline. One of his ancestors had somehow escaped the Priesthood's purge of the Dainetris line, and the descendants had lived under an alias for generations, unaware of their lineage.

So, despite being directly in the Dainetris line herself, Ryan's mother could never see herself as highborn, having already spent a lifetime in poverty and servitude. It saddened Raena to see the woman struggle with her own identity in such a way. Ryan had slowly come into his own as a Dynasty leader, but his mother had insisted on remaining in her small apartment and maintaining a modest lifestyle. The arrangement made family get-togethers a little awkward, to say the least.

"I really want your mom to feel at ease here," Raena said, looking her husband in his eyes. "She's always welcome."

"I'll extend an invitation, but this might not be the best time for her to come, truthfully. I don't expect this to be a particularly restful visit."

"That's a fair point."

Ryan smiled at her from across the table, sensing her souring mood. "Hey, we'd be doing something wrong if this were easy. Being the cornerstone of a galactic empire is complicated."

She chuckled. "Yeah, it is. I never understood why anyone would want to run for president back home, and that was just for a single country!"

"Didn't someone say that not wanting the job should be the top metric for qualification?"

"I'm not sure about the quote, but I think there's truth in the statement when it comes to politics." She wiped the cheese grease off her hands with her cloth napkin. "And, on that note, I was thinking that we should put out some kind of press statement."

"What about?"

"Something to get ahead of this growing unrest in the Outer Colonies."

Ryan leaned back in his chair. "I'll defer to your lead. I'm finally starting to get my head around DGE's operations, but this political ruling stuff… you're a natural."

"Sorry to break it to you, but I'm totally faking it, buddy." She smiled, but it didn't quite touch her eyes.

"Could have fooled me."

"I don't know. I just think about what *I* would want to hear, or what I would want a leader to do, if I was an average person on the street. Whenever there's uncertainty, you want your leaders to step up and tell you it's going to be okay, right?"

"But we don't know for sure that it *will* be all right."

"That doesn't make for a very good press release, does it?"

"No. It's hard for me, though, to not be forthright," he said.

"It's not a lie," she assured him. "It's giving hope. Everyone wants to look forward to a better tomorrow."

CHAPTER 8

AFTER A TERRIBLE morning and even worse afternoon, Jason looked forward to turning the day around by spending the evening with Tiff.

It wouldn't be a date, per se; their relationship wasn't romantic in nature and never would be. 'Intimate friends' is how he labeled it in his mind, not that he ever spoke the term aloud. Honestly, he wasn't sure how she viewed *him*, exactly. Whatever they were to each other, it worked—no strings, no pressure. And on days like this, he needed the physical connection to unwind and forget about the outside universe for a while.

Their relationship had been Jason's lifeline during his early years in the TSS, after Raena left for Tararia; that twin connection everyone joked about was frustratingly real. She had found Ryan, by all accounts her soulmate, while Jason was alone in TSS Headquarters, training for most of the day and studying for the remaining waking hours. In a bold move, Tiff had propositioned him with a 'friends with benefits' arrangement near the end of their first year. He'd eventually accepted, figuring there was no harm in a one-time thing, but they kept coming back to each other.

Over the years, as the intimacy in their relationship grew, Tiff had become his closest friend. Now, they spent at least one evening a week together; sometimes a whole night. Jason had long since stopped caring if anyone found out. Tiff was a smart, attractive Primus Elite Agent. Anyone who judged him for being with her rather than a dynastic heiress deserved a punch in the face—a sentence he'd been known to deal out, when necessary.

The strange thing was, despite their closeness, they rarely spent time together when it wasn't one-on-one. He was sure his other friends must suspect they had a 'thing'. In particular, though Gil had never explicitly asked about Tiff, his friend always got a knowing look on his face whenever her name was mentioned. Jason was glad that part of his life remained private. It had zero bearing on his performance as an Agent, so it wasn't anyone else's business.

Jason headed to his quarters to shower and get in a short nap before Tiff arrived. They'd occasionally meet up in her quarters, but his was the norm—in large part because he was far tidier. In fact, he was fairly sure that half the time she invited him over was to motivate herself to pick up laundry. Word had it she'd been a decent roommate during training, but she had taken the liberty of having her own space as an Agent to do whatever she pleased. However, that was the beauty of their type of relationship: not his problem.

After showering, he managed to get just under two hours of sleep before his alarm woke him, leaving just enough time to grab a quick meal from the mess hall and brush his teeth before her arrival.

He'd just settled on the couch to wait for her when the door beeped softly and slid open in response to her biometric check; as a matter of ease, they'd coded each other as authorized visitors to their respective quarters.

He stood to greet her.

"Hey," she said, removing the elastic tie from her dark-brown hair so it fell loose to just above her shoulders. The door slid closed behind her.

She wasn't stunningly beautiful in the way he had found many of the highborn women he'd met, who had a refined bearing of sophistication that always managed to mesmerize him. Instead, Tiff had downright sex appeal, with a great ass and breasts she knew how to work to her advantage. However, that was never why he was most attracted to her. Her innate confidence and adventurous attitude gave her a frank way of speaking that was a refreshing contrast compared to the deference others paid Jason. He could talk with her for hours, about anything, and be one-hundred-percent confident that what they discussed would never be repeated to another soul.

He moved to Tiff and wrapped his arms around her, pulling her gently to his chest. In an instant, his stress and worries began to fade away. "You're the only person I wanted to see after this disaster of a day."

She hugged him back. "I've been anxious to hear what happened at Prisaris."

He let his arms drop to his sides. "Suffice to say, we have confirmation of alien contact."

"Shite."

"Yeah, so that's going to be a thing."

"What kind of timeline?"

Jason shook his head. "Too soon to tell. There are some aspects of the situation that require more follow-up."

"I take it you're going to be busy?"

"More than likely. But tonight, you're my focus."

He led her to the bedroom and did his best to forget about everything related to the Rift and alien threat.

After years together, they could anticipate each other's wants, even without the added benefits of telepathy. Since their first time, it had been a natural fit—far more satisfying than any of his high school flings on Earth. As their connection grew, they'd reached a level of familiarity and comfort where they instinctively knew what the other *needed*, beyond the expression of conscious desire. And, for a while, he was able to shed his responsibilities and burdens, relishing every moment with one of the people he cared about most in the world.

He was left feeling significantly better than he had earlier that evening. Still breathing heavily, he reached up to brush the hair out of Tiff's face.

She beamed down at him, hands on his bare chest. "That was worth the wait."

"When isn't it?" He grinned.

"Such modesty." She playfully rolled her eyes and slid off of him.

He pivoted his head to the side to face her. "I'm sorry for canceling the other night. You know how seriously Gil takes those dumb tournaments."

"Like you don't get into it yourself."

"Competition is healthy," he said in his own mock defense.

She patted his arm. "Don't worry about it. I know there's a lot of shite going on right now."

"Things could escalate quickly," Jason admitted, hoping to transition to a much-needed therapeutic discussion about his experience with Darin. "I'm not sure what that will mean for our usual schedule."

Without responding, Tiff got up and began dressing.

"Going already?" One-and-done was a rarity for their get-togethers, except for the occasional daytime quickie. Not to mention their usual pillow-talk.

"I can't stay."

Though miffed she was bailing on him so early in the night, he couldn't help admiring her figure from where he still lay in bed. When she caught him watching her, she raised her eyebrows. He took the hint to stop staring and get dressed himself.

"Thanks for coming over. I really needed this after the shit from the last couple of days," he said while pulling on his own pants.

She shook her head and sighed. "You're never going to learn how to swear properly, are you?"

He smirked. "Some things never change."

"I suppose they don't." Sudden solemnness edged her tone.

"Hey, is something wrong?"

Tiff slipped her shirt over her head. "Jason, what are we doing?" The look on her face was more serious than he'd ever seen her.

He was tempted to respond with a joke in his usual tension-diffusing fashion but thought better of it. "I take it you mean more than us getting dressed right now."

Now there was sadness in her eyes. That was a first. She swallowed hard. "I think it's time we end it."

The words struck him like a physical blow to his chest and gut. *Today, of all days?*

He'd promised himself when the relationship began that he wouldn't get attached, but obviously that had been an impossible pledge to keep after nine years together. He didn't love her in the overwhelming infatuation sense he'd witnessed with his sister and her husband, or even between his parents, but he loved her as a close friend. A confidant. Someone he could come home to and be held after a rough day. They may never have formally dated, but they had formed a relationship that was much more than the arrangement for stress-relief sex the way it had begun. Subconsciously, he'd always known that their time together would have an expiration date. Except, he had thought he would have seen the end coming.

"I…" He struggled to find the right words. A major pillar in his support network was being knocked out from under him, and right at a time when he was about to need her the most. "Why?"

She sat down on the bed and placed her hands on her thighs. "It can't go forward, and *we* can't go forward ourselves so long as this is going on."

There was too much truth in her statement to deny. Still, it was a low blow to end things so suddenly. "I can see where you're coming from, but why *now*?"

"There's a promotion opportunity—a posting at Alkeer Station. I was debating whether or not to take it, but all this new shite with the Rift means things are about to get even more complicated. I think it's better I accept the reassignment so we can both be unencumbered for whatever comes."

There it is. He sat down next to her. "Alkeer is a nice base."

"It is. And people have normal lives there. Families." She looked at him briefly and then tore her gaze away. "I know that would never be an option for us, but I don't want to close off that possibility for myself."

"Tiff, it's not your—"

"Please, don't," she cut in. "I was well aware of the reality when I signed up for this. I know your family likes to pretend that they're happy to date commoners, but not one of those was actually the case, as it turns out. I promise you, I'm not secretly a dynastic heiress."

It hurt that she'd reduce their relationship to those terms. He'd been the fiercest defender of the TSS tenet that a person should be measured by their character and accomplishments, not their pedigree. To think that in their time together—the better part of a decade—she considered herself to be lesser than him turned his stomach. "Birthright really doesn't matter. Especially not for me. I'm not in the succession line." He tried to take her hand, but she pulled away.

"You're still a Sietinen. And your grandparents are great people, but no matter what they say, they're hoping you don't end up with a salvage hauler rat like me."

As much as he wanted to argue the point, deep down, Jason wondered if she might be right. He wanted to believe that they would approve so long as he was truly in love. But that was the real issue. They loved each other, but they weren't *in love*.

Tiff met his gaze, and his thoughts were echoed in her expression. "I care about you, Jason. And I've never once doubted that you care about me. But this," she waved her hand between them, "was never about having a romantic happily ever after. You're a good friend—one of my best—and it's okay that that's all it is."

Part of him wanted to fight for her to stay, but that would be selfish. He respected her decision, and her reasoning. He'd be a terrible friend if he offered anything less than his full support. "I want the best for you. If this is what you need to get where you want to go, I won't argue."

She finally took his hand. "It's been on my mind for a while. When I saw the new post open up, I realized it was time. *Especially* now, with the unknowns ahead."

"It could be dangerous out there."

"Potential risks aren't a reason not to live."

He took a slow breath and nodded. "Please don't take my acquiescence as apathy. I'm going to miss you like crazy."

"Me too." She kissed him, and he savored it, knowing it might be their last.

"I really hope this isn't goodbye forever—that we can be friends," he said.

"Oh, stars, yes! Give up my 'in' to the High Dynasties? I'm not a foking idiot." She gave him a light, playful punch in the shoulder.

"We had a good run." A painful twinge struck his heart, even as he tried to smile through it. *We can say we'll stay friends, but things will never be the same.*

"We did. I don't know if I would have made it through the Initiate years without you."

"Oh, hardly! You were in Primus Elite for a reason."

"Maybe. But it was nice to have a real friend to lean on." She patted his knee.

He nodded. "That it was. You gave me grounding when I needed it."

"That's what friends are for."

Unfortunately, he'd gotten too used to having Tiff serve that emotional cornerstone role in his life. While he had no shortage of social friends like Gil, Tiff was the only person he felt he could let his guard down with, to be vulnerable and express worries and doubts. He'd been counting on being able to spend this night with her to talk about his fears about the alien attack and what else might come through the Rift, but the realization that she was moving on to a new chapter in her life closed off that possibility. They could remain friends, but there'd never be that same level of emotional intimacy in their relationship. Once again, he was on his own.

Tiff laughed suddenly. "Stars, you have no idea how

frustrating it is not being able to tell anyone that I've been foking the smokin' hot Sietinen heir for years. How many people I could have slain with that single statement."

"If you were to ever tell someone, I wouldn't deny it."

"You sure about that?"

"You're gorgeous, smart, and a total badass. Who cares if you weren't born into a life of privilege? I'm happy to have been able to have our time together." *And I hate that it's coming to an end.*

She smirked. "Well, I don't have any immediate plans for gloating, but I'll keep it as back-pocket ammunition."

The knot tightened in his chest again. "I really hope you find someone you're head over heels for."

"You too. And I applaud her if she's able to pin you down."

"Geez, Tiff, it's not like I'm a silver fox playboy!"

"Weren't your parents and grandparents married by the time they were, like, twenty-one?"

"That's beside the point."

She raised an eyebrow. "Mhmm."

"You're just as bad as the matchmaking schemers on Tararia, I swear."

She patted his knee. "See, I'm already trying to get you paired up with someone else. Friendship intact."

Jason wasn't sure it would work as easily the other way around, but hopefully that would come with a little time and distance. "You'll be the first to know any new developments, I promise."

"You'd better! I've put in a lot of work over the years to get you trained up, so I've gotta know all the effort is paying off."

"Yes, ma'am."

Tiff turned somber again. "I should go."

They stood, awkwardly judging the space between them

for the first time in years. Jason headed for the door and she followed.

At the exit, they turned to face each other. She met his gaze, and he saw a tearful sheen in her eyes.

"Thank you for these years," she murmured.

"And thank you. I'm glad you were brazen enough to proposition me."

She chuckled. "Yeah… still surprised you accepted, but…"

"You came into my life when I needed you. I'll always be indebted to you for that."

"No debts. You always treated me as an equal, and that's how it will always be with us."

"Deal."

Tiff held out her arms for a hug, and he pulled her in tight. As she started to pull out from the hug, she gave him one last kiss.

It was the end of an era. Bittersweet, as all meaningful endings tended to be. The only way now was forward.

CHAPTER 9

"THE DEMONSTRATION WENT perfectly," Oren announced with a broad grin.

The whole thing was odd to Lexi. They'd been gathering materials for years, apparently, and the 'big event' was putting up some posters and gathering a thousand people to chant about freedom? She didn't buy it. There *had* to be more going on behind the scenes, but Oren still wouldn't tell her anything more.

Her 'promotion' had been a joke so far. Granted, it had only been a day, but Lexi had been hoping for a revealing sit-down with Oren or other leaders of the Alliance. She wanted answers and to finally get a glimpse of the organization's structure she'd been trying to figure out. Instead, the short tour of the underground storeroom had been the extent of it, along with the declaration that she would handle pickups on her own moving forward. Even the latter part of that had proved anti-climactic when Oren had informed her that there wouldn't be a pickup for another week, due to the demonstration activities. So, Lexi had spent the day sitting in the warehouse, watching and waiting for direction, with no clear sense of what she was supposed to do.

Meanwhile, Oren was ecstatic for whatever reason. The tall, thin man was awkward on his best days, but now there was something downright unnerving about seeing him prance around like he'd just scored the greatest victory in civilization's history.

What's the big deal? We didn't do *anything!* Lexi couldn't help fuming with frustration about being kept in the dark. She'd pledged her commitment to the movement, but she wanted to know where the whole thing was headed. That didn't seem like too much to ask. It was beside the point that she didn't care about knowing the goals themselves; all she wanted was to work her way toward the inner circle so she could get answers, and this was just another step in that long, convoluted, and perilous path.

"Oren, could we talk?" she asked. The words came out before she'd made a conscious decision.

When he cast her a disapproving glare, she wondered if she'd made a mistake. "About what?"

Lexi glanced at people gathered in the nearby rec room and those working on projects in the warehouse. "Alone."

He sighed and waved his arm. "If you insist."

Oren led the way down to his office, not bothering to hide his annoyance. She followed him wordlessly. Upon reaching their destination, he leaned against his desk, sticking his feet out at an angle toward the door. It barely left her room to enter and close the door without tripping over him in the compact space.

"I don't understand," she stated.

"What?"

"The rally. How it connects to anything. What made it

such a success?"

Oren crossed his arms and stared at her. The annoyance was gone, replaced with an intensity beyond anything Lexi had seen from the man before. He was in his late-forties, and though she didn't typically think of him as being much older than her, the expression made every crease stand out on his face under the single, stark light centered on the ceiling.

"What do you know of the Taran government's operations?"

The question caught Lexi by surprise. She gave a noncommittal shrug and shook her head. "In what sense? The High Council runs things."

"More specifically than that."

Lexi bit down a snide response. She wanted to talk about the plan for effecting change in the Outer Colonies, not get a civics lesson about the very government they hoped to break free from. "Each High Dynasty is responsible for a corporation, which oversees a major infrastructure element of the Empire. Navigation, communications, food, power, mining, home goods, shipping. The Lower Dynasties have their own corporate arms, many of which roll up to one of the seven major umbrellas. Business and politics are one in the same. Only medical care and banking are independent."

"Precisely. You have answered your own question."

But I haven't. What am I missing? She tended to think of herself as a smart, perceptive person, but Oren's line of reasoning was escaping her. Worse, he clearly expected her to arrive at the answer on her own. If she didn't, that might end any aspirations of advancing within the Alliance on the spot.

There was one option. The risk hadn't been worth considering before, but the conditions were as perfect as they might ever be. *He's thinking about it right now. We're alone, no distractions...* She could glean the answers from his mind without needing to dig around. *He'd never know.*

Still, it was dangerous. She could see something else she wasn't supposed to know about, and then she'd need to pretend she was in the dark. It was why she was always so reluctant to use her Gifts; she'd been burned before by glimpsing secrets that had made her life unravel. Not to mention what might happen to her if she was found out.

The moment stretched on. She needed to respond to him.

Shite, it's now or never. As gently as she could, she reached out to glean the thoughts floating on the surface of Oren's mind.

She was met with a strong, clear narrative. Oren had formed the answer he was hoping to hear from Lexi: High Dynasties controlled the flow of information and resources to all Tarans. Their role was so integral to the fabric of society that one misstep could spell disaster. Trust was a necessity. All that was needed was to sow the seeds of doubt at an opportune time—such as during an unexpected port lockdown due to a security threat. Tie those feelings of worry to a specific target through careful messaging, and people would start asking questions. The Alliance was aiming for the top of the chain— to Sietinen itself. The Dynasty behind the revolution that had freed Tarans from the tyranny of the Priesthood. But, perhaps, it was all a ruse to claim absolute power for themselves.

It was so simple, Lexi was disappointed that she didn't see it for herself. So, it wasn't about the rally or the posters, but about capitalizing on the emotion of outside events and linking those to the messaging. Those emotions could be layered with time, building people into a frenzy.

Lexi rephrased and condensed the thoughts into a response for Oren, "Undermine the trust in the corporation, and the family's political power is on the line."

He smiled. "Yes. You do understand."

And she did, at least in terms of the logic Oren and his collaborators had used. The problem was, she wasn't sure she agreed with their conclusion. *Is disrupting the stability of the Empire's infrastructure really the best way to have our voices heard?*

Ultimately, it didn't matter. She hadn't joined the Alliance to further their mission; she was with them because it was the only lead she had to follow to find her friend. She needed to stay the course. No matter how long it took or how deeply entrenched she needed to become, she wouldn't stop until she found out what had happened to Melisa.

— — —

Jason knew it would take more than a day to process the change in his relationship with Tiff, but he wished he could fast-forward to the part where they were comfortably long-distance friends and everything was great.

Since he, thankfully, didn't have any classes scheduled for the day, he spent the morning and most of the afternoon in his office catching up on the administrative work that had been deferred for his trip to Prisaris. It was the most mundane part of being an Agent. He knew his father hated it, too, which didn't help. Though things were about as streamlined as they could be, entering notes about each student's progress and scores, designing lesson plans, and staying abreast of threat assessment reports was nonetheless time-consuming.

Just as he was feeling like it might be possible to knock out the rest of his backlog by the end of the day, a message from his father flashed across his touch-screen desktop.

>>Come to my office when you have a moment.<<

That meant 'right now', but Jason appreciated that his father wasn't the kind of commander to make everything an urgent order.

Shit, what now? Jason caught himself. *Shite,* he corrected mentally. Tiff was right; he was Taran and needed to adjust his speech. *This is going to be foking weird.*

He sent an affirmative acknowledgement to his father and then quickly locked down his office systems before heading to the High Commander's office down the hall. The doors were closed, so he alerted his father telepathically that he'd arrived.

"Come in," Wil replied.

Jason entered and closed the door behind him before taking a seat in a guest chair. Across the wooden High Commander's desk, his father was tapping out a message on his handheld. He glanced up with a welcoming nod and smile to Jason while he finished whatever he was working on. With a sigh, he set down the device.

"Why does everything always seem to converge? It can never just be *one* thing."

Jason shrugged. "The Universe is testing us, I guess."

Wil studied him. "I saw Tiff's transfer come across my desk. How are you doing with that?"

Leave it to his father to read between the lines. Though Jason had never directly discussed his relationship with her, his parents were frustratingly perceptive, even without telepathy. To them, it had probably been obvious from the start what was going on.

"I'm sad to lose a friend here, but I look forward to staying in touch and hearing how she grows into her new role."

His father nodded sagely. "Some relationships are what you need at the time."

"Yeah. This will be good for her. And me."

"I hope you know, I'm always here for you if you ever need to talk."

"I do, thank you. I'm good. Really."

"Okay." He looked down at the digital reports fanned out on his desktop. "This situation is going to demand our full attention, I'm afraid."

"I'm ready."

"Good," his father said, "because I'll need you to help Michael keep an eye on things around here for a few days. Your mother and I are taking a trip to Tararia."

"Seriously, a social visit *now*?"

"Yes, it's a good opportunity to see your sister, but that's a bonus, not the reason."

Jason burned with embarrassment for jumping to conclusions. He hadn't seen his sister much in the past decade. It was unfortunate that their two paths had taken them apart, but such was life.

"We're going to look through the Priesthood's physical archives to see if there's anything else about the treaty," his father continued.

"There's more you haven't gone through?" When the organization had been ousted five years prior, the TSS had conducted a raid of the island's structures before handing it over to Ryan as the new seat for the Dainetris Dynasty. Jason had assumed that any physical archives found in the depths of the former monastery had been seized at the time.

"I never conducted an inspection myself," Wil said. "There's only one way to find out if the other Agents missed anything."

"I wonder what else you might come across down in the depths."

His father nodded. "The Priesthood kept a lot hidden. Admittedly, I haven't gone to search before because I'm hesitant to find out what else they might have been keeping from us."

"I think it was the right call, at the time, to not dig too deeply," Jason said. "It let us get a fresh start after they were gone. History is great once you have proper perspective, but it can color judgment."

"It can. But now, we need the kind of insights only past experience can offer."

"I hope you find answers."

"Me too. This ancient war is a mystery."

"Do you think the Priesthood intentionally buried the records of that war, too?"

"My impression is that this conflict pre-dates the Priesthood's existence—by a lot. So, any records that may exist would have been locked away simply because no one knew their significance."

That was a strange thought. The Priesthood had an omnipresence in Taran society that made it feel like the organization had been around forever, even though Jason was aware it had only wielded significant influence for the past two thousand years or so. Records from before that time had been intentionally destroyed or altered to help the Priesthood's nefarious ends, so it was anyone's guess what Taran life may have been like during a war a hundred thousand years ago. Finding records about the war would not only help address their current alien problem, but it might offer a fascinating window into their own race's history. That was well worth an exploratory trip.

"I hope you can find the text of the treaty," Jason said.

"It would certainly make things easier."

"I'm happy to go with you, if you want another set of eyes."

His father gave a morose nod. "Under any other circumstances, I'd love for you to come along so we could all be in one place as a family for a change. But... Well, let's just say we're going to leave the *Conquest* here. If there's an incident here at Headquarters while we're away, you know what to do."

When most parents go away for the weekend, they tell their kids not to throw a party. Mine leave me in charge of the deadliest warship in the TSS fleet. He wasn't sure what that said about their lives, but he took it as a compliment. Nonetheless, it drove home the gravity of their situation. "Are you sure leaving Headquarters right now is a good idea?"

"We need answers, and we can't get them here."

Jason nodded. "Okay."

His father looked him in the eyes. "I trust you, Jason. I wouldn't ask anything of you I didn't believe you could handle."

"I know. It's just..." Jason searched for the words, "you've talked about the Bakzen War and how it changed everything. What having responsibility for so many lives did to you. I don't know if I can handle it as well as you did."

"You won't be alone, just like I wasn't. This family—and our extended TSS family—sticks together, *especially* when things get tough."

"I'm in no rush to be making leadership calls."

"And you won't have to right now. Michael will be in charge of TSS operations, but the *Conquest* is yours. You'll be the only one here who can use the weapon to its potential, should it be necessary."

Jason had trusted Michael as a family friend for his whole life and respected him as a leader, so the TSS was in good hands. Still, it was a little exciting to know he was second-in-command. "Will the *Conquest* even do any good against this enemy?"

"I hope we don't need to find out."

CHAPTER 10

TARARIA WAS A sight to behold from above. With its expansive oceans and green lands, the world resembled the best parts of Earth. However, unlike the planet that served as host to TSS Headquarters, massive orbital structures surrounded Tararia to support its role as a commercial and transportation hub. The sprawling spacedocks stood out as reflective gems against the starscape, with sculptural designs that were equal parts form and function. All manner of craft were docked along the concourses, from small surface-to-port shuttles to massive cargo haulers. Even so, Wil and Saera's TSS transport ship, with its clean lines and almost iridescent hull, was a striking contrast to the surrounding civilian vessels as it nestled into its berth.

"Ready?" Saera asked Wil as they prepared to disembark.

He nodded. "I hope we find what we're looking for." *I feel it's here. Somewhere.*

"Me too."

They boarded one of the smaller transports used by dynastic delegates for trips to the planet's surface. Though Wil generally disliked traveling in a craft that he couldn't pilot himself, he'd learned to yield control and enjoy the view on the journey down.

The shuttle descended through the atmosphere with barely any sense of motion, thanks to the advanced stabilizers. Only the immense ocean between the First and Third regions was visible as the craft broke through the upper layer of clouds. As it turned and headed south, Morningstar Isle came into view.

An elaborate white stone estate rose above the sheer cliffs along the northern coast. Its carved towers and terraces contrasted the darker rocks, but the forms were a natural extension of the landscape. The structure wrapped around a courtyard facing the inner span of the isle, which sloped into a lush valley dotted with colorful gardens. On the opposite side, bright red flowers dotted the top of the cliffs—the morningstars that had inspired the island's new name. Smaller structures lined the southern coast, mostly housing for support staff.

The transport ship came to rest on a landing pad positioned near the eastern entrance to the castle-like structure. A handful of attendants stood ready to greet them.

Wil exited the shuttle first, followed by Saera. He breathed in the salty sea air, its somewhat foul aroma of seaweed and fish a reminder of how he had become accustomed to highly filtered environments.

The welcoming attendant quickly came forward with the fluid movements of someone accustomed to working under pressure. "Hello, my lord, my lady." He nodded to each, in turn, and met their gazes. "How was your journey?"

"Uneventful, just like it should be," Wil replied with a cordial smile.

"Wonderful. Well, I'm Jovan, one of Raena's personal

assistants. She asked me to receive you while she finishes a meeting." The name sounded familiar; it was possible his daughter had mentioned the man during one of their video chats.

"We appreciate the welcome, thank you," Saera said. "How long have you worked with her?"

"Just over a year now," Jovan replied. "And quite a year it's been." He chuckled.

"Indeed, it has," Wil agreed.

"The valets will collect your bags. Please, follow me." Jovan beckoned them toward the building's entrance.

A stone pathway led to the arched entry doors standing four meters tall. Like the rest of the structure, the grand scale and intricate carvings emphasized the importance of the place. The Priesthood would have professed that the architectural touches were to demonstrate their commitment to divine truth, though Wil suspected that it was more to elevate their standing in Taran society. He'd always detested such ostentatious presentations of wealth and power; it was the reason he wore his TSS dress uniform on formal occasions rather than the fine suits or robes adopted by most Taran nobles. That was the way of Tararia, though. It again reminded him why he visited so rarely.

They had just made it inside the doors when the brisk click of heels sounded from down the interior corridor. Raena rounded the corner and beamed at them.

"Hi! Sorry I'm late," she called out. "Everything is a freaking crisis with these people, ugh!" Despite her annoyed tone, she laughed.

Wil smiled back. His daughter had come into her own over the last few years. He had no doubt he'd made the right decision to abdicate his position in the familial succession so she could take over the political and corporate duties as dynastic heiress. "No worries. Thank you for letting us come on such short notice."

"You're *always* welcome." She was dressed in a sophisticated, knee-length business dress in a soft blue hue that complemented her teal eyes. As usual, her auburn hair was pulled into a sleek ponytail that swayed with each step.

"We appreciate it all the same," Saera added. "You look happy."

"Yeah, things are good." Raena sighed. "Well, they were."

"Not to worry. By the end of this visit, we hope to be one step closer to a solution to these new problems," Wil tried to reassure her.

"Oh, it's not just the issues with the Rift. Of all times, we've been hearing rumblings of discontent in the Outer Colonies."

Saera groaned. "When isn't there? That's half of what the TSS deals with these days, it seems."

"No, this is different." Raena frowned. "It's more organized."

"We'll look into it, but we have higher priorities right now." Saera sounded calm and confident, but Wil sensed her concern beneath the surface.

"Sorry, yeah." Raena ran her fingers along the hairline of her forehead—a tell for anxious nerves she'd had since she was little. "A lot has hit all at once. You know how it is."

"No need to explain," her mother soothed.

Wil nodded. "We'll try to be quick here so you can get back to your other responsibilities."

"I'm yours for the rest of the day." She smiled. "And grandma and grandpa will be here soon."

"We're looking forward to catching up," Saera said.

"Let's go get a drink," their daughter suggested.

"Sounds perfect." Saera gave her a squeeze before Raena led them down the corridor, deeper into the estate.

Wil had been to the island on several occasions since the Priesthood's fall, but at the time of those previous tours, few changes had yet been made to the estate. The largest building on the isle was the former monastery—though it hadn't served any genuine religious function for thousands of years. The light stone walls had withstood the test of time, still displaying fine, detailed carvings along the peaked archways and embellished window casings. Like almost every aristocratic structure in the Taran Empire, there were sophisticated electronic systems integrated with the handcrafted architectural accents. The resulting effect was timeless and elegant.

During past visits, an eerie energy had hung over the space. Part of it, no doubt, was his memory of seeing the corrupt Priesthood's imprisoned victims and the ultimate confrontation with the Priests who'd become twisted by their lust for absolute power. Their dark deeds had left a taint in the place that was slowly being stripped away through Raena and Ryan's efforts. The young couple was in the process of making the isle into their home. With Ryan's ancestral estate buried, the Priesthood's former administrative center was a fitting place to reclaim as the Dainetris Dynasty's seat of power.

"We don't really have any festivities planned," Raena said as she walked ahead through the airy corridor. "The arrangements being last-minute and all."

"No worries," Wil replied. "We have our own itinerary in mind."

"I also thought that might be the case." She smiled knowingly at him over her shoulder. "What's the deal?"

"You said my parents are en route?"

She nodded.

"Then I'll explain once they're here. No sense going over the same information twice."

Raena sighed softly but didn't push the matter.

"Is Ryan still working?" Saera asked.

"Yeah, an issue came up. The ship dealers keep getting greedier and bolder."

Wil shook his head. "I've never understood why some people feel the need to take advantage of others."

"I know, right?" His daughter shook her head. "Speaking of which, apparently *we're* the bad guys to some people. Can you believe it? If they only knew."

"What makes you say that?" Saera asked.

Raena waved her hand. "New round of civilian protests, this time on Duronis. They put up a bunch of posters about freedom being power, or something, and then scribbled about how Sietinen controls the High Council and the TSS, so what's next?"

Wil and Saera exchanged glances. *"Have you heard anything about that?"* he asked her telepathically.

"No, news to me. But that's the planet where Renfield, the hiring contractor for the Andvari, *is based, isn't it?"*

"Yes." Though Wil hoped there wasn't a connection, they'd need to follow up. "When was this?" he questioned his daughter.

"Yesterday."

"Well, I'm sure we'll hear about it if the situation escalates. That planet is definitely one to keep an eye on," Saera said. *"I'll ask Michael to have the Communications team keep an ear out."*

"We have enough to worry about with this Rift situation, so we'll need to leave the civil unrest management to the Guard for now. However, we should take another look at Renfield once we

get back to Headquarters."

"*Agreed.*"

The silent conversation only took a second, but Raena's advanced senses must have picked up on the energy of the telepathic exchange. "This is a work visit, isn't it?"

"We're very happy to get this chance to see you, but yes," Saera confirmed. "I'm sorry if we're distracted."

"No, I get it." The disappointment came through in Raena's tone, though Wil had no doubt she did understand.

Nevertheless, Wil felt guilty that their time together was tied to other business more often than not. "I know it's only the same transit time as a cross-country flight back on Earth, but I don't like being on the other side of the galaxy and seeing you so infrequently."

"It's not like any of us can easily take time off. I love you guys, and that won't change no matter how long we go between visits."

"Love you, too." Saera hugged her daughter. "I'm looking forward to seeing more of what you've done with the place."

"We can go on a tour when Ryan is free," Raena said. "In the meantime, we can wait out here."

She motioned dramatically with her arms as she stepped from the covered breezeway into a magnificent courtyard planted with rich foliage and vibrant flowers that brought a sweet floral scent to the salty air. A tiered stone fountain at the center offered a soothing babble of background ambiance that fit with the dappled light streaming through the trees. A rectangular metal and glass table with eight padded chairs were arranged under an elegant shade canopy. The table had several pitchers sitting in ice buckets alongside trays filled with fruit, cheese, and other snacks.

"You're really liking this lifestyle of having house staff,

aren't you?" Wil observed with amusement.

Raena grinned. "They're amazing. I thought we would have trouble getting anyone to move out here from the mainland, but we've had people competing for the jobs."

Saera took her seat at the table. "Oh, really?"

"Word has it they love that Ryan grew up as a Ward and spent time working as a servant himself. We're sorta like a celebrity couple—commoners turned nobles. That, or the fact that we're offering payment fifty percent over the standard rates."

Wil chuckled. "I'm sure both help."

"All jokes aside, we have a really good team coming together here."

"It's wonderful to see you happy and settled," Saera said.

"It really is," Wil agreed. "I'm glad you're bringing goodness back to this place."

"We're working on it. The Priesthood left a mess of things everywhere. We figure that their former stronghold was the best place to start with the recovery."

They got their drinks and made small-talk for twenty minutes until Wil sensed the familiar presence of his parents approaching. He rose in greeting when they came into view a minute later.

His parents appeared nowhere near their late-seventies as they were in actuality. Both were quintessential representations of their respective families; Cris with graying chestnut hair and cobalt eyes iconic to Sietinen, and Kate with dark-brown hair and hazel eyes that perfectly matched those of her three older Vaenetri siblings. Born to the two most prominent High Dynasties, they were the pinnacle of refinement in their attractive looks and confident bearing. Thanks to careers spent in the TSS, they'd fallen into more casual mannerisms that weren't easily shaken even after they eventually submitted to the responsibilities of helming the family business. Wil always appreciated that about them; they'd left their comfortable lives of wealth on Tararia in order to serve their people. He was grateful to have them as role models.

"Ah, I see the party is already underway," Cris said with a warm smile.

"Hey, Dad." Wil embraced his father.

"You're looking well," his mother said as she hugged him afterward.

"So are you. I think I'm finally getting used to seeing you out of uniform."

She arched an eyebrow. "It's only taken a decade."

"Just nine years and two months. Give me some credit," he jested back.

They exchanged hugs and greetings with Saera and Raena.

Cris beamed. "It's good to see you. Stars, how long has it been?"

"I've lost track, honestly," Wil replied. "Six months, maybe?"

Kate nodded. "Like most visits here, I take it you've come for more than the pleasure of our company?"

"Yes, though I welcome any chance for all of us to be together."

"Except Jason's not here," Raena said with audible disappointment.

"Next time." More than anything, Wil wished he had both of his children nearby. It was unlikely they'd live on the same planet anytime soon, but he would make a point to arrange a proper family reunion once the current danger had passed.

"And where's Ryan?" Cris asked.

"Still working, but we'll catch up with him soon," Raena replied with an appreciative smile.

Seeing the warmth in their relationship helped ease Wil's misgivings about his daughter having moved away from him at such a young age. If any people were worthy guardians, it was his own parents. He was pleased they'd also taken in Ryan, since the young man's biological father had died before he was born—especially fitting, since Ryan's father had been Cris' former mentor in the TSS and was also Jason's namesake.

Cris turned his attention to Wil. "So, what *does* bring you here?"

"Let's go somewhere more secure to talk," Wil suggested.

Everyone grabbed their beverage and a snack plate, and Raena led them to a nearby conference room with a pleasant view of the garden.

"All right," she said once they were settled, "out with it. Why the short-notice visit?"

"We're here to find the Priesthood's physical archives," Wil revealed.

She tilted her head. "I thought those had already been cataloged."

"We're looking for records that were never digitized. The Priests were meticulous about data collection, and what we've logged from the raid *can't* be the sum of the Priesthood's knowledge. I've known that there were gaps, but there was never a compelling reason to find out what we were missing. Until now."

"The Rift aliens," Raena said.

"Yes. Specifically, we need the text of the treaty between Tarans, the Gatekeepers, and whatever this other race is called."

Cris nodded. "That does seem like the kind of thing they

might have held onto. But where?"

"My guess is somewhere in that labyrinthian basement of theirs."

Raena eyed him. "I hope you're saying that facetiously."

"Of course. Though, based on what little I've seen, the underground complex is at least as extensive as what we can see on the surface. I suspect, with more investigation, we'll find even more."

"That's an unnerving thought." She crossed her arms.

"Have you sensed anything down there?" he asked.

"No. I strongly suspect that if there was something alive down there, I'd have picked up on it. But a bunch of file boxes? I can't say I've made the slightest attempt to look."

"Well, between the lot of us, we'll be able to find any hidden areas equipment can't pick up."

Cris smiled. "Just assuming I'll come along, hmm?"

"Oh, come on, Dad. I know you'll jump at any opportunity to go adventuring—especially now that you're stuck in meetings most days."

"You've always known me too well."

He exchanged glances with Saera. "Still, we may not find anything."

"I have no doubt that you'll find *something*," Cris said. "Raena, you and Ryan never did a deep dive in the underground structure, did you?"

She shook her head.

"Do you know if it's been mapped?" Saera asked.

"Yes, the accessible corridors," Raena replied, "but I don't believe they've done any advanced imaging of the underground structure."

Wil nodded. "So much of it's shielded, anyway. We'll need to go probing ourselves."

"Reminds me of when we went searching for the Dainetris estate," Cris said.

Raena got a mischievous smirk. "I must admit, that was a fun day."

"All of you *really* need to get out more." Wil chuckled, but the reason for the exploration weighed on him. *The fate of the Empire is at stake.*

His family picked up on his shift in mood, and their smiles faded.

"I'll dig up the architectural plans for you," Raena offered. "In the meantime, we can pick up Ryan at his office for the tour and then have a family dinner."

"All right," Wil agreed. "The rest can wait until tomorrow."

"Well, I, for one, am eager to see the new guest wing," Saera said. She added telepathically to Wil, *"Our daughter should come before anything else. It's been too long since we've seen her."*

"No argument here." Wil nodded to Raena. "Please, lead the way."

— — —

Raena's heart warmed as she watched the interactions between her loved ones. Having the most important people in her life together in one place was a rare treat.

However, she couldn't help noticing that whenever her parents and grandparents got together, it seemed like conversations inevitably turned to one galactic-scale problem or another. She wasn't surprised, since holding key positions in both the TSS and Taran government had made the Sietinens the single most influential family in the Empire. Some days it felt like too much pressure, but when everyone was together, Raena believed they could accomplish anything. And, given what they'd already achieved, it was probably true.

Ryan had wrapped up his critical tasks for the day by the time they arrived at his office, so the group proceeded on a tour through the estate. Raena and Ryan traded off leading as they highlighted the places that were special to each of them. It was fun revisiting how much they'd put their personal mark on the estate in just a few years.

By the end, Raena had worked up an appetite and was ready to sit down to dinner—emphasis on the sitting. Her work heels were comfortable, but flats would have been a more sensible choice for the walking tour.

"So, aside from the Sanctuary, pretty much everything else has had some form of improvement," Raena said in summary. "I've enjoyed watching it transform."

"It really does look lovely, Raena," Saera said.

"The building architecture is the same, but the entire place feels so different," Wil agreed.

"It's taken a while to get there," Raena admitted. "I didn't sleep particularly well for the first couple of weeks."

Ryan nodded. "I'm glad we stuck with it, though. It's been nice turning it into someplace better."

"The stuff we know about that went on here is bad enough. I can't imagine what else the Priesthood may have been up to that has remained secret." Raena's thoughts often turned to the island's former occupants in her gloomier moments. Sometimes, her mind played tricks on her, and it was as if Priests were still freely roaming the halls, looking for their next experiment victim—or coming for her.

"There's a lot of history here," Wil said. "I'd like to hope not all of it was bad."

Perhaps there was a time when the Priesthood lived up to its name, but none of that was left by the end. As far as she was concerned, nothing about the organization or the monsters that ran it was holy or good. They'd abused and performed secret genetic experimentations on the Taran people for centuries. That was unforgivable.

"Maybe, while we're digging around, we'll find out more about what the organization was like before it fractured into the Priesthood and Aesir," Cris commented.

Wil shrugged. "I'd be interested to know. The Aesir have been rather tight-lipped about their history before they branched off into their own community."

Raena shook her head. "I'd want to distance myself as far from the Priesthood as I could, too." She couldn't help but resent the Aesir a little. They had known about the Priesthood's genetic manipulation of unwitting Taran citizens for hundreds of years and had done nothing to stop them.

"Knowing the Aesir, getting distance from the Priesthood wasn't their sole reason for leaving," Wil said.

Cris looked at him questioningly. "Why else?"

"The Aesir have firmly held beliefs about how to achieve enlightenment. I suspect they felt... limited by being planet-bound and wanted to leave anyway."

"They're a strange bunch." Cris shook his head.

"But wise. They have reasons for doing, or not doing, everything. It's bomaxed annoying, don't get me wrong, when they refuse to give a straight answer. Except, I've come to trust them that some things need to unfold in a certain way."

"I still hate the cryptic-ness," Raena said. "Like this whole mess with Jason's vision not being about the Priesthood, after all."

"What's this now?" Cris asked.

Raena glanced at her dad and realized that he hadn't yet shared the information with her grandfather. "Um…"

"We've been reevaluating our previous interpretation in light of new information," Wil stated. "It remains a warning with no answer, so there's nothing new."

Nonetheless, her grandparents had lost a measure of their joviality.

"But we have a rare night with the family together, so we needn't dwell on such things," Wil said, giving Raena an encouraging nod.

She smiled. "That's right. Dinner should be just about ready. Shall we?"

Raena took Ryan's hand, and together they led the others to the smaller of the two formal dining rooms, reserved for more intimate gatherings. The other space was more like a massive ballroom, capable of seating hundreds at one time. She had yet to attempt planning an event at the estate with such an extensive guest list, but it was inevitable. For now, though, she enjoyed meals around the oval table in the Gathering Hall, as she'd taken to calling the smaller space. Even without guests, she and Ryan would have dinner with select members of their staff at the end of each week to celebrate their accomplishments together. She enjoyed the new tradition and hoped it would continue even as their lives became more complicated.

A server came around to offer drinks as they got seated, and Raena decided wine was a definite requirement after the day she'd had.

The conversation meandered while they waited for food to arrive. Eventually, Kate asked Ryan about his mother.

"She wasn't able to make it on short notice," he replied.

"We'll get her feeling comfortable here eventually," Raena

told him telepathically by way of support.

"*I know.*"

Kate was the kind of person who'd keep working on Ryan's mother, Marie, until she was her best friend, so it was best not to broach the topic that there was any discomfort there.

Raena understood where Marie was coming from; if she'd found herself suddenly hanging out with celebrities she'd admired as a kid, she'd feel out of place. To anyone on the outside, their little family dinner could be characterized as having an exclusive guest list consisting of the figurative King and Queen of the planet, the most decorated war hero of the past millennium, and the lone descendant of a bloodline that had been resurrected from the ashes. If Raena didn't know them as Grandpa, Grandma, Dad, and her husband, she would have been intimidated, too.

The food arrived, and they served their own plates from the communal platters, how Raena preferred it for these casual gatherings.

"I'm so glad you inherited my taste in what makes a good dinner," her mother said as she finished piling her plate with lasagna—one of the family favorites from her childhood.

Raena hurriedly swallowed an overly ambitious bite. "And your metabolism so I can get away with eating like this!"

Kate took a dainty bite; though her grandmother was never one to complain, Raena knew she was partial to more sophisticated dishes. "Being around the same table is the real delight."

"Indeed. Oh, Kalin and his partner send their regards," Cris said as he began eating.

"Making a former Primus Elite the head of security for your estate doesn't exactly quell the concerns about the Sietinen Dynasty and TSS being too closely entwined," Wil pointed out.

"People can complain all they want, but there's a reason we hold these positions," Cris stated.

"It's the same issue we ran into when considering a new government structure when we overthrew the Priesthood," Kate said. "While a true democracy is appealing, there's too much complexity in the interplay between infrastructure, commerce, and security concerns for the Empire to have an elected leader step in without experience. Legacy leadership is the only reasonable solution."

"Speaking as someone who had to jump in to learn all of this stuff, I can attest that a four-year elected term, or whatever, would be absolutely impossible," Raena chimed in. "Even after all these years shadowing Grandpa, I still don't feel like I understand it all."

"I resented many aspects of my education while I was growing up, but there's no denying that it gave me an incredible foundation," Cris said.

"No one in their right mind would want these jobs." Ryan took out his frustration from the day with a purposeful stab of his fork into his meal.

Cris nodded. "The best leaders are driven by serving the interests of their people rather than a desire for power."

"Seeing so many new dynastic scions enroll in the TSS for training gives me hope for the next generation," Saera said.

"I can't put into words how much it means to me to see that come to pass." Cris had a joyful sheen to his eyes. "Of everything we've done, the most meaningful will always be reversing the Priesthood's ban on the public use of telekinesis. No one should have to ignore an innate part of themselves."

"To my dying breath, I will fight to make sure that kind of oppression never happens again," Wil said.

"I know all of us will," Kate agreed. "It'll take time for the Empire to find its new cultural identity now that the Priesthood's controlling grip has been removed. We can be stewards, but we can't force the process."

"Unfortunately, people are already making calls for independence rather than taking this opportunity to unify." Wil shook his head and sighed.

"They'll come around. I have no doubt," Cris assured him.

"Leave the peacekeeping to the Guard," Saera said. "And we weren't supposed to talk about work stuff tonight." She glanced at Wil.

"Sorry," he said bashfully. "I can't help it."

"We've lived and breathed this life for too long," Cris said. "I guess it's inevitable that you become your career when you're this invested."

Wil nodded. "Like we were saying before."

Born and bred to fulfill a role. Her parents had been crafty about it, but Raena couldn't help looking back on her childhood with new light. Ballet as a toddler leading to martial arts. Violin lessons. Debate team. Science camp. They'd given her the foundation she needed to be disciplined and agile in both body and mind. Without that, adapting to this crazy life at the forefront of the Taran Empire wouldn't have been possible.

They tried to keep the conversation lighter for the rest of the meal, finishing with a chocolate confection for dessert.

"Well, we should call it an early night and get at it first thing in the morning," Wil said when they wrapped up.

"Yes, finding secret stashes is rarely a quick endeavor." Saera rose from her seat. "That was a great meal, thank you. We eat well in the TSS, but this…" She placed her hand contentedly on her abdomen.

"Indeed. Raena stole our best sous chef to head up things here. The guy is amazing," Cris said with an envious smile toward Raena.

"You can come eat here whenever you want." She patted his arm. "See you all in the morning, then?"

They said their round of goodbyes and hugs, then Raena and Ryan headed to their suite.

She kicked off her shoes and collapsed on the couch as soon as the door was closed. "I love them, but playing hostess is exhausting."

"I think it's good that my mom didn't come, given the conversation of the evening," Ryan said.

"Yes, that would have been awkward."

"I hope they find what they're looking for tomorrow."

"Yeah, my parents are more worried about everything than they were letting on today. It seems impossible that going down into the Priesthood's dungeon could glean any useful information."

He shrugged. "Who knows what's down there?"

"I try not to think about it." Though she'd been enthusiastic about the impending journey into the depths of the underground structure, Raena now found apprehension welling in her chest.

The last time she had been there, it had been to rescue the Priesthood's captives, whom they'd been using as subjects in their perverse genetic engineering experimentations. Raena, herself, had almost fallen victim to their vile designs as a teenager.

The experience had altered her perception of life. How could it not? Being ripped from her bedroom at the Sietinen estate in the middle of the night and taken captive in the Priesthood's underground lab. She'd known about the Taran

Empire for less than a week at the time, and yet she had come face-to-face with its deepest levels of perversion and corruption. A cautionary tale about how lusting for power led to terrible ends. Breaking free from them had affirmed her own power and how she could use both her abilities and her social station for good. It was what had shaped her as a young leader, and it's what made her sensitive to the motivations of others. Ryan had been there by her side during the whole ordeal, and it had brought them together not only as a couple but by giving them a shared vision for how they must always work to avoid the pitfalls of power. They had vowed, together, to never succumb to selfish motives, but to always put their people first.

She'd gladly given up her autonomy for that goal. Though it had meant leaving her parents and brother, she'd do it all again to help her people. Not a day went by that she didn't thank the stars she'd helped bring down the Priesthood and put an end to that chapter of Taran history.

Sensing her mood, Ryan moved closer to her. "Awful things happened here. Especially down there. But we can overcome anything so long as we have each other."

"Just like we came together then." She looked into his glowing gray eyes, feeling the strength he gave her now, as he had when they were both captured by the Priesthood as teenagers. They had been the lucky ones, escaping within hours. Many others had lost their entire lives.

Ryan placed his hands gently on her shoulders. "You don't need to go with them tomorrow."

"I feel like I should, but…"

"Raena, this doesn't have to be your fight. There's no sense revisiting those unpleasant events from the past. This, up here, is our home. Everything down there can stay locked away, far from sight and mind."

She nodded. "Okay. I'll sit this one out."

"It's not sitting out. It's being supportive from a distance."

"Nice spin. You really are getting the hang of this politicking thing."

"I try." He kissed her, and her worries melted away.

CHAPTER 11

THOUGH THE PREVIOUS night's festivities had been a welcome reprieve from everyday stresses, Wil awoke in the morning anxious to get to the mission at hand. He and Saera ate a quick breakfast before meeting up with the others to plan out the day's adventuring in the depths of the island.

"I think it's just going to be the three of us," Cris informed him when they arrived.

Wil wasn't surprised Raena had bowed out. After her experience with the Priesthood, going through the underground lab areas would no doubt dredge up painful memories best left buried. She'd tough it out, without hesitation, if her presence was critical, but there was no compelling necessity for her to go. He respected that she felt comfortable establishing those boundaries.

"Mom, don't want to get in on the fun?" he asked.

Kate chuckled. "Digging through dusty chambers in a creepy basement? Not my style."

Three people were sufficient to tackle the task at hand, so Wil didn't press the point. "All right, Dad, we're ready when you are."

Cris smiled. "Let's do it."

Walking through the high-ceilinged corridors together, Wil remembered his first visit to the isle with his father at the age of sixteen. It was the first time he'd seen his father's negotiating prowess in action, as they set the licensing terms for Wil's independent jump drive design. But the most intriguing part of the visit had been when they spotted an entryway to the underground depths of the monastery. They'd known something terribly wrong was going on down there, but it wasn't until decades later that they'd learned the horrific truth.

It was through that same doorway they now traveled. Wil knew now that the elevator shaft was one of several leading into the underground structure, and this was the most centrally located. The door was loosely blocked off with an arrangement of potted plants, and Wil made a careful telekinetic sweep to clear their path.

"How long has it been since anyone went down here?" Saera asked as they entered the elevator.

"At least four years," Wil replied. "Unless some of Raena and Ryan's people have gone."

"Pretty unlikely," Cris said. "They try to keep that part of history out of their everyday lives."

Wil nodded. "As they should."

"We got so lucky they escaped back then," Saera murmured.

Cris shook his head. "Not just luck. Those two are fighters."

It had been the single most terrifying night of Wil's life when his daughter was kidnapped, along with Ryan, and brought to the underground labs toward which the elevator was now descending. It was only thanks to Raena's exceptional telekinetic abilities that they'd escaped and avoided whatever awful fate the Priesthood had intended. Choosing to live above the site of that horrible experience had been a bold move on the couple's part, a symbolic gesture of how the Priesthood hadn't been able to control them or crush their spirits. Wil admired them immensely for taking a stand in that way. Too often, he'd run from his own demons or tried to bury them rather than face the dark truth head-on.

As the elevator descended, he noticed the effect of the strange shielding around the facility. He'd never been able to see past the shield from the outside; now, even within, his extrasensory perceptions were muted. The effect wasn't to the extent experienced when in subspace, but it was enough to make him question impressions he couldn't verify with his eyes. Any space within the facility could have extra shielding, too, so a survey using his Gifts from a central location wouldn't be reliable. They'd need to get up close to be sure.

The elevator stopped five stories down and the doors slid open. A blast of stale air assaulted Wil's senses, bearing an unpleasant combination of mildew, bleach, and death. He was certain that no bodies had been accidentally left after the raid, but it was possible rodents had taken up residence in the dark, secluded environment.

Saera placed her hand over her nose and mouth. "Clearly, the environmental controls have been offline."

"Let's see if we can get everything working," Wil suggested. He recalled there being a control room nearby on that level.

They used the lights on their handhelds to illuminate the path. After checking inside a few doors, they located the desired room. In short order, they got the lights and air filtration online, as well as the terminal for security monitoring.

"All right, we have a map!" Saera declared as she looked over the information on the screen. "Let's see how this compares to the records Raena shared with us." She projected a map from her handheld.

Wil compared the two images. "Looks pretty accurate. She actually may have gotten the map from here."

"The question is, if you were a secret storeroom, where would you be?" Cris mused.

"Bottom level?" Saera suggested.

"Might actually be the opposite," Wil said. "We're looking for the most ancient records here—perhaps even things members of the Priesthood had forgotten about themselves. Generally, if you need to expand an underground structure, you'd keep excavating downward. So, the oldest areas are probably those at the top."

"Good point," Cris agreed. "Except, everything in the central core is probably newer or has been disturbed, so we should focus on the perimeter."

"What about these hallways that seem to go to nowhere?" Saera suggested, pointing to several locations on the map.

Wil nodded. "As good a place to start as any."

"Do we split up to cover more ground or stick together?" Cris asked.

Wil smiled. "You should know by now, never break up the party."

He chuckled. "All right. Lead the way."

The air quality was already improving, and the corridors were decidedly less claustrophobic with proper lighting. Still, there was an ominous energy to the surroundings that set Wil on edge. The satin finish of the stark, white walls reflected the light without adding too much shine. It made the atmosphere feel clinical and impersonal. He supposed that utilitarian design was fitting, given how the Priesthood had operated; relentless efficiency in the name of 'progress'.

His discomfort wasn't from the interior appearance alone, though. Energy could linger in a place, like events burned into the walls themselves. The atrocities committed in the facility had left a stain that time alone wouldn't scrub clean. The upper levels, where the young family and their supporters had focused on spreading messages of hope and love, had been cleansed. Down here, though, the badness had been sealed away where it had festered in the dark.

It seemed he wasn't alone in that perception. Saera and his father held tension in their shoulders and their gazes flitted around the hallways like they believed they were being watched.

"I feel it, too," Wil said.

Saera shuddered. "I hadn't expected this when we talked about coming down here."

"Yes, definitely *not* going to suggest this as a good place for a guest suite."

Wil tensed as their path took them by the shattered remains of glass-walled rooms. The Priests had once held captive women in those cells—surrogates forced to gestate genetically altered clones of the Priests themselves. Though just one of the many crimes perpetrated by the Priesthood during its corrupt reign, it was certainly among the most heinous. If nothing else, Wil took comfort in the knowledge that those cells were only empty now thanks to his family's interventions.

"All right, I think we're looking for more of a false-wall than a hidden-door kind of situation," Wil said as they approached the end of the first corridor they had identified on the map, mostly to break the eerie silence.

"Any guesses about what this hidden archive might look like?" his father asked.

"A storeroom, maybe? There might be data saved to crystalline backups, but I'm thinking of something akin to a treasure room."

"Finders keepers, right?" Saera joked.

"I'll sit on the sidelines for that debate and watch you duke it out with our daughter."

"In all seriousness," Cris interjected, "we should evaluate any items we find on a case-by-case basis to determine what should become of the artifacts."

Wil cast him a sidelong glance. "I'm just trying to lighten the mood, Dad."

"Right, yes." He sighed. "Sorry, I just really thought I was finished with Priesthood business."

"Oh, me too. Believe me, this is one of the *last* places I thought I'd find myself again."

They reached the dead-end that had seemed like it could lead to something not pictured on the map. Wil began inspecting the surface of the wall, looking for any obvious seams. To his surprise, there did seem to be a groove where a door might be.

"Scratch that previous comment about hidden doorways. Look at this." He traced his finger along the edge.

Without waiting for further input, he used his senses to reach out beyond the door, feeling for an open space on the other side. Sure enough, there was a void back there, not a stone wall as one would expect to find in a place with nothing to hide.

Cris' expression brightened. "All right, that's a good start!"

Wil searched for evidence of electrical signals to indicate

where wiring might lead to a control panel, but he didn't detect anything. *Of course not. The Priests all had telekinetic abilities. They'd just swing open the door like we would.*

He tested out his hypothesis. Without any resistance, the wall panel swung toward them, pivoting on a hinge that left just enough clearance from the floor to avoid leaving a scuff mark to give away its presence. The odor of death returned stronger than before.

The area beyond was shrouded in complete darkness, except for what illumination the lights from the hallway offered. The three of them shined their handhelds inside. One of the lights caught a switch on the wall, and Wil flipped it.

Another hallway illuminated, with doors at three-meter intervals lining both sides. Unlike the outer area finished in clean white paneling, this corridor was all poured concrete and metal fittings.

"Definitely older," Cris commented.

"Or at least not a place designed to impress anyone," Wil said.

Saera frowned. "I don't like it."

Wil took the lead down the hall and found that there were no windows on the doors. He hated to think what might be inside; this was definitely not a forgotten treasure room like he was searching for.

With his father and wife standing on either side of him, he swung the first door inward. Inside were stacks of translucent yellow-orange blocks, approximately a meter wide by forty centimeters high on the ends and two meters deep. Each had a plaque on it, which had a distinctive bright-yellow shine of precious metal.

Cris stepped closer. "Is that gold? Why bother for something thrown in a storeroom?"

"It doesn't corrode," Wil replied, worry knotting his stomach. *Something is very wrong here.*

The stacks of blocks that had seemed orderly at first were actually carelessly piled, like the person who'd done it couldn't be bothered to spend time or care in their assembly. The piles rose higher than Wil's head in the back of the room, but the tower was lower to the right. He cautiously stepped forward to investigate.

A layer of dust had settled on the top layer of blocks, and he blew it off with a soft telekinetic wind.

The silhouette of a body inside the block was revealed by the passing breeze. Not peacefully arranged for the long sleep of death, but twisted as though writhing in eternal pain. The woman's abdomen was split open and her intestines piled to one side. Based on the loose skin around the incision site, she had most likely been pregnant until moments before her death.

Realization came to Wil with a shiver up his spine and a sickening twist of his stomach. These blocks were all bodies. Encased in amber to preserve them. The Priesthood's test subjects, discarded the moment they were no longer useful.

"Oh, my stars…" Cris recoiled from the sight.

Saera turned away, trying not to gag.

It took several deliberate breaths for Wil to settle his own queasiness.

Shite, who are all these people? He brushed the dust off one of the plaques, restoring its full shine.

He read the inscription on the foot of the amber block. It stated a full name and family tree back to grandparents along with a 'Subject ID' number, birth date, and death date. *Those foking monsters…* He looked around the room with sorrow, thinking about how many other doors there had been in the hallway. If each storeroom was like this, there were potentially thousands of bodies.

Saera had one hand over her mouth and another on her abdomen. Cris stood with an expression of abject horror.

Sudden anger surged through Wil. He knew the emotion was unproductive, since they'd already brought the Priesthood to justice. But he allowed himself to experience that fury all over again, if only for a few seconds—remembering why they had dedicated decades of their lives to bringing down the organization. When the rage had run its course in the short span he permitted, he released it from him and turned to the task at hand.

"We'll need to get a records team in here. This may provide answers to historical missing person cases." Wil hated how calmly he'd made the statement. That cold professionalism that came out whenever there was an important duty and he was facing something too awful to process in the moment.

How many people did the Priesthood capture and experiment on over the years? They may have an answer soon, or at least an estimate. It had remained a major outstanding question since the organization's fall, and one nobody had been eager to have answered.

He checked behind the other doors in the hallway. Too many doors. As he feared, they were the same. Stacks and stacks of amber blocks. All with a meticulous record of bloodlines.

Cris and Saera took it in with stoic resolve. They had spent their careers as soldiers and had seen death up close. Anyone less acquainted with the harsh realities of war might have broken down at the sight of the evidence detailing the scale of the Priesthood's crimes. Their training and experience prevailed, just as Wil's did. He was infinitely relieved that Raena had decided not to come with them.

"I'll make the arrangements once we're finished here," Saera stated. Like Wil, her tone had turned flat and matter-a-fact.

Cris swallowed. "We should finish the search."

Trying to set aside thoughts of the bodies around him, Wil ran a quick extra-sensory assessment of the wall composition beyond the end of the hall to look for any other hidden chambers. Only solid stone met his probe, so he motioned the group to move on.

They checked several other hallways that had seemed like good candidates on the map, but the next three offered no indication of there being concealed areas nearby. So, they continued their search.

"Seeing what we've done to each other as a race, it's no wonder others have considered wiping us out," Cris said as they walked toward the next place they had identified on the map.

"Really uplifting thought. Thanks, Dad."

"He does have a point," Saera admitted. "I doubt they wrote that ancient treaty without a reason. Even though they chose a peaceful resolution over war then, circumstances have changed."

"There was no doubt a conflict on a huge scale if it involved three races," Wil agreed. "I suspect the Bakzen War was a small skirmish by comparison."

"That conflict dragged on for hundreds of years, though. For all we know, this ancient war could have lasted one day," his father said.

Saera's brow furrowed. "No matter its duration, I'm worried to think about what these beings will do to us now. We have no idea what kind of tech Tarans back then may have possessed or how our modern capabilities compare."

Wil nodded. "The Gatekeepers did tell us, in no uncertain terms, that others would come deal with us. I can only imagine that means the 'others' are less scrupulous and possibly even more powerful."

"For that matter, we don't even know what the Gatekeepers can do—or what their true form is. You interacted with, what, two of the Taran-Gatekeeper hybrids?" Cris asked.

"Yes, it was a strange encounter," Wil replied. "The hybridization is interesting, as an approach of their race. Xenophobic, wary of interaction with outsiders. So, they cope by creating hybrids to actually become *one* with the race they're studying. Forget walking in shoes, they get right up in their skin."

"There is something to be said for being able to understand how another thinks through shared experience."

"Very true." Saera nodded. "How can an energy being understand the life of fleshy meat-bags without living as one?"

Wil smiled at the unexpected phrasing, despite the somber mood after their discovery earlier. "Really flattering way to characterize our way of life."

"Hey, just speaking the truth."

They reached the next point where the map indicated a suspicious dead-end. Wil began his assessment of the wall and area beyond. Unlike the last few places, he didn't sense solid stone this time. In fact, it did seem like there might be a pocket of open space.

All right, now we might be onto something! There were no visible seams to indicate an operable door, and the wall was thick enough that it took conscious probing to see through— not something a Gifted person who was casually looking around might stumble across accidentally. The setup was what Wil had envisioned when he set out on the expedition, but the question remained if it held what they were looking for.

"Over here," he said.

He could visualize the space on the other side of the wall. It was a large cavern, carved into the rock. The composition of the material was unusually dense, masking the presence of the chamber. It occurred to him that it was possible members of the former Priesthood hadn't even known it was there.

They spent centuries hiding information from the public with the hope we'd forget. Maybe they forgot some things themselves. That would explain how they so profoundly lost their way. Such an explanation wouldn't forgive their actions, but it would soften the evil of their deeds to know that they were misguided rather than willfully ignorant.

"Oh yeah, there's definitely a hollow through there," Saera confirmed.

Cris smiled. "Well, this just got interesting."

CHAPTER 12

ROUTINE HAD HELPED Jason ease into life within the TSS after leaving Earth; it's what had kept him centered when Raena had left for Tararia, and it was what would get him through this turning point in his relationship with Tiff. He would adjust, adapt, and move forward. Until he found his new normal, his students would be a good distraction.

As if the mere thought of the woman had summoned her forth, Jason's handheld buzzed with an incoming text message from Tiff: >>Hey, I'm heading out to Alkeer.<<

>>Already? I thought those transfer orders usually took a while.<< He wasn't sure if that was true. Perhaps it had just been wishful thinking that her departure would be delayed because of everything going on.

>>Got the deployment orders first thing this morning.<<

>>Oh.<< While he was trying to think of what else to say on the matter, another message from her came through.

>>I think it would be easier if you don't see me off.<<

He was struck with the impulse to ask her to stay. *Don't be selfish,* he reminded himself. But it wasn't just self-interest; he was concerned about the Rift, and Alkeer was one of the closest TSS outposts. He'd feel better if she was headed anywhere else. At the same time, though, he couldn't tell her to run from danger—not when he would run toward it himself. It was all part of being a TSS Agent.

Putting up a fight would just drive her further away. He valued their friendship too much to risk it. So, he said the only thing he could, >>Safe travels. May the stars be with you.<<

The indicator popped up that she was typing a response, seemingly a long message. When the reply came, however, it simply read, >>Take care.<<

Jason sighed and shoved his handheld into his pocket. They'd figure out the 'just friends' thing eventually without being so awkwardly formal.

He headed to his upcoming class, taking the central elevator down to Level 11 suspended two kilometers beneath the ten primary rings that comprised the Headquarters structure. It was used exclusively for zero-G spatial awareness training and telekinesis practice, so Jason spent a good portion of his time on the level. An added bonus was its substantial distance from his office, making a convenient excuse for dodging last-minute administrative requests.

Unlike some Agents, he didn't have a single, dedicated group of trainees. Rather, he offered specialized training in certain areas, in line with his own interests and strengths. Most of those lessons fell under either flight instructions or telekinetic combat.

His telekinesis students were typically Junior Agents nearing graduation—some of whom were close to his own age. Despite being young, his innate talent had given him automatic seniority in the ranks. In terms of raw potential, he was tied with his father for the highest score on record in the TSS, which directly determined rank; unofficially, it was known that the test had to be aborted for the safety of all those involved, so their actual limits couldn't be measured. People had commented on more than one occasion that they hoped to never find out what that limit might be. After all, the rumors that his father had single-handedly destroyed a planet were true, and even then, he hadn't hit his limit.

Jason had only put his skills to the test on a handful of occasions, but that was enough to give him an appreciation of the immense power of his abilities. He recognized that only his father within the TSS was in the same tier, and his sister Raena was probably the only other living person who came close.

Aside from the Aesir, perhaps… Jason honestly wasn't sure what the people among the Aesir could do ability-wise, just that they didn't suffer from the Generation Cycle that affected other Tarans—the pervasive mutation in their genetic code that made telekinetic and telepathic abilities dormant in the first seven of every twelve Generations. Much of the Priesthood's research had been looking for a patch to that mutation, which they themselves had caused through previous interventions. When no fix was found, they'd decided to make Gifted abilities illegal instead. It was no surprise the Aesir had fled and never looked back.

Given his parents and his exceptional ability score, Jason couldn't escape having a measure of celebrity within the TSS. He'd noticed it with his younger students, in particular. Getting him as an instructor was like winning a lottery, providing an instant promotion in perceived social status. A class with Jason was the next best thing to training under the official Primus Elite designation—and it was, truthfully—but he wished that it didn't also come with the label of making his students the 'cool kids'. That kind of social superiority went against the TSS' culture at the most fundamental level, and he did what he could to dispel that glorification.

At present, Jason only had two consistent groups of students under his tutelage, since his previous group of flight students had just been advanced to their in-field internships. Aside from his newest batch of young pilots, he'd also been training a group of Junior Agents in the unique set of skills known as 'weaponized telekinesis'. They'd been working together for the last year and a half on everything from enhanced hand-to-hand combat to focusing energy into concentrated orbs for offensive attacks. Most of the training had been on the individual level, but they had recently begun exploring what was possible to achieve by working in teams and by focusing energy together through a shared amplifier. It was the foundation for using weapons like that on the *Conquest*, though few would ever wield power of that magnitude.

After the events of the last couple of days, Jason would have preferred a flight training day so he could have some solitude out in the black. As fate would have it, though, it was weaponized telekinesis day. *Well, maybe blowing things up with my mind can be cathartic, too.*

Upon reaching Level 11, Jason walked past the gravity locks leading to the zero-G chambers until he reached the largest training room at the center of the level. The flex space was used primarily for combat training that entailed hurling objects, or people, across the room, but Jason had seen it transformed into a rather impressive party space for special occasions.

His students hadn't arrived yet, so he settled onto one of the large, padded mats and took the opportunity to stretch as a warm-up for the lesson.

Within five minutes, the twenty students had joined him in the warm-up stretches and were chatting cheerfully amongst themselves. Ranging in age from early- to mid-twenties, it was only Jason's black clothing that differentiated him as an instructor rather than a peer next to the dark-blue of the Junior Agents.

He rose to his feet at the designated class start time and clapped his hands. "All right, fall in."

The students arranged themselves in a semi-circle facing him.

"Let's pick up where we left off last week. Lorie, Adam, Paula, let's see how your triad is progressing."

The three students who'd been called out by name stepped forward.

Paula Fletcher half-raised her hand. "Sir, a quick question before we get started?"

"Sure."

"We heard there's something going on around the Rift. Some kind of attack."

He looked at her with his brows raised slightly. "That is a statement, not a question." He had been guilty of the same grammatical infraction countless times while a student himself, but he'd made it a point to require his trainees use precise language in their communications.

"Has there been an attack near the Rift, and is the TSS taking direct action?" she rephrased.

"That's classified."

Paula's lips pressed into a tight line. He would have been equally irked by the response, especially after the previous remark.

Unfortunately, the details actually *were* classified and there wasn't much he could say on the matter. Of course, the statement that there was anything classified in the first place was confirmation of something going on. Even the slowest Junior Agent in the bunch could infer as much. They exchanged glances with each other, and there was a buzz of energy as they engaged in quick telepathic conversations.

"I know that non-answer isn't very helpful," Jason stated. "I will share information as it becomes available. In the meantime, there is nothing for you to worry about."

"Is it true the High Commander and Lead Agent have gone to Tararia?" Jimmy Liang asked from his place in the main lineup.

"Yes, though that's nothing out of the ordinary."

The new round of knowing looks suggested that no one was buying it. This group was too smart; the timing was too coincidental to not be related.

There was little point in Jason pretending everything was okay, even if the events were classified. Misinformation would run rampant if left unchecked, so it was better to head it off with the parts of the truth he could share.

"The TSS faces new conflicts all the time, and we have processes in place to ensure we are always prepared to take informed and decisive actions. It's why we train so hard for years, and why learning is a career-long endeavor. We have contingency plans for everything. So yes, though the High Commander and Lead Agent aren't at Headquarters right now, Agent Andres is overseeing operations, and I have been left in command of the *Conquest* in the unlikely event it is needed."

"You're in command of the ship?" Paula asked, barely falling on the correct side of the line separating question from statement.

"As I just said, yes."

"Can we see it?" she asked.

"Yeah!" others chimed in.

"It's not a toy," Jason stated.

"Right, it's a tool. And we're supposed to be learning about methods of focusing our abilities, aren't we?" Paula tilted her head.

This one is nothing but trouble. He looked over the expectant faces.

Under normal circumstances, he would never cave to their pressure. However, a plan was starting to form in his mind.

The tour could offer an opportunity to see Tiff one more time without violating her wishes. Such tactics weren't his usual style, but he needed to get re-centered and focused as quickly as possible. Nine years was too long to spend with someone and expect to turn off feelings with the flip of a switch. A final chance to reminisce, if only from a distance, would help him get closure. And, if he knew Tiff as well as he thought, her message wasn't what it appeared on the surface.

"All right, just a *quick* tour," he told the group.

Excited cheers erupted along the lineup of Junior Agents. Even a few short years ago, he would have joined them in celebrating such a simple thing. They no doubt took it as a fun field trip where they got to see a piece of history up close. In time, once they'd witnessed events like what Jason had seen over the last few years, they'd find the experience more sobering.

He ushered the students toward the central elevator lobby, and they split into two groups for the long ride up to the surface. Jason left the bench seat open for his students, opting to stand since he'd already warmed up for what was supposed to have been a combat training session.

He checked his handheld for the time stamp from his conversation with Tiff. *She's always hated formal goodbyes. I think this is what she secretly wants.*

Even if he was wrong in his interpretation, it was too late to turn back now. They were on their way to the surface, and he couldn't very well tell his students to forget about the tour.

Upon reaching the moon's surface, they took the waiting shuttles up to the spaceport. Even from a distance, the *Conquest* stood out from the other berthed ships, equal parts beautiful and menacing in appearance.

The *Conquest* was arguably the most famous ship in the TSS fleet. Jason normally wouldn't have agreed to give the students a tour, but it was actually relevant to the work they were doing. They needed to appreciate the magnitude of the power they would wield as Agents, and the best way to do that was to show them the TSS' ultimate weapon.

Designed as a flagship for Jason's father during the Bakzen War, the *Conquest* was equipped with a unique bioelectronic energy relay system. A team of Agents could work together to feed telekinetic energy into a sort of energy buffer in the ateron band around the ship's perimeter, which could then be directed toward a specific target. Ateron was prized for its unique property of oscillating between normal space and subspace; the element's incredible characteristic made it capable of facilitating high levels of telekinetic energy transfer. Since ateron was extremely rare and expensive, such designs weren't possible for other full-scale ships, but a small number of fighters with telekinetic weapons had also been produced. If the conflict brewing in the Rift came to a head, then Jason's students might find themselves piloting such a craft. The *Conquest*, though, could only be utilized to its full potential by Jason or his father. It's why Jason had been left in command, and he was well aware of the implications.

As soon as the group exited their respective shuttles to the spaceport, Jason spotted the nearest terminal listing ship arrivals and departures. Since Tiff wasn't going on a mission, there was no reason her transport ship's itinerary wouldn't be posted publicly. A holographic projection above the terminal displayed the recent departures and upcoming transits. He located the sole ship heading to Alkeer that day; it was scheduled to leave in twenty minutes.

Not too late. He checked the ship's berth and saw that it would be possible to pass by it if they took the long way to the *Conquest.* It was worth whatever razzing he might get from his students if they realized what was going on.

Jason took the requisite route. When the berth for the transport ship came into view, he saw Tiff standing at the base of the gangway with a handful of her friends, chatting and laughing. They were huddled close together, as though hugs had been exchanged and they hadn't fully parted afterward.

Jason's heart lifted at the sight of seeing her so happy. She was about to go on an adventure and couldn't be more thrilled.

As he passed by with the group of students, Tiff looked up at the unexpected crowd. Her softly glowing eyes met his, and her lips parted in a smile just for him. He smiled back, and she nodded before slowly turning her attention back to her friends.

See you around. He didn't send it as a direct telepathic message, but he had a feeling she understood all the same.

Jimmy, one of the older Junior Agents walking near Jason, seemed to notice the silent exchange. "Who's that?" he asked.

"A friend."

"*Just* a 'friend'?"

Jason kept his gaze straight ahead along their path. "Before you continue with this line of questioning, you might consider the fact that I have the authority to add another set of wind sprints to your training regimen."

"She's a very lovely friend, sir."

"Yes, she is."

The weight that had been pressing on Jason for the past couple of days began to lift. Tiff was okay and he would be, too. They had their own adventures to live.

Another two hundred meters down the concourse, they reached the gangway leading onto the *Conquest*. Its semi-iridescent hull gleamed under the station's lights, reminiscent of an oil slick on water. At three hundred meters long, it wasn't the largest ship in the fleet, but it was one of the most fearsome in appearance. Aggressive ridges adorning the side of the oval-shaped vessel flowed into the forked jump drive in the aft. Aside from the blue-hued casing of the ateron band around its circumference, the most notable exterior features were the numerous armaments as well as the fighter launch tubes in the belly of the ship, forming a 'Y' with two in the back and one forward. Rear tail fins served as a heat shield and also added a unique aesthetic echoed in many Taran craft. It was truly one of a kind, and Jason was proud to have it under his command.

"All right, don't make me regret this," Jason addressed his students. "Don't touch anything or neural-link with the ship. It's much more sensitive than anything you've come across."

"Awww, it has feelings?" Paula jested.

"Yeah, and it will spit you out an airlock if you piss it off. Behave."

The statement wasn't remotely true, but it got Paula to snap to attention.

The students' giddy excitement was infectious as the group ascended the gangway. Jason had felt a similar thrill when he'd boarded the vessel for the first time, and even now he had to smile as the ship's bioelectronic link connected with his mind.

They entered toward the middle of the ship. Unlike civilian

vessels or the TSS craft used for basic transport, the piloting and captaining was conducted from the Command Center in the heart of the ship, where it was most protected, rather than a flight deck at the exposed upper bow. In the few occasions he'd commanded the ship into battle, it was reassuring to have the extra measure of protection.

The group traversed the short distance down the interior corridor from the entry hatch to the Command Center's entrance on the same deck. Since the ship was dormant, the Command Center didn't have the same awe-inspiring impact as when Jason had boarded the vessel his first time. At present, the walls and floor appeared plain matte gray. Two tactical consoles at the front faced forward relative to the door at the back, and five command podiums were arranged at the center of the room. Configured as four barstool-height seats surrounding a central station, each was equipped with a retractable handhold for forming a physical bioelectronic link with the ship. The telekinetic weapon charged through that interface, as well as offering control of all other aspects of the ship's operation.

Jason walked up to the pedestal in front of the seat closest to the entry door and brushed his fingertips along the handhold. A subtle electric spark of biofeedback tingled his hand, and a light flashed in his mind's eye as he interfaced with the ship. With a silent command, he switched on the wrap-around viewscreen.

The walls and floor of the spherical room sprang to life in vivid color. A high-resolution screen with holographic augmentations wrapped the entire Command Center, allowing for an accurate rendering of the space surrounding the ship, as though looking through a window. Unlike a window, however, the view could be manipulated and augmented to address the evolving tactical needs of an engagement. With the transparent floor bisecting the spherical space, the resulting effect was like walking through space. All TSS battleships had a similar visualization system, but the *Conquest*'s was the most impressive.

The students took sharp breaths of surprise and delight as they took in the sight. Many looked down at their feet, their legs suddenly unsteady. Though Jason had long since gotten his 'space legs' in the room, he was familiar with the strange sense of vertigo at the convincing appearance of standing among the stars.

"Pretty incredible, isn't it?" he asked.

"Yeah," they murmured almost in unison.

Paula cautiously approached the center of the room. She pointed at the podiums. "Is that how the weapon is controlled?"

"It is."

"I don't suppose we could get a demonstration of that, too?"

"Not a chance," Jason replied. "However, I can walk you through the interface and then take you down to Engineering and the hangar."

Paula grinned. "That will do."

CHAPTER 13

"THE QUESTION IS, what's the best way to get through the wall?" Wil mused as he examined the smooth surface between him and his target in the underground lair.

Even once they got inside, there was no guarantee that they'd find what they were looking for. It was a longshot that the Priesthood would have a copy of the treaty locked away somewhere, forgotten through time. But he had a hunch. And his hunches rarely led him astray.

"It's impossible to know how long a chamber may have been sealed. Any paper in there could disintegrate the moment we introduce outside air," Saera pointed out.

"We could keep a shield up until we can assess the contents," Cris suggested.

"Good call," Wil agreed. "All right, Saera, take the shield. Dad, keep an eye on the structural stability while I cut us an entrance."

They nodded their assent.

Wil instinctively formed a telepathic link with the two of them so they could coordinate their movements. Through the link, he felt Saera probing the space behind the wall to determine where to erect a shield to protect the room's contents. She settled on a placement about a meter beyond the wall, leaving Wil plenty of room to work.

While Cris kept a light telekinetic hold on the wall and ceiling around them, Wil began to slice an opening through the wall with surgical precision. Busting a hole inward would have been a lot faster, but there might not be room for the debris, and he didn't want to inadvertently cause structural damage. So, instead, he formed an energy saw and sliced an archway into the plastic wallcovering and stone behind. Since he was effectively breaking the molecular bonds between the materials rather than actually sawing, there was very little dust but a good deal of heat, which he vented into transdimensional space to keep the temperature under control.

Within a minute, the outline of the archway had been fully cut out. Wil then grabbed the wall segment and began sliding it toward them. The wall groaned in protest.

"This structure is solid rock. It's not going anywhere," Cris said.

"All right." With his fear of a collapse assuaged, Wil gave the chunk another firm telekinetic yank.

The section came free with the rumbling grind of stone-on-stone. A spray of dust, loosened from the friction, prompted Wil to put up a shield between the three of them and the opening to cut off the chalky mist. He guided the wall chunk down the corridor in the opposite direction from their exit and set it down. A thud reverberated underfoot as it came to rest.

Through the archway, Saera had her shield intact. Invisible to anyone without Gifts, it showed up as a silver shimmer to Wil's enhanced senses.

"It feels like there was a good seal in here," Saera reported. "The air is stagnant."

As the dust settled, Wil dropped his temporary shield. "I can't say I know much about document preservation," he admitted.

"Uh," Cris shrugged, "I think moderate humidity and temperature."

Wil assessed the conditions inside the chamber. "Feels okay, I think?"

"I'll start slowly equalizing the air." Saera made her shield slightly permeable and allowed the air to begin mixing from the hallway into the room, rather than billowing in with a single gust.

While they waited for the process to complete, Wil shined his handheld's light inside to start taking visual inventory of the contents.

At first glance, there wasn't a lot to see. A thin layer of tan dust covered everything in the room. The objects appeared to be in cluttered piles and had no consistency in size and shape. Statues. Crates. Pottery. The only thing uniting the mismatched collection was that it all seemed *old*. Though no books or other paper were out in the open, he was thankful they had taken precautions while accessing the space.

No energy signatures jumped out at him. But a cursory glance wasn't sufficient.

"Would something important like an ancient treaty end up here?" Cris asked.

"I don't have a good reason why, but my gut is telling me 'yes'." The feeling had been insistent since Wil first got the idea to visit the island—almost like he was being drawn by a preternatural force to the place. Having looked into the nexus, he respected the universal energies and the patterns woven in complex paths. So, when he was nudged in a direction, he tried to follow the threads to see where he was being led.

"What would this thing even look like?" Saera asked.

It was a good question, and Wil didn't have a lot to go on. During his prior conversations with the Aesir, they suggested that it would have been a physical record, probably etched in something that could stand the test of time. One would think something like that would stand out, though, and not have been tossed into a random storeroom. Except, Wil didn't know where else it might be. The Priesthood's many, many artifacts had already been meticulously cataloged, and there wasn't anything that fit the description. So, either it was buried somewhere down here, or the Priesthood never had it and the treaty record might be lost forever.

"We're probably looking for something durable," Wil said. "I know it's not helpful, but I think we'll know it when we see it."

They began going through the items as carefully as they could, using telekinesis to move around objects rather than their hands as to avoid unnecessary contamination. Nearly half an hour passed, and Wil had yet to see anything valuable.

"These items are totally random," Cris said, echoing Wil's thoughts.

Saera nodded. "Yeah, this all seems like useless junk. Like stuff that was dumped in a storage shed because no one knew what else to do with it."

"Yeah." Cris nudged a plain, bronze vase with his toe. "Things can get lost over time, but the Priesthood sealed off this room for a reason. It was the reject stuff—items that weren't even worth removing."

"I just can't shake the feeling that it's close. I don't know why." Wil shook his head.

"I trust your instincts," his father said. "There could be another room like this. We haven't yet completed this level, and there very well may be others."

"No, I'm missing something." He looked around the room again. All old, ugly things. *None of this fits the Priesthood's style.* "Maybe I've been going about this all wrong. We agreed that a treaty of this importance would have been documented on a material that would last. Gold. Crystal. We're talking about something maybe a hundred thousand years old. The Priesthood, themselves, used amber and gold to preserve those bodies." He paused for a few seconds to swallow while his stomach turned over at the thought.

"So," he continued, "there's a measure of innate worth to the material itself that we're looking for, even behind the value of its content. One thing we know for certain about the Priesthood is that they enjoyed being ostentatious. Anything 'pretty' or valuable would be on display, not locked in a forgotten room with a bunch of reject junk."

"Where, though?" Saera held out her arms. "You said yourself, everything else was cataloged."

Cris pursed his lips in thought. "Could it have been sealed in a shrine or something?"

"Oh, shite." Wil froze. "Stars, why didn't I think of it before? We already have the foking thing!"

"What?" Cris asked.

"It's been right there all along. Stars!" Wil ran back toward the elevator.

"Wil, what are you talking about?" Saera questioned as she ran after him.

"A material with utility. Crystal. Specifically, toradite crystal is often used as a focusing aperture for telekinetic powers; some types are the next best thing to ateron. When we seized the island and the Priesthood made their final stand, there was that column of energy. I was so focused on the telepathic link, and, well, *not dying*, that it never occurred to me they may have been using a relay hub, in the way we use the *Conquest*."

"Okay, but what does that have to do with this?" Cris asked as he jogged behind Wil.

"The position of that beam. It was a beacon pointing us right to where we need to go. We're almost directly under it."

Saera's brow furrowed. "So, it's...?"

Wil reached the elevator and waited for the others to get in before hitting the door controls. "*That's* why I had the feeling it was here. Subconsciously, I probably detected the properties of the material, and I may have even seen inscriptions. I bet the thing is written in some form of Old Taran, which was the Priesthood's language, so it wouldn't have stood out at the time."

Saera was starting to look excited. "Okay, but what object are you talking about?"

Wil smiled. "I saw it during the tour yesterday! And it didn't even occur to me it might be what we were looking for."

"Where?!" Saera and Cris asked in unison.

"In the Sanctuary. The foking centerpiece." Wil couldn't help laughing to himself. *I walked right past it and didn't think twice. I was so intent on the idea that it was hidden away in a locked room that it never occurred to me it might be there in plain sight.*

"Stars!" Cris breathed.

Saera laughed. "Okay, I feel like an idiot for missing that."

"Oh, me too," Wil agreed. "Of *course* a treaty with a race of transdimensional beings would be inscribed on a rare material with such unique properties."

It made perfect sense. The Priesthood was corrupt, but they were never stupid. Their historians were always thorough in their accounting of Taran history through the ages, filtering what made it out to the public. But they knew the 'truth', as they chose to interpret it. So, the notion that something as important as the treaty had simply been *lost* was ridiculous, and he felt silly for ever thinking that was a possibility. Far more reasonable was that the Priesthood would have known the significance of the artifact and wanted it close at hand. More than that, though, they would have appreciated the utility of it. Seen it as a tangible connection to the higher dimensions, to help them achieve the ascension they so desperately wanted. So, they used it as a tool, placed at the center of their operations.

The moment the elevator doors opened, the three of them dashed toward the Sanctuary. As Raena had noted during her tour, it was the only space that had remained largely untouched since the Priesthood was ousted. By far the most striking remnant of the Priesthood's theological roots, the Sanctuary reminded Wil of the ornate cathedrals he'd seen on Earth in historic European cities. The paintings and engravings on the walls and arched ceiling were priceless works of art, and Raena and Ryan had been right to leave it intact.

Centered in the middle of the room, positioned beneath a skylight to catch the light, was a life-sized prismatic glass statue of a robed figure with one arm reaching toward the stars. The statue was on top of a pedestal, capped with a circular piece of pale blue toradite crystal divided into thirds, each with beautiful engravings that had stood the test of time. Much of the circle was covered up by the sculpture, so it naturally wouldn't draw attention.

Now, primed for it as they approached, Wil felt the energy

radiating from the circular piece at the base. *Perhaps the most important document in Taran history, and they used the thing as a bomaxed tabletop.* He laughed again, shaking his head. *So typical of the Priesthood. Fokers.*

"Stars, that really could be it!" Cris approached the statue with new reverence.

There was a strange humor to it. The statue depicted an imagined version of the Cadicle—the symbolic figure Wil was in the flesh, as far as the Priesthood and Aesir were concerned. According to their doctrine, the Cadicle represented the next stage of Taran evolution in terms of superior genetics and abilities; though, while Wil's Gifts were undeniably advanced, he'd never considered himself particularly iconic. Nevertheless, it figured that this ancient avatar of himself would be standing on the exact pivotal piece of history he'd been trying to locate for months.

The irony wasn't lost on Cris and Saera, and they exchanged amused glances.

Wil sighed. "You don't need to say it."

Saera smirked. "What, that the fate of the galaxy is at your feet?"

"Or that you stand up on principles?" Cris chimed in.

Wil resisted the urge to wipe his hands down his face. "Yeah, something like that."

Before any more wordplay could threaten to derail their mission, Wil telekinetically lifted the statue off the pedestal and placed it gently on the floor out of the way.

The three of them huddled around the inscribed toradite crystal. Two-thirds of the circle were incomprehensible symbols, but the other did appear to be Old Taran, as Wil suspected.

"It's like a Rosetta Stone," Saera said.

Cris cocked his head. "What's that?"

"A tablet on Earth—allowed translation of a dead language. If this is Old Taran, then you might be able to make some sense of these alien languages."

Wil nodded. "In written form, anyway. We have no idea how it's supposed to sound."

"Oh, good point." She frowned.

"But what matters now is what our side says." He began reading over the text to make sure it was what they suspected. The language was difficult to make out but readable. It appeared to be a variation of Old Taran—a language hardly spoken outside the Priesthood—and could be even an older dialect of the language than that. While he'd always been partial to mathematics over linguistics, he knew enough about the roots of Taran language to fill in the gaps.

Cris' face lit up while he read the text while Saera looked confused.

"Looks like the treaty text to me," Cris said.

"I can only make out the occasional word. What does it say?" Saera asked.

"Today we strike an accord," Cris began the rough translation in slightly stuttered cadence as he worked out the words. "Peace will… endure so long as the terms are upheld. The… destructive Gates will remain sealed. Each race will stay in its… designated realm. If ever the Gates are reopened by Tarans, they will be destroyed."

"I think that last bit is more 'wiped out for all time'," Wil said.

"Uh, I'm not a fan of either of those translations." Saera scowled at the inscription.

"Me either, but this is helpful. We know for certain that our violation *is* tied to that tech, specifically."

"But why?" Saera asked.

Wil reread the text. There was no further explanation. "It doesn't say. Bomax, I thought there'd be more here."

"There might be." Cris looked closer. "Does that look like micro inscriptions to you?" He pointed to the vertical height of the circular disk.

Sure enough, it looked like it could be rows of tiny text.

"We need to magnify that." Wil captured an image of the band on his handheld and projected it as a holographic image, zooming in until the characters were easily read.

Wil pored over the text. There were pages and pages of information—all of the details they'd been missing. "Stars! I can't believe it."

"What?" Saera asked, peeking over his shoulder.

"Those Gatekeeper-Taran hybrids? Apparently, they're not new. That's how the Gatekeepers first made contact with our Taran ancestors, by going to live among them. But they were found out, and the Priesthood started studying them. They were fascinated by them being impervious to telepathy, but that they still possessed a link with one another."

"That sounds familiar."

"The nulls. That side effect from the Priesthood's neurotoxin." The pieces began to fall into place in Wil's mind as he reflected on the tech the Priesthood had deployed during their last stand and bid for ascension. They had deployed the neurotoxin as a means of telepathically networking the masses across multiple Taran worlds. "If I had to wager, I bet you they used this research as a foundation for the neurotoxin—tried to isolate the 'networking' component, but it also made a small percentage of people nulls in the process."

She shook her head. "We've had evidence of aliens right in front of us for decades and didn't know it."

"That explains why we couldn't identify many of the sequences in the neurotoxin."

Saera crossed her arms. "This is so messed up."

Cris scoffed. "The Priesthood would do *anything* to further their own ends. I can't say I'm shocked by this."

"You realize what this means, though," Saera said.

He tilted his head, not sure what she was getting at.

"They knew about higher-dimensional life. They understood that such beings were networked as one to move beyond their physical forms."

The realization hit Wil like a punch in the gut. "This text is where the Priesthood got the very idea of ascension."

"Taking inspiration from a war that almost wiped out Tarans once."

He shook his head. "And willing to do it all again with no regard for what would happen to everyone else."

Saera stared with disgust at the documentation. "Not that I needed a reminder about why they had to go, but wow. Kind of makes me want to take them down all over again."

"I second that." Cris took a deep breath. "It all makes perfect sense. We should have known there was more."

"We wanted to close that chapter and never look back. I won't blame us for not wanting to dig too deeply at the time." As TSS High Commander, Wil knew that was too dismissive an approach. Duty should come before personal feelings. But the Priesthood's depravity made it difficult to remain objective.

"All right, so we have confirmation that the treaty violation is for the Gate tech itself," Saera summarized. "Arvonen and his Gate research cronies obviously won't be an issue anymore, since the Gatekeepers dealt with them. But we can't be certain they were working alone. If this tech is the crux of the whole issue, we need to root out anyone potentially pursuing that kind of research and put a stop to it."

"Yes, agreed." The TSS' resources were about to be stretched very thin. Wil had been in that situation before, but he hadn't expected to find himself faced with that challenge again. *Our people are well-trained and capable. We're ready for this,* he tried to assure himself.

"There's something else strange in here," Cris said, continuing to scroll through the text while Wil and Saera talked.

"Good or bad strange?" Wil asked as he tried to catch up to what his father was reading.

"More a curiosity. It's about Earth. It's mentioned in these documents."

Wil snapped to attention. "Wait, what?"

Saera looked between the two of them. "That doesn't make any sense."

"I'm as surprised as you are." Cris paused in thought.

"It raises an interesting point, though," Wil jumped in as he began thinking through the branching possibilities. "Why have the Taran government and the Priesthood gone to such lengths to protect the planet?"

"Humans are of Taran descent, regardless of whether they know about us or not," Cris surmised.

"Yes, but there are other rogue colony worlds that aren't provided the same protections. What makes Earth special?"

"I always figured it was the proximity of TSS Headquarters," Saera said. "The moon would be in bad shape if the planet blew up."

Wil cocked his head and looked at her. "Well, yes. What I mean is, Tarans have gone to great lengths to keep the Empire's presence hidden. It's always felt like there must be a reason for it. The cost and labor associated with that secrecy is astronomical."

"I suspect you have a hypothesis," Cris stated.

"More of an inkling, at the moment. I wonder if it has something to do with this ancient alien tech from the galactic war."

"What makes you wonder that?"

"There's no shortage of ancient alien stories on Earth. In the time we lived down there, I figured most of it stemmed from former Taran interaction—and that's certainly part of it. But I wonder if there was also something else going on. Perhaps even one reason colonists from so many disparate planets settled on Earth to make it the cultural melting pot it is today."

"What could be there?" Cris wondered aloud.

Wil shrugged. "I have no idea. But, what if all of those ancient sites on Earth were built in those locations because there's something important there? Buried deep beneath the pyramids or Stonehenge, or any number of other historic sites."

Saera raised an eyebrow skeptically. "I think you watched too many of those conspiracy shows on TV. Wouldn't something have been found, if it exists?"

"Has anyone bothered to look? Taran researchers, I mean," Wil clarified. "Everything I've ever heard is that modern-day people write off Earth as a nothing backwater world. But there must be *some* reason the specialized stewardship we show the planet started all of those years ago. We go through the motions now because that's how it's been done as far back as anyone can remember, but *why*?"

"I must admit, you raise an interesting point," Cris admitted. "To my knowledge, Earth is a no-fly zone except for sanctioned military and political operations—and, naturally, some space tourists occasionally skirt the law and mess with the local humans. But research historians? No."

"The mystery continues," Saera said dramatically.

"Unfortunately, I don't have a good suggestion for how to begin an investigation on Earth," Cris said.

"It's something to keep in mind, anyway." Wil gazed at the toradite crystal record. "At least we got what we came for. We'll get some other eyes on it to make sure we didn't miss anything. On that note, we should return to Headquarters."

"Stay the night," his father suggested. "Fill everyone in on the discoveries. It might be quite a while before we have another chance to be together."

"We shouldn't delay," Wil said to Saera telepathically.

"The research team at Headquarters can get started on the image analysis without us. One more night here won't make or break things."

"All right, one more night," Wil yielded. "Then we have to get to work."

CHAPTER 14

SOMETHING HAD CHANGED. Only a short while had passed since Lexi had met with Oren about the grand vision for the Sovereign Peoples Alliance's movement, but she'd noticed a shift in the energy around the office. People were more serious and fervent in their actions. They sat huddled in small groups talking rather than watching vids on the main viewscreen. When they did watch anything, it was flipping through the official media broadcasts to see the spectrum of political coverage.

The rally on Duronis was no longer the focus, but the political commentary had persisted. They had sparked a conversation, which was the point.

So, why doesn't anyone seem happy? Lexi looked around the lounge room at the serious faces. She was by no means the lowest-ranked person in the organization—especially not now, after her promotion—but everyone seemed to be picking up on something she wasn't. It was frustrating to continually feel like an outsider. And she knew she wasn't stupid. *What the fok is going on?*

"Lexi!"

The sudden call of her name from Shena made her jump. "Yeah, what?" Lexi replied.

"You're late for the meeting."

What meeting? Lexi rose from her seat to see Shena motioning for her to follow. "No one told me there was one."

"Oh, oops." Shena shrugged. "I guess I forgot to pass on the message from Oren."

Forgot or didn't care to? Lexi followed the other woman, as requested. "What's the meeting about?"

"Next steps."

"Is this meeting a new thing…?"

"You mean this one specifically, or these kinds of tactical discussions?"

"The latter," Lexi clarified.

"Oh, we have them every couple of days." Shena said it so casually, Lexi almost felt silly for asking.

But she was well aware that she was right to feel surprised. The people she slept next to, ate with, talked to every day, had been having secret meetings 'every couple of days' for who knew how long, and she hadn't had a clue.

It was obvious, then, that the others in the Alliance probably learned something in their last meeting that had set them on edge. That's why everyone had turned somber and she was still clueless about *why*. The explanation made her feel better, but only marginally. It still didn't offer any insight into *what*.

Think about Melisa. She reminded herself. *You need to stay the course for her.*

If it wasn't for that singular drive, Lexi would have run far away from the Alliance after the way things had been going the last few days. The mounting tension was the sort that could only be released from a physical altercation. She wanted political change, but not through violence.

Naturally, she couldn't say any of that out loud. She needed to play along, be an unwavering supporter of the Alliance and its quest for independence in the Outer Colonies. Sovereignty of the planets. So, she followed Shena downstairs… and directly through the door at the end of the hallway, which she'd recently gone through with Oren. The door that Shena said was always locked when Lexi had asked her about it.

As they passed through, Shena must have noticed Lexi's expression of confusion and annoyance. "Sorry, I had to lie. Only those who've been initiated get to come down here, and we don't like newbies getting too curious."

"How many are on the inside?" Lexi asked.

"You're about to find out."

Incidentally, it was a lot. When Lexi got to the bottom of the stairs, she found the secret storeroom was filled with at least half of the people she interacted with on a daily basis. Many of them were people whom Lexi had asked about the bigger picture, and they'd denied knowing anything. *Has everyone been lying to me?*

She had no idea what to believe anymore. The layers of secrecy and compartmentalization reeked of shadiness of the highest order. Not for the first time, she had a horrible sinking feeling that the Alliance's plans were building toward something awful.

The low hum of conversation in the crowd quieted suddenly as a figure stepped up onto one of the crates, which had been positioned at a central point in the tunnel.

"Our first phase has succeeded. People are talking," an older woman's voice easily carried in the acoustics of the space. She had the accent of someone from the Central Planets, oddly enough. Lexi couldn't make out many physical features from the distance in the dim light, but she had graying black hair, mahogany eyes, and carried herself with confidence.

"You are one critical part of our path to victory for the independence we all seek. You have joined the Alliance because you believe things can be better. That the Taran elite have lived in their manors for too long without understanding what it means to be a citizen of this great civilization."

No, actually, Lexi thought to herself. *Not the leaders of Sietinen and Dainetris, anyway. Don't they get any credit?*

"...and that's why we must make our voice heard! We started with the demonstration on Duronis, and others will soon follow. This is only the beginning. We have a long road ahead of us, but the greatest victories are won with the hardest battles. Play your part. Trust in our mission. Together we are unstoppable."

The crowd burst into applause—almost deafening in the confined space—as the older woman stepped down from the crate and disappeared down the tunnel.

Wait, that's it? The speech was frustratingly cryptic and short. Not to mention, the content was dubious.

Unlike the skepticism souring Lexi's mood, Shena was beaming, apparently energized by the speech in a way Lexi had never seen her.

"I can't believe she actually came to talk to us! Wow." Shena's eyes had the starstruck sheen of someone who'd just met their idol.

Lexi was officially lost. *Who the fok was that and why is everyone so excited?* Nothing was making sense. "Yeah, great speech. Who is she?" Lexi asked, suspecting she was *supposed* to know—if only someone would tell her something useful.

"Magdalena," Shena said with zealot-level reverence.

"She's the founder of the Alliance."

Lexi nodded and smiled, doing her best to fake that she cared. *It's official, I'm in a cult.* Unfortunately, there was no backing out now.

—   —   —

By the end of the day of staring at his viewscreen, Jason needed to clear his head and burn off some energy. Without a class to keep him occupied, he'd been stuck all day buried in administrative tedium. Maybe some time at the gym would do him good.

He headed to the workout arena on Level 10, which was shared by Agents and Militia members alike. A track circled the perimeter of the large space and a wide assortment of weight equipment was arranged in the middle. Other open areas had padded floormats for stretching or sparring. Though it was a communal space, the Agents and Agent-track trainees tended to keep separate from the Militia members, just as officers wouldn't typically fraternize with the enlisted in Earth's military. There was no specific regulation against it, but rather it was simply the way the TSS' culture had shaken out. Jason tried to dispel that division, whenever opportunities presented themselves; they were all people working together toward a common goal, so different abilities or ranks shouldn't divide them.

His most common 'in' with the Militia crowd was through Corine, whom he'd grown up with on Earth. She was Michael's daughter and had also been raised without knowledge of the Taran Empire. They were never particularly chummy growing up, but the shared experience of learning there was a galaxy-spanning civilization had brought them a little closer over the years. However, though both of Corine's parents were Primus Agents—Michael a Primus Elite, even—she didn't have abilities.

Through unfortunate timing, she'd fallen on 1st Generation in the cycle of Gifted trait expression. Since only those 8th through 12th exhibited telekinetic and telepathic abilities, it would probably be close to a couple hundred years before any of her descendants could train as Agents in the TSS.

It was heartbreaking when Jason thought about it. Those abilities were so much a part of himself, that Jason couldn't imagine life without them. If he ever had a child of his own, he'd look forward to the day of their Awakening when he could begin guiding their exploration of those new abilities; it had certainly brought him closer to his own parents. Though Michael had never said as much, Jason imagined that it must be difficult not to have that kinship with his daughter—for her to know she was missing something. Joining the TSS in the Militia division kept them together as a family, but it wasn't the same.

Jason looked around for Corine but didn't see her. There were other Militia members at various stations within the facility, but he recognized them as those who weren't keen on starting a conversation with an Agent. That was okay. To each their own.

For that matter, he didn't feel much like talking at the moment. He hit it hard alone, running laps after warming up and then completed a full set on the weights. It was a welcome task now, but he would have needed to do it regardless; artificial gravity wasn't as strong as planetside, and the workouts were an important part of preventing muscle atrophy.

Feeling a pleasant level of worn-out, he exited the gym and

headed toward his quarters. Halfway to the elevator, his handheld buzzed with an incoming vidcall. Still sweaty and flushed from the workout, he didn't particularly want to answer it, but he saw it was coming from his sister's personal account. He spotted a munitions storeroom nearby. He palmed it open with the biometric lock and ducked inside to answer the call.

Raena beamed the moment her face materialized in the holoprojection. "Jason! I wish you were here." She stuck out her lower lip in an exaggerated pout.

Behind her, his parents, grandfather, and Ryan waved.

"Good to see you," Cris said.

Jason smiled. "Looks like you're having quite the party!" He hadn't spent appreciable time with his grandfather, so there wasn't much closeness in the relationship in the way he had with his parents. While he was used to things being the way they were, he couldn't help but feel like he was missing out by not being on Tararia for the gathering.

"We spent a good portion of the morning digging through a musty basement. It's not as glamorous as it seems," his mother said.

"But wine!" Raena grinned. She was definitely a little tipsy; he wasn't used to seeing her that way.

"Rough day?" he asked her.

She took a gulp from her glass before replying. "Oh, wait until you hear the story about what they found!"

Jason perked up. "Did you find what you were looking for?" he asked his parents.

"Yes, we got the treaty," his father replied. "Along with another unpleasant discovery."

"Stars! You actually found it?"

"Yes, and we confirmed that it's the Gate tech usage that

was prohibited. There's more documentation we're still evaluating. I'll fill you in when we get home. Everything okay there?"

"Yep, nothing to report."

Wil nodded. "Good. Well, we'll be heading back first thing in the morning. Let's touch base early-afternoon."

"Okay."

"You really need to come visit once this situation is under control." Raena's brows drew together. "I miss all of us being together."

Jason smiled. "I'm ready for a vacation. No arm-twisting needed."

"Thanks for holding down the fort. We'll see you soon," his father said.

"Anything I should do to prepare, now that you've found the treaty?" Jason asked.

"Rest up while you can. This is just the beginning."

CHAPTER 15

ANALYSIS OF THE treaty text was well underway by the time Wil and Saera returned to TSS Headquarters. The flight back gave Wil ample time to review the translation their researchers had made overnight, and the findings were both helpful and confounding.

On the one hand, it became clear why the Gatekeepers had been so upset about the use of their Gate technology, since it was explicitly prohibited in the text. However, they still didn't know *why* that technology presented such an issue. The Engineering team was conducting another review of the scan data from the Gate sphere from when it had been in the TSS' possession, so there was little he could do but wait for their report.

Meanwhile, Wil met with Jason to fill him in on what they'd learned, and Jason gave an account of what he'd been up to while Wil and Saera had been away. It was good to hear that Jason had thought ahead about sharing the *Conquest* with his students; the IT-series fighters that used the same direct neural link would be an important piece of the TSS' defense against a transdimensional threat, so now was the right time to introduce them to the technology.

When he'd finished the recounting, Jason fell silent with a contemplative look Wil recognized, meaning there was something else on his mind.

"What?" Wil prompted.

Jason sighed. "I've been thinking a lot about the Rift… with Tiff heading out that way, you know."

Wil nodded.

"I dunno. It might be nothing, but I keep wondering what the *Andvari* was doing out near the Rift at all," Jason continued. "I wasn't going to bring it up, but I was thinking it might be ancillary to the unrest that's going on in the Outer Colonies."

"Why?"

"Something Darin said about how the job came through. Nothing solid to go on, just…"

"I get hunches, too. I know how it goes." Wil straightened in his seat. "Well, I maintain that dealing with that civil disruption is the Guard's domain, but we'd be remiss to withhold information from our investigation into the *Andvari* that might relate to their peacekeeping efforts."

"Exactly."

Wil steepled his fingers. "What are your thoughts on the matter?"

Jason shrugged. "In terms of why the ship was out there, the easiest answer is that everyone's trying to make a living. It's harder in the Outer Colonies than most places."

"But going through an off-limits former war zone?"

"A rich harvest for someone willing to take the risk."

"There are a lot of easier places to get scrap metal."

"It's not just scrap metal though, is it? Aren't there whole ships out there?" Jason asked.

"Well, pieces of them, anyway."

"Okay, so first of all, we're talking about TSS wreckage here. The tridillium in the hulls alone is worth a ton. Then there's the drives."

"Jump drives are notoriously fragile," Wil pointed out. "If one of the prongs breaks, which they often did in battle, it's easier to manufacture a new one than effect repairs."

"I didn't mean those. The energy cores."

Wil considered the suggestion. "That's true. The distribution cells are valuable and usually well-protected, so they often survive when a ship is damaged. And the PEMs themselves…" Most starship components sported a high price tag in secondhand markets, but the Perpetual Energy Modules at the center of every vessel's operation were prized for their versatility. Powering everything on ships from the jump drive to subspace communications, PEMs also had numerous applications on space stations or planetside to support all manner of offensive, defensive, and general operational needs.

"I can think of a *lot* of good uses for a robust PEM in the Outer Colonies," his son said. "But the circumstances don't add up for this being a pirate operation, especially since Darin indicated that they had a salvage contract with Renfield."

"Ah, I'd meant to follow up on that lead but haven't had time yet."

Jason raised an eyebrow. "That's why you have a team. You can ask for help, you know."

I've always been bad about that. Wil smiled. "And rob you of the opportunity to take the initiative?"

"Uh huh, sure, Dad. Anyway, I did some digging while you were on Tararia. Turns out that Renfield was working as an intermediary… for MPS."

"Monsari?" Wil's smile faded.

"Not directly, of course. But the chain of subcontracts can be traced to Monsari Power Solutions corporate. That's weird, right?"

"Very." Wil folded his hands on the desktop. "High Dynasties always exert minimum effort in their dealings. They're so wealthy, their business models are based on speed and efficiency. So, ordering a salvage from a remote location like this goes against all of those things."

"Typically, I'd suggest that this was a clean-up effort to hide something," Jason said.

"Eliminating evidence of a past dealing out there, perhaps?"

His son shrugged. "I can't imagine it would be related to anything tracing back as far as the war. They've had decades to address it, if that was the concern."

"And MPS had very little involvement in the war. Aside from the TSS purchasing power cores."

Jason sat in quiet thought. "Unless…" he said, barely above a whisper.

"What?"

His son shook his head. "No, never mind."

"I brought you in because I wanted another perspective. Please, share."

"I was thinking, if MPS' only tie to the wreckage in that area is the power cores, then that, logically, is what they were after. And, following your statement that the High Dynasties always take the most efficient path, then that would mean that all other avenues would have been exhausted already. So, either they want the power cores themselves, or they need some component from the cores."

"It doesn't make sense, though. Out there?"

"You've said thousands of ships were destroyed over the centuries, right? The Kryon Nebula is a cosmic graveyard— everything in the region works its way toward there. At a certain point, salvage does become an easier endeavor than mining."

"Not the way they have mining operations set up. The ore goes straight from the mines to the refineries and production plants."

"As long as those mines are producing, at least."

"That's never been a concern." Wil faltered. "In the past, anyway."

Jason gave a slight shrug. "Like I said, it might not mean anything."

The situation defied conventional logic. Monsari was one of the most powerful of the High Dynasties, with resources to rival those of Sietinen and SiNavTech. In fact, since SiNavTech had relinquished its ship manufacturing division to its rightful Dainetris ownership, the argument could be made that Monsari now held the *most* power. After all, everyone needed energy cores.

Everyone needs them... The civilization had always operated under the assumption that there would be an endless supply of cores to fuel the Taran Empire's expansion. Wil had fallen into that same mindset, having no evidence to suggest otherwise. Perhaps, though, that hadn't been the correct assumption.

"What if they can't keep up?" He met his son's gaze. "After all, *we* hit a production capacity limit for starships during the war. There's no reason energy core manufacturing would be any less restricted."

"So, they're trying to salvage old cores?"

"It would be an easy way to keep up with demand in the

less sophisticated markets that wouldn't know old from new. I mean, an old core really *shouldn't* make a difference."

"Even those from a critically damaged ship?"

He thought about it a little more. "I should say, in *most* cases it wouldn't make a difference. But MPS has a reputation to uphold, so I'm not overly concerned about safety. Regardless, I don't want to make any accusations without allowing MPS the opportunity to explain their actions."

"Going to them offers the opportunity for them to sweep it under the rug if there's anything shady going on."

"It does, but the TSS is already in a precarious enough position politically. If we're wrong about this, it could damage our standing."

"Go through Ryan, perhaps?" Jason suggested.

"I don't know that he's cozy enough with Monsari yet to get an honest answer from them. I'd say my dad would have enough sway, but DGE does significantly more business with MPS than SiNavTech does."

"It's your call. Either it's a business matter or a public safety one."

"When you put it in those terms, it's our TSS responsibility to see it through."

"I suppose it is."

Wil nodded. "An exploratory call will be very telling."

— — —

Jason had hoped that his father would dismiss his hunch about the *Andvari* being connected to a larger issue. They had enough going on already. But, if it *was* connected to the civil unrest or an issue with one of the High Dynasties being unable to fulfill their duty, then it was an important lead to chase down. People did crazy things when they felt cornered and desperate. The *Andvari* venturing into a forbidden former war zone on an off-the-books contract may be a symptom of the greater sickness they were trying to root out.

He could hardly believe how much had changed about the outlook for the Empire in just a few days. There had been peace for years. Prosperity. Hope. As far as he knew, no one had seen this kind of unrest coming.

With a twinge in his chest, Jason realized this was the kind of time when he would have messaged Tiff to meet up and talk about everything that was going on. *Wait, why should now be any different? Either we're still friends or we're not.*

Sure, the physical aspect of their relationship had ended, and some emotional intimacy would go along with it, but that didn't mean they couldn't vent to each other about life's bad moments. The sooner they could establish a rapport under the new normal, the better.

He typed out a message on his handheld. >>Hey! I hope you're settling in okay. Don't feel pressured to respond, just wanted to wish you the best.<<

To his surprise, he got a response right away. >>Available for a video chat?<<

>>Sure.<<

His screen lit up with an incoming vidcall. He accepted it on the holographic display.

An image of Tiff appeared, a light in her eyes as she brushed her hair behind her ear. "I had been wondering if you would show up at the port anyway."

He shrugged. "I was just passing through."

She flashed a coy smile. "I'm glad the timing worked out. It was perfect."

"You know, if you wanted me to see you off, you could

have just asked."

"Nah. It's better to know you care."

"Tiff, of course I do. You're one of my best friends, no matter what."

She beamed. "You too. I was afraid… things would change."

"Yes, it will. But I'm never going to stop caring."

"I won't, either."

They could be happy together, he knew. Their relationship had a more solid foundation than a lot of marriages he'd witnessed growing up. Nonetheless, there would always be something missing there. That romantic spark that elevated a couple from good partnership to one where life would become meaningless without one another. It was a rare, powerful thing; Jason had seen it up close with the couples in his immediate family, so he knew it was possible. He'd never particularly aspired to have that for himself, but if he was going to commit to someone for life, that's what it would take. To stay with Tiff would mean closing off the possibility of either of them finding that kind of connection for themselves. They were too young and had too much life ahead of them to settle for anything less.

"This distance thing is going to take some getting used to," he admitted.

"Yeah, I know." She sighed. "It… it is what it is."

"You don't have to explain, Tiff. I get it. I feel it, too. I just don't want to see anything come between our friendship. So, just like you did what needed to be done, I'm here now making sure we push through until this is no longer awkward."

She laughed softly. "Okay, thank you. So, uh… how are things?"

"Oh, nothing unusual. Trying to figure out how to prevent an alien invasion and simultaneous collapse of the Empire.

Everyday stuff."

"Nice. About what I expected. Glad things haven't fallen apart without me."

"Yeah, who would have guessed you being at Headquarters was the singular thing holding the Empire together? The day you decide to leave… BAM!" Too bad he was only half-joking.

"I think the civilization will recover."

"At least, if it doesn't, we won't be around to worry about it anymore."

Her eyebrows drew together in concern. "Are you doing okay?"

"I'm not projecting relationship woes on the galactic state of the Empire, if that's what you're asking. There's serious shite going on."

Tiff grinned. "Hey, look at you! Swearing like a proper Taran now, huh?"

He chuckled. "Yeah, I'm working on it."

"But in all seriousness, I know you'll find a way to beat whatever fokers are trying to take down the Empire. The High Commander is foking Wil Sietinen—the guy who won an unwinnable war and solved the unsolvable equation for subspace travel. You're his son, and you're every bit as capable. If I had to put money on a team who could do the impossible, it would be you."

"I'll try not to let you down."

"I know you won't."

It wasn't much of a pep talk, but it had eased some of the heaviness in his chest. "Thanks, Tiff."

"Anytime." She grinned.

"Now, I want to hear all about your new post."

— — —

Is it possible MPS is in trouble? Wil had always placed faith in the stability of the High Dynasties. It was the foundation of the Taran Empire, really. They were a monolith of society. Dynastic heirs were raised from infancy to be effective leaders. The services the family members and their corporations provided were the cornerstones of the civilization's operations.

Wil's position in the TSS had kept him away from the politics on Tararia for the most part, especially once Raena had stepped in as Cris' official scion. Therefore, his relationships with the Taran elite were cordial but distant.

In the case of Monsari, Wil had loose blood ties via his paternal grandmother, but he wasn't close with his distant cousin who now sat as the Head of the Dynasty. Nonetheless, a personal connection—albeit third cousin once removed—was better than nothing at all. Even so, he would be hard-pressed to overcome Celine Monsari's profound distaste for those with telekinetic abilities. Before the Priesthood's fall, she'd even gone so far as to say the Gifted were 'abominations' that should be removed from the gene pool. She'd had to change that tune with the birth of her 8th Generation granddaughter recently, particularly with scions of other High Dynasties now publicly joining the TSS. Perhaps, as a result, their next conversation would be more pleasant than the last.

Wil opted to settle on the couch in the center of the High Commander's office, facing the large viewscreen on the wall, rather than initiate the communication from his desk. He reasoned the cozier backdrop might make him seem more approachable.

Thirty seconds passed while he waited for the call to be accepted. When the screen resolved into an image, it was of a young man rather than Celine.

"Office of Celine Monsari. How may I assist?" the man asked.

"Williame Sietinen, High Commander of the TSS. I'd like to speak with Celine."

The young man's olive eyes widened the slightest measure at Wil's name and then narrowed when he spoke of the TSS. "She's asked not to be disturbed."

"Is she meeting with anyone right now?"

"No—"

"Then please put my call through." Wil had to work to keep the annoyance out of his tone. Almost anyone else would have immediately passed through a communication marked from someone of his social station. He didn't like to pull rank on people, but common decency was expected.

"One moment."

Wil couldn't help noting the lack of a 'sir' or 'my lord'. He disliked honorifics as a rule, but this felt like an intentional personal slight.

The screen went to the Monsari crest of a glowing orb against a black backdrop.

When the image returned, a stern woman in her fifties was staring back, looking none too pleased. "Williame Sietinen. I'm surprised to hear from you."

"Hello, Celine. I should state upfront that I'm calling on behalf of the TSS, not my family."

"I never know with you lot anymore. You seem to have worked your way into every corner of the Empire's dealings."

"We serve the people. If they decide they don't want us in those roles, we'll make no effort to cling to them."

"You must be pleased with the latest election polls."

"Our only pleasure is in a job well done."

She gave a mirthless smile and slight nod. "Yes, of course."

The Monsari Dynasty had had more leadership turnover than most. It wasn't uncommon for Heads to remain at their post into their eighties or nineties, skipping a generation and passing on leadership to their grandchildren. Monsari, however, tended to only have a Head remain for twenty-some years before the next generation took over. By contrast, Wil's grandfather had remained as the Head of Sietinen for six decades. It would be interesting to see how tenure evolved under the new governance system established after the Priesthood's fall.

"As I was saying, I wanted to reach out on behalf of the TSS," Wil continued. "We've begun an investigation into the incident involving the *Andvari*."

Celine tensed too quickly at the mention of the name. "Oh? What does that have to do with us?"

"Based on the documentation we've reviewed, it appears that the *Andvari* was under contract with one of your subsidiaries."

"We have dozens of subsidiaries and thousands of independent contractors. I don't keep track of all of their dealings."

"But you have heard about this particular incident?"

"Yes. The board makes a point to be aware of any situations resulting in a serious injury or casualty. For continuous improvement purposes."

Right, 'continuous improvement'. More like ass-covering. Wil nodded. "Naturally. So, I imagine that this review included a briefing on the nature of the ship's contracted business."

"An overview."

"How do you account for the *Andvari* being in the Kyron Nebula?"

"Salvage."

"Yes. But it was in restricted territory."

"They weren't authorized to go there."

"I wasn't suggesting you or any of your subsidiaries would skirt legality in such a manner. I'd only like to know what they had been contracted to do," Wil pressed.

"Salvage, as I said."

"Salvaging *what*, though? They were in a remote, restricted area."

"Ship scrap." Her gaze was slightly unfocused, as if she was resisting the urge to look away. No doubt, her statements were lies.

"I could see DGE ordering that kind of operation, but what interest does MPS have?"

"That's not relevant. They had a quota to deliver, and the consequences of how they went about accomplishing that objective is on them alone."

Wil wasn't sure what to make of the woman's hedging. It didn't take a telepath—or even a trained investigator—to tell that she was hiding something significant. Frankly, he expected more poise from a seasoned politician. "I was in no way suggesting their deaths were your fault. I'm simply trying to understand the circumstances."

"I have nothing more to say on the matter. Best of luck with your investigation." She ended the call.

Wil leaned back in his chair, staring at the blank screen. Whenever the High Dynasties weren't forthright, much bigger issues weren't far behind. *Time to take another tactic to get answers.*

CHAPTER 16

JASON SAVORED THE crisp air flowing into his flight mask as he soaked in the view of the starscape around him. No workout would ever provide an outlet for his nerves in the way running maneuvers in a fighter could. He'd rather be out in the real thing, but the simulator was an acceptable substitute for now.

"I saw a lot of sloppy maneuvers out there on the practice course, so we're going back to basics, tighten up your turns," Jason said. "Get in your squad formations and watch."

He moved his simulated craft in an example pattern through the course. "See how the curves connect? Always be looking at least two moves ahead. Set yourself up for the next maneuver."

He backed off his craft to a good vantage for watching the students run the simulated course. In turn, he had the members of each squad go, offering real-time feedback to each student.

"That's better. I can tell you're more confident in these sims than out in the black. Practice will improve that," he said after the final student had completed their run of the course.

"For now, though. Let's mix things up."

Jason loaded in a new course, this time one that required more aggressive transitions between the different obstacles. He'd noticed that several of the students were too loose, so this would push their comfort zone. Alisha should excel, so long as she didn't try to clip the corners.

The students started their run-throughs in the same order.

"Good job, Hamlin. That was much tighter, but don't baby your throttle. You've got the thrust; use it next time," Jason said.

"Yes, sir." His voice was lacking some of his usual enthusiasm.

"Delroe, you're up."

Alisha took her craft out from formation and dove into the course. To Jason's relief, she seemed to have taken his feedback last session to heart, striking the ideal balance between aggressive lines and safety. In short order, she completed the course without a single misstep.

"Really well done," Jason told her. "That's exactly what I was talking about."

"Yes, sir!" The pride came through in her voice.

He worked the group through several other courses and offered notes. On the whole, the group was coming along exceptionally well. If he could get them to fly that way in real fighters, they'd be in business.

They may need to put those skills to the test sooner than later if we find ourselves in another war. It was a grim thought, and he was quick to dismiss it. With the discovery of the original treaty, there was a renewed chance for a peaceful resolution.

Jason completed the lesson with practice flying in formation, turning as one. The students were much less adept at the synchronized movements than they were at running a course individually, but they'd come a long way since when he'd started working with them. It would be rewarding to polish their skills and see them come into their own.

With the practice complete, Jason ended the simulation and the pods popped open with a hiss. To maximize the simulation effect, they were kept pressurized just like a real cockpit.

Jason hopped out of his pod and waited for the students to line up. "You're doing great," he told them. "I'm feeling good about these improvements. I think we can resume the space flights next week, as I'd hoped."

There were broad smiles from half the students, but the others ranged from mild enthusiasm to expressionless.

"What's wrong?" Jason asked.

"Nothing," Bret muttered at the same time Wes said, "What's going on with the protests in the Outer Colonies?"

That's not what I expected them to be thinking about right now. Jason tucked his helmet under his arm. "I couldn't give you any specifics. I don't know any more than what's been in the news reports."

"Does that mean the TSS isn't responding?" Wes asked.

"It means I don't know. Why does everyone think I'm privy to each decision the TSS makes?"

"Because the High Commander is your dad."

"Like any officer, he briefs me when I'm needed, and the rest of the time our other very capable field Agents take care of the rest."

"I have family on Duronis," Bret said. "I can't help being a little worried."

"Naturally. And I sympathize with your position, but I don't have any additional information to share. I will say that, typically, that kind of domestic disturbance is handled by the

Guard." Even if Jason *did* know more, he wouldn't be able to share anything classified with the students. Withholding information like that was his least favorite part of being an Agent—aside from paperwork, perhaps. However, his father was about as open and honest as leaders came, so rarely was Jason placed in a position of needing to overly temper his statements.

The students still looked worried. Jason softened. "Nothing has come through official channels. Let's not get ahead of ourselves and worry about nothing," he tried to assure them.

As far as he knew, right now that was true. He could only hope it would stay that way.

—   —   —

Lexi descended the stairs into the underground storeroom tunnel. The place gave her the creeps. *People always joke about plans being made in the shadows. I didn't think it would be so literal!*

Oren had summoned her to another cryptic meeting. There'd been no discussion of the odd mini-speech from that Magdalena woman afterward, and everyone had just gone back upstairs like they were having a perfectly normal afternoon. The only indication that the gathering had been real was that Shena's awestruck expression had persisted for the rest of the day. Lexi had wanted to ask for more information about the mysterious leader but had thought better of it; questions might be taken as question*ing*, and it was better to fake reverence. The woman was clearly some sort of idol for the Alliance's movement, so that was all Lexi really needed to know for now.

Oren and Shena were waiting in the tunnel when Lexi

arrived, and Josh came down the stairway soon after. The staggered movements were, apparently, a tactic to keep the uninitiated from picking up on the secret meetings. *Stars know it worked on me!*

But for being one of the 'initiates', Lexi wished she had a better handle on what was going on. She'd been saying that for days now, and she didn't expect it to get better. She was caught up in a surreal daydream that was quickly trending toward a nightmare.

Melisa wouldn't have supported any of this. But that had never been in question when Lexi had caught wind of the Sovereign Peoples Alliance and how several women had gone missing in their wake—her dear friend included. Melisa was more than a friend, though. She was a sister. Even more so than her half-sister, who was her solitary living blood relative of any note.

So, when Melisa had disappeared on Duronis, Lexi had gone to investigate. There was no sign of Melisa at first blush, but Lexi's telepathic gleanings told her that she had been a part of the Alliance before she went missing. In that same silent probing, she'd also learned that the Alliance was on the lookout for young, unattached women like her with Gifts. So, she'd kept her own abilities secret and started looking around. She kept thinking that she might be on the cusp of discovering what happened to Melisa, and then she'd have another bizarre twist thrown her way that would set her back. Only sheer determination kept her pressing forward.

What are they planning, and is any of it related to Melisa? She had to stick around until she got answers, no matter her concerns about the Alliance. Earning their trust would be the only way to get the truth. And, at all cost, she must keep her abilities hidden. Fortunately, she was good at that.

"Thank you for including me," Lexi said to the small group as they gathered at the center of the tunnel.

"Our mission is bigger than any one of us," Oren replied. "We must grow our numbers with those who share our vision."

"I am happy to pledge my support to a cause worth supporting." The statement itself was true. *Never said I thought the Alliance was worthy.*

Oren and the others nodded with approval. "Now that the word is out and others are starting to wake up to the injustices, we must continue to open their eyes."

A crate had been taken off one of the shelves to serve as a makeshift table for a holoprojector. Oren activated the device and brought up a rendering of Duronis. More than a dozen red dots appeared around the globe.

"Here's where we've had the most activity to date," Oren said. "We've been advised to set our aspirations higher."

"Easy," Josh said. "We need to disrupt the planet's supply line. The connection to the outside worlds. That's what will make people realize how important it is to be self-sufficient."

"What do you mean by 'disrupt'?" Lexi asked.

"You know, just make life a little difficult."

Oren was staring with intense concentration at the three-dimensional rendering. "No, this is about showing them the High Dynasties are not our friends. It can't come back on us as causing 'disruption'."

Shena crossed her arms. "They need to be responsible."

"There are ways to arrange that appearance." Oren nodded slowly in thought. "Perhaps an accident at one of the facilities?"

"One that the media would have to cover," Josh said. "I can help nudge them in the right direction."

Shena nodded. "That's the key. We need the story to get out there, get people talking. And then we can guide the narrative."

"What kind of 'accident' could do that?" Lexi asked, not sure she really wanted the answer.

"No need to worry about that. Our tactical team will take care of the details," Oren said dismissively. "Now, let's work on the narrative. Once we have that, we'll know exactly what we need to do."

Lexi bit back the follow-up questions that flooded into her mind. *We're just crafting a story? We're going to trick people into believing it? What happened to sharing the truth about life in the Outer Colonies?*

She didn't like it one bit. But at least she was part of the conversation. Maybe, in time, she'd find a way to really make a difference. And, if nothing else, she was one step closer to gaining their trust and finding her friend. *Hang in there, Melisa. I'm going to figure out what they're up to and find you.*

— — —

The conversation with Celine Monsari left Wil confused and concerned. Everything from the woman's rude assistant to her evasive non-answers suggested she and her corporation were up to something shady.

Do MPS' dealings with Renfield have any connection with the other activity on Duronis? That potential funding web was too convoluted to unravel yet.

Before he could proceed with any line of investigation, Wil needed to know how the MPS energy cores actually worked.

Like most tech controlled by the High Dynasties, the proprietary secrets were closely guarded. Only a small handful of people understood the finer points of the SiNavTech beacon navigation network and nav consoles, just like the confidential operations of VComm's telecommunications network. MPS was no different. If anything, the energy cores were the most secretive of all.

Wil knew how they functioned in a theoretical sense—essentially, drawing energy from a pocket universe. So long as the connection was maintained, there was near infinite energy potential. The Perpetual Energy Modules—or PEMs, as they were typically called for short—could be scaled to fit any number of applications. Most critically, they were the energy source for all starships and shuttlecraft. It was the only existing technology within Taran purview capable of fulfilling the astronomical energy needs of propulsion and maintaining spatial disruptions to vent exhaust into subspace.

Without PEMs, there would be no interstellar commerce. No more Taran Empire. End of story.

The seriousness of the circumstances made it critical that Wil learn everything he could about the technology and anything that might hinder production capacity. The problem was getting accurate information. Without question, no one within MPS would share secrets about the PEMs' operation. There was only one other place Wil could turn to potentially find out more about the technology: the Aesir.

Wil's relationship with the Aesir was one of the most complex and challenging to navigate in his life. In terms of raw ability, the group was closer to being peers than other Tarans. Having left the rest of the Empire before the Priesthood's widespread genetic interventions, they offered a window into the race's past. Wil had been welcomed among them as the Cadicle, heralded with almost religious reverence for his advanced abilities being the next phase of Taran evolution. But with Saera and his other personal ties to the rest of the Empire, going to live among the Aesir wasn't a viable option.

The temptation was there, though. Life would be a lot

simpler amongst a population of people who were all Gifted and embraced their abilities. Plus, their advanced tech was designed with bioelectronic interfaces to enable telepathic linking with machines. Everything felt *right* when he was with the Aesir. Yet, their magnificent cities hidden in spatial rifts near the galactic core would never be his home. He limited himself to short visits to ensure he never got too comfortable. His responsibilities to the Taran Empire had to come first.

He'd fostered a number of relationships with members of the Aesir over the years, but his most trusted friend was Dahl. The man was over twelve-hundred years old and still looked forty. Such incredible longevity was one of the most striking aspects of the Aesir's culture. Cellular renewal therapies had extended many of their lives beyond a thousand years, making death a choice when a person felt they had lived a full life rather than being a ticking clock beyond their control.

The life-extending therapy was one of many technologies the Aesir had shared with Wil five years ago in an Archive of their collected knowledge—a gesture of goodwill for improving relations between the branches of Tarans. Wil had held many lengthy discussions with Dahl about how best to share the technologies with the rest of Tarans, but there were significant implications to making such things available to the general public. He hated the pressure of it, literally deciding if something lifesaving on the surface might ultimately do more harm than good. Dahl, in his frustrating ancient-mystic ways, had told Wil 'he'd know what to do when the time was right'. As if Wil had any clue what that meant. He kept waiting for a grand epiphany, but none had come yet.

So, Wil had held onto the information contained in the Archive within his trusted circle, weighing what to do with it. The most frustrating part was that Wil was certain the Aesir had given him the Archive as a test—much in the way they'd tested him as a young man when he'd gazed into the nexus. They were crafty like that, always gauging and studying. He had no idea what they hoped to see, or if there even was a 'correct answer'. Stalling his participation in their game remained the best option for now.

Even so, he couldn't avoid contact completely. The Aesir knew too much and had such valuable insights that he found himself turning to them whenever he felt stuck. And now, with this transdimensional alien threat on the horizon, he needed their opinion more than ever before.

Wil brought up his backdoor communication protocol to connect directly with Dahl, established after the Priesthood's fall.

The secure subspace link connected after twenty seconds. Dahl smiled serenely at Wil from the holoprojection above his desk. "Hello. I thought you might reach out."

"Hi, Dahl. Yes, it's been quite a week." Wil inclined his head in respectful greeting.

"A great test is coming. We have felt it."

"This is what Jason saw, isn't it?"

Dahl nodded. "The truth of the nexus is always revealed in due time."

"Can you tell me anything about these beings beyond the Rift?"

"No more than what I have already shared about the treaty, I'm afraid. That conflict predates even us."

Wil smiled. "We found the hardcopy."

"You did?" Dahl's eyes widened in a rare show of surprise.

"That Cadicle statue in the Sanctuary? It was sitting right on top of the thing."

The old Oracle chuckled—a strange sound, coming from

him. "I should have known."

"It didn't give us a lot, aside from confirmation that the Gate tech is the point of conflict. We're trying to figure out why."

"I cannot offer any more insight."

"I know. That's not why I called," Wil said. "Please forgive what may seem like a strange question, but how do the Aesir handle power generation? Do you use PEMs like other Tarans?"

Dahl paused in consideration for a moment, tilting his head slightly as he studied Wil. "We do. It is the most efficient power system known to us."

"That introduces an interesting logistical question. MPS provides all of the PEMs for the colonized Taran worlds. Do you have a means of replicating their process?"

"We took a large number of PEMs with us when the Aesir originally broke from the Empire."

"But your numbers were in the thousands then, right? Now, with a hundred million, surely your power demands have grown beyond the original capacity—not to mention system failures."

Dahl nodded. "Yes, we have needed more to support our expansion. While we have reverse-engineered our equipment that interfaces with the PEMs, so we can manufacture replacement parts, we still acquire the modules themselves from dealers within the Empire when the needs arise."

The answer shocked Wil more than he was expecting. "So, with all of your advanced tech, you still rely on MPS for your power cores?"

"In short, yes."

"Because it's easier that way, or because you've been unable to replicate the PEMs?"

The Oracle seemed reluctant to answer him. "We have theoretical models for how the PEMs operate, but we have been unable to produce a module that is as efficient or stable as the MPS versions."

"So, they really *do* have proprietary tech."

"We've studied them. The issue is not simply the design, but also the materials. The voydite crystals are the only thing we are aware of with the capability to contain a stable connection to a pocket universe as a perpetual energy source. Everything else we've tried either breaks down quickly or is unable to reliably channel the flow of energy."

"All right. So why don't you get your own voydite?"

"We haven't found any. To our knowledge, Monsari has complete control of the sole source of the crystals."

Wil's heart sank. "And they've been working that mine since before the Aesir broke from the Priesthood? A millennium, or more."

"Correct."

"Fok." The curse slipped out involuntarily, and he gave Dahl an apologetic look. "In your estimation, is their supply finite?"

"I have no direct knowledge to inform such an evaluation."

"Humor me."

"Given that we, with all of our knowledge and travels, have not come across any other voydite veins, I can only assume that their creation was under a set of very specific, and I dare say *lucky*, circumstances. Such rare conditions are in an isolated area. So yes, I would expect the supply to be limited."

"And the fact that it's lasted this long—"

"Is, frankly, astonishing."

It was the absolute worst answer imaginable but also the one that made the most sense. No wonder MPS would be hiring crews to salvage ship wreckage—the old PEMs contained voydite for them to recycle. But there was only so much scrap to be found.

Once the voydite deposit is fully depleted... Wil breathed out between his teeth. "Thank you, Dahl. I appreciate your candor."

"You, however, are not being as forthright, as usual."

"I would like to conclude my investigation before I raise unnecessary alarm."

"Very well. We trust your judgment, Cadicle."

The title still sounded strange to Wil's ears, like talking about himself in the third person. "I'll be in touch when I have anything concrete," he said. "And please, if you find out more about these beings coming through the Rift, I hope you'll share."

"Tarans are not as divided as they once were. If this is what we fear it might be, our continued distance will not benefit anyone."

That was as close a statement of 'we have your back' as Wil was likely to get. "Thank you. We'll talk soon."

Dahl bowed his head and ended the commlink.

Wil wilted into his chair. *We are so foked if Monsari is running out of voydite.*

It might be the single most destructive piece of information in the entire Taran sphere—if it was true. He had to verify the claims.

There was one person on Tararia always at the top of his list for vetting sensitive information. He made the call.

"Hey, Dad," Wil greeted as soon as his father's face appeared on the screen. "This is going to seem out of nowhere, but have you heard about MPS having any... issues?"

"Hi to you, too." Cris smiled and then shook his head. "I

can't say I've heard anything about MPS, no."

Wil frowned. "It was worth a shot. Sorry to bother you."

"Wait, hold on. You can't just call me up, drop a question like that, and not explain."

"It might be nothing."

"Weren't we *just* talking about your hunches?"

Wil cracked a smile. "Fair point. Are you alone?"

"I can be. Hold on."

Wil waited while his father found a private place to talk. When Cris was secure in a conference room, Wil continued, "We're still looking into the *Andvari*. They were working for an MPS subsidiary, doing salvage, and I can't get a clear answer about *what* they were looking for. I mean, MPS doesn't deal with ship salvage."

"No, they don't."

"The evidence seems to be pointing toward MPS ordering the salvage of old cores to get the voydite."

"That's, uh… a lot of work." Cris frowned.

"Yes, that was my thought, too. But there are some rather worrying implications if that type of salvage has become appealing."

"Quite an understatement."

Wil nodded. "So, I'm not sure. All I know is something isn't adding up."

Cris' brow furrowed in concentration. "My father talked a little about MPS, before my parents handed me off full-time to the tutors when they realized I couldn't care less. But I was listening. What was made very clear is that the single most valuable thing MPS has is its process for turning voydite crystals into the nanotube shell structure for PEMs. That and, well, the voydite crystals themselves. Funny how businesses flourish when they have a monopoly on raw materials, hmm?"

"Do you know where they mine the crystals?"

"Haven't a clue. If everyone knew, it wouldn't be much of a secret."

That was sounding an awful lot like what Dahl had said. "So, *one* location?"

"I don't know, honestly."

Wil asked the difficult question. "Do you think it's possible they might be running out?"

His father laughed once then quickly turned serious. "If they really do only have one mining location…"

"Surely, they've developed a lab process for growing more of the crystals, though. They couldn't have just been working with a single natural supply all of this time. That would be— I can't imagine how they could have gotten this far if that was the case."

"Yeah, I…" None of the humor remained in his father's face. "Wil, if there's even a hint of truth to this, it is an issue on a scale we've never faced. And that's saying something. I mean, PEMs are critical to almost every aspect of Taran life. Transportation, planetary shields, food production. Yeah, the PEMs don't fail too often, but if we can't make new ones, we can't expand, and we can't replace them. We'd stall out."

"With the new colonization efforts that are underway now—"

"We've been counting on an unrestricted supply of power cores, able to scale as the Empire grows. MPS has never indicated that would be an issue."

Wil shook his head. "They couldn't. It would be the end of them."

"Could they really have been faking their ability to deliver?"

"You would know more about that than me."

His father took an unsteady breath. "I can't say I've been looking for any signs of them failing. I can dig around. See if anything jumps out, knowing what to look for."

"Obviously, keep it *very* contained. If this is actually happening, it'll—"

"Be catastrophic."

"I was going to say, 'unleash a foking shitestorm', but yes."

"Let's keep level heads," Cris said. "It might not be anything remotely so grim."

"I hope not."

CHAPTER 17

WIL'S GROWING PILE of concerns had made for a poor night of sleep. Nonetheless, he was forging ahead with his investigation. Wil was midway through a review of MPS' publicly available annual reports when Michael rushed into his office.

"Something is happening," Michael announced without preamble.

Wil minimized the work on his desktop and turned his full attention to his friend. Though Michael was often straightforward with his communications, he rarely barged in—and never without urgent reason. "What and where?"

"It might be connected to the other business near the Rift," Michael explained. "Alkeer Station is reporting strange activity in their vicinity."

"Strange how?"

"Erm, the best way to describe it might be 'spatial ripples'. See for yourself." Michael swiped information from his handheld to Wil's desktop, and it popped up on the holoprojector.

The information was, indeed, odd and difficult to

classify—much like everything related to the alien contact through the Rift. There was an array of rolling spatial distortions heading toward the Alkeer Station, one of the more remote TSS outposts. The 'waves', as Wil saw fitting to call them, appeared to originate at the Rift and then flow toward Alkeer. There wasn't any consistency to it, and any given wave didn't form a continuous line. However, looking at the composite image Michael had displayed, showing all of the information recorded within the past three hours, a defined path was beginning to form between the two locations.

Wil frowned at the holodisplay. "Agreed, there's definitely something strange going on, and it does seem to be connected to the Rift. The relative distance to Alkeer is far greater than to the site where the *Andvari* was attacked. So, given that the timing and placement of the spatial distortions exceeds lightspeed transit, it means there's a transdimensional component to whatever is going on."

"I haven't been able to get the image out of my head of that leviathan wrapped around the ship," Michael said, concern tinging his voice.

Wil studied the composite image of activity, seeing where his friend was going with the observation. When he let his vision go fuzzy, the spatial distortion points were reminiscent of the curves where huge tentacles could be reaching across space from the Rift toward the station. *No, the scale of that…* He dismissed the thought. "These entities are no doubt large, but this would be absurd! We're talking dozens of lightyears in span here."

"It doesn't have to be *one* of them. Ants make bridges by linking together. Gophers carve tunnels. This could just be a bridge or super-highway."

"Not unlike what the Bakzen did with the Rift's

expansion," Wil realized.

"Obviously, this is different, but…"

Wil took a moment to collect his thoughts. They'd strongly suspected that the event with the *Andvari* was just the beginning and that the beings would make their presence known again on a larger scale. Based on the limited information at their disposal, they had been working on preparations for that inevitable contact. However, they weren't nearly as far along in that process as he would have liked. The problem was that they simply had insufficient information to make informed decisions. Every new encounter would give them greater insight, but that meant going into each of those engagements at an extreme disadvantage. No matter how he looked at it, they had no choice but to face the entities head-on.

"Okay, we'll go talk with them," he decided.

"Talk how? It's unclear if there's anyone there."

"There's *some* kind of presence," Wil insisted. "I have no doubt that someone—or, more appropriately, some*thing*—is watching and listening to everything we're doing."

"I suppose it wouldn't hurt to try," Michael agreed. "The *Andvari*'s crew destroyed their own ship. Based on everything we know, these beings just mess with people's heads."

"That's my thought."

"This whole thing is crazy, for the record."

"It is, but we play the hand we're dealt." Wil stood up.

"Your pep-talks are normally more eloquent than that," Michael quipped.

"I'm saving my creative energy for convincing these beings that this is all an unfortunate misunderstanding. The Gatekeepers listened to us and were willing to keep the peace, so let's hope these others respond in kind."

"Except, the Gatekeepers said that the 'others' *wouldn't* be so forgiving. So, if these *are* those others…"

"The previous conflict was a long time ago. Things change."

"Let us hope. Be safe," Michael said. He hesitated, seemingly on the verge of saying something else, then left the office.

Wil could guess at what he might have said, but the two of them had been through too much for the words to need to be spoken aloud. It was a dangerous mission; they both knew it. But they would fight for freedom to the end, and there was no point in admitting early defeat by saying goodbye.

They needed to depart for Alkeer as soon as possible, but certain preparations were required. Wil called Saera and the Lead Engineer to his office to coordinate.

"It's go-time," he said when both had arrived, waiting in front of his desk.

"For what?" Saera asked.

He directed her attention to the image on the holoprojector.

Rowan, the Lead Engineer, reacted first. "Fok! What is that?" Not the most professional response, but Wil couldn't blame him. The stocky man's face had flushed up to his hairline, dark eyes wide.

"It would seem the aliens are making their grand entrance after the prelude."

Saera groaned. "Naturally."

"How is that imaging solution coming?" Wil asked.

"We're not finished yet," Rowan replied. "It sounds a lot easier to do than it is in actuality. The way that the *Andvari* pulled off that capture wouldn't be safe for the people on the station. I mean, they basically produced a bomb blast. To do this in a controlled fashion, we—"

Wil held up his hand to stop the rambling. *I should have been working on it myself.* He respected the TSS' engineers, but it was a point of fact that he could see solutions no one else did. It was why he'd cracked the 'uncrackable' code for the independent jump drive, not to mention a dozen other engineering marvels over the course of his career. But time, not intellect, was his limiting factor. "Grab what you need, and we can work on it in transit."

Rowan paled slightly at the prospect of heading toward the enemy, but he nodded. "On it, sir." He ran off to finish the preparations.

"Who are we taking?" Saera asked once they were alone.

"I'll go with Curtis and Jason."

She frowned. "I'm not staying behind."

"Saera, the High Commander and Lead Agent shouldn't both go. Not this time." He left the subtext unspoken.

He expected her to fight him, but instead she nodded. "Are you sure you only want two Seconds?"

"More wouldn't make a difference. If it comes to that point, it'll all be on Jason and me, anyway."

"True."

"All right, I need to get going. It'll be at least five hours for transit. As it is, we might not even make it before they do whatever they're going to do."

"If anyone can find a way to communicate with them, it's you." Saera took his hands. "Please be careful."

"We'll do our best."

— — —

An alert for immediate mobilization popped up on Jason's

desktop and handheld simultaneously. Not a second later, he heard rushed footsteps coming down the hallway.

The Lead Engineer went running by as Jason read over the details.

Shite! They're coming through the Rift?

He locked down his desktop and was about to head to the central elevator when he heard his parents leaving the High Commander's office.

"Has something happened?" he asked telepathically from a distance, not wanting to shout down the hall.

The information they shared in his mind turned his stomach. *How are we supposed to go up against that?* He didn't ask the question aloud, but the expressions on their faces mirrored his concerns.

After well-wishes and a hug from his mother, he and his father made their way to the *Conquest*, bringing only the clothes they were presently wearing. If it came down to an extended trip, they could manufacture more on board; for now, time was of the essence.

Jason started the pre-flight initiation in the Command Center while his father went down to Engineering to review the work that had been done on a transdimensional imaging solution. Curtis Jaconis, another of the original Primus Elites, and Rianne, the ship's usual tactical officer from the Militia division, were already in the Command Center when he arrived.

"Hey, Jason. This is some pretty crazy shite, eh?" Curtis said. He ran his hand through his dark, curly hair.

"Not how I expected my week to go, no." Jason swallowed the bile rising in his throat. *Of all the places, why did it have to be Alkeer? Tiff could have gone anywhere...*

He shut off the line of thinking. It wasn't productive, and

there was nothing he could do to change the situation.

Instead, he focused on going over the *Conquest*'s systems to make sure they were ready for a potential engagement. Once they had passed checks across the board, he had Curtis pilot the ship from port and initiate a jump to their destination.

We're coming. Hold on. Until they arrived, there was little else to do but wait.

—

When the ship dropped out of subspace a little over five hours later, Jason was relieved to see the Alkeer Station was still intact.

The structure consisted of three rings rotating around a central shaft. Several starships were docked at a connected port, with only a single destroyer and the rest transport vessels of various sizes. Not long ago, this location would have been filled with a substantial contingent of warships. So much for the peace that had enabled that demilitarization.

His father had come up from Engineering moments before they dropped out from subspace, not looking particularly happy. "Well, at least we're not too late," he muttered upon seeing the view.

"What about the imaging?" Jason asked.

Wil shook his head. "Close, but nothing reliable yet. Rowan's still working on it."

So, we're blind. Jason slumped in the front right seat in the middle of the Command Center, where he'd settled for the voyage.

While his father conversed with Rianne and Curtis about the sensor data, Jason reached out his senses to the minds of the people on the station. It didn't take long to single out Tiff.

He gave her a telepathic hail that was the equivalent of a door knock. She jumped in surprise but then let him in.

"*Hey from afar,*" he greeted telepathically. "*I swear, I'm not stalking you.*"

"*Sounds like something a stalker would say,*" she jested. "*I take it you're here because of the… weirdness?*"

"*Yeah. I wasn't expecting to be out this way any time soon. Sorry to intrude.*"

"*Glad you're here. We were pretty relieved to hear the* Conquest *was coming with the High Commander himself. I suppose you're okay, too.*" She winked in his mind.

"*Still liking the new digs?*"

"*It's great, aside from these bomaxed neighbors that are trying to destroy the neighborhood.*"

"*We'll see what we can do about that.*"

With the speed of the telepathy, Jason hadn't missed much of the conversation about the sensor data. The gist of it was that they could detect the spatial waves but had no idea what was causing them.

Wil paced next to his chair. "We're still blind up here. How is that imager coming?" he asked Rowan over the comm.

"Still working on it." The Lead Engineer sounded a little defeated to Jason's ear. "This synchronization issue is a beast."

"I know." Wil groaned under his breath as he ended the commlink. "I should go back down there to help."

"If these guys make a sudden appearance, we need you here in the Command Center," Curtis said from the front console.

"Besides, you said yourself that there's nothing more you can do right now. It's down to letting the configuration models process," Jason added. While he didn't share his father's passion or aptitude for engineering, he understood enough about what the team was doing to know that their work was at a standstill until the computer found a feasible scenario to meet the conditions his father had programmed.

The display on the wraparound screen shifted to include a holographic overlay of the spatial distortions that weren't yet visible to the naked eye. The waves seemed to be closing in on the station.

Jason's chest tightened. *"We're going to figure this out, Tiff."*

Wil leaned forward in his seat. "Any sign of a ship or something we can talk to?"

Rianne held up her hands in a helpless gesture of what was on the screen. "Take a wild guess." Any other Militia officer wouldn't have gotten away with talking to an Agent that way, but she'd been through enough with Wil and the others that it was fitting for the situation.

"Okay, stay back from the station, outside the zone of the distortions," Wil instructed. "As soon as they make an appearance, we'll try to open a dialogue."

"What's the plan?" Tiff asked.

Jason wished he had something more reassuring to tell her. *"We're trying to figure out a good way to get a look at the bad guys."*

"I must say, I'm curious."

"Me too. The only thing I've seen is foking nasty."

"Well done! You've gotten the hang of swearing like a normal person."

"I'm more adaptable than we thought, apparently."

She hesitated in her response. *"If this is some kind of gesture about how things could be different with us—"*

"No, I was just ready to fit in properly. I've been holding onto Earth for too long."

"Okay."

"But I do miss you, Tiff."

"I miss you, too. Maybe we can—"

The space surrounding the station suddenly became unfocused with the telltale appearance of a localized spatial distortion beginning to form.

"We need that imaging *now*!" Wil shouted into the comm.

"Tiff, something is happening!" Jason warned telepathically.

The station began to vibrate. It took a second for Jason to realize that it wasn't actually oscillating, but rather the structure was coming apart. Not pieces, but as if the individual molecules had released their bonds to one another and the thing was dissolving before his eyes.

"Jas—" The telepathic link cut out. There was only emptiness where her presence had been moments before.

He stood in horrified silence as the station dematerialized in the span of three seconds. Space was once again smooth and still.

Even after the structure was gone, as if it had never existed, no one spoke.

"Tiff?"

He reached out telepathically for her, but there was nothing outside the presence of those on the *Conquest*. The space where the station had been felt wrong. Empty. Reality dropped out from under him.

She was gone. *No…*

CHAPTER 18

WHAT THE FOK? Fear gripped Wil in a way he'd never experienced. The hum of thousands of minds on the station had been extinguished in a moment. His immense abilities had always afforded him confidence that he could control a situation through force when diplomacy failed. But this... *How is this even possible?*

Next to him, Jason gaped at the place on the screen where the station should be. "Wha...?" He slowly dropped to his knees.

The blackness where the station had been somehow seemed darker than the surrounding space, though that was probably his imagination trying to cope with the sudden horror of it all. For a split second, Wil tried to reason that the station had been taken from this place and moved elsewhere—transported or transitioned outside visible spacetime. But he knew that wasn't the case. It had been destroyed, utterly and completely. And, along with it, everyone on board. *Including...*

Jason was staring silently at the spot on the viewscreen where his friend had been.

His heart broke for his son. He was all too familiar with the agony of loss, and especially the feeling of being powerless to stop it. But there wasn't time to grieve now.

Wil snapped himself from his own shocked daze. "Curtis, back us up fifty thousand kilometers. Rianne, order all other ships to leave the area immediately, and then take a thorough scan of the vicinity—everything we've got."

"Aye," they acknowledged.

"Let me know as soon as the scan is complete." He then added to Jason telepathically, *"Hold it together. We'll figure out what happened."*

His son hadn't moved from where he'd sunken to the deck. "Where'd they go?"

"I don't…" Wil faded out. He didn't want to voice his thoughts that the station had been destroyed, because that would make it real.

"That wasn't a conventional weapon," Curtis said to him telepathically.

"It was like the molecular bonds gave out," he agreed. *"Perhaps at an even smaller level."*

"Shite, all those people…" Curtis shook his head.

Wil's chest constricted with thoughts of the tragic loss of life. But the commander in him was focused on the larger issue. *I don't know if this is an enemy we can fight.*

Next to him, Jason's brows were drawn together with fear and confusion. "Dad, what—"

"Maybe you should go wait in the lounge," Wil suggested. Once the shock wore off, Jason would realize his longtime friend and lover had been dematerialized along with the station. That wasn't a scene he wanted to handle while in the Command Center.

"I'm not going anywhere." Jason rose to his feet, somehow

maintaining composure despite the catastrophic loss.

Wil couldn't help feeling a swell of fatherly pride about the fine officer Jason was becoming; he knew many great soldiers who would have cracked. It was one thing to see strangers die, but losing a close loved one could send anyone over the edge.

"We've got the results," Rianne stated.

"Are you sure you want to be here for this?" Wil confirmed with his son.

Jason nodded. *"I need to know."*

"What's the verdict, Rianne?"

She took a shaky breath. "It's as if the station was never there."

A sob caught in Jason's throat and he turned away.

Wil swore under his breath. "Open an external comm broadcast, all frequencies."

Rianne nodded when it was ready.

He looked forward, resolute. "You've shown us what you can do, and we acknowledge your power. But a war is not in either of our interests. There's no need for those losses. Let us find a way to maintain this longstanding peace." He gestured with his hand to cut the broadcast.

Wil resisted the urge to pace while they waited for a response.

After a minute, none had come.

Rianne gave Wil a nervous look over her shoulder. "Orders, sir?"

This must have been a demonstration. And if they don't want to talk, we'll just make ourselves the next target. Bitter anger swelled in him, frustratingly without direction since their enemy had no face it was willing to show. He suspected they were out there, watching and waiting to see what they would do. Any action beyond the scan was likely to make matters worse.

"Take us back to Headquarters," he instructed.

Jason wordlessly rushed from the Command Center.

"Jump whenever you have a course, Curtis," Wil called out as he followed his son out into the corridor.

Jason hurried into the small conference room directly across the hall from the Command Center, used for strategy sessions. He made it halfway across the room before the tears came.

"Jason, I'm so sorry," Wil murmured.

"She can't be gone," he stammered between choked breaths. "She…"

Wil embraced his son and held him as he sobbed into his shoulder. He hadn't seen Jason cry since he was a young teenager, and he'd always been thankful his children hadn't needed to endure the grief of loss in their lives. Now, he wished he could do something to take his pain away.

As they stood there together, the dark starscape transitioned to the ethereal light of subspace. For once, Wil was happy for the dampening effect of subspace on his abilities, lessening the emotional turmoil he sensed in Jason. While it wasn't the same closeness of the bond he shared with his wife, he was more connected to his children than other people. Through that tie, he felt Jason's raw grief, shock, and confusion about what had transpired, magnifying Wil's own emotions. But he also sensed Jason's strength and grounding. He *would* be okay.

Eventually, Jason's tears subsided and he pulled away to wipe his face. It was only then that Wil realized his own cheeks were wet.

"I don't think I ever told you, I had a complete breakdown in this room during the war. Right after we lost Cambion." Wil let out a bitter chuckle. "I guess we should go ahead and label it a designated therapy space."

Jason managed a strangled laugh. "Good call." He finished wiping his eyes.

"I know there are no words that can make this better, so I'll just say that I will always be here for you, no matter what." He squeezed his shoulder.

"Thanks."

Wil returned to the Command Center to allow Jason time to process on his own. He'd learned long ago that his son was like him in that way.

While Wil knew many of the Agents who'd been stationed at the Alkeer outpost, none were more than acquaintances. The emotional distance allowed him to make an objective assessment of the issue at hand in terms of military response and security. The enemy hadn't even shown its face, and yet they'd been able to un-make a massive structure in seconds. If that was possible, could they also destroy a planet? Or an entire system? The galaxy itself?

He re-focused his thoughts to keep from going down an unproductive tangent. *Address the here and now, what's in your control.*

Rather than taking his seat in the Command Center, Wil headed for his office connected to the room. "I'm going to prepare a TSS-wide communication. Find us a good stop-off point half an hour from now so we can transmit the message."

"Will do," Curtis acknowledged.

The announcement that Wil needed to craft was the exact message he'd hoped to never have to deliver again. Death. Danger. Impending war. It was nasty business, but he was the TSS leader so it could only come from him.

He first prepared a briefing with the full sensor data and

visual record of the incident for his senior officers. They'd need
to strategize about how to respond to the enemy action, and he
wanted them to have all of the information he was working
with.

Next, he prepared a simplified brief for the High Council—
little more than a statement that a TSS facility had been
attacked and there was loss of life. His father, as the former
High Commander, would read between the lines and help
manage the council's reaction. He'd wait to send that one until
they were back at Headquarters, so he could be available to
field the replies that would certainly come in right away. Since
the Alkeer base was so remote, it was unlikely news outlets
would get any notice of the destruction before then, buying a
little time to formulate a response.

The final message, to the TSS as a whole, was the most
difficult for him. A few years ago, he'd given an address
welcoming in a new era of peace and prosperity. These were
supposed to be the good years where they could relax and
celebrate their victories. Instead, he needed to tell them that
they were in more danger than ever. Some of their friends and
colleagues had already been killed by an enemy that didn't yet
have a face or name. He wanted to offer reassurances that
they'd prevail and that he had a plan. But he couldn't lie. Not
to them.

He crafted the statement as well as he could to underline
the seriousness of their situation without causing a panic.
There'd be questions, but the statement would buy time until
they had devised an official response strategy.

Beyond that, they'd need to notify next of kin. Saera could
help with that; she always had a softer touch when it came to
those sensitive matters.

Once the communications were ready for sending, he

stared out the viewport at the swirling light of subspace until the ship arrived at the waypoint. He sent off the messages to their respective recipients and then returned to the Command Center for the remainder of the journey.

"Messages are sent. Let's get home," he said to Curtis.

The Agent reinitiated the subspace jump at his front console. "What did you say in the communication?"

"There has been an attack, and we've tragically lost many of our own," Wil repeated from memory. "The exact nature of the enemy is unknown, but it's clear they mean us harm. Despite our losses, we are still hoping to find a resolution that will keep us from war. However, we will respond with appropriate force at such time it becomes necessary. TSS Command is working on a coordinated response. Until you receive further instruction, remain vigilant."

"Well put," Curtis said softly.

Everyone fell silent. There was nothing else to say.

— — —

None of it seemed real. Jason was still floating outside himself, watching the events unfold. He remembered leaving the Command Center and then being comforted by his father, but it felt like it was happening to another person.

What was she about to say? That we could... 'what'? He'd never know. They'd left things on good terms, but it was never meant to be 'goodbye'.

He slumped into one of the chairs around the conference table. Having the support against his back helped ground him a small measure. He was safe. His family was okay.

But she's gone, and she's never coming back.

This time, though, no new tears wet his cheeks. Crying

about her death wouldn't solve anything. She wouldn't want that.

Instead, he tried to think about their happy moments together. Even though everything still seemed unfocused, he was warmed by Tiff's presence in his thoughts. She would always be with him.

He formed his arm into a pillow and laid his head on the tabletop while he stared at the swirling blue-green light of subspace. He had no idea how much time had passed until the light transitioned into a starscape and the TSS spacedock came into view.

Jason looked up when he heard the hiss of the door opening. His eyes still itched, but a bit of the tightness in his chest had eased.

His father stepped inside and waited for the door to close. "I'll walk down with you."

Jason stood up slowly, finding his legs unsteady after being slumped for so long. "Thanks for letting me have some space."

"I know more about this kind of thing than I care to."

The knife twisted in Jason's gut. "I still can't believe it."

"Sudden loss is the worst kind. I've found it helps to think about the good times you shared."

Jason gave a weak nod. "I am, and it does. Stars, I didn't think I'd be needing to follow the advice I gave Darin just a few days ago."

"I'm sorry."

His breath caught in his throat. "I knew it in my gut, and I let her go anyway."

Wil stepped closer, his brows drawn with concern. "You can't think that way, Jason. You have absolutely no guilt to bear for being a good friend and letting her go live her own life."

"Still, if I'd asked her to delay—"

"No." Wil gripped Jason gently by his shoulders. "You did everything right, and this isn't on you. It's a terrible situation. It sucks! But please, believe me when I say there is nothing you could have done. We act based on the information we have at the present moment, and you have shown exemplary care in your thoughts and actions. I am very proud of the man and leader you have become. And I'm going to need you now, more than ever, for whatever happens next."

Jason dropped his gaze and nodded. *I need to honor her memory.*

Wil gave him a hug. "Take a couple of days off. Rest. Process. Keep perspective. Being fueled by guilt or vengeance isn't the answer."

While a nice offer, there was no way Jason was going to stay on the sidelines. *We can't afford any down time. We need to bring the fight to them.*

— — —

As he took the transport shuttle down to TSS Headquarters with his son, Wil relayed telepathic instructions to several friends to make sure the pathway to the Primus Agent wing was clear. The last thing Jason needed right now was to be bombarded with well-meaning questions from his friends.

Once Jason was safely inside his quarters, Wil walked down the hall to the suite he shared with Saera.

The moment the door closed, Saera embraced Wil and held him in silence, waiting for him to speak. He considered sharing his impressions telepathically but decided against it. Over their many years together, they'd found a balance between spoken and telepathic exchanges. Even though it was slower and less intimate, there was something about talking through things out loud that helped them work through issues and get new perspectives. This was one of those times where he needed any burst of inspiration he could get.

In time, he released her from the hug. "It's bad."

She nodded, likely having watched the video recording of the incident a dozen times by now. "That was a good message you sent out."

"You know I'm one for transparency. I'd rather our people hear we're at war directly from me than through the rumor mill."

"Has it come to war already?"

Wil shook his head. "I don't know for sure. If we can't open a dialogue, fighting might be our only option."

"Who—or *what*—are they?" Saera asked.

"Proof that there's so much more out there than we understand."

"That's not really an answer."

"I'd tell you if I knew, but I don't. All I can say for now is that their form of 'life' is beyond what we experience here in spacetime. What that means in a practical sense, in terms of their perception and abilities, isn't something we can begin to explain with the information we currently have."

"I've forwarded the readings to the research team and have them working on a more comprehensive analysis," Saera said. "From what I can tell, we have enough to maybe offer the breakthrough Engineering needs for an imaging solution."

"That is my hope."

Saera squeezed his hand. "They clearly don't *want* to be seen. But no beings are powerful enough to stop us."

"This isn't like anything we've faced," he murmured, reliving the scene of the station dissolving. Until then, the battles during the Bakzen War had been some of the worst moments in his life. For something to top those experiences underscored the dire nature of their situation.

She took a steadying breath. "It's awful to feel helpless when something we care about is destroyed."

He shook his head, realizing that she'd misinterpreted his point with the comparison. "No, 'destruction' is something we can comprehend. However terrible it is to perpetrate, it's a part of the natural order as we understand it. What I witnessed today was something being… 'un-made'."

"The data doesn't track," Saera admitted.

"I don't understand it, either, and that's what scares me. This wasn't a weapon blast or anything like that. It was as if the target," he held out his hands, fingers wide, "never existed."

"And that's what the scan data shows. But *how*?"

He shrugged, genuinely mystified. "They're controlling matter—our reality—on a scale that we can barely even perceive despite all of our advanced tech, let alone manipulate. To destroy or create at the subatomic level…"

"It's like they're tapped into… primal energy."

"Sort of. We literally don't have a term for what they can do or what they are. The very fundamental stuff that makes up the universe." He drew still. "*Aesen*."

"What does that mean?"

"Old Taran for 'origin' or 'essence'. It's the root word the Aesir drew on for their name when they split from the Priesthood, denoting themselves the seekers of truth in accordance with the organization's founding. *Aesen* is the source, the thing out of which everything else comes. It's the only term that fits."

"You're talking about these beings like they're gods."

"They may as well be. They manipulate *aesen* the way we breathe air. If that isn't a god, what is?"

CHAPTER 19

THE LOUNGE WAS abuzz with frenzied conversation when Lexi walked in after breakfast.

"Stars! Can you believe what happened to that station? Obliterated," Josh said to Shena.

She shrugged. "I don't know how much stock we can put in the scan data. Lidaer is a long way off from the station. Lots of interference from the nebula. The official news reports are still just saying there was an 'incident'."

"The station was there on the scan one minute and gone the next. Sounds pretty definitive to me," Josh insisted.

"But what caused it?" Shena asked.

Josh held up his hands. "Whatever it is, I hope it doesn't come our way."

Oren began to laugh.

"What's so funny?" Lexi asked, horrified by what little she'd heard. There was no humor in the destruction of a large facility like that.

He regained his composure. "I'm sorry, it's too perfect."

"It is!" Josh exclaimed. "Even a foking station! They'll

think it's connected."

Lexi looked around the faces, knowing she had once again been left out of a critical decision. This wasn't a good-natured inside joke. Something bad was going down. "What am I missing?"

Oren smiled. "Our plan that we've already set in motion couldn't dovetail more beautifully with this turn of events."

Lexi's heart dropped. "What are you going to do?"

"Oh, it's just a little push to speed things along."

She couldn't let that slide. Despite the risk, she dove into Oren's mind to see what he was thinking about.

The thought wasn't immediately on the surface, but it wasn't deep. There was a package. A bomb. And it was on its way to the main Duronis shipping port.

Lexi had to resist the urge to yell at Oren then and there, to condemn his actions. *A bomb will kill people. Maybe a* lot *of people!* She schooled her face as she'd conditioned herself to do. An outburst citing this information would reveal her Gifts. She couldn't afford to do that. But, she also couldn't sit on this knowledge knowing what it meant for the people on the station. She had to do something.

"I'm sick of the news," she declared. "I'll see you later."

The others didn't pay her any heed as she dismissed herself and headed toward the dorm. But rather than flop onto her bunk, she continued through the space to the back access point for the office. The door opened to an alley that didn't tend to get much traffic, so it was her best chance to slip out without drawing unwanted attention.

As soon as she was free from the building, she broke into a dead sprint. People on the street gasped with surprise as she sped by, but she didn't care that she stood out. For all they knew, she was late for her train.

She ran as quickly as she could to the port. There was only one contact who might listen to her.

No, no, no. This isn't what I signed up for!

Sure, she wanted to see change in Taran politics, and especially in the quality of life for those in the Outer Colonies, but she never intended for innocents to get hurt. Planting bombs in orbital stations wasn't part of the deal. There were workers there who had nothing to do with the controlling corporation aside from getting a paycheck to feed their families. It didn't make them complicit to the perpetuation of power structure. And it certainly didn't mean they should get hurt or die.

Even those who *were* willingly playing a part in the system didn't deserve to be bombed. That kind of violence wasn't ever the answer.

But it was a spectacle. And Lexi was coming to the dark realization that Oren and whoever he reported to wanted as much attention as they could orchestrate. Big, splashy events got media coverage, and media coverage provided a platform for spreading their message. As soon as people could see, you could make them listen. And once they listened, they could be turned into allies. Grow the movement. Fight for freedom. Then, with that freedom, seize power.

I helped make this happen. She hadn't known where it would lead. There were probably signs of this very act that she'd chosen to ignore, but she hadn't made a conscious choice to be a part of it. It had been like sitting in a pot slowly being brought to a boil. Only now that she was already burning did she realize the heat was on.

There was still a chance to prevent loss of life. To undo her part in what was about to transpire. Her lungs and legs burned from the sprint, but she couldn't delay for even a moment. If she got to the port quickly enough, she could pass on the message that—

Fok! What can I say? Admitting there was a bomb would implicate her.

With a further sinking feeling, Lexi realized that she had no way to get in touch with Niko. She just showed up at the back door at the pre-arranged time; Oren handled the details. And even if she could talk to him, she didn't know if he'd help her. Maybe he was in on it. Or...

There were too many possibilities. Debating with herself wouldn't get her anywhere. She needed to try.

She briefly considered whether it was better to go in through the front door or if she should go to the back door and hope for the best. In the end, she decided that tried and true was the safer bet.

Lexi dashed through the dank alley and began pounding on the door where she usually retrieved her pickups. *Come on, Niko! Please be here.*

An agonizing minute passed with no reply. "Niko!" she finally shouted, unsure if her voice would penetrate the thick metal door. "It's urgent, please."

Still no reply.

She was about to abandon the tactic and try barging in through the front door, instead, when there was the sound of the internal lock clanging open.

The door swung outward and Niko peeked out. He rolled his eyes when he saw her. "Shite, Lexi! We try to keep a low profile around—"

"Listen," she interrupted, "there's a package that was—"

An alarm suddenly blared, and a red light sprang to life.

Lexi's chest constricted. *No...*

Niko swore. He looked back through the door as workers

inside stopped what they were doing.

Her heart pounded in her ears. "What's that?" The words were spoken at a whisper. She already knew the answer.

"Lockdown order." He checked a readout on his handheld. "Shite! There was an explosion at the port."

I'm too late. Lexi dropped her hands to her sides and stepped back.

Niko looked her over. "Why did you say you were here?"

"Nothing. Never mind." She started to walk away.

"Lexi, wait! Do you know something?"

She fought back tears that threatened to sting her eyes. "No. I don't know anything at all."

—   —   —

Raena checked the time on her desktop, surprised to see it was still morning. She'd gone into the zone and had addressed most of her inbox to-do items already. *Hey, today might not be so bad!*

Recently, the little things had been piling up to one massive headache, but perhaps they were through the worst of it. Even so, news reports had continued to circulate in the Outer Colonies about organized rallies calling into question the validity of the High Council's rule and the worth of their corporations. While she considered the views shortsighted, people were entitled to their opinions. Her job was to turn those perceptions around.

Her most immediate concerns were SiNavTech and DGE.

She could see an argument in the case of DGE that starships could be manufactured by any number of companies. Having baseline safety standards would be important, but the construction beyond that wasn't critical to have centralized. What the general public didn't seem to realize is that DGE *was* that regulatory authority first and foremost. Yes, they had their own shipyards, but the corporation's biggest function was quality control oversight for ship manufacturing and maintenance; they were in the business of keeping people safe and preventing vendors from excessive price-gouging. The same thing went for VComm with telecommunication regulations and Makaris with food quality standards. Did anyone truly believe things would be better without them?

The case of SiNavTech's value was even clearer. Commerce and travel would be impossible without the SiNavTech navigation beacon network. Sure, a handful of people were in possession of ships with independent jump drives, but eliminating SiNavTech would mean concentrating the power in that small number of hands. It would be a disaster. Moreover, all of SiNavTech's recent initiatives had been to reduce costs for everyday citizens and put the onus of infrastructure maintenance costs on wealthy businesses and dynasties. They'd worked hard to make it as equitable as possible.

Until a week ago, she hadn't heard about anyone being dissatisfied with the system. If anything, approval ratings had been climbing over the past five years. It didn't add up.

Unless those behind this movement want *that small handful of people to have control… because they are in on it.* That was a terrifying thought. *Are they trying to take down the High Council to install their own regime that will control who has access to resources?*

Her thoughts were interrupted by a chime on her desktop. It was her father calling from TSS Headquarters.

Given the sequence of events following her father's last

unexpected call, she debated whether she might be better off leaving it unanswered. Of course, that wasn't a viable option.

"Hi," she greeted when the image of Wil materialized on the wall viewscreen. "How's it going?"

"It's been better." He looked down before returning his focus to the camera. "I'm sorry, Raena. I don't mean to only call you with bad news."

Her stomach dropped. "What happened, Dad?"

"I've sent off the official briefing to the High Council, but I thought you should hear it from me rather than secondhand."

She steeled herself for whatever was about to be said.

"There's been another attack. The TSS Alkeer Station was destroyed. One hundred percent casualties."

"Stars! What?" The energy sapped from Raena. For a few seconds, she forgot to breathe, everything too tense to think or react.

"We still have no idea what they look like or how they move. I wish I hadn't seen it with my own eyes, but there was nothing we could do. One second the station was there; the next it was gone. There's nothing left, and all crew were killed. It also pains me to report that your former Trainee friend, Tiffani Farrow, was on assignment there."

"Oh, my stars…" Time seemed to stand still as a flood of memories flashed through Raena's mind. Her first days in the TSS, with Tiff adopting her as a friend and teaching her about the Taran Empire. Training together. Late nights talking in their shared quarters about their dreams and aspirations. They'd been good friends, and Tiff had had such a promising future as an Agent that it was devastating to think of her life being cut short. But Raena's loss of an old friend was nothing compared to what her brother must be going through right now. He'd never openly talked about the relationship, but she knew. "How's Jason holding up?"

"As well as can be expected."

"You know they were… close."

Her father nodded. "Yeah, their relationship wasn't as secret as they pretended. I was always fond of her. She was good for him."

"Terrible about picking up after herself, but such a good heart… Gah!" Raena shook her head, her shoulders slumped. "I hate to think of how many good people like her were on the station."

"One-thousand-three-hundred-twenty-seven."

Raena closed her eyes and took a deep breath. The TSS hadn't suffered a loss on that scale since the end of the Bakzen War—not even in the violence surrounding the Priesthood's fall. It would be horrific enough on principle, but the personal connection made it even worse.

"I'm really trying not to freak out here." Even as she voiced the words, her chest swelled with anxiety and her pulse quickened. The tension about the issues facing the Taran Empire flooded into her mind. *It could all fall apart. We were so close to bringing everyone together, and now they're more divided than ever.*

"This is a challenge, but one we will overcome."

How can he say that so calmly? The answer was clear, though. *He needs to say that because we have no choice but to fight for our lives.*

Breaking down wouldn't save her, and it certainly wouldn't help her people. She suppressed her anxiety and returned her attention to her father. "What are you planning to do?"

"Since we have been unable to open a line of communication with the perpetrators, at this point we have no option but to declare them an enemy force and take any necessary military action to ensure the security of the Taran worlds."

"I understand." Raena barely felt herself say the words. Everything in her mind was fuzzy.

Still in the fog, it took her a moment to realize there had been a knock on the door.

"It's me," Ryan said in her mind, grounding her somewhat. *"Come in."*

Ryan took one look at her father's image on the viewscreen and nodded gravely. "I saw your report about Alkeer. My condolences."

"Thank you," Wil said. "But I'm afraid the memorial for the fallen will need to wait. There's another story that's about to hit the media streams, and I wanted to give you advanced warning, though it's not much."

"That explosion at the Duronis spaceport?" Ryan asked.

Raena's eyes widened. "What?"

"It's been a bad day." He added telepathically, *"It looks like sabotage, or possibly a terrorism demonstration related to the protests going on planetside."*

"Was anyone hurt?"

"Two dead. Half a dozen injured. It could have been a lot worse."

"Like the Alkeer Station…" Raena was glad it was said in her mind for fear of her voice cracking.

"I saw the TSS briefing come through while I was reading the report from the Duronis Stationmaster. Despite proximity, they aren't connected. What happened on Alkeer was something else entirely."

"I know. This is shaping up to be everything we feared."

Ryan moved to stand behind her desk chair. "What's the news?" he asked Wil.

"The TSS concurs with the Stationmaster's findings that the explosion was due to an incendiary device on a pressure regulator. However, a leaked draft from the Colonial Herald media outlet is saying that the 'accident' was due to poor maintenance practices at the port. Those operations were regulated by DGE following the operations manual inherited from SiNavTech when the ship manufacturing arm branched off."

Ryan paled. "Huh?"

"It's not true, right? This wasn't an accident!" Raena exclaimed. "They planted a freaking *bomb*."

"That doesn't matter," her father replied. "It's being presented as fact that this all happened due to shoddy maintenance protocols, and a good number of people are going to believe it."

"The Herald is hardly the most reputable publication. They're known to have a fair amount of slant," Ryan said.

"But they are well known throughout the Outer Colonies, and even on some of the Middle Worlds. It carries more weight than a clip in the Sensationals."

Raena's brows drew together. "The 'facts' can easily be refuted, though. They're just sowing disinformation."

"The problem is that saying it is disinformation will make people believe it's true even more fervently. History shows that time and time again. People will look for confirmation of their established beliefs and it's very hard to change minds."

"It doesn't make sense! Say something once and then it becomes the immutable truth?" A hint of worry edged Ryan's voice.

"Primacy effect, I guess," Wil said. "If the source is perceived as trustworthy, then all others afterward will be seen as the opposition."

"Except the Herald *isn't* all that trustworthy," Raena pointed out.

"Perhaps 'trustworthy *enough*' would have been better phrasing," her father amended. "The point is, they are a known quantity, so there's enough there for people to take notice."

Ryan exchanged a concerned glance with Raena. "What are we supposed to do, then?"

Wil shrugged slightly. "Say nothing. Let it play out."

Raena's mouth dropped open. "No! It's wrong. We have to release a statement or do *something*!"

Her father shook his head wearily. "But by taking that defensive stance, people will dig into their position harder that you're trying to hide the truth."

"Remaining silent will do the same."

"Except, you won't lose credibility that way. If you try to take a stand against what the masses believe to be true, you'll paint yourself as an 'outsider'. In other words, an enemy."

"Silence leaves hope for redemption," Ryan murmured.

Wil nodded. "Yes, it's the only way to play this for now. Wait for the right time to make a statement, when people will be receptive to it. Because once you're painted as 'the other side', there's no going back. The best option is to remain neutral. At least then you are still part of the conversation."

"Except for the fact that they are trying to get rid of us," Raena muttered. *Has he always been this perceptive about political positioning? I thought he hated this stuff!* Regardless of her father's dislike for politics, he did bring up a valid point.

"They have no power to actually unseat you, though. Who else would take your place, really? Play along, and eventually their case will unravel."

Raena's cheeks flushed. "It goes against everything in my

nature to play along with such a farce."

"What is true and what is right are not always the same thing. We must find a balance we can live with."

The sage words carried even more weight coming from her father, knowing what he had been through and what kind of awful decisions he'd had to make as a leader. Nonetheless, Raena was surprised to hear him so willing to concede truth in the matter. *We fought to free Tarans from the Priesthood's corrupt messaging. And now it's okay for others to make up stories?* It didn't sit right.

"Doesn't VComm have a responsibility to make sure people are getting accurate news?" she asked. "I feel like we should cut into the news broadcasts and shut down the misinformation. The *lies.*"

Her father raised an eyebrow. "And thereby wield the very power your accusers claim you have? *Any* action in your own defense will be viewed as confirmation of the claims. *Especially* if it's saying what is or is not reliable information."

Raena crossed her arms. "Well, that's a frightening thought."

"It is."

"No, not that in and of itself." She paused. "I was running with the thought. In this matter, silence is an option. The *best* option."

"Yes."

"But what if there were to be a situation where we *couldn't* afford to remain silent? If inaction would be even worse than doing nothing and taking the beating."

Wil leaned forward as he seemed to realize where she was going. "Then they would get the 'confirmation' they needed in order to get their soundbites proving we're the enemy. But if we refuse to give them that, then we would be equally lambasted for not helping when we had the power to do so."

"Yeah."

"Shite." Ryan breathed out through his teeth.

"The question is, what kind of scenario could be orchestrated that would meet that criteria?" Raena pondered.

"Any number of the civil unrest situations growing in the Outer Colonies," Ryan offered.

Raena nodded. "Peaceful protest is well and good, until it turns violent. But that's the Guard's responsibility."

"And who does the Guard report to? The High Council," Wil continued. "Create a confusing enough situation, the Guard is going to take action, and that action is going to piss off one side or the other."

Raena caught the lead. "And that will get run up the chain—"

"—until someone breaks a story that the High Council *ordered* it," Ryan finished the thought. "And the public consciousness was already primed to trust that source, and have all naysayers be the opposition."

"Leaving us…" Wil started.

"Completely screwed any way you look at it." She sighed. "So, what do we do? If the endgame leaves us on the outside and powerless, should we try to take action now?"

"I believe buying time is still better than cutting off our arms and legs right out of the gate," he replied.

"I agree, but…" Her face contorted, at a loss for words. She could see everything playing out, just the way the case had been presented. The specifics were vague, but the logic tree was all there in plain sight. Take little, seemingly innocuous actions and layer them until a movement took on a life of its own. Whoever was behind it was brilliant. A plan beautiful in its simplicity.

She took a steadying breath. "I won't give up. We haven't lost yet. Far from it."

"Nor will I. Having an inkling of the end game that's in store for us will go a long way toward heading off the moves."

"And, to that end, I'm left with a big question of 'why'? What's the goal to all of this?" Ryan asked.

"A very good question," Raena mused. " 'To remove the High Council' doesn't tell the whole story. It's always about money and power, right?"

Her father nodded. "Usually. Either those who have it are trying to keep it at any cost, or those who don't are trying to claim what they deem to be rightfully theirs."

Raena got down to business. "Okay, so prime suspects. Anyone *currently* on the High Council who doesn't like to play nice with others?"

Ryan let out a dry chuckle. "Several."

"Okay, so who has the most to gain?" she asked.

"Doing an exhaustive exploration of each High Dynasty and their network of contacts would take years," her father cut in. "As would exploring the Lower Dynasties who might be looking to elevate their social standing. And then there are those who don't believe in our governance structure at all and wish to upend it to let anarchy reign and take advantage of the power vacuum to rebuild society to their maximum benefit."

Raena frowned. "You're jumping ahead."

"Yes, but only because it's a pointless thought exercise. Trying to narrow it down by who has something to gain would yield infinite motivations and possibilities."

"I'm just trying to do something productive," she retorted. "I can't sit back and watch the Empire crumble around me."

Her father smiled. "I wasn't suggesting that. Simply taking a different approach."

"Please, enlighten me."

"Rather than asking who has the most to gain, ask, 'Who has the most to lose?' "

CHAPTER 20

THE SENSATION OF his heart being crushed in a vise had given way to a hollow ache that made Jason wonder if he would ever be whole again.

He'd managed to avoid interacting with anyone on his way back to his quarters the afternoon before. With the TSS-wide announcement made about the attack, the other Primus Elites from his cohort would no doubt want to have a memorial for Tiff. He had several unread messages in his inbox from some of them—probably questions or condolences—but he'd tried his best to stay offline and instead focus on coming to terms with his new reality.

Hypothetical thoughts kept creeping in about how he could have asked her to stay at Headquarters, so she never would have been on Alkeer. The guilt gnawed at him. Everything he could have done differently. *Except, anything else wouldn't have been right. I can't wallow in regret.*

Sitting around in his quarters wouldn't do any good. He needed to push through.

He was scheduled for work with his flight students again,

but the classroom side of their training rather than direct flight practice. Though the academic study wasn't as fun as being in the simulators or out in a real fighter, he enjoyed spending time with the students and seeing their enthusiasm about learning new things. Most of the course involved going over combat tactics and maneuvers for novel situations, so they got to watch footage of pilots pulling off amazing feats. On the whole, there were far worse ways to spend a few hours.

Since he didn't feel much like lecturing, Jason decided it would be a good day to play a pre-recorded analysis of three key engagements from the Bakzen War and then have a group discussion.

His hopes for a quiet, distracting class session evaporated as soon as the students entered the room, talking in low voices to each other and glancing at Jason.

They want to know the inside story about what happened. He'd noticed similar interactions when he'd gone to grab breakfast from the mess hall. The announcement from the High Commander about an attack and prospect of a new, large-scale conflict had put everyone on edge. He was a senior Agent—and a well-connected one, as they were always quick to point out—so naturally they'd be looking to him for more information.

He braced himself for the inevitable barrage of questions. *I really should have taken the day off like Dad suggested.*

Bret was the first to speak up. "Sir, are we at war?"

"A state of war would need to be declared by the High Council," Jason replied. "Until such a time as that happens, the TSS is officially in a state of high alert."

Samantha took her seat. "The whole thing is awful."

"Some kind of new conflict was inevitable in our lifetimes," Wes said.

"No, I mean what happened to the station," she clarified. "I heard there wasn't time to do anything." Her look to Jason said it all—wanting him to share what he'd seen firsthand.

"Yes, it happened very quickly," he said, not knowing how to say any more without breaking down.

With the knowledge of hindsight, they could have taken action sooner. They had almost six hours from the time the spatial distortion waves appeared to when the base was destroyed. Evacuating the station wasn't logical based on the information available at the time, which was why the order hadn't been given. Now, though, knowing what they did, it was difficult to not think about everything that could have been handled differently.

Before the students could dig in deeper and threaten his tenuous composure, he decided to pivot the conversation into the lesson. "In battle, a lot happens quickly. As much as we try to look ahead at the possible paths stemming from each action, we are often forced to make decisions based on the information available in the moment. Sometimes, we will learn later that there was a better course, but we must remind ourselves that we're not omniscient. As long as we make the best choice available to us at each juncture based on what we know, we can accept the outcome. Though you won't always like it, it's justified. We can't dwell on what we can't change. However, we can be informed by history and set ourselves up for the best chance of long-term success by learning from the outcomes of others' decisions."

Jason queued up the first video. "Let's take this engagement, for example."

He played the video and then led the students through discussion of the tactics at the individual and squad levels. He was happy to see the students picking up on the subtleties and where he was going with the explanation of making informed choices.

They then went through another example. For a time, at least, the discussion offered the kind of distraction he had been hoping for. Now, he only wished he could believe his own statements about not dwelling on the path not taken.

It wasn't like he could snap his fingers and have everything be okay. He'd lost his best friend and longtime lover. He could still hardly acknowledge that fact, let alone have had time to work his way to acceptance. Worse, he'd seen it happen—had actually been linked with her mind. And there hadn't been any pain on her end… she was just *gone*. Somehow, that made it worse. Like she'd never existed. But she had, and he'd loved her.

Emotion unexpectedly swelled in his chest again, closing his throat and stinging his eyes. He wasn't sure what they had even been talking about. Close-quarters engagements, maybe? He took a deep breath and tried to re-focus on what the students were saying, willing himself to hold it together. Breaking down in front of his dad was one thing, but not here with a group of Initiates who looked up to him as a mentor. He was stronger than that.

"So, I guess the neural link is sort of how you cheat at omniscience," Alisha said.

Wes smiled. "Yeah, it kinda is, huh? Getting a feed from what the other pilots in the squad are seeing, so you can take action *together*, not simply based on what makes the most sense from your vantage alone."

Jason swallowed the lump in his throat. "Yes, exactly."

Shite. There had been a little crack there—enough that the most perceptive students in the group caught it.

"Let's go over one more," he quickly added, trying to sound

more confident.

The conversation was less lively than those about the previous examples, but at least the content was valuable. When the discussion started to wind down, Jason dismissed the class.

Not surprisingly, Alisha hung back.

I can't deal with her right now. Jason took a steadying breath, willing himself to hold it together long enough to get back to his quarters.

"Sir, are you okay?"

No! he shouted in his mind. "We have jobs to do," he said instead. "How we feel doesn't matter."

"Except it does, sir. You told us yourself that our emotions color our perception, even when we don't want them to. But a good officer knows how to acknowledge that and compensate."

Fok, I did say that, didn't I? He evaluated the statement and decided that it was still good advice, as much as he hated it right now. "It's been a difficult few days. One of my best friends was on Alkeer."

"Shite!" Alisha's eyes went wide. "I'm so sorry. Why didn't you say anything?"

"Because talking about it won't bring her back," he snapped.

Alisha took half a step back. "At the risk of sounding patronizing, sir, you also told us that keeping things bottled up isn't productive in the long-term."

"Thank you, Alisha, I'll take it under advisement." Jason walked away before he said something he'd regret.

In any other military-type organization, she'd have never been able to speak to a superior officer like that. But, as much as it pained him to admit, she was being as TSS as they came. The TSS drilled into their trainees how important it was to have each other's backs as *people*, beyond their responsibilities dictated by the chain of command. Alisha was observant and not afraid to speak up when she sensed something was amiss. She'd make a good officer one day.

Regardless of her well-meaning intentions, talking about Tiff with a student acquaintance wasn't any way to go about healing. He'd need to dig a lot deeper to come to terms.

Being alone wasn't going to help, though. Not with everything going on. He needed to recover quickly; he didn't have the luxury of mourning on his own time frame.

He had people he could turn to. Tiff may have been his best friend, but she wasn't his *only* friend.

Jason pulled out his handheld and typed out a message to Gil: >>Game night tonight? I feel like killing some bad guys.<<

— — —

There was too much work to do, but Wil had to step away and call it an early night. He couldn't dismiss the magnitude of the events on his psyche, and he knew he needed to take the proper time to process the loss.

The people on Alkeėr had been under his command. He had been in a position to order an evacuation that may have saved their lives. It didn't matter that they hadn't known the danger at the time; he still bore responsibility for their deaths, as much as anyone but the perpetrator. If anyone was to be blamed, it would be him.

No one would—at least not within the TSS. There was no reason for him to have given any other orders.

Saera sat with him on the couch in their quarters, offering what comfort she could. She understood better than most the parallels to what Wil had been through in the war and how those decisions had eaten him alive. This wasn't as bad, but the similarity dredged up the past to make it worse.

"I keep wondering if I should have taken action sooner. Tried to talk to them," he murmured.

Saera squeezed his hand. "I've watched the replay over a dozen times, Wil, and I wouldn't have done a thing differently. There was nothing to talk *to*."

"Still." He hung his head.

"Hey." She rubbed his back. "Engaging sooner may have gotten the *Conquest* destroyed, too. I suspect they were going to take out the station regardless of what else happened. Dwelling on what 'could have been' doesn't alter the present."

"I know. It doesn't change the feeling like we've been here before."

"And, as we learned from that, sometimes inaction is the best strategy to win the bigger war."

"It hurts all the same."

She nodded and hugged him, bringing his head to her chest. "It does. But those feelings are what assure me we can trust ourselves as leaders. Though we may push back our emotions in the heat of battle, we feel every choice afterward. It's how I know, in the moments that count, we'll make decisions we can live with."

Wil took a deep, steadying breath. "Some decisions let me rest easier than others, despite best intentions."

"No matter what, we can lean on each other. Just like before."

"I couldn't do it with anyone else." In these moments of doubt, uniting as a team was what kept Wil going. He never would have made it through the Bakzen War without Saera and his friends, and he needed to remember he wasn't alone now, either.

Like in the war, they were at a disadvantage in firepower.

Tactics and intellect were what had gotten them to a place where they could make the final push. He needed to start thinking like a strategist again.

Dwelling on losses won't save anyone else. With renewed determination, Wil sat up and started planning next steps.

"We need to try to think like the enemy." And they were the 'Enemy' now, not just vague 'beings' or 'entities'. They'd attacked and killed his people. The fight was on.

"The obvious question is, why do they have an issue with the Gate tech?" Saera pondered.

"Maybe what seems innocuous here wreaks havoc in the higher dimensions somehow. I mean, it makes a tunnel outside of spacetime, so there's no telling what that might do to beings that exist in those higher dimensions."

"Fair point. But how can we begin to understand the impact?" She settled in, recognizing Wil's shift to brainstorming mode. Over the years, she'd helped him work through a multitude of issues, patiently listening to him ramble and offering counterpoints while he talked out problems.

"It'll all be speculation, since we're bound by the limitations of our native reality. Even when we enter a subspace state, we're just temporarily punching out of spacetime into an encompassing super-manifold. We always maintain a tether to spacetime via fixed reference points, such as nav beacons. That connection will always be our frame of reference."

"Right. Buoys along a flowing river, as you so adorably explained it when we first met." She smiled at him while sharing a reflection of the memory in his mind.

He smiled back. "Exactly. But we have to try thinking about what existence would be like if a being *didn't* have a tether—if it wasn't restricted by the constraints of spacetime. To them, spacetime would only be a representation, in the way we might regard a two-dimensional drawing."

"We can't escape the immutable laws of our native dimension."

"No, but we can bend the rules a little—such as using subspace to bypass constants like the speed of light."

Saera pursed her lips. "On that note, I always thought 'hyperspace' would have been a more accurate term."

"Oh, don't get me started!" Wil groaned. "That naming mess has been around for too long to change now. But my point is that for everything we take for granted in spacetime, there's a representation of it in the lower dimensions, so the same would go for anything on the higher dimensions looking down on us. Consequently, under the right conditions, we can catch a three-dimensional glimpse of what happens on higher dimensions, such as that image taken when the *Andvari* was attacked. But it's only a shadow, or a reflection. On the flip side, the higher-dimensional beings trying to perceive our spacetime reality can only glimpse an equally poor representation—like seeing a photograph versus walking around a room."

Saera's brows knitted. "That doesn't bode well for building a relationship with these beings. We'll never really know their true form."

"And they'll never understand us. Our perceptions are too different."

"Regardless, we have to try," she said. "Our respective dimensions are intertwined, so we must find a way to coexist or they could simply stomp us out. The way we would crush unwanted ants."

"Worse. More like erasing a stick-figure drawing. Or burning the piece of paper." Wil waved his hand. "We don't think about the interaction of individual molecules in the matter around us. Why would our lives be any more meaningful to a being of their power?"

"It's wild to think about."

"It is," Wil agreed. "And it's made me realize how much I've taken for granted. Our abilities, for example."

She cocked her head. "How so?"

"Well, we generally teach that telekinesis, telepathy, and the general skillset we call our Gifts are basically electromagnetic sensitivity. That's a greatly oversimplified explanation, but the essence is that certain people have the innate ability to sense and manipulate energy fields at the foundational level.

"Now, I don't know if it's the same *aesen* energy that these aliens wield, but we Agents and others like us must have some form of connection to a higher dimension than spacetime. It's the only explanation for us being able to do what we do. The enormous amounts of energy we wield has to come from *somewhere.* I've thought about it a lot, especially after seeing the tear left in the Rift after the war. It makes perfect sense why we always felt more powerful in the Rift rather than normal spacetime—it was blurred with a higher dimension, closer to that energy source we draw on."

"All right, I can see that." Her brows drew together. "But if our Gifts are a manifestation of this higher-dimensional connection, then why are some people's abilities more powerful than others?"

"No clue." He shrugged. "There's a genetic predisposition, obviously, but how does that biology interact with a connection to a higher dimension? Could be that some genetic structures are simply more conducive to tapping into that extended aspect of our being."

"As natural as our abilities feel to us, most people would

perceive them as magic."

"Just more rule-bending by reaching outside spacetime," Wil admitted. "The funny thing is, I think we feel the higher-dimensional connection in other common ways—like what we'd call 'gut feelings' or 'intuition'. That very well may be us sensing that there's been a shift in the universal energy pattern. Though the full range of Gifted abilities aren't widespread anymore, Tarans and their subspecies may have always maintained that aspect of their higher-dimensional connection."

Saera wrapped her arms around her leg and rested her chin on her knee. "That makes me wonder… You've spoken about your vision in the nexus, of seeing a vast energy web stretching through the universe. Is that the *aesen*, in some kind of structured form?"

He thought for several moments. "I look at it this way: the *aesen* itself is neutral. It is the definition of potential. The very existence of the universe has a natural order to it, keeping everything in balance. That 'energy web' is a representation of the *aesen* comprising and connecting everything."

"That's a nice thought—why we feel connected to certain people, to our home. In the most tangible sense, our bond."

"Exactly. And it's what gives me hope that we'll be able to find a way to communicate with these beings. Despite being natives of spacetime, we *can* extend ourselves beyond the normal confines of this reality. Maybe we can somehow meet them in the middle."

"Like the realm of telepathy or astral projection?"

He nodded. "But my worry is that these beings have such a low opinion of us that they don't want us reaching outside spacetime, let alone touching the power of *aesen*."

"I hope they're not some sort of cosmic overseers that

intervene if us lower-dimensional troublemakers get out of line."

He shrugged. "Well, if they are, and what happened at Alkeer is their idea of police action, I reject their judgment. Just because someone has authority, it doesn't mean they will wield it in the right way. You know the adage about absolute power."

She nodded. "No matter what they are and their reason for returning to our dimension now, we need to do everything we can to survive."

"Absolutely. And the first step toward doing that is to get eyes on them." He crossed his arms. "We were trying to replicate the novel circumstances on the *Andvari*, but we maybe should have taken the parameters and seen what other ways we could get the same result using more reliable means."

Saera nodded. "With what we learned from the scan data captured at Alkeer, we now have more options."

"Yes. Let's take a step back. First, it's clear at least part of these beings' essence exists in another dimension. We also know that they hate the use of Gatekeeper tech, which draws energy from another dimension. What do you want to wager that the two are connected?"

"Odds are good enough that I'm not betting against you on it."

Wil's face lit up. "I'm pretty sure we did a full analysis of the Gate sphere that opens the portals before we handed it back to the Gatekeepers."

Saera raised an eyebrow. "Don't look so excited."

"Sorry, but we might actually be able to approach this as an engineering problem. That's not only something that I can manage, but I *enjoy*."

"It's worth exploring," she agreed.

"I don't know what else to suggest. If the Gate tech is what makes these aliens so angry, then maybe it's the solution to interacting with them." Wil sent a quick message to the Engineering team so they could get working on a fresh analysis from the new angle. *We may be able to solve this, after all.*

CHAPTER 21

A SEA OF people passed by Lexi while she observed from the edge of an alley. Her chest knotted tighter each time she overheard a member of the fervent crowd repeat one of the Alliance's catchphrases. *Would they be so eager to join the movement if they knew what the Alliance has done?*

Tensions on Duronis were escalating at an alarming rate, and Lexi was finding it increasingly difficult to keep her nerves in check. The Alliance's narrative had taken hold.

Despite her direct knowledge that the spaceport's deadly explosion was caused by a bomb, every other account she'd heard—both word of mouth and news reports—were repeating the lie that the incident was the result of poor maintenance practices. Technically, the more reputable news outlets were stating that it was 'still under investigation', but 'sources' had come forward in support of the prevailing narrative. Lexi strongly suspected that those sources were Alliance operatives, and she wouldn't be surprised if people at the news outlets had been bribed or strongarmed into running the story.

Whatever steps the Alliance had taken, it was working. People not only believed the narrative, but they had internalized it. Genuine anger against the High Dynasties was building in the public consciousness, and the gathering today was the latest evidence that talk would only take them so far. People were slowly being worked into a frenzy, and that kind of tension could only be released through action. And it wouldn't be peaceful.

Lexi had gotten Oren's permission to attend the event under the guise of 'research' for her work within the Alliance. In truth, she wanted to get a firsthand look at the people who'd been swept up in the movement. Broadcast footage could easily be edited, and she wanted an unfiltered view.

To her surprise, a broad range of people were represented. The news reports had selected footage of mostly young people to show, but in actuality, the crowd was a close mirror of the city's demographics—minus small children. She suspected that was because the older people still remembered the High Dynasties as they were while the Priesthood was in power, and the younger people were of an age where revolutionary thinking and rebelling against the status quo was the norm.

Lexi, herself, fell into the university-age bracket, but she couldn't share their perspective on these issues. There had already been a revolution, and people needed to give the new system time to shake out. The changes would most immediately be felt in the Central Worlds, then work outward. A planet like Duronis, at the outermost fringes of the civilization, would be the last to feel the effects. To decry the new system so soon after its implementation was shortsighted.

The tension in her chest turned to annoyance and then anger as she watched the mob shout venomous words about the people who'd given Lexi the freedom to be herself. *For the*

*first time in memory, we have leaders who've used their power
for the common good. What more do they want?*

As if on cue, a woman started chanting one of the
Alliance's popular lines nearby, "What do we want?
Independence. When do we want it? Now!" Several people
joined her, repeating the phrase in unison.

Lexi sighed at the banality of it all. *But what are the
benefits? Can't they see they're being manipulated?*

If she wanted any chance of making people see reason,
then she had to understand where they were coming from. She
decided to break from her hiding place in the alley to walk with
the group, hoping to covertly learn more about their rationale.

Lexi regretted her decision the moment she stepped out. A
mass of bodies closed in around her, propelling her forward.

She fought against the crowd's movement. Despite her
efforts, she found herself being directed toward the middle of
the street. Initially, she was concerned about where everyone
was headed. But this was what she'd wanted—to be part of the
experience, to understand what was alluring about the Alliance
to everyday citizens. With that in mind, she made a conscious
effort to suppress her worries and focus on her other senses.

People were talking around her. Several conversations
were ongoing, seemingly between groups of friends or possibly
family members.

The first discussion Lexi tuned into was between two
women close to her age.

"I'll believe it when I see it," a blonde was saying.

"Yeah, I know. It might just be talk. But at least someone is
finally saying what we've all been thinking," her dark-haired
friend replied.

"I guess."

"May as well hear them out, right? It's not like we had

anything better to do today."

The larger play started to come together in Lexi's mind. For as long as anyone could remember, citizens in the Outer Colonies had been distrusting of the rulers on Tararia. During the Priesthood's reign, those sentiments were reserved to quiet grumblings, fearing retribution. Now, no one feared speaking out against the new 'compassionate' nobles leading the Empire. Yet, people were used to being resentful and distrusting toward authority in general, so they had redirected longstanding frustrations toward the new figureheads. The Alliance had simply tapped into deeply engrained perceptions and offered their own solution to the problem.

This was not the time or place where Lexi would be able to unmask the Alliance's ill intentions. The best she could do at present was gather information for later use.

Lexi picked up her pace a little to come alongside the two women she'd overheard. "Hey, do you know if there's going to be a speech today?" she asked, hoping the question was vague enough to elicit more information.

"Not sure," the brunette replied. "A saw a social post about there being a rally in Evanwood Park at noon, so I figured I'd check it out."

The park was the largest greenspace within the city limits, suggesting the Alliance was hoping for a big turnout. Beyond that, the response confirmed Lexi's suspicions that the Alliance had done more than only put up posters. She'd been too paranoid to run any searches online about the Alliance's activities for fear of Oren or others questioning her reasons for the research. So, to avoid suspicion, she'd elected to avoid social media, or even browse sites, since joining the Alliance. Consequently, she'd never been sure about the extent of the Alliance's online presence.

She risked a follow-up question. "Where did you see the notice posted?"

"I think it was a forum for upcoming local events. It popped up in a few places on my Feed."

"Yeah, same. Didn't want to miss it." Lexi smiled. *So, they're advertising heavily.*

That certainly helped explain the large number of people at the gathering. But without promise of a specific speaker or other structured activity, it still seemed strange that so many people would attend. Not *everyone* could have nothing better to do.

Lexi suspected that there would be more to the event. A centerpiece. The Alliance would take every opportunity to further their objectives.

"Head toward Parkway," a man to Lexi's left said. "We should have a better view from there."

She cued in on the lead. Discussion of a 'view' implied knowledge of a specific demonstration. With a nod of thanks to the women she'd questioned, Lexi began tracking the man who'd mentioned Parkway. When he began working his way to the right, she followed.

The crowd continued slowly weaving through the city streets, passing by some spectators while other people merged with the crowd. It was unclear if everyone knew what the gathering was about, but there were enthusiastic smiles from most people, all the same—simply excited to be a part of the event.

They're so easily swept up in the emotion of it. The Alliance has figured out exactly how to get people excited, and they'll go along with anything. The realization was concerning for Lexi, not only because she had a good indication that the Alliance was dangerous, but also because she'd seen public sentiment manipulated like this before, and it never ended well.

She'd watched the Priesthood employ many of the same tactics. They'd painted themselves as an infallible authority, and people went along for the ride because they'd been conditioned to trust in their leadership institutions. The sudden removal of the Priesthood had left a void, and people no longer knew which authority to trust. The High Council was supposed to have filled that vacuum, but how could people fully rely on the leaders who'd shattered their worldview by ousting the previous rulers?

For lack of another option, they'd gone along with the High Council for a time. But now the Alliance was offering an alternative. These new figureheads spouted all the right talking points, reenforcing the lingering uncertainty about the High Council and their intentions. 'Think locally, forget about Tararia!' was a perfect message to capture the hearts of people who'd been missing direction and certainty in their lives, torn between the competing messages from the Priesthood and High Council that they should trust, but also distrust, centralized leadership. Both of those messages had originated on Tararia. But *local* leadership—that was something new.

Were it not for her direct knowledge of the Alliance's nefarious dealings, she could imagine herself getting swept up in the excitement of the sentiment, herself.

Abruptly, the buildings that had been penning in the crowd gave way to open space. The mass of people spilled out into a boulevard, which encircled a large park. Trees covered the outer boundaries of the greenspace, and there was an expansive grassy area within. A decorative fountain also rose up above the crowd.

Many people had already gathered in the park. As the crowd Lexi had been following through the streets began to merge with the other spectators, movement slowed and bodies began pressing closer together. The tight quarters prompted the people around Lexi to stick out their elbows to maintain their personal space, causing her to get prodded in her ribs and back.

Tension gripped Lexi's chest. Her pulse spiked as the bodies surrounded her. There were no open spaces in sight. *It's okay. You're okay,* she told herself, forcing down her anxiety.

The crowd continued to propel her forward to an unknown destination. She kept track of the man she'd been following and matched his movements as best she could. As the ground underfoot changed from pavement to grass, the man and some other people around her started to aim in the direction of the fountain.

What's over there? Lexi couldn't see a stage or anything specific to make that area special. Nonetheless, if that's where people wanted to go, then that seemed like the place to be. She carefully set a path in that direction.

The group stopped a couple dozen meters from the fountain when they ran up against too dense a crowd to pass through. Everyone was standing with their attention fixed on the fountain. Its broad basin and multi-tiered waterfall made a nice centerpiece for the park, but it hardly seemed like the best stage for a political rally. There was nowhere dry to stand, let alone the sound.

Lexi checked the time on her handheld. It was five minutes to noon.

She shifted on her feet while waiting for the rally to kick off. Strangely, she hadn't seen any Enforcers patrolling the area. This many people packed into such close quarters was asking for an incident.

More people continued arriving behind her. Even if she'd

wanted to leave now, there'd be no way to make a quick exit.

When noon arrived, the murmur of conversation in the crowd noticeably diminished. Everyone's attention was focused on the fountain.

A new sound of splashing water drew Lexi's interest, but she couldn't see the fountain well through the mass of bodies. Then, she spotted a man scaling the tiered stone form to the top of the fountain's central waterfall. He was soaked by the time he reached the top.

The man straddled the upper tier and surveyed the crowd.

Lexi was swept up in the collective curiosity of everyone in the park as they waited for him to speak. The air hummed with anticipation—eerily still and quiet for so many people.

The demonstrator held his arms wide. "Unless we claim our freedom, this will be our fate." He let his arms fall to his sides and dropped something into the top tier of the waterfall.

A wave of red cascaded down the fountain's height, flowing from one tier to the next. Lexi couldn't fully see from her vantage, but she assumed the entire basin would turn to crimson, as well.

She groaned inwardly at the cheesy demonstration. Water turning to 'blood' was about as clichéd as it got. She actually found herself feeling a little embarrassed for the Alliance; they were diabolical, no doubt, but normally they went about their evil designs with ingenuity. This was subpar.

Disappointed, she turned to go. She'd only gone three steps when shouts sounded from across the park. Lexi glanced back over her shoulder to see what was happening.

A wave of movement was passing through the crowd, beginning at the outer edges and sweeping inward. People were trying to get away without having anywhere to go. It was unclear what was causing the panic.

Then, Lexi spotted helmeted heads within the crowd. *Oh, now the Enforcers show up?*

The local peacekeeper division of the Guard had been Lexi's enemy more often than not. The authorities were too often one-sided and heavy-handed with dealing their brand of justice, and she had no interest in getting tangled with the law—especially in her present circumstances.

Lexi tried to spot her best escape path. However, no matter which way she looked, she was penned in by the crowd and the Enforcers. Her pulse spiked again, recognizing that she was trapped.

What did you think would happen by coming here? she chastised herself. But curiosity had gotten the better of her.

A team of four Enforcers had made it to within Lexi's earshot. "Please disperse," one of them was saying to a particularly agitated-looking group of women.

"We have every right to be here!" a redheaded woman shouted back, linking arms with one of her friends.

On its own, the exchange wasn't noteworthy. However, Lexi noticed that none of the Enforcers had made any effort to remove the man who'd climbed up on the fountain and dyed the water red. In fact, they seemed to be forming a subtle perimeter around the fountain to keep anyone else from climbing up.

The back of Lexi's neck tingled in warning. Something about the scenario was suspicious. *Is this all planned?*

She reevaluated the scene. The Enforcers weren't trying to empty the whole park, but they were clearing the area around the fountain. There was now an unobstructed view. A focal point.

People had their handhelds out, all pointing in that direction.

Only then did two of the Enforcers approach the fountain. They climbed the waterfall, turning their gray uniforms dark-red from the dyed water. Together, they grabbed the man and yanked him down. Each taking one of his arms, they then dragged him through the lower basin—sending up a spray of crimson water.

Lexi swore under her breath, realizing what a perfect photo op the spectacle would make. The Enforcers had no doubt been paid off to set the perfect scene for showing the unfair treatment of central Taran authorities against the innocent citizens of this border world. No doubt, the propaganda image would be captioned with a bold statement like, 'The streets will be covered in blood if their power is left unchecked.'

Her stomach twisted. *They know how to control the narrative. How can I compete with that?*

All that was clear is that she had to get away from here as quickly as possible.

She put up her hands to try to move people out of the way so she could get through. Bodies jostled around her, preventing her from moving forward.

Something hard and pointed struck her back and she stumbled forward. In an effort to avoid hitting anyone, she tucked her arms to her body. She tripped on the uneven, grassy ground and fell to her side.

Legs surrounded her in an oppressive, moving forest. Feet were coming down dangerously close to her head and limbs. She tried to lever her arms under her to get up, and she got a boot in her ribs.

Lexi's skin tingled. Instinct told her to tap into her Gifts and throw the people away from her. Such an action was well within her ability. Her body screamed at her to draw on her power in defense, as she had during the most desperate moments in her life. But her intellect told her to resist.

Telekinesis may be legal now, but it wasn't safe to use so close to the Alliance. Someone else in the crowd may very well be in the organization, and she couldn't risk word getting back.

Even so, she was being driven into the ground. She needed to do *something*.

Lexi grappled the leg of someone stepping over her and held on. He flailed in an attempt to save himself from coming down, kicking Lexi's jaw in the process. Her teeth clacked together from the impact and stinging heat spread across the left side of her face.

Ignoring the pain, she clung to the man—committed to her plan. His balance finally gave way. As he fell, the man knocked into several nearby people. The action caused them to pause, and that was the opening Lexi needed.

She quickly scrambled to her feet. Once upright, she extended a hand to the man she'd pulled down. "Sorry."

He brushed off her offered hand and stood up. "What the fok?" He swept his arms outward in challenge.

Engaging him any further wasn't bound to improve her situation, so Lexi turned to go. Unfortunately, the wall of people made it difficult to go anywhere quickly.

"Hey!" A strong hand roughly gripped her arm, holding her in place.

A glance over her shoulder confirmed it was the man. Clearly, she'd picked the wrong random person to grab.

"Sorry, I don't want any trouble," Lexi said, jerking her arm away from his hand. She spun back to face him so she could watch his movements. In an effort to defuse the situation, she held her hands up in front of her. He had enough of a size and weight advantage that Lexi didn't want it to come to a brawl.

"Everything okay here?" a male voice asked behind her.

The speaker stepped into Lexi's periphery. It was an Enforcer.

Lexi froze. *I can't have there be a record of me being here!* She kept her face turned away from him to minimize how much of her image could be captured by his body cam. "All good," she said. Her stinging face indicated that wasn't quite true, but she didn't want to invite more questions.

"She—" the man Lexi had tripped started to say. He cut off and sized her up. After a pause, he scoffed and walked away.

"Are you sure you're okay, miss?" the Enforcer asked.

Lexi dusted herself off as an excuse to bend over and keep her face concealed. "Yes, thank you. I just want to get home."

"Good idea." The man turned his attention to two young men who were shouting and competing for footing on a park bench. "Hey, get down! Now!"

Lexi didn't need any more encouragement to leave. *I never should have come here in the first place.*

As quickly as she could navigate through the sea of people, she worked her way in the direction of the Alliance building. By the time she was past the boulevard surrounding the park, the crowd had dispersed enough for her to have a clear walking path.

She took several slow breaths in and out to help release the tension in her chest. Her pulse normalized.

With the reduced adrenaline, the ache in her face intensified. She dipped off the street to examine her reflection on a window. Her left jaw was red and swollen, and there was a line of dried blood where the skin had split. She carefully opened and closed her mouth and moved her jaw side to side. Though the motions hurt, nothing felt broken or out of place. All things considered, she'd been lucky.

She next probed her left side with her fingertips through her shirt, finding a painful area toward the bottom of her ribs. Though she couldn't rule out a cracked rib, the injury was nothing her medical nanites couldn't address. They were no doubt already hard at work. A booster injection would be nice to speed up the process, but she had no interest in inviting attention by seeking out that remedy.

Instead, Lexi took the back streets to the Alliance building and entered through the rear door. She'd hoped to sneak into the bunk room without encountering anyone, but Shena was in there when Lexi arrived.

The other woman evaluated her from across the room. "You okay?"

Lexi gingerly touched her bruised jaw. "It's nothing."

"What happened?"

Even though Lexi had had Oren's permission to attend the rally, she didn't feel like explaining the whole backstory to Shena. "There was only one piece of fried leeca left. Don't worry, I got it."

The other woman raised an eyebrow. There was no way she believed the explanation, but she didn't question further.

Lexi eased onto her bunk, drawing in a slow, deep breath. Her ribs ached in protest to the movement. The temporary discomfort was worth it to have glimpsed the Alliance's propaganda in action. Understanding the narrative was the first step toward forming a counter-offensive.

Justice will be served. She just needed to survive long enough to see it through.

CHAPTER 22

WIL SAT ALONE in his office in the morning, running through the most likely scenarios for how the coming weeks and months would play out. Too many variables prevented an accurate prediction, but one thing was clear: no matter what happened, the Empire would be better off if the TSS and Guard were working together.

The rivalry between the two organizations went back as far as anyone could remember. The Guard was, without question, older—tracing back to when the Taran Empire was confined to a handful of settlements across the territory now known as the Central Worlds. The police force and military had no doubt been separate at one point, but the Guard and its Enforcers had become a joint symbol of Taran law and order.

Meanwhile, the TSS had spent much of its existence on the fringes of society. The Priesthood had formed the TSS only a few hundred years prior in order to train Gifted soldiers—a necessity upon realizing the danger the Bakzen posed. But, with such abilities outlawed among civilians, those in the TSS were equal parts awe-inspiring and pariahs. They set up the

TSS in old structures previously occupied by the members of the Priesthood who broke off and became the Aesir. It was no wonder so many people viewed the TSS and its Agents with apprehension. Wonder, fascination, respect, too—but there was also fear there, knowing the power they wielded.

Only within the past few years, following the Priesthood's fall, had such abilities been legalized for common use, as they had been before the Priesthood's meddling. However, changing the public consciousness took more time than rewriting the law. Many people grew up learning that Gifts should be hidden and ignored. It didn't matter how open a handful of Dynasties were with their abilities; many civilians would continue to denounce those with Gifts, no matter what. Only time and patience would heal the divide.

As a result, the Guard was viewed as trusted protectors while the TSS remained a strange quasi-military-but-also-academic institution. Their strengths were complementary, and each held value. Yet, it was still too soon after the broadcasted images of TSS ships facing off against the Guard during the final fight to bring down the Priesthood; people weren't ready to fully move past their differences.

But if we don't, this fight is already lost. Wil felt it in his core. *I have to try.*

The best way to work toward unity was by reaching out. He briefly considered running the idea by the other senior Agents but decided that there wasn't anything worth discussing. It was the most sensible action—and it was prudent to confirm that the Guard was willing to play nice before anyone else was brought into the conversation.

He'd only spoken with the Tararian Guard's leader, Admiral Jakob Mathaen, on a handful of occasions over the years. Their last exchange had been professional but curt when the TSS had been asked to lend a hand in dealing with an incursion in a remote Outer Colonies system. Hopefully, the successful outcome of the joint operation had established a measure of goodwill.

Wil called Admiral Mathaen's personal handheld, not wanting to have to explain himself to an administrative assistant.

The TSS logo swirled on the main viewscreen while Wil waited for the vidcall to connect. No doubt, the admiral was cursing under his breath while he tried to figure out why the TSS High Commander might be calling.

After nearly a minute, the image on the screen resolved into a hardened older man with squared jaw, close-cropped graying hair, and dark eyes that were pinched in intense focus. "High Commander Sietinen, what can I do for you?"

"Hello, Admiral. It's past time we have a frank conversation, one-on-one, leader-to-leader. Are you somewhere private where you can speak freely?"

The admiral inclined his head slightly. "I'm listening."

"I'm sure you've already been informed about the destruction of the Alkeer base."

"Yes. My condolences." His deep voice held genuine sympathy; a good sign there was a heart beneath the gruff exterior.

"Especially now that the unrest in the Outer Colonies has escalated, my intention is to minimize future Taran loss of life. It goes without saying that we are facing an unprecedented external threat."

"I suspected that might be why you were calling."

"It shouldn't have taken a tragedy to open this dialogue, but here we are. We need to set aside our differences and start working together."

Mathaen drew in a long breath. "The differences have been significant."

"There's no point dancing around our friendly rivalry over the years. The Guard has been the butt of many of our jokes, as I'm certain we have been of yours. But underneath that, I know there's a foundation of mutual respect. We're both committed to protecting the interests of the Taran Empire, even though we've sometimes found ourselves on opposite sides of conflicts. However, in this case, the civil disputes pale in comparison to the outside danger. Our very existence as a race might be at stake. We'll need to be a united front in order to stand a chance against what, by my estimation, will be a full-on invasion."

The admiral didn't reply at first. He rubbed his chin, studying Wil on his screen. "Have you talked about this with anyone?"

"No. It's a non-starter if you don't have any interest in putting our petty differences aside."

"It's strange, isn't it? The two people in charge of the Empire's most preeminent armed forces and we've never had so much as a friendly chat." The admiral shook his head.

"Like a relationship with a bad relative, isn't it? Only calling when one of us needs something."

He chuckled. "We should really change that."

"That's why I wanted to reach out now. I think a lot's been left unsaid. The way everything went down with the Priesthood was… awkward."

"It was." He sighed. "And for that, I owe you and your people an apology. I was following orders, and I know you won't fault me for that. Still, I should have been more willing to listen when you began presenting evidence of the Priesthood's corruption."

"The TSS was launching a coup. You were right to resist."

"Even so, I'd felt in my gut that there was something rotten going on with them for years. Part of me regrets not taking action sooner to be on the right side of history. You made a courageous move, and the Empire is indebted to you."

"No one owes me anything," Wil said. "All I've ever wanted is to work toward a better future for my loved ones. This case is no different."

"And, to that end, I agree that we're facing a tremendous threat. Possibly the most significant of our lifetimes."

"This is far worse than the Bakzen, trust me."

"You'd know better than anyone."

"So, we're in agreement to move forward as a unified front?"

"Heartily." Mathaen nodded. "But one question: who's in charge?"

"I think we'll need to see how that plays out." Though Wil didn't want to press the issue, he had rather strong feelings that it should be him. With the transdimensional nature of their enemy, the TSS was in a far better position to assess and respond.

Based on the way the admiral was looking at him, the thoughts may as well have been spoken aloud. Still, he didn't seem ready to admit as much. "As a team, then?" he proposed.

"Agreed." Wil nodded. "Now that we're in alignment, there's some information you should know about this enemy, and it won't be easy to hear."

—

The rest of the conversation with Admiral Mathaen went surprisingly well. As it turned out, the admiral had been wanting to reach out to Wil for some time to begin building rapport. Though he had almost two decades of experience on Wil, he made no attempt to diminish Wil's authority of command. If anything, he'd been shockingly complimentary.

Unfortunately, joining forces with the Guard wouldn't be enough on its own to prepare the Taran Empire for the confrontation to come. The aliens would no doubt be back, and likely in greater numbers. Too many Taran worlds would be utterly defenseless. Maybe *none* of the worlds would stand a chance against them, but the TSS and Guard needed to at least make a show of support so their people didn't think they'd been abandoned.

The Taran Empire was at a crossroads. Wil could see it plainly before him, as much as he wished that wasn't the reality. They'd been heading toward the inflection point for centuries, though the interventions of various players had done a good job of delaying the inevitable. Now, they faced not only a potential civil war over the appropriate form of Taran leadership, but also were squaring off against an outside threat with capabilities beyond their comprehension.

Part of him wondered if the Aesir had anticipated that things would come to a head in his lifetime. When he'd first met with them decades before, they'd indicated that he was positioned to be a guiding voice for the Taran people. It was a role he was reluctant to fill, fearing his own shortcomings, but he kept finding himself in situations that necessitated he speak for the collective well-being of his people.

Now, the transdimensional aliens—whatever they were— would force him to take action at an unprecedented level. The TSS was the best equipped to deal with their unique nature, and he was the organization's leader. The responsibility fell to him.

He'd been sitting at his desk in the High Commander's

office for the last hour trying to figure out the best way to proceed. There were countless political and military factors to consider, and he was running through the possibilities to determine the best way for the pieces to work together. Slowly, a plan was forming. No doubt, it would take work to convince others it was the most sensible approach.

A knock on the door roused him from his thoughts, and Michael entered at his indication.

"Am I interrupting?" his friend asked.

"No, just thinking." Wil straightened in his seat. "In fact, there's something we should discuss."

Michael closed the door behind him and took a seat across from Wil. "I'm all ears."

"This alien threat is going to test us in new ways," Wil began. "We need to have a coordinated front to fight them."

Michael scowled. "I've been dreading this conversation."

"Why?"

"Because it's confirmation that we're facing another war."

Wil nodded. "If we're lucky, it won't come to that."

"I worry we used up all of our good fortune with the Gatekeepers. I wouldn't count on that strategy working a second time."

"Agreed, which is why preparations are in order."

Michael looked down at his hands in his lap.

"Can I count on you to follow me again?"

"Always." He looked up. "But stars, do the wars always need to have you at the center?"

Wil laughed. "Sorry."

"All right, so what's the plan? How do we protect against an enemy this powerful?"

"I'm not sure, but we certainly don't have a chance to look out for worlds that don't have any of their own defenses."

"I hate to think of a planet being un-made as easily as they dispatched the Alkeer Station."

"We can't rule out anything, but precautions are common sense."

"Planetary shields, orbital fortifications…" Michael began listing off.

"Exactly—not that we can be sure conventional shields will be effective against this enemy." He sighed. "Nonetheless, we need to do what we can. And, unfortunately, our very own TSS Headquarters is vulnerable at present. If anything happens to Earth, the base inside the moon would, obviously, be compromised."

"Yeah, good luck installing a planetary shield in secret."

"It would be impossible. There's only one viable option."

His friend gaped at him. "No, you can't be suggesting—"

"We need to bring Earth into the Taran fold."

Michael shook his head dismissively. "They're not ready."

"Will there ever be a good time?" Wil asked.

Humans had already moved beyond the confines of their planet. The year was now 2055 by Earth's calendar, which was far longer than anyone had expected the secret about the Taran Empire to last. Wil had watched Earth's technology evolve over the years, and while Taran shields could still hide the TSS' presence, the sheer number of humans now roaming space was becoming an issue, both logistically and the resource cost to maintain cover. Aside from that, he disliked secrets on principle, unless it was absolutely necessary. There was no *reason* for Earth to remain unaware.

"There's still so much conflict—" Michael started to protest.

"I know." Wil let out a long breath. "I watched it play out during the years I lived on Earth, and I've continued to watch from afar since. Those issues don't change the fact that we can't properly protect the planet until they're aware that the rest of the Empire exists. And, moreover, that we aren't the only space-faring race."

"I worry that revealing ourselves might spark a world war."

"I hate to be callous, but if it does, so be it."

"How very diplomatic of you."

"It's a matter of adaptation and survival," Wil stated.

"Rather cold to speak that way about the world that was your home for almost two decades."

"I resided there, but that soil was never my real home. I care for Earth and its people, don't get me wrong, but it's one planet among fifteen hundred. And the humans... it's interesting to see how petty people can be when they don't have proper perspective about their place in the universe."

"They've fought bloody wars over a difference in opinion about a few lines of scripture. I can't imagine how they'd react to an alien race," Michael pointed out.

"It'll go one of two ways: either they tear each other apart in short order, or seeing that they are a mere drop in the cosmic ocean will unify Earth's countries under a common banner. What greater test of humanity's will to survive than to show them there are others roaming the stars?"

Michael drummed his fingers on the chair's armrest. "All it would take is one politician getting twitchy, and the world could be lost to nuclear war."

"That's no different than everyday life. At least this way, there's a chance to push the planet toward its next stage of evolution. Give Earth's people a path ahead."

"I get the impression that there's more to this than altruism."

Wil nodded. "Aside from the benefits of freeing up the

resources currently dedicated to keeping the Empire hidden from Earth, there are other considerations. I didn't want to bother you with the details of the treaty text, but I should note that there were references to Earth."

Michael's eyes went wide. "What?"

"It's confounding, I know. There's no explanation about *why* the planet is important, but letting it get blown up because it doesn't have a simple shield installed isn't in our best interest."

"No, you're right. And we can't get a shield in place without buy-in, which means open contact." He groaned. "This is going to release a shitestorm."

"In the short-term, yes. But I maintain it's also an opportunity for the planet to come together. I'd like to believe that country borders and social divides will take on new perspective when compared to a civilization spanning the galaxy."

"In all fairness, though, there's infighting within the Taran Empire."

"True, and some conflict is inevitable in any society. The people of Earth will have a lot of work ahead of them," Wil replied. "We'll need to strategize about how best to roll out the information, but I feel it must be done. Honestly, we've probably already waited too long to begin."

"They might hate us for having sat on our hands while the world went through wars, pandemics, and natural disasters. So much of that would have been mitigated by our technology."

"Yet, it wasn't our place to intervene. We've remained at a distance because we've wanted to give them a chance to come into their own—despite the missteps." That had been a particularly difficult part of life on Earth for Wil. There were a lot of smart, compassionate individuals, but society as a whole had taken some questionable actions. But, as his friend had pointed out, Tarans weren't without their own issues, as the current unrest in the Outer Colonies exemplified.

"Not to be a pessimist, but dropping the 'there are aliens' truth-bomb isn't likely to fix those issues," Michael said.

"No, but it can show them a model for coexistence on a scale that they could have never before imagined."

"It'll be a new scale, all right! Most people probably won't believe it."

Wil leaned back in his chair. "Convincing them we're for real will definitely be an initial challenge. But as we build trust and respect, coming from such different places, I hope some of that will transfer to how humans think about each other. Too many social movements have taken on a 'you're either with us or you're against us' stance. In the end, those tend to create further divides rather than bring people together. To unite, there must be mutual respect—even when someone holds a viewpoint in fundamental opposition to yours. For everyone to be on equal footing, you need to respect your enemy's perspective and recognize that they hold their opinions with as much conviction as you hold your own."

Michael frowned. "But some perspectives are just plain *evil*. After what happened to Alkeer, how could we ever be friends?"

"It's either find a way to get along or go to war. No doubt, finding common ground with aliens will be more difficult than solving a civil dispute."

Michael drummed his fingers on the armrest. "Considering that our own disputes are rarely resolve without hurt feelings—or bloodshed—that doesn't inspire a lot of confidence, I'm afraid."

"We can't control how the aliens will react, but I'm hopeful that we can at least show humans that there is a way to come together while still protecting personal autonomy.”

“Respect differing opinions.”

“Exactly. If you ask others to accept you as you are and respect *your* viewpoints, doesn’t that mean you should extend them the same courtesy?” Wil asked.

Michael crossed his arms. “In other words, maybe the best we can do with this new enemy is ‘agree to disagree’?”

Wil nodded. “I mean, even within the Taran Empire, when you’re looking at a population in the trillions, statistically you’re going to have too many competing perspectives to get everyone on the same page in all matters. If the same species can’t come to accord, there’s no hope for being in complete alignment with aliens who aren’t even native to our dimension. The best outcome would be to accept our differences and let each other live in peace.”

“Historically, if people couldn’t reach an agreement, a planet would simply elect to leave the Empire. I guess it’s not really an option to leave this dimension, huh?”

“I wouldn’t count on it.”

Michael sat in quiet thought. After a while, he looked up. “It stands to reason, then, when enough time has passed, it’s only fair that a world who’s left the Empire should have the opportunity to return.”

“And I think Earth’s time has come.” But Wil realized his enemy might be thinking the same thing. *What if these transdimensional beings once resided here, and now they’ve come to reclaim what’s theirs?*

CHAPTER 23

THE LAST TWO days had been a waking nightmare for Raena. *The Empire is falling apart, and there's nothing I can do about it.*

She recognized that was overly pessimistic thinking, but that was part of her coping process. She needed to have a proper freak-out before she buckled down and dove into the task at hand. Unfortunately, a mysterious summons to the Sietinen estate in the Third Region on Tararia wasn't helping her process.

The High Council usually rotated its meeting locations, though for special sessions, they defaulted to whomever had called the assembly. In this case, her father had asked for the gathering on behalf of the TSS and her grandfather had volunteered to host. Normally, she wouldn't attend the meeting since she was still only a scion of Sietinen and wife to the Head of Dainetris, but spouses and scions had been asked to attend this particular event—even more irregular.

As she exited the shuttle onto the landing pad on the western side of the estate, Raena did her best to push the worries about Duronis and the Rift to the back of her mind.

"I hope there's some good news mixed in with the bad," she said to Ryan as they began walking along the path leading to the massive white stone estate atop the hill overlooking the lakeside city of Sieten below.

Ryan took her hand. "If the expanded council is being called together, then that means there's a plan of action to be discussed. We can finally move past the 'wait and see' part."

"Can't come soon enough."

They met up with her grandparents outside the largest of the conference rooms in the western administrative wing of the Sietinen estate. The circular table with an open center could comfortably seat thirty, making it ideal for council sessions and other gatherings where the hierarchy lines were blurred.

"Hey, good to see you again," Raena greeted.

Kate gave her a hug. "How are you holding up?"

"Well enough."

"The others haven't arrived yet," Cris said. "We may as well get settled." He motioned them toward the room's interior.

"What's the meeting about?" Raena asked her grandfather while they took seats on the far end of the table with the best view of the door.

"I have my suspicions, but it's best I don't engage in idle speculation."

"Come on, it's us," she urged.

"That's precisely the point. Your father called an assembly of the High Council to make a formal statement to all of us at the same time. To speak with us privately is in direct conflict to the TSS' responsibility to serve everyone equally."

Raena looked at him skeptically. "Like we haven't used backchannels before."

"If he's making a concerted effort to avoid those now, it must be grave."

That angle hadn't occurred to Raena. "Oh."

"I won't worry until I know I should. I advise you to do the same," Kate said.

Raena nodded faintly in response.

She looked out over the two halves of the table, each a curved rectangle positioned to form a circle with an open center and aisle. The emblem for Tararia was embossed on the tile floor, indicating it as a place where the world could come together in unity rather than broadcasting the branding of the Sietinen Dynasty specifically, like some other conference rooms. Ornate lighting mounted along tracks in the ceiling accentuated the circular shape and cast a warm glow in the room.

Soon, small groups began to enter through the open wooden double-doors. Raena had met each of the Dynastic Heads and their scions on various occasions over the past several years. All had been mandatory guests at her and Ryan's formal wedding, naturally. Each Dynasty had their own unique look and style, preserved through careful partnerships over the generations. The whole thing was ridiculous and archaic to Raena, but it was the kind of superficiality she expected the Priesthood to have encouraged. Changing mindsets would take time.

When the final attendees had taken their seats, the lights dimmed and a holoprojector at the center of the circle activated. A lifelike rendering of Wil stood at the center of the room, dressed in TSS formal attire. He spun around to face every person at the table, in turn.

"Thank you for coming together today. I wish I could have been there in person, but current circumstances preclude travel. I am acquainted with the Dynastic Heads, but for anyone I haven't met, I am Wil Sietinen, TSS High Commander. I am speaking with you today in that capacity."

There were nods and murmurs around the table.

"I don't need to tell you about how we have faced adversity as a united Empire," he continued. "In the five years since the Priesthood's fall, we have been stronger together than ever before. We will need all of that strength to face what's coming next.

"We are under attack from an outside threat, the likes of which we haven't seen for a hundred thousand years. Even though our ancestors reached a truce with these beings, I don't know if we'll be so lucky. Rogue actors within the Empire unwittingly broke the treaty. The terms make it clear that the penalty for doing so is our complete destruction."

Gasps of distress and opposition rang out in the room as Raena tensed in her seat. Somehow, hearing the news in that formal setting made it feel more real.

Wil waited for them to quiet down before he continued. "I recognize how outlandish that sounds, and far too dire to be true," he said, walking in a small circle as he spun to face the attendees. "However, I have seen the power of these beings firsthand. I was there when they destroyed the Alkeer Station in a matter of seconds—unmaking it at the foundational level. This level of control defies our understanding of the universe. Even so, we cannot stand by while our civilization is wiped out. We need to take a stand. And we need to do so together."

"What are you suggesting?" Kaiden Vaenetri asked. He had always been the most vocal supporter of the TSS aside from Sietinen, no doubt because he was Kate's older brother and they had maintained a close relationship over the years. Unfortunately, now over one hundred, he was showing his age and would no doubt pass the mantle to his son or granddaughter soon.

"We usually think of the Taran Empire as beginning and ending with those under the official seal, but the reality is that there are several Taran-settled worlds that operate at the outskirts of our society. These planets are particularly vulnerable. We can't have weak targets waiting to be conquered. I move to bring these worlds under the stewardship of the Empire, extending the protections we would offer any member planet."

Celine Monsari scoffed. "Those savage worlds? Why bother?"

"Some are more sophisticated than you might think," Wil replied. "Earth's population is in the billions—significantly more than many of the Empire's planets. Would you doom all those people to death?"

The woman shifted in her seat as the attention of everyone in the room turned on her. "I wouldn't wish death on anyone."

"My official military recommendation, and Admiral Mathaen is in agreement, is that we immediately commence the integration of these outlying planets. Doing so will enable the installation of planetary shields and orbital defenses. It's unclear how effective these installations will be against the enemy, but at least we'll know that we did everything within our current capabilities to protect them."

"This proposal includes Earth?" Ellen Taelis asked.

"Yes. In fact, its role as host to TSS Headquarters makes it the most critical planet of all in this proposal."

She nodded. "Please allow us time to discuss this."

"We'll be in touch soon," Cris said.

The holoprojector deactivated, and the attendees looked at each other as the lights returned to their former brightness.

Cris addressed the group. "This is a lot to take in. I'd like to state for the record that my previous role as TSS High Commander has granted no special privilege in regard to inside information about this threat."

"It goes without saying that you bring a unique perspective to this matter," Ellen said. "I think it's reasonable to assume you will have a measure of bias in this matter. However, I, for one, would like to hear your impressions."

"As would I," Kaiden seconded.

Not surprisingly, Liam Makaris and Eduard Baellas kept quiet—always ones to see how the sentiment was going to play out before they attached to the prevailing side. In an even less surprising move, Celina Monsari outright scoffed.

"How is it even a matter for consideration? Those planets are not in the Empire and are not entitled to our protection," she declared.

"This isn't a political matter. It is one of ethics," Ryan spoke up. "They are no less Taran because they do not acknowledge the rule of Tararia."

"To that end, the modern residents of Earth don't even know Tararia exists," Cris added.

Ryan nodded. "Yes, you can argue all you want about the worlds who've made a conscious choice to leave the Empire within the last several hundred years, but going back tens of thousands? Even longer? The Taran Empire was very different back then. The people of Earth, if no other world, deserve a chance to *choose* whether or not they want to return to the Empire. It is unjust to make that decision for them."

Raena's heart swelled with pride to see her husband defend her homeworld. It wasn't long ago that he would have remained a quiet observer in the High Council meetings, but he was really coming into his own.

"I agree, offering a choice is the most equitable option," Ellen said.

"Is it a real choice, though?" asked Kaiden. "It sounds like rejecting the offer of protection would make the world a target. So, when they accept, we cannot be confident that they are joining the Empire for the right reasons."

Cris sat in consideration for a few seconds. "That's a good point. As much as I'd like to see unity, we want to ensure we are taking a step forward in our relations."

"So, what do you suggest?" Ryan asked.

"I believe we need to break the planets into two classifications: those aware of the Taran Empire and those who aren't.

"For those who already know about our breadth and resources, we can simply offer a factual statement about the looming threat. If they *ask* for protection, we will grant it; otherwise, we can rest assured that we spoke of the danger and allow them the independence and freedom they desire. They will be easy targets for the enemy, yes, but we cannot force the will of the Empire on those who want nothing to do with us. They can decide their own fate, as is their right.

"In the case of Earth—for I believe it is the only known colony with next to no knowledge of Tarans, outside the highest levels of government—we must take a different approach. Speaking of a prospective galactic war would begin the relationship on a note of fear and dependence. Instead, I propose we approach the world with a message of peace and partnership and leave the external threat out of it. We can provide stewardship and protection to the world under the guise of first contact."

Raena thought through her grandfather's suggestion. *Earth would be crazy to turn down access to this kind of tech.*

We could defend them without them needing to know there was an urgent need. They could enter the choice freely.

Ellen nodded thoughtfully. "I like that."

"I could potentially agree to those terms," Kaiden concurred. "How many planets fall into the first category—being independent but aware?"

Cris brought up a holographic map of the Empire in the space between the curved tables. "Here are the fifteen-hundred-odd member worlds of the Empire." White dots appeared across the rendering of the galaxy, concentrated near Tararia, and becoming more intermittent further out. "Based on current information, these are the other known worlds." Approximately a dozen additional dots showed up in red. "The good news is that those worlds are at the boundaries of the Empire's territory at the edges furthest from the Rift."

Raena spotted the location representing Earth, in the least populated area. Seeing the concentration of inhabited worlds on the opposite side of the galactic core, she could see how the Empire could have gone unnoticed for so long.

"So, fourteen," Kaiden said, counting the red points. "Do we have the resources to offer planetary shields and other defenses if they accept our offer?"

"Emergency provisions aren't an issue," Liam Makaris stated on behalf of Makaris Corp, the overseer of food production and distribution throughout the Empire.

"We can re-task one of the DGE ship manufacturing facilities to construct orbital defense satellites, if needed," Ryan offered.

"I know there's a stockpile of shield generators, so they'd only require power," Cris said.

"Most are powered by geothermal, right?" Eduard asked. Baellas, as a textiles and home goods company, didn't have much to offer in terms of defense, but they would no doubt be pleased to have new sales markets open to them.

Cris nodded. "That's a large construction undertaking, though. A PEM array would be much quicker to set up."

Celine gave a prim nod. "Don't some of these worlds already have planetary shields in place?"

They checked over the records in a data table next to the map. Almost half of the worlds did, but eight were defenseless aside from asteroid-spotter turrets.

"I think we can swing it in short order," Cris assessed. "They've been staging materials on Phiris for a set of new colony worlds out that way, right?"

"Yes, DGE has been handling the shipments," Ryan confirmed.

Celine was looking decidedly unhappy as the attendees waited for her to confirm that MPS could provide the necessary PEMs for the project. Raena didn't understand her hesitation.

"What's going on with her?" she asked her grandfather.

His outward expression remained neutral. *"Shite, your dad might be right. Keep this to yourself—there's concern that MPS' production capacity is at its limits."*

She followed his lead and remained outwardly serene. *"How is it possible this is only coming to light* now?"

"This expansion campaign is the largest the Empire has undertaken in recent history. More ships, more shields, more cities. Their production limits might never have been tested before."

"But don't they have a stockpile?"

"I guess we'll find out." Cris returned his attention to Celine, though only a second had passed during the telepathic exchange. "When can you have the PEMs ready for delivery, Celine?"

"I'm not convinced this course of action is the right move at all," the woman replied.

Eduard waved his hand dismissively. "Those worlds knew what the danger was when they stepped away from the Empire. Their fate is their own to bear."

"My sentiments exactly." Celine inclined her head. "I would, however, be happy to provide the PEMs to support a planetary shield grid for Earth. The situation of that planet—and its strategic importance to the TSS—make it the priority."

"This is all a cover, isn't it?" Raena said to Cris. *"Celine has enough to help Earth but not the others, and she's making it about political allegiance."*

"I fear that may be the case. And if that's true, the worries about PEMs are far from over."

"To a vote, then?" Kaiden proposed. "All in favor of bringing Earth into the Taran fold?"

The hands of the seven High Dynasty representatives all raised.

"The motion carries," Kaiden stated. "We can revisit the matter of the other worlds at a future time."

"Thank you all for meeting on short notice." Cris bowed his head to the group before standing. "I will record the results of the vote and forward the decision to the TSS."

The representatives filed out of the room in short order, leaving Raena, Ryan, and her grandparents alone.

"That went pretty well," Kate assessed.

"We've come a long way with being civil to each other," Cris said. He telekinetically swung the conference doors closed. "However, we might have another problem."

He filled them in on the conversation he'd had with Wil. It was all speculation, but Raena had to admit that Celine's behavior during the meeting reinforced the other observations.

"What can we do about it?" Ryan asked when Cris had finished his account.

"They'll need to admit there's a problem before we can make an accurate assessment," Cris said with a heavy sigh.

Kate shook her head. "I always knew something was off about that Dynasty. The comparatively quick leadership turnover. How cagey they are."

"This would explain a lot," Raena agreed. "They had to have seen this coming."

"I'm afraid we'll have to table the concerns for now, but we'll keep an eye on the situation," Cris said. "This matter of Earth is going to demand a careful touch, and you're in the best position to advise, Raena."

"Me?" She realized how silly that sounded. "Yeah, I guess I am."

Since learning about the civilization spanning the galaxy, she'd dreamed about the day when the people who'd been close to her as a child on Earth would finally understand why she'd disappeared from their lives. The technology, medicine, and interstellar reach was the stuff of fantasy. She'd been looking forward to sharing the wonder and excitement with them. Now, though, the threat of an alien invasion cast a shadow on the upcoming revelation.

"Knowing your father; I'm sure he's already thinking about how to approach it. Why don't you coordinate with him and then let us know what support you need from the High Council?" Cris suggested.

"Yes, I will."

"Good luck. And stay in touch."

They exchanged goodbye hugs before Raena and Ryan headed back toward their shuttle.

"This freaking week." She couldn't help but laugh.

"It'll be okay, Raena. We'll get through this."

How can he sound so calm and collected with everything going on? She appreciated his measured presence, but stars! It would actually make her feel better to see him flustered, too. "When did you become the one to talk *me* down?"

"Oh, come now. We have a long history of alternating roles. Admittedly, though, you were always more confident during our early years together."

"The enthusiastic over-confidence of youth," she huffed. "Now, I know better."

He beamed, seeming almost satisfied.

"What's so amusing?"

Ryan chuckled softly. "I know this is part of your process and you're about to crest the curve. The freak-out followed by a renewed wave of determination. A good challenge is definitely among your Top Five favorite things."

She rolled her eyes. *He really does know me well.*

He took her hand. "We've got this."

"I know. But this whole thing is a nightmare."

"It is, no doubt," he agreed. "However, sometimes it can be good when circumstances force your hand."

"I much prefer having the opportunity to plan."

"Certainly. But hey, were it not for unusual twists of fate, we may never have met. I might still be a random Ward working as a servant to the Sietinen Dynasty."

"That's true."

"So, this business in the Outer Colonies and with these aliens could lead to great things on an even larger scale." Ryan squeezed her hand. "Adversity has a way of showing you what's really important."

— — —

"We're going to do *what*?" Even though Jason had heard the statement clearly, he couldn't believe it.

"I know, this isn't how I pictured Earth's reintroduction, either," his father said. "I wish it was all of the unincorporated colonies and not just this one, but I suppose we should be thankful for the small victories."

"I don't know if I'd call it a 'victory', exactly. This is going to be rough."

"Which is why it is so important that we're involved. All of our inside knowledge of the cultural nuances will be critical to making this integration a success."

Jason winced. "I suggest keeping expectations low. For that matter, maybe rather than 'integration', just 'maintaining peace'."

"Fair."

"This is going to be crazy, Dad."

"No crazier than when we announced that the Priesthood had been removed from power. If anything, this will be easier because we're only dealing with one planet."

"There is that."

Jason had watched the political ramifications of the Priesthood's fall play out from afar. Earth might be a smaller group of people than the Taran Empire as a whole, but that didn't make its political and socioeconomic dynamics much simpler. Sides would no doubt be chosen. People would lobby for their place in the new, expanded scope of life. Perhaps not right away, but the power struggle would happen eventually.

"How are we going to approach this?" Jason asked.

"The High Council has agreed to your sister serving as a political liaison, given her firsthand knowledge of the 'local culture', so to speak. We may as well bring her into the conversation before we go any further."

"Sure."

Wil dialed through to Raena's office.

The image of her appeared on-screen, and she folded her hands on her desktop. "Hey. Are we really going to do this thing?"

Wil smiled. "I think so."

Raena looked over at Jason. "Hi, Jace. I'm so sorry about Tiff."

Bringing it up doesn't make it any easier. He knew she meant well, but not thinking about what had happened was the easiest way to cope right now. "Yeah, thanks."

His father picked up on the shift in mood and jumped in to move things along. "So, Raena, have you given any more thought since we spoke about how to approach the disclosure?"

"Well, it needs to circumvent political boundaries somehow. We don't want political leaders to think that whoever makes first contact somehow owns the relationship above all others."

"Agreed. It needs to be an international event. An opportunity for unity," their father said. "Earth has been through a lot in the past several decades. Disease, war, civil disputes. The people on the planet seem intent on finding any excuse to rip each other apart."

"I never saw it that way—that they wanted division," Jason countered.

"I was being facetious."

"Even so. Don't take this the wrong way, Dad, but you always looked at Earth from an outsider's perspective."

"I did, no doubt about it."

"Speaking as someone who grew up there," Raena jumped in, "my opinion is that in the attempts to make sure everyone is represented, in some ways, people have lost sight of the bigger picture: the shared humanity. There's such a focus on uniqueness and differences that it has divided people more than bring them together. What's needed now is a big, outside demonstration to remind people that they're in it together on their little planet Earth."

"In other words, we need to make a big splash?" Wil asked.

"Yeah." Jason nodded. "Make an undeniable show of it being Earth against the rest of the galaxy."

Raena's face lit up. "I think I have an idea."

CHAPTER 24

WIL WAS KNOWN for a multitude of professional accomplishments, but being the person to officially invite Earth into the Taran Empire would be one of the most significant. Sure, the independent jump drive and his command of the TSS forces had had far-reaching impacts, but he was about to open up a veritable universe of possibilities to billions of people who'd been trapped on their world.

It was a big responsibility he took seriously—but that didn't mean he couldn't have fun with it. Stars knew they needed a happy moment with everything else going on.

He'd talked with his children at length about the best way to approach the disclosure. They'd walked through the official military and government response plans on record, collected by the TSS Agents who'd been doing their part over the decades to maintain distant relations with the planet's key influencers. There was nothing in the Earth armory that could threaten a TSS ship, so the biggest concern was taking an approach that wouldn't spark an immediate world war.

The best way, therefore, was to make the first contact very

public and highly watched. World leaders were far less likely to take adverse action if everyone was in a simultaneous state of shock.

What it came down to was they needed to make a spectacle of first contact. Wil had spent enough time on Earth to know how much humans loved their big-budget movies about alien encounters. Though most of those films ended with lots of explosions and the vanquishing of the would-be extraterrestrial invaders, he was optimistic that first contact with the Taran Empire would go more smoothly.

"It's a bit much, isn't it?" Saera asked with a raised eyebrow as she reviewed the manifest Wil had prepared of ships to encircle Earth.

"Do you really think the media would be satisfied with anything less?"

She took another look at the lineup of vessels. "We should probably take the *Conquest*, too."

He smiled. "That's what I thought."

No matter what they did, some people would freak out, many wouldn't believe it, and some would be excited. Wil's bigger concern, though, was the backlash about why Tarans hadn't made contact sooner; millions of lives could have been saved with the medical technology he took for granted in everyday life, let alone the specialty tech. They'd need to tackle those bigger issues in time; for now, his immediate concern was simply making the presence of the Taran Empire known to all.

"Have you finalized the landing details yet?" Saera asked.

"Yes, and I was trying to settle on phrasing to send to our government and media contacts that our field Agents have been working with."

She looked over the draft language. "Fairly casual, isn't it?"

He smiled. "Come on, Saera. This is me. There's no way this is going to be a formal affair of pomp and circumstance."

"Good point." She read it again. "I think that's a reasonable list of requests and clear instructions. Send it."

"All right, no going back now!" He delivered the written message and attached instructions: >>Greetings from the Taran Empire! Upon review of your planet's state of development, we have determined that you are now eligible to join the rest of the galactic community. Our liaisons will land at the attached coordinates at 12:00 local time to initiate formal relations. Please send impartial members of your press instead of government representatives. We are making contact with the *people* of Earth, not the planet's governments, specifically. We look forward to meeting you soon.<<

"Do you think they'll go along with it?" Saera asked.

Wil laughed. "Not a chance."

—

Sure enough, when the designated meeting time arrived, a swarm of military personnel had descended on the specified landing field in the Virginia countryside. However, along with the military was a large contingent of international press.

Wil took in the scene displayed on the viewscreen in the *Conquest*'s Command Center. "This should be interesting."

"Are you *sure* you want to go in-person?" Saera asked not for the first time.

"I'll have a dozen Agents watching for security threats and my own personal shields will be up. It'll be even safer than when we were living there."

"Okay," she agreed, though apprehension still sharpened her features.

He'd fantasized about what it would be like to reveal the truth about the Taran Empire to the people of Earth since he'd first visited the planet as a young man with Saera. At the time, the world was reeling from political unrest and recovering from a worldwide pandemic, though that hadn't directly impacted their travel. However, reviewing the news reports had revealed to him that humans were a passionate race with good intentions but prone to tribalistic thinking. They were similar to other Tarans in that way, and at least that offered a common frame of reference for how best to approach the integration.

It wasn't until he'd lived on the planet while his twins were growing up that he'd learned to appreciate the intricacies of Earth's cultures. He knew it would be impossible to approach each of the major governments in an identical manner and expect the same, welcoming result. That was why he'd made it a point to address the citizens of Earth as a whole, not any single governing entity. It was about promoting commonality. He sincerely hoped it would work.

But, to hedge his bets, he wanted to also make the most spectacular show of power they could with their already stretched resources. If he was to convince Earth that they were better off unified with the Taran Empire, then they needed to make the Empire look like the shining jewel of the galaxy. And he was prepared to put on a bomaxed good show.

All of the TSS ships they could spare were set to simultaneously jump into Earth's airspace and take up low orbit. Though the craft wouldn't be particularly visible from the ground, an array of new lights would join the night sky on the opposite side of the planet from the meeting. Government and military surveillance would see the full picture, though, and some of those images would no doubt make it onto worldwide media outlets, probably along with headlines like, 'ALIENS!' and 'They Have Arrived!' in bold letters. He couldn't help but smile thinking about it.

The door to the *Conquest*'s Command Center opened. Jason and Raena entered together, not nearly as in sync as they'd once been with each other.

"Go time?" Raena asked in English. It had been a while since Wil had spoken the language, but he was fluent from the years spent living as a local.

"All good on this end," Wil confirmed.

She rubbed her hands together and grinned. "All right."

He was glad to see her focused and excited. When he'd last visited with her on Tararia not long ago, she'd been too tense. However, the spark had returned when she'd offered to travel to Headquarters and be a part of the big show. She'd always thrived in challenges when she had control over the action, so she was in her element; the business with the Outer Colonies was different, requiring her to remain hands-off. Perhaps this project with Earth was a therapeutic displacement of those frustrations.

Jason smiled slightly. "I wish we could see their faces when we jump in."

"I'm sure there will be plenty of ground-level footage captured," Wil said.

Jason, likewise, was doing better than he had been since Alkeer. It was only natural for him to be despondent after witnessing something like that, and especially after losing someone who'd been close to him for so long. However, he seemed to have inherited Wil's ability to compartmentalize and commit to the task at hand, no matter what else was going on. It would serve him well in what was to come.

Wil checked the reports from the other ships in the fleet.

Everyone was in position and ready to jump. "Okay, let's go make contact."

The *Conquest* executed a short-range jump from behind the moon, within the shielded zone out of sight, into broad view. Simultaneously, the rest of the fleet popped in, speckling the surrounding space with flares of blue-green light from the spatial distortions. The ships took a coordinated flight pattern to drop into low Earth orbit, concentrating most of the vessels on the side of the planet presently cloaked in night, so the appearance would be visible to anyone watching with magnification.

"Any military response?" Wil asked.

Rianne kept a close eye on the scan data. "We're picking up orders to stand at the ready, but no incoming fire."

He released a relieved breath. "Good."

"Our Agents on the ground have checked in and given the go-ahead," Saera stated.

"I guess it's almost that time, then." Wil brought up some of the top network video feeds to see if anyone was talking about the appearance of spaceships yet. A handful of the live broadcasts were starting to react, expressing surprise that the 'strange message' seemed to be panning out.

"Good luck," Saera bid Wil and gave him a quick kiss.

"See you soon." Raena gave her mother a hug, and then she and Jason followed Wil down to the hangar in the belly of the ship.

They boarded a shuttle they would take to the surface along with a contingent of Agents as a security detail, not that Wil was overly concerned. Still, better to be overly cautious in such matters, especially with his children.

Wil kept a close eye on the scan as they descended through the atmosphere, looking for any potential threats. Fighter jets appeared in the vicinity, but they made no offensive action.

"Escort?" Jason asked.

"More like watchdogs, I suspect," Wil replied. He looked over at his children. "I'll go out first. If any crazy person out in the crowd tries to take a shot, I'd rather it be aimed at me."

Raena frowned. "You don't think that will happen, do you?"

"No, but I'd rather proceed with caution. I'll test the waters with a welcome interview, and then you can join in once we know it's going well."

Jason nodded. "There is the possibility this fails spectacularly."

"I hope it doesn't," Wil replied, "because TSS Headquarters will be in a bad situation if we can't establish good relations with Earth."

Raena straightened in her seat. "Then we'll charm them into submission."

The shuttle was on its final approach to the specified field. It wasn't far from where their family had lived when the twins were young, near Saera's relatives and hometown, in the Virginian suburbs a short drive from Washington, D.C.

Figures it would be one of the most stereotypical places for first contact, Wil thought with an inward chuckle. *But we chose it because it was home.* At least they weren't landing a ship on the White House lawn.

The instructions had urged the local humans to make the event an international affair. No matter where they landed, one country or another would try to take the lead, since the middle of an ocean or Antarctica certainly weren't viable options. So, they may as well go with a place they knew well.

As the shuttle approached the field, Wil caught his first sight of the crowd through the viewport. A mass of well-dressed professionals, armed security, and civilians circled the quartered off landing area. Per the instructions, no official government representatives were supposed to attend in an official capacity, though he suspected at least a handful were intermingled in the crowd. At cursory glance, the security presence was within the established guidelines—enough to keep attendees in check but not so much to make it a military affair. Again, he imagined many of the 'civilians' in the crowd weren't quite what they seemed.

"So far, it looks like they're actually following instructions. I must admit, I'm pleasantly surprised," Wil commented.

"I'm shocked anyone showed up," Raena said with a chuckle. "I mean, I read that message you sent out. It sounded like a joke."

"It probably would have been taken as such if we didn't have a *little* official presence established. Not to mention testimony from astronauts and everyone else who's been sworn to secrecy over the years. All it took was a handful of leaders saying, 'This is it!' to make the world listen." *Truly, it's amazing our deception didn't come crashing down decades ago.*

Raena smiled. "If they weren't listening yet, they certainly are now."

The shuttle landed on the grass in what was certainly a wonderous display to the locals. While nothing special by Taran standards, the craft's propulsion no doubt seemed otherworldly as the vessel touched down quietly and with minimal turbulence. Many jaws in the crowd were slack with wonder, eyes wide as they waited to see what would happen next.

"Have any visuals of the Empire been released publicly?" Jason asked.

Wil smiled. "None. I must admit, I toyed with the idea of

manufacturing some robots to look like aliens from popular culture and sending them out first."

"Dad…" Raena rolled her eyes.

"It would be hilarious and you know it."

Jason smirked. "Now I'm disappointed you didn't."

"Stars, you two! Go on, get out there." She shooed Wil toward the shuttle hatch.

"All right, I'll see you soon."

He straightened his TSS formal uniform and took a deep breath. *Here goes nothing.*

The hatch hinged upward, and a ramp extended to the ground with a soft mechanical whir. He took a few seconds to let his eyes adjust to the brighter natural light—which also served for dramatic effect—and then began descending the ramp. Not knowing how people might react, he kept a shield raised around himself; though invisible to anyone but trained Agents, he would be impervious to any attack.

A hush fell over the crowd as he walked toward the greeting party. Their unguarded thoughts were so loud that Wil couldn't help catching snippets of internal monologues expressing their confusion about how this 'alien' looked remarkably like them.

Wil stopped ten meters after the end of the ramp and the security detail of Agents flowed out from the shuttle to take up defensive positions between him and the audience. He waited for someone to emerge from the throng to meet him. The instructions had specified that Earth should agree on a single interviewer to represent the planet; though a tall order, it seemed like the best way to keep the governments out of it.

Eventually, an older man stepped forward and stopped a conversational distance away from Wil. Based on the press credentials badge the man wore around his neck, he was from one of the leading European news outlets regarded worldwide as a neutral, fact-based reporting authority.

Wil extended his right arm, palm up, in traditional Taran greeting for new acquaintances; the gesture was meant to show there was no weapon in hand and good intentions were meant, but the person was not yet a friend trusted enough for touch.

The reporter looked awkwardly at the outstretched hand, seeming to weigh whether it was intended as a handshake. He ultimately settled on mimicking the gesture. "Welcome to Earth." The words were amplified and played back over speakers positioned in towers throughout the crowd.

"Thank you," Wil replied in English. "It's a pleasure to be here."

The audience murmured in excited and surprised tones. No doubt, this wasn't the kind of alien contact anyone anticipated.

"Where have you come from?" the reporter asked with the clear intonation of a seasoned interviewer. The question, however, left a lot to be desired as an opener.

Oh, stars, this isn't a great start. Wil forced a friendly smile. "Well, that's a multi-layered question. In short, space."

The older man's gray brows drew together. "Do you have a home planet?"

"Me personally, or our race in general?"

"Um, both?"

Well, this quickly went off a cliff. There wasn't a straightforward answer to the question, but Wil did the best he could. "I actually grew up in a secret military base inside Earth's moon, so that's as close to a homeworld as I have. The seat of our civilization, however, is the planet Tararia. It's on the other side of the galaxy."

The reporter blinked rapidly. "Your English is very good,"

he managed to say at last.

"If you mean I speak English well, then yes. I did live on the planet for sixteen years while my children were young."

"Oh. So, your kind have walked among us?"

Really, they chose this *guy?* A quick gleaning of the man's mind revealed that he was used to being in a studio—and was well-respected in that capacity—but he hadn't conducted an on-the-fly field interview in two decades. It was understandable why the world would have nominated a known, trusted person to serve the role—probably one of several candidates selected via a lottery—but he was unfortunately stumbling in this novel situation.

Wil looked around the growing crowd of press and spotted a reporter he recognized from his time as an Earth resident. She wasn't the best investigative journalist he'd seen, but she had a calm confident energy even amid the current frenzy. "You." He pointed at her and beckoned her forward. "Jessica Rodriguez, right?"

The middle-aged woman looked down at the press credentials hanging around her neck as if she needed to verify her own name. "Yes, that's right."

For a moment, Wil wondered if he'd made the correct call to invite her over. "I remember watching you on the evening news," he replied to her unspoken question. "Let's see if we can have a more productive conversation."

The original interviewer made little effort to hide his disappointment and annoyance at the turn of events as Jessica took his place near Wil.

"Why don't we start over," Jessica suggested, to Wil's relief. "Who are you and who do you represent?"

Much better. He smiled. "My name is Williame Sietinen, and I'm here to reunite Earth with the Taran Empire."

— — —

"Ouch, that was an awkward start," Raena said to her brother as they watched the interview unfold from the otherwise empty passenger area of the shuttle.

In all fairness, her father had cut off the original interviewer before he'd had a chance to get his legs under him, and his abrupt answers hadn't helped the situation. However, there was no guarantee the conversation would have gotten on track after the rocky beginning, and they would only get one chance at this first impression. She had been over the talking points with her father and they knew what needed to be said in order to set the tone for what was to come.

"We share a common ancestry," Wil was explaining outside. "Tarans have sought to honor the wishes of those who settled on Earth to allow your free development. However, you have reached a level of technological sophistication that it is no longer feasible to keep our presence hidden from you." That particular line was stretching the truth, but they'd agreed that it would make humans feel more special.

"I detest the pandering," Jason said, shaking his head. "The only reason we're making contact now is because of imminent doom."

"Oh, and that would make such a great first impression?" She eyed him.

"We're starting out the relationship by hiding key information. Not great."

"Nothing about any of this is ideal."

The interviewer had taken Wil's response and expertly rolled it into the topic of opening cultural relations.

"She's pretty good," Raena commented with a smile.

"I remember Jessica," Jason said, watching the interviewer. "I'll deny it if you ever try to tell another soul, but I had a little crush on her when I was, like, twelve."

"Oh, I know. No twelve-year-old is *that* interested in suburban traffic incidents."

He smirked. "Right. Just like you were *fascinated* with the weather there for a while."

She crossed her arms. "Shut it."

"Yeah, that's what I thought." He sat back with a smug smile.

They were quiet for a while, half-listening to the interview outside.

"I've missed this. Us," Raena said.

"Me too. But life took us in different directions."

"We could have tried harder to stay in touch."

He shrugged. "You were off learning to be a princess with your Prince Charming. I was living in Dad's and Mom's shadows in the TSS, trying to prove myself in my own right. There hasn't been a lot of time for socializing."

"That's not an excuse, Jason. We could have easily exchanged more messages here and there. I made an effort. Why didn't you?"

"This is really not the time."

"Then when will it be? Isn't that the issue? We're always putting off conversations rather than saying what we can when we have the opportunity."

He glared at her. "We're making freaking first contact with Earth right now, and you're starting an argument with me about how I could have been a better brother? Are you hearing yourself?"

She pursed her lips, realizing she hadn't come across in the way she'd meant. *I don't want him to feel like he's alone. He just lost his girlfriend of nine years and he hasn't said a word about her.*

"What I mean to say is," she tried again, "I'm always only a call away if you ever need to talk."

He looked her over, evaluating the statement. "I hope you know how good you have it."

An amazing husband. Wealth. Power. I know I do. She nodded.

"I don't mean that tangible stuff," he countered, picking up on her open thoughts. "You have this natural way about you that lets you slide into any situation and, almost magically, know exactly how to act in order to get your way. I've always been envious of that."

"You're plenty adaptable."

"Not like you, though. I take things in first and then want to test the boundaries. You just *know* what those confines are and then turn the situation to your favor. At least, that's what it always seemed like to me with our friends."

"It doesn't work like that on a galactic scale for the Empire," she said wistfully. "I wish it did."

"Maybe it's that you haven't found the right way to play to your strengths," he suggested.

"I don't know. Perhaps." When he didn't offer any more, she asked, "So that's why you pulled away? Because you were envious of my adaptability?"

"What? No." He shook his head. "I saw you were on a meteoric trajectory and I didn't want to match that pace. I pulled back so you could do your thing."

"Jason, I would never think of you as 'holding me back'."

"I didn't mean it like that. Just… attachments change how we approach situations. We *always* did things together, but with our respective duties to the Empire, that couldn't continue. We both needed freedom to grow in different areas."

"It did force me to find my new 'normal' once I got to Tararia," she admitted. *And help me get even closer to Ryan.*

"Hey, and now you're an ambassador for the Taran Empire to bring Earth into the fold. I'd say it worked out pretty well."

"And we're here together, when it counts the most."

"I wouldn't have it any other way."

Outside, the conversation was progressing. Raena had been half-listening while she talked with her brother, but now she fully tuned back in to make sure everything was on track.

"What are your proposed next steps?" Jessica was asking.

"Humans and Tarans diverged a long time ago, but we have an opportunity to move forward together. We are prepared to begin offering access to our technology to aid in your planet's continued development. We hope this can be the start of a new, prosperous friendship between our people."

"And how do you propose to do that, given your instructions to leave government out of this conversation? You may represent your people, but I can't speak for mine." Jessica really was a pro; she'd no doubt be getting a nice promotion after this.

"Nor can I speak for mine in all regards," Wil said. "We are very fortunate, however, to have liaisons who understand the nuances of both cultures and can help navigate this transition."

Jason nodded toward the shuttle hatch. "Hey, I think that's our cue."

CHAPTER 25

RAENA WAS STRUCK with an unexpected wave of nerves. She smoothed her dress and quieted her thoughts. *This is going home. Nothing to worry about.*

She walked with Jason down the shuttle's ramp. Fully exposed, the crowd seemed much larger than it had from within the shuttle.

"Speak as you would to your friends," her father said in her mind.

She stopped next to him, and Jason stood on her other side.

"My children, Raena and Jason, grew up here," Wil introduced. "I lived here, but it was never my home in the way it is for someone who was raised on this soil. *They* know what it's like to find out about the Taran Empire and begin integrating into that much larger civilization."

"It seems crazy, right?" Raena began. There were a few chuckles in the audience and many nods. "I thought the whole thing was a massive prank when I found out, too." She motioned to the sleek shuttle. "Seeing ships like that helped make it real, but it's all so… big. I don't think you're ever really ready to hear about something like a galactic empire when you've lived your whole life here on Earth. It's the stuff you read about in books or see in movies. And the concept of aliens is something totally foreign. To know that there's a race that looks like you but has all of this advanced technology—and they want to share it… It's like a dream.

"But I'm here to tell you, it's true. I completely understand feeling skeptical right now. I would, too. All the same, I urge you to keep an open mind. Let us prove ourselves to you. Because, I'll be honest, there are bad things out there. Tarans—and our human cousins—are not alone in this universe, and not even in this galaxy. So, we need to work together. We have our differences, but we have far more that unites and binds us.

"Let this be the dawn of a new age for our Empire, reborn under a shared mission of advancement. We will earn your trust, just as you will earn ours. Please, give this partnership a chance. Let us close this many millennia-old divide and take a step into the future, together."

When Raena finished, hearty applause sounded in the audience.

Jessica gave a warm smile. "Well, that says it all, doesn't it?"

More clapping and cheering rose from the crowd.

"We are here to unite with the people of Earth, not any single government entity," Wil reiterated. "Of course, integration will take time. We come to you now to open the door. I'm sure you'll have many questions, and we'll do our best to answer them. Ms. Rodriguez, thank you for the thoughtful dialogue. I'd like to open it up to the rest of the press now to start getting into specifics."

She bowed her head and stepped aside.

"Great speech," Wil said in Raena's mind.

"Thanks. You got them all warmed up!"

"A team effort, for sure. Thank you for being here for this."
"I wouldn't miss it for anything."

— — —

Breathing the air of his homeworld brought Jason back to his childhood. He'd been down to the planet on several occasions since officially moving away, and each time, he felt more removed. *How could this have once felt like where I belong, but now I just have memories?*

Watching Raena and his father interact with the press confirmed the nagging feeling that the TSS was now truly his home. It was strange, given that there was no divide between his 'work' and 'home' lives. He was an Agent. The two couldn't be separated, in the same way Raena was a dynastic heiress. Some roles transcended the normal boundaries in one's life.

I may as well embrace it. When he thought about it, though, he realized that he already had. *That* was why he'd let Raena go all those years before. Instinctively, he'd recognized that they would need to give their full selves to their roles. Though there was certainly overlap in their respective duties to Tararia, both mandates were too important for there to be any reservations. Sharing their day-to-day lives would have introduced distractions. Thoughts of 'maybe politics aren't so bad', or 'perhaps staying in the TSS for another year would be helpful', which could have set each of them on different paths. In truth, each of them had needed every second of preparation to bring them to this juncture.

It was sad, putting it in those terms. His best friend for the first seventeen years of his life—his other half, in many regards—and they'd parted ways in the interest of fulfilling plans set in motion before their parents were even born. Yet, he'd do it all again. Sacrifice was a key tenet of duty.

The press circus went on for almost two hours before Wil finally cut it off. Jason got off easy, only having to answer a handful of questions aimed specifically to him, while his father and sister had fielded the rest. For all his father's talk of not being a politician, he knew how to spin narrative like the best of them. Given he'd spent most of his life with Cris and Kate, though, that wasn't a surprise. Just because a person didn't like something, that didn't mean they weren't good at it.

Jason breathed out a long breath to ease the tension in his chest as soon as they were back in the sealed shuttle. "Raena, I can't believe you do this on a regular basis."

She laughed. "Oh, normally the audience isn't so complimentary!"

"Well done, both of you," Wil said. "I don't think we could have hoped for much better than that."

"You did sort of skirt the question about what happens next," Jason pointed out. "Intentional, I'm sure."

"We don't know yet, so I didn't want to commit to anything."

The deck of the shuttle vibrated as the craft took off. Jason strapped into his seat.

"The important thing is that people seemed receptive and there was no violence," Wil continued. "The dialogue is open, and now we can nurture that relationship."

"A proper planetary shield needs to be installed ASAP," Jason said.

"That will be our top priority, for sure. Defensive tech is a pretty easy sell."

"Unless someone decides to call it a cage designed to keep humans *in*," Raena countered.

"Oh, stars, that would be a terrible spin. It could tank the deal right out of the gate." Wil shook his head. "Do you think it's likely?"

"That someone will say it or that the idea will take hold? The former, definitely. Ultimately, I don't believe it's worth worrying about."

"Okay, then we'll move forward with expedited implementation. We'll throw some low-level medical tech toward the UN to get things going and offer to install the shield. If we make the pledges public, the leaders will have to agree if they want to save face."

"They'll certainly try to get weapons out of it—but an exclusive deal only for their country and allies," Jason said.

Wil bowed his head. "Naturally, and we'll politely decline. Medical and defense are all I'm comfortable handing over to Earth right now—and the Agents that have been dedicated to keeping the Taran Empire secret can now re-task their efforts on making sure those advances make it into the hands of common citizens."

There was a bright future ahead for the planet, and that gave Jason great satisfaction. *Assuming we don't all die in an alien invasion.* He pushed the thought away.

The shuttle docked with the *Conquest*, and they flew back to the TSS space dock in short order.

"I should get back to Tararia," Raena said as they prepared to disembark.

"Already?" Jason asked.

"As soon as word about Earth hits the news streams, we're going to be inundated," she replied.

"If you can spare a couple of hours, the Primus Elites have been wanting to do a memorial for Tiff. It would be nice to have you there. We could pull something together in short order," Jason said telepathically. He'd been stalling about the

memorial, not wanting to let go. But it was time, and he didn't want to face it alone.

"Of course, Jason. I'd love to." Raena turned to their father. "But I can delay for a bit. It would be nice to see everyone while I'm here."

Wil smiled. "That would be great."

"Thank you," Jason said in her mind.

"I appreciate you inviting me. Let's go give her a proper sendoff."

—

The memorial gathering was short and simple, just how Tiff would have wanted it. Tears were shed, laughs were shared. Though Tiff had left the mortal coil, she was far from gone. She'd touched many people's lives, and she'd continue to live on with them.

Jason was slowly coming to terms with that perspective. It would take time, and he'd feel the emptiness from her loss, but he could try to live his best life on her behalf.

After the service, Jason and Raena met up with their parents to say goodbye.

"I'm sorry I can't stay longer, but please let me know what I can do to support the transition," Raena told them.

"Thank you for coming. I think your presence made all the difference with winning over the crowd today." Wil gave her a hug.

"I watched the whole broadcast. They loved you." Saera beamed.

Always stealing the spotlight. Jason knew their parents loved them equally, but Raena sure had a knack for drawing the most praise. He embraced his sister. "It was great to see you." And he added telepathically, *"Thanks for being here for me. I didn't want to say goodbye alone."*

"Please, don't be a stranger," she replied in his mind. *"We're both where we need to be now. We can support each other from afar."*

"And we will. Thank you." He gave her another tight squeeze before they parted.

"I'll walk you to your transport," Saera offered.

"Sounds good. See you around," Raena said to Jason and their father as she headed off toward the central elevator with Saera.

Wil patted Jason on the back. "How are you feeling?"

"A little better."

"Good. It's important to find peace in the ways we can. Today was a big day—ends and beginnings."

Jason looked down. "Yeah, it's one for the record books." He had conflicting emotions; joy from seeing his homeworld united with the Empire, sadness from finally saying goodbye to his friend. It was a turning point in many ways. One of those days he'd look back on decades from now and recognize as a critical juncture in his life.

He stood in quiet contemplation with his father, the two of them alone in the corridor. Eventually, their gaze met.

"We actually did it. Earth, reunited with the Empire." Wil shook his head with disbelief.

Jason smiled in spite of his heavy heart. "Congratulations. You've made history yet again."

"I'm glad you could be a part of it. When we made the call to raise you on Earth, I wasn't sure you'd ever be able to talk with people from your childhood about the truth."

"Mom's side of the family must be freaking out right now." Some of his tension released as Jason laughed, thinking about his extended family who were always so skeptical about global conspiracy theories.

"Oh, yeah. They've already started calling. Speaking of which, I should probably stay on top of that while your mom's with Raena."

"All right. I'll catch you later."

Jason headed to his quarters, hoping to get time to decompress after the turmoil of the day. However, not long after he'd settled onto the couch, his phone lit up with an incoming call. The caller ID, pulled from the contacts list on the phone he'd had on Earth as a teenager, indicated that it was Seth. They'd been friends during middle and high school, and he'd briefly dated one of Raena's best friends.

Ah, shite. Here we go.

Jason considered letting it ring and dump into the generic voicemail that existed for this very purpose, but that wouldn't accomplish anything. The point was to integrate Earth with Taran culture. He was in a rare position to be a bridge.

He answered. "Hey, Seth. Long time no talk." To his surprise, speaking his native tongue of English was strange within TSS Headquarters.

"Holy shit. You actually picked up," Seth said.

"Yeah, well, how often do you get a phone number ending in 4-3-2-1? I couldn't ever give that up."

"Right. Yeah." His friend's voice was deeper than Jason remembered, but that was to be expected now that they weren't teenagers. More striking was the uncertainty in Seth's tone. He'd always been confident, often to the point of being brash. None of that was evident now.

"I can guess why you're calling," Jason began, hoping to help the other man get comfortable.

"Um, it's…" Seth sighed and let out a little laugh. "It's

crazy, man. We thought it was a joke, and then we recognized you. So, we decided one of us should reach out. Just wanna know, is it for real?"

"Caught me by surprise, too, when I found out," Jason replied. "But yes, it's all very real."

"A couple of us were messaging back and forth, arguing about if it was really you or not. But twins with the same names and looked that similar to you—I knew it had to be."

"Yeah, a lot can change in a decade."

"You've been living with aliens this whole time? We'd wondered what happened to you."

"They're not *aliens*, exactly," Jason said. "Extraterrestrials might be a better description."

"I guess." His old friend paused. "So, the 'Taran Empire', huh?"

"I'm sure that's where terra is derived from. I'm not sure why there's a difference in spelling. Lost in translation, perhaps? But yeah, Tararia is the center of it all. Raena lives there full-time now."

"Huh."

"Hey, I know this is a lot."

"It's, uh… No one knows what to say."

"That's understandable."

"I mean, there are aliens! And they look like us. And they want to help us?"

Jason didn't bother to correct the use of 'aliens' again. "It makes sense, though, doesn't it? In a weird way."

"I don't know. It all seems pretty out there to me. But I figure it has to be real if I have a personal connection to it."

"Once the initial shock wears off, it's pretty amazing."

"I'll bet! Those ships look epic."

"Oh, they are."

Seth chuckled. "I know we haven't talked in forever, but we were friends for a long time, ya know? It's weird thinking back on things. I keep wondering if there were signs I should have noticed, or whatever."

"Hey, man, even *I* didn't know. Seriously, one day everything was normal, and then I was living in the moon. Mind-bending shite. Shit," he hastily corrected. *Figures* now *I finally get the hang of it.*

"I can't imagine."

"I had to see it to believe it, as cliché as it is. Actually, our first night here, I snuck out to go up to the surface port. It wasn't until I saw the walls of the crater and the stars that it started to sink in."

Seth laughed. "You totally need to take people on ship rides to show you're for real."

"We might have to, if seeing a shuttle land isn't enough."

"Hey, if that program ever happens, I expect a spot on the first flight."

"You bet."

"So, how've you been?" Seth asked. "Seeing anyone?"

Jason's heart was struck by another pang of sadness about Tiff. "Things are good. No one right now. But I'll say, the dating pool just opened up by a few trillion to everyone on Earth, so there's that."

"I won't complain." There was a contemplative silence. "Should we be worried?"

"How do you mean?"

"About Earth becoming part of the Empire."

"This is the best thing for Earth," Jason assured him. "Tech. Resources. Opportunities. I hope it brings the people of the planet together."

"Me too. But people are worried. It seems too good to be true."

Because it is. We're doing this as an act of desperation to protect you because we're facing an enemy we have no way to fight. Except, he couldn't say any of that. "You have nothing to worry about with the Taran Empire," he said instead. "We're the good guys in this, I promise you."

"As a friend, I'll take your word for it."

It's a start. "Thank you. Please try to spread that message to others. We're going to need all the help we can get."

CHAPTER 26

NEWS ABOUT EARTH being brought into the Taran fold had taken over screen time in the news broadcasts, pushing the civil unrest on Duronis and surrounding planets into the background. While the rest of the Alliance was annoyed, Lexi found herself drawn to the message of unity. Unfortunately, that sentiment was in direct opposition to the objectives of the Alliance.

I can't abandon Melisa. If I don't look for her, who will? Soon, though, she might be forced to abandon the search in fear for her own safety. When she'd decided to personally investigate the Alliance, she thought they were a small local organization and she'd quickly be able to locate her friend. Then she'd learned the scope of their reach was global, and now the revelation about Magdalena's leadership had made it clear the Alliance's network was actually on an interstellar scale. It was too much for her to take on alone.

Worse, now that she had been brought into the Alliance's planning, she was certain that they wouldn't let her walk away freely. As much as she didn't want to go forward, backing out wasn't an option. *I'm in deep shite.*

The tense mood around the office had persisted over the past several days, making Lexi wish she could hide out on her bunk and avoid interacting with anyone. She couldn't un-see the excitement in the eyes of her friends and colleagues when they'd seen the footage of the station's explosion. Relishing the death of others. It was downright barbaric. What kept threatening to push her over the edge, though, was that she needed to play along. She couldn't reveal herself as an outsider, so she forced herself to cheer alongside them. Each time it happened, a little bit of her died inside.

Lexi wandered into the lounge room in her continued attempt to keep up appearances. It was where she should be at that hour, having already completed her latest pickup from Niko. The other Alliance members were winding down for the day, enjoying drinks at the tables or lounging while they watched the evening news broadcast.

It only took a few seconds for Oren to spot her after she entered. He beckoned her over to one of the standing-height tables near the door.

"Lexi, just who I was hoping would walk in!" he said. "How did the pickup go today?"

"Nothing to report. Niko is behaving himself," she replied. She left out any mention of going to see him before the explosion in her failed attempt to stop the attack. To her surprise and relief, Niko had also pretended like that had never happened. Perhaps he wasn't as irredeemable as she would have thought.

Oren picked up a stack of posters printed on plasheets and handed it to her. "Here."

"What's this?" she asked.

"For our next round of recruitment efforts. Put them up

around the transit station, would you?" Though spoken as a question, it was clearly an order.

"Sure." Not wanting to seem overly curious, Lexi resisted the temptation to read the poster on the spot. "I'll get these up tonight."

"Also, expect another planning session tomorrow. Shena will get you the details." Oren walked away.

Lexi sighed inwardly. *I don't know how much longer I can keep this up.*

She'd been going through the motions for a while, but now the stakes had changed. People had died, and she'd been a part of it. It made her sick.

At least putting up the posters would get her out for a while. She grabbed the thermal stapler they used to affix the plasheets to the sides of buildings and then rushed out of the office before anyone could rope her into another task.

She waited until she was two blocks from the office before ducking into a side alley to read the poster. Her stomach turned over when she saw the text: 'Join the fight for independence! Use your skills to start a new world free from the oppressive rule of the Central Worlds.' Beneath the bold header lines was a list of specialist positions in various fields of biology, genetics, chemistry, and engineering.

Since when do we need people like this? The answer was obvious, as much as she didn't want to admit it to herself. Those people would be very useful in designing and building weapons of war.

Fok! This is even worse than I thought. She was at a loss for what to do. Defeat started to edge in on her mind. The Alliance was already too big and powerful for her to have a reasonable chance of slowing them down, let alone stopping them. Even answering the relatively straightforward question of what had happened to Melisa was looking impossible for her to answer alone.

For now, she had a job to complete before Oren got suspicious. She bundled up the posters, put up her hood and pulled the cowl neck of her shirt over her face, and then resumed her walk toward the transit station.

What was extremely clear was that she shouldn't offer any resistance if she didn't want to end up disappeared or dead. She could run, but it would be a last-ditch move, and she would need to be certain she could live with the decision to never come back here. She wasn't there quite yet.

Nevertheless, her worry continued to build while she hung up the posters along corridors in the transit station, keeping her face tilted down to avoid any potential cameras from getting a good look at her, despite her coverings. *More people mean they're going to do something even bigger.*

She didn't want to run, but she decided that she had to do *something.* The Alliance was too powerful and up to something too nefarious to leave unchecked. Yet, her options were limited.

Lexi needed help, and quickly. The obvious choice was to report the known crimes to the Guard. Though the Guard's Enforcers were responsible for civil peacekeeping, she had yet to see them take meaningful action to address the situation. She didn't trust them to follow through on whatever information she might give. Assuming she would only have one chance to send out a tip, she needed to make it count.

If not the Guard, then who? Part of her wanted to write the Taran High Council directly, but it was unlikely that would go anywhere. The TSS, on the other hand, would have a mandate to look into potential leads. *Are they any more trustworthy than the Guard?*

Ultimately, she decided they must be, simply because if they weren't, then that would mean there was no one to step in and help. She couldn't let herself believe that she was doomed.

The question then became *how* to reach out. There were plenty of reporting channels, from written correspondence to vidcalls. Some promised anonymity while others were designed for insiders to share information in exchange for witness protection. Neither option appealed to her. What she wanted was help—backup with the ability to get in deeply enough with her to get answers and then be in a position to do something about it.

Her only viable option, then, was direct contact. A personal plea. She couldn't very well go offworld to the nearest TSS field office, but she could send a video message securely enough.

With the last of the posters hung, she began working her way back toward the Alliance office. Midway on the trek, she spotted a particularly secluded side street she'd been down before. It was likely the most private place she could get access to quickly.

Lexi jogged down the alley until she found a dead-end alcove between two buildings. No one was around. *This is my chance.*

She pulled out her handheld and began recording a video.

"My name is Lexi Karis. About a year ago, a friend of mine, Melisa Zedra, went missing. I tracked her to Duronis and found out that she had joined up with a group that calls itself the Sovereign Peoples Alliance. This is the organization behind the recent attack on the spaceport.

"The news reports about it being an 'accident' are lies put out by the Alliance itself with the intent of damaging the reputation of the High Dynasties. The Alliance says that the

High Council has too much power and that we're better off without it. Too much centralized power breeds corruption. Maybe they're right, but I don't think the Alliance's methods to get out that message are in the best interest of the Taran people.

"I didn't know what the Alliance had planned when I joined up; I only wanted to find my friend. This violence is awful, and I want it to stop. I'd try to leave, but I worry about what might happen if no one is watching from the inside.

"I don't know if you can do anything to help, but I needed to say something to someone who might be able to make a difference. The Alliance is one part of something bigger. I don't know *how* far it goes. All I can say is that I doubt Melisa is the only person to have gone missing.

"My branch of the Alliance is based in the neo-industrial district of Duron City, intersection of Meridian and Fairmont. They've started putting up ads for new recruits—all kinds of specialists, like molecular biologists and geneticists. I don't know what they're planning, but it can't be good. Please, if there's anything you can do, send help."

Lexi replayed the message to confirm that she'd touched on the relevant points. It was all there. Her handheld may as well be a nuclear bomb.

Before she could lose her nerve, she sent the message directly to the contact for the nearest TSS field office and then scrubbed the evidence from her handheld. All she could do now was wait. *Stars, I hope this is the right move.*

— — —

The happy buzz from the successful contact with Earth hadn't lasted as long as Raena had hoped it would. Though relations with that one planet were trending in a positive direction, conditions in the colony worlds near the Rift were quite the opposite.

"Our silent approach doesn't seem to be getting us anywhere," she commented to Ryan as they sat down to their joint evening strategy session. It had become their daily ritual to debrief after their respective workdays and see how they could help each other with their overlapping governance responsibilities.

He shook his head and ran a hand over his dark hair. "It's playing out just like your dad said it would. Saying DGE should be held responsible for negligence. It's unbelievable people will swallow a story like that without any evidence."

"I'm sorry you're in this position. That *we're* in it."

"I want to make a statement so badly. What kind of leader stays silent after people have died?"

Raena nodded. "You're right. I get what my dad was saying about how it could be spun, but maybe there's *something* we can say to walk the fine line. I can't stand seeing the Empire like this."

She brought up the latest compilation of footage from the Outer Colonies. Her throat tightened as she took in the images of the riots spreading through the fringe worlds. *We've been at peace. Why is this happening now?*

It's not like the years since the Priesthood's fall had been wholly without discontent. Despite high satisfaction polls, there were always those who complained—an annoying regulation, a burdensome tax, an antiquated law. But no matter what might change, people would find something new to latch onto that needed fixing. Perhaps it was simply in the nature of people to find dissatisfaction. It could be an evolutionarily selected feature to make a person always strive for advancement. Get too content and complacent, and nothing gets done.

She didn't have another explanation for what was happening, because everything—at least, on the surface—seemed to be going well.

"I don't get it," she muttered, shaking her head.

The statement was rhetorical, but Ryan responded, "It didn't come from nowhere. The messaging is too uniform. Someone is driving this behind the scenes."

"But why?" she asked. "This is the most prosperous the Empire has been in centuries. Why plunge it into chaos?"

"The usual reasons. Power. Pursuit of wealth. It's not like these are respectable business people. When things are good for the rule-followers, criminals don't have as many opportunities. Apparently, someone decided to do something about it."

"You think a bunch of thugs are behind this?" Raena waved her hand at the videos of the expertly orchestrated protests.

"Not all criminals are 'thugs', as you put it," he said. "Select criminal organizations are probably managed better than some dynastic corporations."

"That's an unnerving thought."

"But it's a reality that we need to be prepared to face."

She massaged her temples with her fingertips. "We had enough to worry about with the Rift without adding this mess, too."

"I'm certain that's not a coincidence. Which is what makes me think these people must be well-connected and efficient operators. They're smart."

"It's true. If I was trying to sow discontent with the High Council, I'd make a move toward Dainetris first. It sucks for us, but you're the youngest leader by several decades and are still rebuilding the family name and business. A lot easier than trying to unseat an institution like Vaenetri."

"And those opening jabs about Sietinen set the stage, given our relationship. Dragging Sietinen through the mud by association with Dainetris is probably the only way your family would ever get bad press, aside from the ongoing baseless complaints about the ties to the TSS."

Raena sighed. She was sick of going over the same material time and again. *Can't they just believe we're genuinely trying to do right by our people?*

"I know it's frustrating, my love." Ryan reached across the table and took her hands in his. "We'll get through this."

"I know we will." She paused. "Let's prepare a statement and run it by my parents, grandparents, and the press team. We can express our condolences to the families of the people who died without taking responsibility. Say an investigation is underway."

"There's probably a way to word that to make it work."

"I have some ideas. I'll draft it up tonight and we can send it out for review—aim to release midday tomorrow."

He nodded. "Sounds good."

"All right, next issue…" She scrolled through the conversation points on her handheld. Before she could select an item, Ryan spoke up.

"Something you said a little bit ago got me thinking. You're right that Dainetris makes the most sense as a target on paper, but DGE's assets are actually very stable. There's another High Dynasty that's a less obvious choice."

Raena set down her handheld as she caught on to where he was going. "Monsari. Stars, you're right! *They're* the ones that have the most to lose."

"Is it possible they're behind this unrest, to serve as a distraction?"

"I'm willing to explore every possibility. It would make sense, in a twisted way."

Ryan leaned back in his seat and crossed his arms. "Celine Monsari was hedging during the council meeting, that's for sure."

"Even if *this* isn't what they're up to, there's *something* going on behind the scenes that doesn't bode well for the rest of us." A shiver ran down her back.

"We need to be careful, Raena. Players this powerful don't respond well to others getting in their way."

— — —

Wil's crash course in dealing with Earth's politicians revealed that they were even higher maintenance than those on Tararia. *What was I thinking agreeing to this?*

Being the first Taran to be interviewed had made him the de facto face of the integration efforts, though he'd intended for Raena to serve that role. However, with DGE in the crosshairs, she had needed to return to Tararia sooner than he'd hoped. That left him to deal with the reporters and government officials.

The latest interview, conducted in English, was for an in-depth public relations piece called 'Getting to know the Taran Empire', or some such equally hyperbolic title. So far, the questions from the interviewer had been superficial, at best. Wil was playing along for the sake of making a good impression, but he hoped they'd get to some meaningful content soon.

The well-dressed man on the other end of the video conference nodded thoughtfully as he looked over his notes. "So, were the governments of Earth aware of what's been going on?"

"The government is *always* in on it when there's something of this scale," Wil replied. *Finally, getting to the meat of it.*

"Nothing you've said made it sound like they were part of the coverup."

"Well, not actively, perhaps. But they were aware of the truth. It's no coincidence that humans set their sights on Mars more fervently than the moon, despite the significant proximity difference. The TSS had claim to the moon well before humans possessed the means to venture beyond the planet's atmosphere, and we've made a point to discourage exploration and colonization. The exploration and settlement of the moon that is permitted stays as far away from TSS Headquarters as possible, and our presence is scrubbed from the records."

"I can't begin to guess how time-consuming and challenging that must be," the interviewer said.

"Oh, extremely. And there have been several times when it seemed like it was inevitable the ruse would collapse, but it's managed to persist."

"I have to ask… Roswell?"

He smiled. "Yes, that was one of ours, though it didn't happen quite how everyone thinks. It's interesting, actually. There have been a number of leaders over the years who've vowed to make a formal disclosure of everything they learn about alien collaboration during their time in power, but not one has followed through on that promise. We—being the Taran Empire—haven't outright *forbidden* disclosure, but we always lay out the case for why public knowledge of the Empire's existence hasn't historically been in the best interest of the people of Earth."

"And why is that?"

"Because, before now, Earth wouldn't have been granted a

seat at the table. It's a simple argument, which is why it was successful for so long. What it came down to is that once people found out about the Empire and all of the technology and mobility it could offer, they'd want to be a part of it. To have it so close and be denied would be torture. The world would tear itself apart, with groups blaming each other for being the reason Earth wasn't allowed back into the fold."

The interviewer's brows drew together in thought. "Why the change of heart now to grant that role on the galactic stage?"

"It has become too time-consuming and expensive to maintain the old ways," Wil stated. It wasn't the whole truth, given the alien threat, but it was still accurate. "If global war breaks out, so be it. I'd be saddened, mind you, but I have more important battles to fight right now. Every culture needs a defining crisis. This will be Earth's greatest challenge. Can the people unite for the sake of survival, or will petty differences prove too divisive to overcome?"

"I hope it brings everyone together. I believe I speak for the planet as I share that sentiment."

"It is my sincere wish," Wil agreed. "What gives me faith is that many people have been learning to think for themselves. The more adamant official reports were that there weren't aliens made people convinced that there was a cover-up. Funny how that works. It's why, as a leader, I've always tried to be as open and transparent as possible. The more adamantly you try to get people to look one direction, the harder they'll look in the other. So, the real secrets aren't mentioned at all.

"Notice the stories of close encounters on Earth were all about little gray aliens, or reptiles in human skin-suits, or any manner of other exotic forms. But rarely were there claims of alien people who looked almost indistinguishable from humans; those stories existed, of course, but they were never the first thing that came to mind when someone said 'alien'. So, the TSS and others charged with maintaining the secret were able to remain in the shadows. The mystique of the 'men in black' was the most notoriety we ever got, but even that was so warped from the reality of the situation that people became blind to the truth."

The interviewer nodded. "The reality is so contrary to everything else. Most alien lore centers about Earth being an island, which exotic alien beings found and began studying humans like a novel species. But the knowledge that the Taran ancestors of Earth humans willingly gave up their galactic lives to be isolated on that island is a whole other matter. It flies in the face of the outward-looking mentality that is so important in modern culture."

All right, I think I like this guy. Wil considered his response. "Everything is cyclical. We've seen vacillation between expansionist and isolationist cultural tendencies throughout the Empire's existence. It so happens that Earth's present interests align with the rest of the Taran Empire's, so this is the best opportunity we've had for millennia to reunite these divergent branches of people."

"I, for one, am looking forward to seeing what our people can share with one another."

"As am I." Wil bowed his head. "To that end, we will soon be rolling out implementation of a planetary shield for Earth to protect against asteroids and other potential hazards. It is but the first of many advanced technologies we will begin sharing with you. Your world health authorities are also vetting medical nanotech we would like to make available. If approved, it's fair to say that common disease will be a thing of the past."

"Remarkable." The interviewer smiled broadly. "Can you

tell us a little more about how this technology works?"

After another fifteen minutes, the discussion finally wrapped up.

"Thank you for the enlightening conversation," the interviewer said. "I appreciate your thoughtful insights."

"Gladly. I hope your report helps set people at ease."

"It's been quite a ride over the last few days, that's for sure!" He laughed. "I think we'll get there."

"I believe so, too. Please, reach out if you have any follow-up questions."

"I will. Thank you again."

Wil ended the transmission and collapsed back in his chair. *"I don't know how many more of these I can do this week,"* Wil said telepathically to Saera; she was in her office a short way down the hall.

A few seconds later, she entered his office with a smile. "You're doing great." She closed the door behind her and walked over to his desk.

"I appreciate your cheerleading."

She sat down on the inside lip of his desk, facing him. "You're pulling off an incredible thing. I never thought my homeworld would get to be a part of this deep, ancient culture I now get to live in every day."

"It should have been you making contact, not me." He looked into her jade eyes.

She shrugged. "Nah, not my scene. You're way better at speeches. Plus, it needed to be handled by a full Taran— someone who could really represent the Empire."

"Well, you were there at my side in spirit."

"Always." Saera leaned down and gave him a kiss. "Honestly, I'm amazed by how peaceful the contact has been so far. We were all braced for the worst."

He smiled. "It gives me hope that the rest of the Empire can take a nonviolent approach, as well."

"I guess this means that we can start sending researchers down to Earth to look for hidden alien tech? Whatever our ancestors found important enough for them to keep vigil over Earth."

He nodded. "On it. I suspect it will be quite some time before we know anything definitive, but I'm excited to see what they might find."

"Me too. Where are we on the security front?"

"We should be able to begin installing the shield around Earth within the next few days. Still no sign of the enemy."

"Good news, then," she assessed.

More like the calm before the storm. He could feel the tension building—the kind of shift in cosmic energy that foretold impending danger. He squeezed his wife's hand, savoring the warmth of her touch. "We can, and should, celebrate this victory with Earth, but I don't expect the peace to last."

— — —

Calls from people in Jason's past on Earth kept coming through. Several he was certain shouldn't even have his number. Whenever he found himself feeling irritated with the intrusion of inane questions, he reminded himself that he would have reached out to an old acquaintance he saw show up on global television, too. It was human nature to want to connect, especially to draw links between oneself and anyone with perceived celebrity status. He was famous now, whether he liked it or not.

He ignored yet another call as he strolled to his father's

office for their check-in meeting. "Have you been getting random people reaching out to you, too?" he asked his father while he sat down in his usual chair.

"Oh, it's been constant. I want to be nice about it, but it's to a point where I've needed to start sending calls straight to voicemail."

"Me too. I can't blame them for being curious, but a person can only take so much!"

Wil chuckled. "I suppose we could be wrestling with worse issues."

"Speaking of which…" Jason turned solemn. "Anything new from the patrols around the Rift?"

"No, which has me more concerned than if we were seeing activity."

"Is it possible that destroying Alkeer was enough to get even, and that was the end of it?"

"I think believing so would be wishful thinking." Wil sighed. "The treaty was clear: *all* Tarans will be destroyed."

"So, where are they?"

"A very good question. Planning a larger-scale attack, I fear."

Jason sat in quiet reflection for a few moments. "Are the shields going to do anything to stop them?"

"Between us?"

Jason nodded.

His father shook his head. "Based on the analysis of the attack on Alkeer, that… weapon—I don't even know what to call it—will cut through anything we have. The *only* potential countermeasure would be generating a spatial disruption field with a large-scale focusing aperture, such as the ateron band on the *Conquest*."

"But that's the one ship we have with that capability to do

anything on a meaningful scale."

"*Our* only ship, yes. But the Aesir have offered their assistance; our common Taran ties put them at the same risk as us."

"How large is their fleet these days?"

"As usual, Dahl wouldn't give me a straight answer. My guess is they have a few dozen ships with that capability, at most. We could perhaps protect ten planets, optimistically."

"Ten of fifteen hundred isn't a great percentage."

"No. Worse, we can't maintain a disruption field for long."

Jason's heart sank. "Where does that leave us?"

"We continue trying to find a way to communicate with the enemy and attempt to open diplomatic relations. Any combat scenario would result in unacceptable losses, in my assessment."

"And if they won't talk?"

"Then we'll do everything we can to prevent our race's extinction."

CHAPTER 27

GETTING BACK INTO a normal routine, if there was such a thing in the TSS, was proving difficult for Wil. In the week since Earth's induction into the Taran Empire, there'd been reactions ranging from celebration to protests across the galaxy. *Strange that one little planet could spark such strong feelings.*

He tried to focus on Michael's latest operational report, but his mind kept flipping through the multitude of high-priority issues. Tensions were rising everywhere. It would only take a tiny push to send the Empire into chaos.

"Where are we with the transdimensional imaging?" Michael asked, setting his tablet on his lap while he awaited the reply.

Wil sighed. "I wish I had better news on that front. Using the new scan data, we *did* figure out a way to replicate the conditions used by the *Andvari* to capture the image, but even CACI can't come up with a way to maintain those conditions for a continuous video observation. So, it looks like the best we'll get is bursts."

"How rapidly?"

"Approximately thirty-second increments. And it'll take almost the full instantaneous output capacity of the *Conquest*'s PEM, so communications and jump capabilities will be interrupted during each burst."

Michael frowned. "That's disappointing."

"We have limitations, as much as I hate to admit it. And seeing a fraction of these entities is the bare minimum. What do we do with that?"

His friend shook his head slowly. "I don't know, Wil. When we're face-to-face in the moment, you'll think of something, like you always do."

"I appreciate the faith, but this time… I don't know."

"No sense worrying about matters beyond our control."

"I suppose so," Wil agreed. *Not that it'll stop me.*

"Which brings us to the matter of Earth and the general unrest throughout the Empire," Michael said.

Wil didn't know what the big deal was, honestly. He knew firsthand that humans and Tarans were remarkably similar in their mannerisms and life outlooks. Sure, the planet was lacking technological sophistication, but so were many of the Outer Colony worlds. And humans were industrious and adaptable. Give them the tools, and they could turn Earth into a power to rival the influence of the Taran Middle Worlds in short order. So, he didn't put a lot of stock in the objections. People resisted things that were new; eventually, they'd realize their complaints were ill-placed.

Given that outlook, Wil was concerned by Michael's seriousness. He knew his friend to be cautious in his assessments—which made him a fantastic officer to have as a top advisor—but there must be something else going on to warrant the present level of pessimism.

"What about the unrest?" Wil asked.

Michael frowned. "There's a developing… situation."

"Meaning?" He braced for the worst. Whatever 'developing situation' might be, it couldn't be good.

"That attack on Duronis seems to be part of a growing separatist movement."

"Yes, old news. The Guard is handling that."

Michael nodded. "Which is why I wasn't going to say anything…"

"But…?

"We received a message sent to one of the TSS field offices near Duronis by a woman claiming to be a part of the movement who's behind the uprising on the planet. She's made assertions that they're connected to something larger, and she's looking for a friend who went missing after joining them. She doesn't want to be a part of what they're doing, but she's afraid about what might happen if no one is watching from the inside."

Is she a standup citizen or is this a trap? Wil met his friend's gaze. "Do you have a copy of the message?"

"Yes." Michael forwarded it to Wil's account. "I know this is the Guard's domain, but their response hasn't been proportional to the magnitude of this potential threat. The rumblings are becoming louder and more persistent."

Wil pinched the bridge of his nose. "I thought the recent approval ratings for the Taran High Council were favorable?"

"They are. And that joint statement from Dainetris and Sietinen has been getting positive press. So, it's possible this may turn out to be nothing."

It's never 'nothing' once you have a seasoned Agent taking notice. Those whispers would turn to shouts sooner than later, if history was any indication. "What are our people in the field saying?"

"They've tried to ask around, but you know how it is around Agents—people see us coming and get far away."

"Apparently, our presence is no longer deterrent enough."

"The problem is, the events on Duronis have been timed to what's going on with the Rift, tracing all the way back to the *Andvari*'s salvage contract. They seem to have a response ready for our every move."

"Do they have an informant within the TSS or Guard?"

Michael shrugged. "I haven't seen anything to suggest insider intel. They're just smart."

"That's worse. It would be nice to know who is driving the message that the Outer Colonies are better off without Tararia. At least, I assume that's what the separatists are calling for?"

"In a nutshell."

"Well, pulling away from the Empire won't get them in a better place, regardless of what some may think. Every time a planet has seceded, they've fallen into a Dark Age."

Michael studied him. "Like Earth?"

"Of course—the Empire's favorite cautionary tale."

"I think there was a concerted effort to leave Taran technology behind, in that case."

"Yes, but look where that got them—a divergent genetic branch with lost ability potential, technologically hamstrung, and barely able to look after the health of their planet. Yet, they were venturing out into the solar system and wanted to spread those problems. We'll have a chance to guide them toward a better path now that we're reunited, but it goes to show what's possible. If we get too many rogue groups like that…" He didn't need to complete the thought.

"Right." Michael nodded. "So, that's why I thought it prudent to follow up on the tip. See what you make of it."

"Thank you for raising these concerns. I'll go over the

available information with Saera and figure out a plan."

"I'll be standing by." Michael showed himself out.

Wil sent a telepathic summons to his wife, and she joined him in his office. Once she was seated, he played the video message received from the informant, who had identified herself as Lexi Karis. They listened to it three times to confirm the details.

"This isn't good." Saera frowned at the final frame of the video, showing the attractive brunette's concerned face. "Wil, I'm worried. They have a case."

"What do you mean?"

"The arguments about power dynamics in the Empire. After all, these protests directly impact your parents and our daughter, and we're using our influence in the TSS to 'monitor the situation', and we'll use that information to report back to them. The altruistic intentions don't matter. There's enough validity to the messaging that it may take hold."

"I can't deny being invested beyond an official capacity," Wil admitted.

"What do we do about it? Step aside?"

"No. The truth is that *anyone* will have bias in their position. At least we're aware of ours and openly acknowledge it. That's why we've surrounded ourselves with good people who'll make sure we don't let those feelings factor into our decision-making."

Saera nodded. "That's true. But how do we convince the public of that?"

"With tensions running so high at the moment, we certainly can't make any open move right now."

"And covertly sending in an Agent to follow up on this lead is out of the question, because they won't trust anyone with abilities."

"Not to mention, after what happened the last time we sent someone in undercover, I'm hesitant to try again."

She grimaced. "Yeah, that one is still a little raw."

"The easiest thing to do would be to kick this tip over to the Guard. However, I'm not sure if their approach would align with our own preferred methods."

"If they don't handle this, is it the TSS' place to intervene?"

"Who else could?"

Though Wil always tried his best to stay clear of Taran politics, it was inevitable that the TSS needed to get involved in certain matters. While the Tararian Guard was the military and police force of the Empire, the TSS was recognized for its diplomatic aptitude. Their reputation allowed them to intervene without it being seen as an overt application of force on the part of the government; instead, their involvement was often welcomed as a sign of good faith for fair negotiation.

Any separatist group had a reason for wanting to pull away from the Taran Empire, valid or not. The TSS was in the best position to find out why and see if an amicable agreement could be reached that would maintain a measure of harmony between the Taran-occupied worlds. Though true equity remained a lofty forward-looking aspiration, there were at least little things the Empire's leaders could do to improve citizens' lives. The trouble was, with a population in the trillions, they needed to be made aware of specific issues in order to address them. As unfortunate as it was, trying to manage fifteen hundred worlds meant that sometimes people fell through the cracks in the system.

Saera leaned back in her seat. "So how do we proceed?"

"I can't ignore testimony like this with everything else that's going on. We need ears out there—someone who can get the real story."

"Who could we send?" she asked.

"Since when does the High Commander need to make those kind of staffing decisions?"

"Since you ordered Michael and me to subscribe all available field units to monitoring the Rift."

"Ah, right." The tension rose in his chest. *We're already stretched thin and the real conflict hasn't even begun.* However, just because he didn't fully trust the Guard's methods, that didn't mean they couldn't draw on their resources. "I have an idea."

—   —   —

Jason cautiously entered his father's office. Cryptic summons almost always meant bad news or a mountain of work. Either way, he already had enough on his plate between the Rift situation and trying to convince his old acquaintances on Earth that the Taran Empire wasn't attempting a hostile takeover of the planet.

"Hey, what's up?" he greeted his father.

Wil looked up from behind the High Commander's desk and motioned for Jason to sit. "Complications."

"What now?"

"Disruption in the Outer Colonies, naturally. Because we need another civil war in the midst of this other shite." He sighed and combed his fingers through his hair. "Sorry, this is reminding me too much of the years after the war. I hadn't anticipated the need to mentally prepare for another crisis."

"Dad, are you okay?"

"I will be. But fok! We can't get a break, can we?"

This was the last thing Jason had expected when he walked into the room. He'd known the situation with the Rift was serious, but seeing his father's nerves frayed drove home that things were far worse than he'd realized.

"Is there something else you haven't told me?"

"Things in the Outer Colonies are getting heated, and the Guard isn't handling it well."

"We don't have jurisdiction, do we?"

"It's not an issue of jurisdiction but of resources and leadership."

Jason nodded. "The Guard is often lacking in finesse."

"We have been able to work together and unite our unique skillsets in the past, and we need to do a lot more of that going forward. I'm thinking of one soldier, in particular, who can help create that bridge."

He had no doubt to whom his father was referring—an acquaintance from the joint op two years ago with the Tararian Guard. Conventional weapons had been wholly ineffective in their engagement, and they'd only prevailed thanks to the heroic actions of one Guard soldier who'd been modified with experimental nanotech and an embedded AI. Aside from her modifications, she also possessed telepathic abilities, though through different means than most Tarans, making her skills unrecognizable, unlike those of Agents.

Jason crossed his arms and leaned back in the chair. "Kira? Yeah, she's good." He was intentionally downplaying it. Truthfully, he thought she was a total badass.

Wil nodded thoughtfully. "Have you stayed in touch with her?"

"No. I'd meant to, but you know how it goes."

He nodded. "Well, I was thinking that she might be helpful in this situation with the Outer Colonies."

Jason sat up straighter. "What did you have in mind?"

"The Guard is more likely to quell rebellion through force,

but I believe that would make things worse. So, the TSS is ultimately in the best position to intervene diplomatically, except our Agents can't sniff around, because everyone can see them coming and won't open up. Even so, we need someone with an enhanced skillset to get the whole truth, in this case. As far as I know, Kira is the only covert ops Guard officer who's also a telepath."

"That she is. And that nanotech she has… Suffice to say, she can go into a fight alone, and I feel sorry for whoever wrongs her."

"That's exactly what made me think of her for this mission," Wil said.

"If she's still in General Lucian's chain of command, I'm not sure he'll be willing to loan her to the TSS."

"We loaned him a ship; it'd be in poor taste for him to deny the request."

Jason winced. "He kinda hates me."

"Lucian is an arrogant prick who can't admit he made a fool of himself with you. Don't worry, Mathaen can put in the order straight from the top. Before that, though, I'd like to see if Kira is amenable to working on our behalf."

"Any mission parameters I should pass on?"

"Posing as a civilian, investigating a potential separatist group in the Outer Colonies. Possible connections to contractors, such as Renfield, with ties to those with deep pockets and more power than they should rightly have. And, that geneticist boyfriend of hers might be handy to have along. I'll forward you the tip we received."

"All right, I'll reach out to her." Jason paused. "And, Dad, we'll figure out this thing with the Rift. If these aliens struck a treaty with ancient Tarans, that means the odds were even enough that they called a cease-fire rather than one dominant force wiping the others out."

"As much as I want to believe that, we have no idea what kind of technology our ancestors had. Just because they were able to stand up to the enemy back then, we have no way of knowing if we can do the same now."

"Yeah, that's true." Jason smiled. "But they also didn't have us."

—

Some people left a lasting impact, even knowing them for a short time. For Jason, Major Kira Elsar was one of those individuals.

Throughout his time in the TSS, he'd encountered few people who could challenge his telekinetic abilities—and all of those were immediate family members. Granted, there were many powerful Agents, but he, his father, and his sister were in a unique class of their own. Kira, on the other hand, had no Gifted abilities in the traditional sense, but she was augmented in a different way that had posed a genuine challenge when he'd sparred with her.

It wasn't that he couldn't beat her; it was that she'd been able to catch him by surprise. Such a simple thing, but to someone who'd rarely been challenged, he relished the feeling of someone finally being able to get one over on him. More than that, she'd treated him like any other colleague while she'd done it. Perhaps it was because she'd grown up on a world outside of the formal Taran Empire where the Sietinen name didn't command immediate deference. No matter the reason, he appreciated that he'd needed to *earn* Kira's respect.

Jason went down the hall to his office to place the call. He pulled up Kira's contact info; it'd been almost two years since their last exchange. *Hey, still not as out of the blue as these calls I've been getting from people back on Earth.*

He sat up straight in his chair and initiated the vidcall, expecting it to be forwarded to a message inbox. To his surprise, the call was accepted.

Kira's smiling face filled the screen, her hazel eyes bright and red hair still styled in a casual pixie cut. "Stars! Jason Sietinen. Not who I expected to hear from today." The video on the other end had a bounce and waviness to it, indicating that she was probably on her handheld.

"Hi, Kira. I owe you an apology for not staying in touch like I said I would."

"Oh, psh!" She waved her free hand. "I was just as bad. I've been too busy to really notice. No offense."

He chuckled. "None taken. I'm shocked I caught you."

"Yeah, lucky timing. We just got back from a field op. I was actually on my way to the gym to work out some unspent energy."

"If you don't mind me delaying you for a few minutes, there's something I wanted to discuss with you."

"Yeah, go for it."

"Can you get somewhere private?"

Kira looked at someone off-camera and nodded. "Yeah, gimme a sec."

The camera pointed down at the deck, accompanied by the sound of jogging footsteps. Subsequently, the video panned up to her face again. The background looked to be a compact office similar to the study rooms found throughout TSS Headquarters.

"All right, there." She tilted her head and looked him up and down. "So, how've you been?"

He was about to respond in the way he normally would to

the question when asked by a casual acquaintance, saying things were good but busy. Generally, people didn't want a genuine answer to the question; it was asked as a pleasantry to feign a sense of caring and closeness. A gesture of civilized society. Though Jason had been through a trying experience with Kira, they hadn't spent enough time together to be the sort of friend where he'd bypass small-talk and jump to the heart of real issues. However, given what he was about to ask her to do, he also didn't feel right pretending that everything was okay. So, he struck a balance between the two. "Life goes on, the good and the bad."

Kira nodded. "I hear ya."

"You've probably heard about what's going on with the Rift?"

"Yeah, bits and pieces."

"I lost a good friend on Alkeer."

"Ah, shite. I'm sorry." Genuine sympathy clouded her face.

"No one ever said things would be safe and happy in this line of work."

"Yeah, I know that all too well. Doesn't make it easier when you lose someone, though."

"No, it doesn't," he agreed. "How've you fared since we last saw each other?"

"Better than most. The worst part has been being on a new team since my promotion to major. They're good, but it's not the same dynamic. At least I still have Jasmine; she says 'hi', by the way."

"Hi, Jasmine," Jason greeted Kira's neurally embedded sentient AI, which had been paired with her to control her unique nanite augmentations. "Glad you've been keeping Kira out of trouble."

"She says she hasn't entirely succeeded." Kira laughed.

Jason smiled. "Well, you did have an exceptional team

before. I'm glad I got the opportunity to meet them."

"They're all the rock stars of their own units now. Apparently, we did our job *too* well and the Guard decided to spread the goodness around."

Jason nodded. "I've seen it happen. It's bittersweet."

"Yeah."

"And what about that boyfriend of yours? Leon, right?"

She smiled. "He's great. And fiancé now, actually."

"Oh, congratulations!"

"I don't think we'll ever get legally married, but there was no sense kidding ourselves that we weren't in it for the long haul. The official paperwork doesn't matter to either of us."

"That's common in the TSS, too."

"Look at us, finding all of these similarities! Maybe this whole 'integration' thing between the TSS and Guard will work out, after all."

"Hopefully, because there's a lot to take on."

"Yes, to business," she said. "What's the deal?"

Jason had been authorized to share the details of the attack on Alkeer as well as the other information that was still classified within the TSS. Since Kira had had direct alien contact herself and was, in fact, carrying a variant of alien nanotech within her, she was in a unique position to understand the circumstances and need for discretion. Plus, there was no way he could ethically send her on a mission without her having a clear understanding of the risks and stakes. They needed complete buy-in from their key people on the ground.

"We're facing an invasion by transdimensional aliens who probably want to wipe out the Taran race."

Kira raised an eyebrow. "That it? So just a regular day at the office."

"Exactly."

"Well, fok."

"Yeah. But it's actually a little worse than that, because there appears to be a separatist group in the Outer Colonies that's taking advantage of the present disruption to make a move. And that's where we'd like you to come in. The TSS is going to be beyond tapped out dealing with this alien threat, and we need someone reliable to gather information about what's going on from a civil unrest standpoint. Someone who doesn't stand out like an Agent."

"You're thinking an undercover op inside whatever organization is behind the movement?"

"That's the idea."

"Hmm." She pursed her lips.

"We got a tip from someone on the inside. Sounds like she would make a good point of contact, assuming the whole thing isn't a trap."

Kira nodded thoughtfully. "I could probably make that determination easily enough."

"There's another wrinkle," Jason continued. "This 'Alliance' is recruiting new members—specialists, this time. Engineers, biologists, the works. Leon is a geneticist, from what I recall."

"Oh, I see." She shook her head and looked away.

"If you don't want to get involved—"

"No, I'll do it. Jasmine's in. Leon will, too; I'll talk to him."

"Are you sure?"

She shrugged. "Beats most of the boring shite they have me do. Assuming Command signs off on it."

"My father will make the formal request with Admiral Mathaen. We wanted to check with you first."

"That's not really how this works. I'm a soldier. I go where

I'm told to go and do what I'm ordered to do."

"I appreciate that," he said, "but we do things a little differently in the TSS. For any kind of high-risk undercover op, we like to get buy-in. It's a choice, not an assignment."

"How 'high-risk' are we talking here?"

"The informant's friend disappeared. The Alliance has planted a bomb on a station and killed two people. Extrapolate from there."

Kira bit her lip as she considered the information. After several seconds, she gave a resolute nod. "We're still in. It's nice taking out the one-off baddies, but it's not every day there's an opportunity to tackle something big like this. I want to know what they're up to."

"You might be in for… *months*."

"With Leon there with me, it'll be a nice vacation."

Jason nodded. "Okay, I'll pass it up the chain. Thank you."

"Sure thing. It's good to talk to you, Jason. Take care."

"You too. In case I don't talk to you again before you head out, best of luck."

"Thanks. And good luck with those aliens. You know, saving the Empire and all that."

He smiled back. "Like you said, just another day."

CHAPTER 28

"THANK YOU FOR lending Kira's unique abilities to our investigation," Wil said as he concluded his check-in with Admiral Mathaen. "I'm glad you were able to send her out to the field so quickly."

The admiral nodded. "It's fortunate the timing worked out. Admittedly, I've heard a lot more about her than an admiral should ever hear about a major. Her commanders haven't known what to do with her."

"Then I'm glad we can put her skills to full use. She'll be an asset in this endeavor."

"I hope you're able to get the answers we need to stay ahead of this thing."

"Indeed. I'll keep you apprised."

The admiral nodded. "Thank you."

"On that note," Wil began, shifting gears, "with all this talk of unity, it's occurred to me that both of our organizations are due for name changes."

"How so?"

"Well, they're 'Tararian'. It's very capital-centric. We serve

Tarans as a whole."

"That's a good point." Mathaen stroked his chin.

"I suspect others have thought about it in the past and then promptly realized what an utter nightmare the paperwork would be for a rebrand of that scale."

"An even better point."

Wil shrugged. "I don't know. It's something to consider in the future."

"The sentiment is important now, though, given the political climate." Mathaen paused in thought. "I wonder if there's a way to present a new umbrella that encompasses both the Guard and TSS. Not anything official to the point of needing legal name changes or reorganization, but more symbolic."

"I like that idea. But what to call it?"

"I'm about as far from a marketing expert as one can be. Don't ask me!"

"I'll get some input," Wil stated. He wasn't much for branding himself, but he knew many people who were. *It would be nice to show up in a more inclusive way. I don't blame the Outer Colonies for distrusting us when everything down to our name points to the Central Worlds.*

"Sounds good." The admiral paused. "And Wil, I'm glad we're finally working together. We should have done this a long time ago."

"Better late than never, as they say."

"And just in time. The storm is brewing."

— — —

Lexi couldn't help looking over her shoulder at every turn. *Sending that message to the TSS might get me killed! What was*

I thinking?

She had been acting independently, and that was the problem. The Alliance expected her to fall in line and do whatever they said without question. She wouldn't, couldn't, do that—not knowing they were killers and were behind her friend's disappearance. Now, if only the help she desperately needed would arrive.

Yet, she couldn't wait around forever hoping someone would swoop in to take out the Alliance. She needed to keep digging deeper and learn everything she could.

The past week had been tense around the office. She'd been instructed to take the hovercart for each of her daily pickups from the port, and the heavy crates had almost maxed out the equipment's capacity. The inventory duty had been passed off to a new recruit, so Lexi hadn't had the opportunity to see inside. Based on the little snippets she'd dared to glean from people's minds, she had gotten the impression that it was something destructive—either weapons or explosives. The Alliance was gearing up to make a big statement.

Lexi went about her tasks around the office, listening and gathering information whenever she could. She kept getting pieces, but she didn't have nearly enough to get the bigger picture.

"Oren wants to see you, Lexi," Shena said as she came up behind her.

Lexi jumped at the sudden address. "Where?"

"His office." Shena walked off to do whatever else. Lexi still, for the life of her, couldn't figure out how everyone passed their time throughout the day.

Not having a real choice in the matter, she went down to the basement.

Oren was working at his desk when she arrived. She

knocked twice on the open door to get his attention.

He motioned to the seat across from him, and she took it.

"So, I hear you've been asking questions."

Lexi's heart dropped to her feet. She swallowed and forced herself to breathe. "I just want to do my part to the best of my ability. Understanding the larger goals helps me prioritize and be effective in my tasks." Her voice didn't quaver, thankfully.

"I appreciate your attitude. You know we keep things compartmentalized for a reason."

"Yes, I know. Just… everyone was so excited to see Magdalena speak, and I was hoping to know more about her."

Oren cocked his head. "Why didn't you come to me and ask?"

She shrugged sheepishly. "I didn't want to bother you. It seemed silly."

"You shouldn't feel that way at all. There is *some* information we need to share with our trusted members."

That phrasing was encouraging. *I'm still on the inside, it seems.*

"The Alliance is a piece of something much bigger," Oren continued. "Magdalena is one of the visionaries behind what is known as the Coalition. I will simply say that there are very powerful players working behind the scenes to make sure we have the resources to be successful."

Lexi nodded. "I've gotten the impression that we have moved from a time of talking to a time of action."

"Indeed, we have. In fact, our biggest move is about to be set in motion."

"May I ask what that is?"

He studied her. "It's a significant responsibility to be brought into the next level. Are you sure you're willing to commit?"

"Have I done anything to make you question my loyalty?"

He was silent for longer than Lexi would have liked. "No," he said at last. "And we're going to need more people to help see us through the next phase."

She kept her expression neutral. "Tell me what you need."

"We're expecting an important shipment. Rather, Duronis is. Two freighters are arriving tonight, and we need to secure them."

Her heart skipped a beat. "How?"

"A team from another office will be leading that portion of it. The reason I called you here, though, is we need to prepare messaging to the citizens of the world, to deploy once our task is complete. You've had great ideas in our recent strategy sessions, so I thought you would be perfect for leading that communication effort."

It was a lame assignment, and she would have been offended if she'd actually cared; a simple copy-paste from previous materials would get the job done in short order. "That sounds great. What should this communication say?" Her pulse pounded in her ears with fear that Oren would detect her disingenuous intentions.

"It should focus on how Duronis has achieved its independence and now we have the chance to lead the charge for other planets in the sector and beyond. We will be the hub of something new and great."

Shite! What are they doing to make that happen? Lexi was having difficulty keeping her rising panic in check. She had an awful feeling that a lot of people were about to die, and she couldn't stand by and do nothing while that happened. If ever there was a time to risk reading Oren's mind again, it was now. She reached out telepathically to see what she could glean on the surface.

The first impression was a thirst for power and control. It didn't map over clearly to a plan, only a strong emotional charge. Oren felt it so strongly it was like they had already carried out the act; an independent Duronis, at the hub of a new, rising power. He fancied himself a lord in this future scenario, reaping the benefits from years of hard work and sacrifice.

Lexi pushed deeper. *How does Oren think that future will come to pass?* The two cargo freighters were fixtures in his mind. They were filled with supplies on a massive scale— enough to let the entire planet get by without any off-world contact for at least a month.

Why would that matter? She had to risk rooting around. As carefully as she could, she peeled back the layers of his subconscious mind, praying to the stars he didn't notice the intrusion. There was something about preventing outsiders from interfering. *Just a little more—*

"Lexi, are you all right?" Oren's voice brought her back to the present.

She quickly withdrew from his mind and realized that she must have appeared to be staring off into space. The delve had only been a few seconds, but any length of time was awkward for someone to be sitting there expressionless in the middle of a conversation.

"Yes, just contemplating all the wasted time and wishing I'd come to you sooner," she said.

She hadn't gotten enough. She needed to go deeper, in spite of the danger. *If I could distract him with something while I dig...*

Before she could think of a good question to prime his mind, footsteps sounded behind her, followed by a knock on the door frame.

"Sorry to interrupt," Josh said. "There's been a change in the timeline. Operation Nova needs to commence right now."

"That's two days early!"

"I'm only passing on what I've been told. They expedited processing."

"Shite." Oren shoved his chair back from his desk abruptly and stood up. "Do you have what you need?"

Josh held up a sealed case in his hand, which Lexi recognized from their contentious pickup with Niko a couple weeks prior. "I'll manage."

What is Josh's part in this? Lexi could only catch the briefest gleaning of a command console from his mind. *Some kind of logistics coordinator?*

"Get in position. I'll make the other arrangements," Oren instructed. "Lexi, we need that communication plan ASAP. Don't let me down."

"I won't." She was reluctant to leave his office with so many unanswered questions, but she wasn't in a position to protest.

Josh rushed toward the door leading to the storage tunnel.

Could that be where the control room is? If he was involved in the logistics, he might have as good of a sense of what was going on as Oren. "Hey, anything I can do to help?" she called after him.

"Your part," was his only reply.

During the brief interaction, she caught a mental flash of the space surrounding Duronis.

All of these pieces, but how do they fit together? She needed to go somewhere she could think. And to get as much other information as she could.

Stars, I swore I wouldn't do this! Yet, telepathy was the only thing that could give her an edge right now. She couldn't bear the thought of more lives being lost if there was *anything* she could have done to prevent it.

Lexi jogged upstairs. At the top, she slowed her pace and sent out a low-level telepathic probe to search for relevant thoughts on the surface of the minds nearby. She wasn't particularly practiced with the technique, so a flurry of images and sounds came back as a jumbled mess. She winced at the sudden din. *That's not going to work.*

Her only other option was to skim the thoughts of everyone she could find, one by one. Dangerous if they caught her, but she was desperate.

She kept her gaze down and opened her Gifted senses she had ignored for so long. It was like finally being able to take a full, deep breath again after wearing a too-tight shirt—allowing her to pick up on details in her surroundings that she'd missed after months of staring at the same walls. Background mechanical sounds, distant conversations, scents of cleaning supplies and body odors. Even the colors seemed more vibrant.

The most striking aspect of the sensory expansion, though, was the atmosphere in the place. Her subconscious had picked up on part of it, when the mood was particularly happy or serious. Now, she caught the nuances to it. People were charged up. The focus toward a common goal, and there was a noticeable energy to those unified thoughts. A buzz in the air. As she assessed the feeling, she realized that some individuals had a sort of glow to them. After coming across a few people with that distinctive aura, she realized that all of them were at the meeting where Magdalena had spoken. *They're the ones who are in on the plan!*

That narrowed down her efforts considerably. She began tracing the energy fields throughout the office, searching for those buzzing with excitement.

There weren't as many as she would have liked to collect a

broad sampling of information, but anything was better than nothing. The gleaned snippets didn't make much sense on their own. The cargo ships—those came up a lot. A nav beacon. Weapons. A shuttle. Riots. *How* everything fit together, though, was elusive.

As she walked through the halls and common rooms, Lexi tried to keep her gaze away from the person she was targeting. Even so, telepathy had the potential to give people the feeling that they were being watched, especially when delving deeper than surface gleaning. Some were more sensitive to it than others, likely due to their own genetic potential for abilities as a dormant Generation. So far, everyone had seemed perfectly oblivious. It emboldened her to dig deeper with the hope of finding information to tie all the threads together.

One woman had a bright aura around her, and Lexi zeroed in. The blonde woman was in front of her, facing away, making it an ideal setup to dive deeper without detection. Lexi started to peel back the layers, picking up thoughts about the cargo ships and snapshots of a plan for an armed group to secure the dock.

The woman whipped around stared directly at Lexi. "What are you doing?"

Lexi pulled back her mental probe and instinctively snapped up a telepathic wall around her own mind. *Shite!* The woman was more sensitive than most, apparently. Way too much so.

There wasn't anything she could offer as an explanation. Lexi spotted a table nearby and decided that a physical distraction was her best play. She intentionally hooked her right foot on one of the legs as she passed by, knocking her off-balance.

She went down hard on her left shoulder, pinning her arm

at a funny angle. Radiating pain shot from her elbow down to her wrist and up to her back. That wasn't part of the plan. *Fok!*

"Stars! Are you okay?" the woman exclaimed.

Lexi rolled to her side and used the table to help herself up. "Only hurt my pride." She did her best to hide the pain of the injury; any indication of actual harm and she might be forced to see a medic, and she couldn't afford any delay. Besides, her medical nanites would mend the injury almost as quickly as any other care.

"I can—"

"I'm fine," Lexi assured her. "Just need to pay closer attention to where I'm going."

The woman nodded, looking over Lexi with concern, the observation of Lexi's suspicious behavior seemingly forgotten. She turned back around and left with the person she had been talking to.

Not exactly the way I wanted to handle that. Lexi gingerly opened and closed her hand and rotated her joints. It didn't feel like anything was broken, but at least a slight sprain was likely. *I also need to learn to fake-fall better.*

The other people continued to disperse. By the time Lexi circled back to the workshop, she was alone in the room. It was as good a place as any to work on the 'messaging' project Oren had assigned her, so it would also serve as a suitable place to sort through the information she had learned.

She laid out the disparate pieces in her mind and started looking for connections.

The two cargo ships had been the most common thought. They were clearly central to the plan in some way—probably carrying valuable materials the Alliance was hoping to claim for itself. Or, she realized, the Coalition as a whole. She couldn't forget that important tidbit she'd gotten from Oren about the Alliance being a unit within the larger Coalition that Magdalena helped run.

The freighters were massive targets. Despite the resources on board, though, it was an odd choice to seize them. Taking over was one thing, but *holding* them was quite another. The arrival of a single Guard destroyer would change the equation in a big way.

Unless backup couldn't arrive, she realized. Except, no backup would mean taking out the nav beacon to make the planet challenging to access via subspace. *Shite!*

She considered the other snippets of information. *There was a shuttle...* Small, difficult to detect. A craft like that could get close to a target without drawing too much attention.

Like a nav beacon floating out in space.

She started piecing together the plan. Destroying the nav beacon would temporarily cut the world off from any vessel that wasn't equipped with an independent jump drive. Of course, one of those ships could bring a new nav beacon to install, but that would take time to initialize. The question was, what was the Alliance planning to do in the interim? It was too large and complex a distraction to pull off for their mission to not be something significant.

What am I missing? She pored over the observations, trying to see the connections between the seemingly disparate pieces. *Why would they take out a nav beacon?*

Stars, it's a temporary distraction! It came to her in a sudden moment of clarity. *They're going to hack into the planetary defense network.*

CHAPTER 29

LEXI'S HEART POUNDED in her ears as the Alliance's intentions crystalized in her mind.

A plan to hack the planetary defense network was the only thing that made sense, given everything she knew about their operations. With control of those orbital weapons, they could take out any ships that were approaching the planet during the moment they were most vulnerable leaving subspace. The best of the military vessels could weather the attack, surely, but how many would it take to overwhelm the defense grid and bring it down? Certainly more than either the TSS or Guard could spare with everything else going on. It wouldn't be worth the time or effort.

Duronis would be on its own—free to serve as a base of operations for the Alliance and the larger Coalition. Given how well everything else was planned out, the members of the organization almost certainly had access to contraband independent jump drives of their own, so the lack of the nav beacon wouldn't impact their own transit abilities.

Fok! What can I do? She needed to find out who was

supposed to hack into the satellite network. If she could stop them from gaining control there, the rest of the plan would fall apart.

It could be anyone, and they might not even be part of this office. If the plan was going down now, she wouldn't have time to vet potential suspects.

Except... She had seen a control room in Josh's mind. That seemed like the kind of place where someone might hack into a defense network. If it wasn't Josh himself, he might know the person who would lead the act. A flimsy lead, but it was all she had.

Unfortunately, following up on that lead would mean abandoning the work that Oren expected. Or maybe not. She had a lot of material from the previous rallies. A little bit of reworking and embellishment, and there would be a decent narrative to present. Really it was a consolation assignment— the sort of thing given to someone not trusted with important work.

She brought up an assortment of old messaging materials on the workstation and began hurriedly knitting some of them together into a smooth narrative. With some word-vomit embellishments based on the instructions Oren had given her about what this particular piece should communicate, it was a sufficient rough draft. She'd go back to add more polish if there was time. But for now, it would serve its purpose to make it look like she'd done the work.

The question then became how to find the control room. Most likely, it was accessible via the underground tunnel network, since that's where Josh had been heading. She couldn't very well walk into the room unexpectedly, though. *And how do I stop them from taking over the defense grid?*

She wasn't a programmer or even that great with

technology beyond the level of a proficient user. So, any option necessitating countermeasures from a tech standpoint was off the table.

Mind-control wasn't reliable and also had a high probability of her getting caught. While she could take on one person and manipulate their thoughts to not carry out a particular action, it was unlikely she would find the hacker alone.

The only viable option was to render the entire control center inoperable, if there was such a place, as indicated in Josh's mind. A disruption so significant that it would throw the whole plan off.

There are weapons in the storage tunnel. The major problem was that each was carefully cataloged and inventoried. Granted, she had done those logs herself and could doctor them, but that would take time and add another layer of risk. There was a much more straightforward solution, though risky in a different way: she could take out the control room with telekinesis.

It had been years since she'd done anything significant with her abilities, and her training had been spotty, at best. Trying to do anything on the fly might fail. But it was the most sensible option, given the alternatives.

If I can even find the bomaxed control room. That was Step One.

Lexi closed out from her writing on the workstation and thought about the best way to get down to the tunnel without anyone asking questions. To hedge her bets, she put a note on her workstation that she was going out to field test some messaging before writing a final draft; weak cover, but again, better than nothing. That was rapidly becoming her motto.

She knew that the tunnel entrance was potentially

unlocked with people on the move for the big operation, so getting down there might not be too difficult; she could reset the bolts with telekinesis if it came down to it. That left the significant problem of locating the control room.

It would need to be easily accessible to people in this office. And it would use a lot of power.

She shook her head and let out a long breath. There was too much riding on her set of cobbled-together assumptions. Still, her gut told her this was the right thing to do.

A power-consumption-heavy location would give off a distinct energy signature. In the underground tunnels made of stone with minimal other wiring, there was a good chance she would be able to trace the electromagnetic signature all of the way to the control room. Such a feat would be easy for a trained TSS Agent, but an out-of-practice street rat like her…

Bad people are going to take over this planet if you sit on your hands and leave the problem-solving to other people. You got yourself into this mess, so you need to do something about it. She gripped the edge of the desk. *Do it for Melisa.*

Her mind made up, Lexi placed her handheld offline so her location couldn't be geo-tracked, in case anyone got too curious about her whereabouts. With the note on her workstation about leaving the office, she instead headed downstairs.

As a precaution, she generated a low-level electrical field around herself to disrupt the footage of any security camera that might be watching her movements within the office. While it would draw suspicion if anyone reviewed it, at least it would be an extra layer of protection to keep the events from tracing back to her.

On the lower administrative level, the office doors, including Oren's, were thankfully closed, so she had a clear shot to the tunnel entrance; everyone was already in their designated places.

She tried the door handle. Locked. *Bomax.*

Well, at least it would be a good opportunity to refresh her telekinesis skills. She opened her senses again, assessing the lock with her mind. She identified the location and position of the physical bolts holding it in place. Carefully, she tugged at the mechanism. It clanged to the side—much harder than she'd anticipated.

Shite. The entire mechanism was busted, but at least it was now broken in the open position. She was immensely thankful for her foresight to disrupt the camera feed.

She slipped through the doorway and closed it as best as she could behind her with the broken lock. The dim stairwell leading down to the tunnel now seemed even darker and more ominous than normal.

Toward the bottom of the stairs, she slowed her pace and listened for any sign of voices or movement. Not hearing or feeling anything, she continued forward.

A careful visual inspection confirmed that the tunnel was clear.

How can everyone disappear like this? Nothing about the Alliance's operations made any sense.

She walked to the center of the tunnel and closed her eyes, focusing her extrasensory perception on the energy fields in the corridor. The first thing to jump out at her was the wiring running in the ceiling to the lights. She noted how it felt and then let it fade into the background, trying to sense something more powerful in the distance.

There was nothing. Just quiet and cold.

Come on! Where could it be? It was possible she was too far away to detect the control room. *Logic, then. Which direction makes the most sense?*

She studied the physical features of the tunnel, looking for indications of movement. After a minute of searching, she spotted a recent disturbance in the dust on the floor. It indicated people walking to the right, which was the same direction Magdalena had gone when she left after her speech. The logic tracked.

Okay, to the right. Lexi took off at a deliberate yet cautious pace, watching, listening, and feeling her way to make sure nothing caught her by surprise.

After what felt like two hundred meters or so, Lexi sensed a different energy in the air. It was the kind of intense electromagnetic signature she had been hoping to spot that would suggest a high-intensity power usage. She headed in its direction.

After another hundred meters, the signature increased in intensity. She was close now. A mechanical hum and the distant murmur of voices entered her awareness.

She crept closer, staying near the wall where she would be most hidden if someone came out the door up ahead. It was open; no one would be expected down here aside from those working for the cause.

There was no way to get a look inside without potentially revealing herself, so she listened.

"Remote pilot initiated," a woman stated. "Taking control now."

"Take them out," a man instructed.

"The area hasn't cleared yet. There are children—"

"All part of the sacrifice for our independence."

"On it," she confirmed without hesitation or remorse.

"When will we have access to the grid?" the man asked.

"Almost there. Gimme two minutes," a voice she

recognized as Josh replied.

Stars! I need to do something right now. She thought about trying to cut the power, but that wouldn't be enough. They might have other communication devices that would be able to get out a message about what had happened. They might even locate *her.* She needed to do something that might look like an accident when it was investigated—something that would abruptly end their activities without providing an easy transition for others to continue the work.

These walls are old. I could cause a cave-in, she realized. The thought of it turned her stomach. *That would kill everyone here.*

It wasn't a decision she wanted to make, but she was faced with a hard reality: these people were willing to kill innocent children without a second thought, and she could help save those lives.

They're monsters and need to be stopped. This wasn't just people doing their job. They were *choosing* to go about achieving their ends this way. There wasn't an excuse for hurting innocents like this in any context, but especially not while claiming it was to help people.

The anger welled in her, fueling her abilities. A charge of energy built up in her, waiting to be released. When she felt like she was about to burst, she focused the energy at the ceiling inside the control room, breaking the bricks free from their mortar.

As the room began to crumble, Lexi was greeted with the sound of breaking monitors and the thud of bricks pelting the people inside. There was an initial cry of surprise before the roar of falling bricks, concrete, and dirt drowned out other shouts of pain or fear. Once the ceiling gave way, a cloud of clay-scented debris poured into the tunnel as the walls fell inward in a cascade of structural failures.

It all seemed too quick and quiet for ending lives, but Lexi didn't feel anything except relief. *They needed to be stopped.*

The ceiling in the tunnel trembled. With a lurch in her gut, she realized that she may have destabilized the entire place. *I need to get out of here!*

Lexi pulled her shirt up over her mouth to help filter the dust. She couldn't go back the way she came because she was supposed to be outside the office. So, she'd need to find another path to the street and then return to the office that way. *You know, like a normal person that didn't just kill a bunch of people!*

She recalled seeing a ladder a little ways back, hanging halfway down the wall and rising to a hatch in the roof. Squinting against the dust and flickering lights, she ran back that direction to find it. Fortunately, the structural damage hadn't reached that far.

Negotiating the ladder with only one good arm proved challenging, but she managed to shimmy up. At the top of the ladder, she found herself in a basement. Based on the musty smell, no one had been in it for a long time. It was unlit, and only thanks to her enhanced senses was she able to perceive some features. Her footsteps were soft underfoot in a thick layer of dust, which wafted up and tickled her nose.

One benefit of the dark was that any light source was obvious. She spotted the faint outline of a door half a story above her—the right elevation to be at street-level, given how far she'd descended initially and had come back up since. *How do I get up there?*

It was then she remembered that she had her handheld in her pocket—still safely offline but powered on.

She pulled out the device and activated its flashlight. Piles of old crates suddenly sprang into view in the pool of illumination as well as sheets draped over old equipment. The only thing that mattered, though, was the concrete staircase leading to the doorway.

Lexi jogged up the stairs and felt along the door for a way to open it. There was no handle or even a sign of a bolt. She shoved against it, only to find it solid. *Just my luck.*

She backed up a few steps. *Well, there's one way to deal with this!*

With a burst of telekinetic energy, she shoved against the door. It groaned on its hinges but remained firmly in place. She gave it another shove, harder this time. Part of it gave way, bending with a loud groan of rending metal. A jagged triangle of light in the upper left showed where it had started to give way.

Come on! She kept beating at it with all the strength she could muster. She was still exhausted from earlier and out of practice. Even at the height of using her abilities, she had never done so many intensive feats in such a short span of time.

She kept at it, beating with telekinetic blows as the door slowly pulled away from its bolts. *Almost there...*

At last, Lexi broke through the final section. She stumbled out into the well-lit night street amidst a cloud of dust and rust. The sound of the door giving way reverberated on the hard surfaces, sending a clanging echo down the alley. She coughed as the grit hit her lungs and waved her hand in front of her face to clear the particulates while she jogged away, wishing she'd kept her shirt raised.

She sagged against the concrete wall where the air was clear, finding the cool surface refreshing after the intense physical activity. Her head pounded from exertion, and her limbs trembled and throbbed slightly, like she'd just run a marathon.

After resting for a couple of minutes, the dizziness had subsided enough to move. She brushed herself off with a telekinetic breeze to remove any evidence of dust from the incident. Figuring that the racket must have called attention, she should get as far from the site as possible—if not to avoid anyone on the outside, then to steer clear of those underground who were no doubt already investigating the odd cave-in and might spot her escape path.

She went out to the main street, realizing she was across from the transit station closest to the Alliance's building.

Leaning against a wall on the opposite side of the street was a woman with short red hair, staring at her; from that vantage, she would have had a view of the door Lexi had busted out of during her escape. Based on her interested expression, the act had not gone unnoticed.

Shite, was it obvious I was using telekinesis? Probably, if she was being honest with herself. There was no chemical explosion, and a door had been flung from its hinges. The only reasonable explanations were telekinesis or advanced augmentations.

The woman had been leaning against a wall with one foot up, and she now was tracking Lexi from a distance as she walked toward the office. After another two blocks, she was still shadowing Lexi.

Fok, this is all I need. Lexi picked up her pace while looking for a good side street to duck down. However, she was close to the office now and didn't have a lot of options without going out of her way. She broke into a jog, causing her sprained elbow to throb with each stride.

The red-haired woman matched her pace and then started to overtake her. Finally, she crossed the street. She was pretty in a tough sort of way and looked to be around thirty. "Hey," she called out as she approached, "you look like someone who could use some help."

Lexi cradled her injured arm. "I'm fine."

The woman followed her. "You really did a number back there. Don't see skills like that too often."

"I don't know what you think you saw, but you're mistaken."

"You should be proud of Gifts like that."

"No!" Lexi wheeled around to face her. She dropped her voice to a harsh whisper. "Don't say anything, please."

"Why? It's legal now."

"The people around here make people like me disappear." Lexi pivoted on her heel and resumed walking back toward the office.

"I'd really like to help you. Sometimes, when you have nowhere to turn, someone answers your call."

Hold on, that's not something a normal bystander would say. Lexi stopped and turned back slowly. "Wait, are you…?"

The red-haired woman smiled and shrugged. "Oh, me? I'm here to get involved in a cause. I heard the message loud and clear and want to be a part of it."

Lexi couldn't be certain, but it seemed like this woman was speaking in code. *Is she working undercover?* She didn't detect any abilities, so she couldn't be an Agent. But the TSS also had the Militia division. If that was the case, this might be the answer to her desperate plea. "You're late."

The woman looked her over. "Sorry, just got here. But I take it you've had a bad day?"

"Let's just say I did a big thing, but no one can know I had any part in it."

"I've had plenty of those kinds of days myself."

That certainly seemed like the kind of response someone

with a military background might give. Lexi looked her over, not sure whether to laugh or cry; she really could have used someone like her about half an hour earlier. "Well, the Alliance is looking for committed people with skills."

"I like to think I can handle myself in combat. And my fiancé happens to be a geneticist. I heard that might be one of the skillsets you're looking for?" She tilted her head questioningly.

Lexi's heart leaped. For the first time in months, she felt a glimmer of hope. "Uh, yeah. Yes. You sound like exactly the kind of people the Alliance is looking for."

"Great! How do we join up?"

CHAPTER 30

WIL AWOKE TO the chime and vibration of his handheld, a tone reserved for urgent communications. He sleepily grabbed the device to check the caller. Immediately, he snapped to full alertness.

"Dahl, what can I do for you?" In all the years they'd known each other, the Oracle had never messaged Wil in the middle of the night.

Saera sat up next to him, listening intently.

"We have sensed something coming," Dahl stated. "It is close."

"What do you mean?"

"The beings beyond the Rift. We believe they intend to use one of the rifts near the galactic core as a doorway."

Wil's heart pounded in his ears. *I should have thought of that possibility.*

The largest known rift, and the one that demanded a good deal of his attention, wasn't the only spatial tear in the galaxy. It was unique and attracted so much interest because it was manufactured—ripped open by the Bakzen before the start of the centuries-long war. There were, however, smaller, natural rifts. These other pockets were essentially thin spots in the dimensional veil, and the Aesir had taken up residence in some of them in order to be closer to the cosmic energies. It made sense that the transdimensional beings would be able to use *any* rift as an access point to spacetime.

Fok! What can we do? He realized that he hadn't acknowledged Dahl's statement and the ancient man was waiting for a response. "Is this something you witnessed in the pattern, or have you seen physical evidence?"

"For now, we have only foreseen it. But, as you know, those visions are glimpses of the pattern's threads that have already been pulled."

Wil had learned long ago how to decipher the metaphorical language used by the Oracles. He knew Dahl spoke of the cosmic energy web connecting places and people at critical junctures; he'd seen it for himself when he'd looked into the nexus as a young man.

His glimpse of the web had changed his perception of the universe, but the greater impact was the realization that he was one of the focal points in the energy network. The Aesir had spoken of him restoring balance for Tarans and how he must fulfill his role; it was the motivation that had seen him through the war in the final push. He'd taken solace in the thought that defeating the Bakzen and seeking justice with the Priesthood would free him from his place in the web. These recent events, though, had changed all that. *I'll never be free. Even now, the Aesir are turning to me. Before now, it was I who turned to them.*

He was embedded deeper than ever. No escape. The realization struck him as a physical weight.

"It has to be you, Cadicle," Dahl said in the hushed silence. "You must be the one to guide us."

"I don't know anything about them. What am I supposed to do?"

"You will know the path when you see it."

Wil wished he could terminate the call and have that be the end of it. The cryptic statement was one of Dahl's favorites, and it annoyed Wil to no end. The only thing that kept him calm was the irritating truth of the statement: somehow, Wil *did* know what to do when it mattered most. Those instincts had saved him and his people in countless engagements. This felt different, though. None of the other enemies or conflicts had been anything like these transdimensional beings.

"I'll go to Tararia," Wil said. "I'll try to speak with the beings."

"We are behind you." Dahl bowed his head. "May the stars favor us."

The communication ended, leaving the room dark and quiet. Wil could feel Saera watching him, waiting for a reaction.

He spoke the only truth he could at the moment as the fate of his people once again fell on his shoulders. "I will say to you what I can't to others: I have no idea how to fight them."

Saera moved closer and wrapped her arm around his middle. "We'll figure it out."

"That's the thing, though. I don't know if we can." He shook his head. "We remain limited by the scope of our own experience."

"I'd argue that many of the things we do are at the borders of those limitations," Saera pointed out.

"Perhaps. But I'm not sure it will be enough."

"If we can't fight them directly, then we'll find another way forward. Not everything has to be about shows of might."

Maybe there is another way to go about this. He nodded. "You're right."

"You can handle this, Wil," Saera said. "I believe in you." She hugged him tightly.

"I wouldn't want anyone else by my side. What do you say we leave Michael in charge around here and tackle this one together?"

"Bring it on."

—   —   —

Raena checked the time when she saw the image of her grandfather stifle a yawn on the viewscreen. It was after midnight for her, and he was in a time zone two hours ahead. "Stars! Sorry, I didn't realize it was so late."

"No, it's all right," he replied. "These kinds of matters take priority."

"Not our first late night," Ryan said.

They'd been going over the information from Duronis for hours. The events didn't add up. Armed private mercs had seized control of two supply freighters at the planet's primary spacedock, and then everyone had spontaneously walked away. Reviewing the security and scan footage, they had detected a lone shuttle had circled the planet's nav beacon and then returned to port at the same time as the other mercs left. The only conclusion that they'd been able to draw was that a takeover attempt had been aborted, but it was unclear why.

"I don't get it," Raena murmured yet again. "They were in position. Why did everyone walk away?"

"I suspect there was another piece of the plan we don't know about, and that must have fallen through," Cris stated.

Ryan frowned. "A failure like this will make them want to hit even harder the next time."

"No doubt," Cris agreed. "At least now we know what to

look for—and the kind of resources they wield."

"Which are significant." Raena hadn't personally dealt with mercs, but she had a cursory understanding of how much quality armor and weapons cost on the black market. Given the number of mercs and their gear, there'd been a hefty price tag associated with the operation. No one spent that much and then walked away mid-act without a compelling reason.

Cris rubbed his eyes wearily. "This close call reinforces the hypothesis that there are major players behind this disruption. Those with credits to burn in order to get their way."

"Like Lower Dynasties with grander political aspirations?" Raena suggested.

"Arvonen certainly wasn't an isolated case."

She sighed. "What do we do about it?"

"For now, monitor the situation. The Guard has taken renewed notice of the planet's activities in light of these events, so it will be a while before the perpetrators have the breathing room to try anything else."

"All right, we'll let you get to bed."

"Thank you for going over this with us," Ryan added.

"Anytime." Cris smiled warmly at them. "We're on the right track. Stay the course."

She nodded. "Talk soon." She ended the vidcall.

"Well, it wasn't as bad as it could have been." Despite his upbeat tone, Ryan still looked concerned.

"I suppose so." If it wasn't one thing, it was another. *At least a crisis was averted today.*

She was about to lock down her desk and suggest they head for bed when a message came in from her father's handheld. The desk lit up with the urgent communication.

"Fok! Of *course* there would be something else," Ryan muttered.

Raena answered. "Hey—"

"They're heading for Tararia," he cut in. "Dahl gave me a heads up. Nothing on scan yet. We're headed your way on the *Conquest*."

Ryan froze. "Oh, my stars…"

"I want you up here with us," Wil continued. "Ryan, you're welcome to come along."

Raena's heart pounded in her ears. "Okay."

"We'll be there in five hours. See you then." The call ended.

Ryan swallowed. "By 'they', I take it he means the aliens?"

"I assume so." Her stomach flopped. *They're coming* here? *How?*

"I thought they came through the Rift? How are they getting all the way over here?"

"I have no idea."

His brows furrowed. "Do we warn people?"

"What could we say? An invisible enemy is coming to vaporize our planet?"

"No… I don't know."

Their eyes met. Fear. Concern. But also determination.

"We'll stop them," Raena said. "I not sure how, but we'll find a way."

He gave a resolute nod. "Let's get ready."

— — —

The initial traces of spatial distortions had begun to form around Tararia by the time the *Conquest* dropped out from subspace. Two dozen other TSS warships were waiting for them, along with four times as many from the Guard.

Wil assessed the preliminary scan data with Saera. "Well, I guess this is it."

"Time to find out what we're really up against," Raena said from behind him. She stood hand-in-hand with her husband, both looking worn. They'd only arrived on board a few minutes prior and had yet to settle in.

Wil, Saera, and Jason occupied the middle seats in the Command Center. They'd telepathically linked with the ship to get a real-time feed of the scan data so they could monitor the situation. It was feeling eerily similar to the conditions around Alkeer before the attack.

"Come on, join us up here," Wil suggested, motioning to the two remaining seats on the central dais.

"Even though we're not TSS officers?" Raena asked.

"You graduated from the TSS. That's enough qualification for me."

They obliged, though they didn't seem entirely comfortable. Granted, the situation didn't lend itself to feeling at ease.

"Any movement around the other Rift?" Wil asked.

Saera brought up a galactic map with status indicators of various incidents as well as locations of ships. No red was showing near the Rift in the Outer Colonies.

All the same, Wil wanted to confirm with Michael. He initiated a vidcall in a window at the base of the front viewscreen.

"We're in position," Wil reported as soon as the call connected. "The spatial distortions are growing."

"We've been monitoring from here. What's the plan?" Michael asked.

"We're going to attempt to make contact. Still working out the 'how'."

"Okay. What about the fleet by the Rift?"

"Keep a quarter of the ships there. Have the rest disperse

to the most populated colony worlds nearby."

Michael nodded to acknowledge the order, thankfully not protesting to the unspoken subtext. Breaking up the fleet wouldn't offer protection to those worlds, but it would make the people feel better. That was all they could do.

"We'll be in touch," Wil said.

"Good luck."

The call ended.

"What is the plan?" Saera asked telepathically.

"We try to talk in terms they'll understand." Wil's greatest regret from the last encounter at Alkeer was that he'd waited until the aliens had fully emerged before they'd tried to make contact. Under normal circumstances, that would have been the right move. But these aliens were different. This situation was different. 'Wait and see' wasn't a viable approach.

They had no idea how to pronounce the alien language, or if it even could be spoken aloud, but they did have the tablet of the dialect in its written form.

"CACI," he addressed the onboard AI, "can you generate a written translation program for the alien languages on the Treaty Tablet?"

"The tablet contains enough language to translate with eighty-two percent accuracy," CACI replied.

"All right, ignore the Gatekeeper language for now, aside from using it as a reference point for translation accuracy. In the other unidentified language, please attempt to translate the following message from New Taran: 'We come in peace. We wish to speak with you. What is the name of your race?' End message."

"Processing."

A couple of seconds later, a text message in foreign characters appeared on the lower portion of the viewscreen.

"All right. Let's get their attention." Wil accessed the ship's controls using the bioelectronic interface. "Ready to see how this new imager works?"

"Yes, let's put a face to these guys," Jason replied.

"Entering momentary communications blackout."

Wil activated the imaging protocol, drawing enough simultaneous energy from the PEM to cut out all but life support systems. The front viewscreen refreshed as soon as the burst was complete.

"Well, they should know we're onto their game now," he said.

The resulting image from the transdimensional scan appeared onscreen, showing not just the spatial distortions from the regular sensor data but something stirring within them. The initial image resembled shadow art, as if a figure was standing behind an opaque screen. Only, the figure in question was ten times the size of the *Conquest* itself.

Everyone stared with dismay at the image.

"How big are these things?" Raena asked.

"Remains to be seen," Wil replied, not looking forward to the answer. "Let's see what else we can learn."

He took the text from the message CACI had translated and modified the next scan to be focused beams in the shape of the message characters. *No idea if this will work, but worth a shot.*

Saera looked over at him with surprise when she realized what he'd done. "Good thinking."

"It's a longshot, but you never know."

Wil let the same modified burst cycle two more times, and then he switched back to the full protocol. The distortions were continuing to grow. If anything, the movement was accelerating.

On the next flash, the forms finally began to emerge. Unfolding in stop-motion in the transdimensional images, he watched inky tendrils unfurl from the micro-rifts, invisible to the naked eye. One of the tendrils was heading directly for the *Conquest*.

"Orders, sir?" Rianne asked from the tactical station, visibly inching back in her seat.

"Hold steady," he instructed, hoping it was the right call. Not that they could do anything else but run. And that wasn't an option.

The tendril made contact. As it did, the visualization system in the Command Center shuddered. Text in the alien language appeared on the screen.

"Oh, my stars!" Raena breathed.

"CACI, can you translate?" Wil requested.

"Negative."

Saera scowled. "What is it?"

He smiled. "An answer: the name of their race. It wouldn't have a direct translation." *Now we're making progress.*

They stared at the string of nonsensical characters displayed on the screen.

"Uh... I don't think I can pronounce that," Jason said.

"Yeah, that's not going to work," Wil agreed. "We need another name."

Raena thought for a moment. "What about 'Erebus', the Greek god of darkness."

"I'm impressed you could pull that off the top of your head," Saera commented.

"I went through a mythology phase." She shrugged. "What do you think?"

"I can say it, so that one hundred percent gets my vote over," Jason frowned at the screen, "whatever *that* is."

Wil nodded. "Erebus, then."

Saera smiled. "We have contact. That's a good sign."

"CACI, translate and send the following message: 'We want to negotiate peace. Stop your invasion.'"

"Isn't that wording a little harsh?" Raena asked.

"Any other word than 'invasion' could have too many meanings. 'Advance', 'approach'. Need to keep it simple," he replied.

"Good point."

This time, no response came from the Erebus. The dark tendrils continued to spread from the micro-rifts in the image snapshots, crackling with ethereal energy.

"Okay, we need to let them know we're serious," Wil suggested.

Saera nodded her agreement.

"Charge weapons. Hold," Wil instructed the fleet over the comm. *Stars, I hope they don't take this as cause for an immediate assault.*

The status indicators next to ships on the vicinity map switched to 'offensive', ready to take action.

"CACI, translate another message. 'Withdraw, or we will attack'. Overlay on next image burst."

The computer complied. Several seconds later, a reply came. A single character this time.

Wil frowned. "CACI, translate."

The result on the screen chilled Wil to his core: 'No'.

Raena paled. "What do they mean, 'no'?"

"They've already decided our fate. They won't back down."

Everyone in the Command Center watched as the *Conquest* kept taking snapshots of the Erebus as the being continued to emerge through the spatial rift. Each image was more horrifying than the last. What began as small tears had widened to kilometers-wide chasms through which tendrils were extending. The tendrils branched and thickened as they reached out toward everything in the vicinity. The sickening freeze-frame of the imaging chronicled their advance, enveloping ships and then the planet itself.

We can't win. Everything across Wil's TSS career had tuned his senses to approach every engagement as a potential life-and-death battle. Weighing the different engagement strategies, the probable injuries and loss of life, the enemy casualties. He ran through every possible scenario with the information at his disposal, and there was no conceivable way for the TSS to end a combative engagement intact. At best, a fifth of the fleet might escape. The loss was unacceptable.

He gave the only order he could. "Stand down!"

The command was met with expressions of confusion and shock from the crew, but they complied without hesitation.

"*Why?*" Jason asked in his mind.

"*This is an unwinnable fight. Diplomacy is the only option. We must find a way.*"

He saw Jason doing his own mental exercise of how things could play out. Having not been through a war himself, the process was slower, but his determination turned to somber stoicism as he reached the same conclusion.

Raena stood, unwavering, at the middle of the Command Center. "We need to reason with them."

"No. Surrender." The statement didn't feel real, even as Wil said it. Everything they'd been through—the Bakzen War, the overthrow of the Priesthood, facing the Gatekeepers—it was all prelude to this moment. At this critical junction, he found himself helpless.

No, not helpless. We have power beyond physical might. He and his children had the most formidable Gifts of anyone in the Taran Empire, living or dead. They represented both the political and military strength of the Empire, condensed into three individuals at the center of their civilization. They were the first, and last, line of defense.

"We need to go to them on their terms," he told his children.

They instantly understood his meaning. They needed to approach the Erebus without their physical forms, in the same essence that the alien beings existed.

There was no need for Wil to spell out the danger of the act. The Erebus could strike while they were separated from their physical selves and sever the connection. Or they could attack the essence of their consciousness itself. But it was their only chance. That, or meet the same brutal end as those at the Alkeer Station.

"Okay," Jason agreed aloud, and Raena nodded her assent.

"What are you doing?" Ryan asked.

Raena looked at him, and there was the buzz of a telepathic exchange.

One look in Saera's direction, and she knew what Wil was planning. There was no protest in her eyes, only silent understanding.

"I love you always," he told her.

"I love you, too. Come back to me."

"I'll try."

Wil took the handholds at his command seat and linked with the ship, establishing it as an anchor for the astral projection to come. He sensed Raena and Jason establish their own links, and then they networked with each other. The joining was like grabbing hands to form a triad, only without the physical forms. Together, they left their physical selves behind and ventured into the void.

Normally, Wil found astral projection to be like a flight

through space. He could roam freely, the immensity of the universe stretching around him as a pristine starscape in every direction. In the span of moments, he could soar across the galaxy. The part of himself that could journey in such a way extended beyond the limitations of spacetime. There was the energy of more, out of sight, but he'd never extended himself further than exploring the rifts.

This time, as he began venturing outward with Jason and Raena, there was more than the black starscape spread out before him. Invisible to the sensory perception of those existing solely within the confines of spacetime, he now saw the physical form of the being enveloping the *Conquest* and the rest of the TSS fleet; however, the rest of its essence remained hidden in the higher dimensions, beyond the scope of Wil's understanding. Its tendrils wrapped around each ship and connected to a central form reaching down through the cosmic veil from its native dimension. The entity dwarfed Tararia— what portion he could see of it through his extrasensory perception—and that was only the part they could perceive. Energy crackled and swirled around it, as a tornado would break through a storm front, with a funnel extending to bring devastation on all it touched. Wil and his children were grains of sand on a beach compared to the star that was the being. And yet, they needed to get its attention and make it listen.

It was then he noticed that the being's form was pitted and deformed in places. The entity kept the tendrils in those areas wrapped around itself, as a hurt animal might cradle a wounded paw.

"Are you injured?" he asked. The question was a risk, but he didn't know what else to say. They were losing the discussion and needed to do something different to have any chance of staying in the conversation.

The Erebus' energy aura shuddered. Wil wasn't sure it was from surprise or anger, or perhaps a bit of both.

"You did this."

The force of the statement in Wil's mind struck like a physical blow. Never had he experienced a presence so powerful, so ancient. It enveloped him, as though he was not only hearing it in this present moment, but across time— becoming a part of his past, present, and future self. Like some forms of telepathy, he didn't receive the message as words, but rather sensed the meaning of the statement, which was then interpreted into narrative in his own mind. There was such sadness in the mental tone, only spoken as a faint whisper despite landing on his perception like a deafening shout. The anguish from the being flooded through him in the brief contact. In that moment, he knew that what the Erebus was doing wasn't an unprovoked attack, but an act of self-preservation.

It took all of his strength not to fall back from the immense force of the being pressing against his mind. He held firm, knowing this open dialogue might be his one chance. *"Please, explain what we did so that we may understand. We didn't mean to hurt or offend you."*

"We had a treaty."

"You made that agreement with our ancestors over one hundred thousand years ago."

The being's aura rippled again. *"Has that long passed for you?"*

"Yes. Our civilization has transformed since then, and we have few links to the past. We didn't know there was a treaty."

"That doesn't absolve you from punishment for what you did to our kind."

"Ignorance does not make us blameless, but it should not

automatically condemn us to the same fate as those who would act with malice."

The Erebus considered the position. *"Your kind has always wielded too much power for how little you know."*

"Teach us, so we may learn," Raena chimed in. Wil could feel her straining under the being's presence, but she was resolute.

Jason joined the front. *"You already destroyed one of our stations and killed thousands of innocents. For what? Killing those of us here and now won't address the underlying issue. Explain what we did wrong so we may share the message."*

"Your kind are spread throughout this galaxy?" the Erebus asked.

"Yes, on many planets," Wil confirmed.

The Erebus seemed to pull back for several moments. Were it a person sitting across a conference table from them, he would have taken the act to be a whispered side conversation with a colleague. *"We will speak with you,"* it said when its presence returned full force.

Tentative relief flooded through Wil. *"How?"*

"We will create a representative."

The Erebus vanished from Wil's mind.

He beckoned for Raena and Jason to follow him back to their bodies on the *Conquest.* The conversation was over, as far as he could tell. He had no idea what would come next.

CHAPTER 31

JASON TOOK A deep breath as he returned to his body. Every autonomic function was briefly at the forefront of his mind as his senses readjusted to the physical form.

"That was… wow," he said.

Next to him, his father sat with a distant gaze, like he was still looking beyond his physical self. "It was incredible."

'Terrifying' was more the word Jason would use to characterize the interaction.

"What happened?" Saera asked, eyes wide with anticipation.

"We made contact," Wil reported. "It said they would send a representative."

"Whatever in the stars *that* means." Jason focused on his breathing in a vain attempt to calm his racing heart.

"What did it look like?" Ryan asked.

Raena shook her head. "Words can't… it's a leviathan. No, that doesn't do it justice—it's encircling the planet."

He gaped at her. "What?"

"Things could get strange," Wil said. "Whatever happens,

don't take offensive action until I give an order. Pass it on to the fleet."

"Aye," Rianne acknowledged.

"Did they say *when* they would—"

Saera cut off as a shimmer of light sparked in front of them.

A figure began to materialize behind the two forward consoles. Rianne almost jumped out of her seat but managed to maintain her composure.

The being looked vaguely Taran but had a bluish glow and slight transparency, like it might be a projection rather than a living creature. Its agelessness reminded Jason of the Aesir, though the proportions of this being's features were distorted enough to give it an alien appearance—too small a nose and ears, extra-large eyes with no lashes, and thin lips. Its long, slender limbs were draped in a shimmering tunic.

"Hello," Wil greeted.

Jason was impressed he had been able to find his voice. His own heart was in his throat.

"You represent Tarans?" the Erebus representative asked.

"We do, yes."

An intense telepathic screech filled Jason's mind. Everyone in the Command Center winced and started to double over. The screech faded into the background as Jason's vision was replaced with darkness. He wasn't sure if he'd lost consciousness or if his senses had been blocked out.

There was a presence surrounding him in the dark—not unlike what he'd felt two weeks before during the flight lesson with his students. It walled him in, making him unable to move. The sheer power of it terrified him. He'd sensed this before, when he was reading Darin's memories. In those memories, though, the entity had been curious. Now, it was vengeful. The TSS' attempts to communicate had made the ancient beings angry. No, that wasn't quite the emotion radiating from the dark... it was pity. The being pitied the pathetic weakness of the Taran race and how foolish it was to think its people could wield the cosmic powers.

Then, as quickly as the darkness had come over him, Jason's vision returned. He was still standing in the middle of the Command Center facing the Erebus' avatar.

"This one has borne witness before." The representative focused on Jason. "Do you not yet understand what you have done?"

"No, I don't. But I do know that you killed someone I loved, and she'd done nothing to harm you. Did they suffer?"

"It was over quickly. We would offer you the same kindness."

Jason scoffed. "A merciful death? Great. Maybe rather than jumping to the stance that we all deserve to die because a handful of people out of trillions messed up, we can open a productive dialogue." When the Erebus representative didn't say anything, Jason continued. "We know we have broken the treaty, and that was wrong of us—regardless of the fact that we, personally, were unaware such an accord existed. We are very sorry for that. But we don't understand what happened in the past to necessitate the agreement. Why is the Gatekeeper's technology forbidden?"

The avatar stared at him, dumbfounded, as one regarded a dog failing to maneuver a long stick between fence posts. "You truly don't know?"

"You've seen inside my mind," Jason replied. "I am hiding nothing. We want to understand."

"Before two weeks ago, we didn't even know your kind *existed*. Please, educate us," Wil implored.

"The Gates harm us. They pull energy from our essence."

Jason reflected on what he had seen while astral projecting—how the being had seemed injured, with pits and holes across its form. So, they were wounds from the Gate tech, some ancient and others new. Even the old injuries hadn't healed completely after all those millennia since the previous war.

They can *be hurt.* The realization made the beings seem a little less godlike, but it didn't change the fact that harming the entities wasn't the same as killing them. They didn't even have Gates in their possession to mount an attack against the Erebus, nor would he want to. The Tarans hadn't meant harm.

His father seemed to be coming to the same realization next to him. *"The* aesen*. The Gates must draw on* aesen *itself as their power source, ripping holes through these beings in the process. It's barbaric."*

"None of us knew," Saera murmured in their minds, her anguish coming through the telepathic connection.

Jason's stomach turned over with the thought. *Those people casually used the Gates and didn't have a clue they were hurting these incredible beings. No wonder the Erebus think we're awful.*

"We are so sorry," Wil said aloud. "It was a mistake for our people to activate the Gate. An isolated incident, done without knowledge of the pain it would cause you."

"You repeatedly used the Gates."

Wil turned to Saera for confirmation.

She shook her head. *"According to our intel, a Taran traversed a Gate just one time,"* she said telepathically to everyone in the Command Center.

"Maybe they mean every time a Gate activated?" Jason suggested.

Wil returned his attention to the Erebus representative. "I

think there has been a misunderstanding about our role in all of this. Yes, we must admit that a rogue group within the Taran Empire used a Gate, but only successfully once. Any other activations were not by our hand."

"Multiple Gates were open for days, at great cost to us. That is why we have come."

Realization dawned on Jason. *"The Gatekeepers set us up,"* he said to the group. *"They opened those Gates not to destroy our planets, but because they knew it would anger these guys. They* wanted *them to come deal with us so they didn't have to."*

Saera paled. *"So, that whole standoff with the Gatekeepers before was just a ploy?"*

"It's sounding that way," Raena replied.

"Devious alien fokers," Wil grumbled.

Jason tuned out his mental curses as he desperately tried to think of what to suggest for how they could proceed. Diplomacy was Raena's wheelhouse, not his. Even she looked at a loss for what to say.

"We know the others as the 'Gatekeepers'," he said. *"They* were the ones to open those other Gates."

The representative stared at him with unblinking eyes, like looking into the depths of the cosmos itself. "We will deal with them. But it was the actions of Tarans that prompted their involvement."

"Yes, one group of Tarans used a Gate, and we'll own up to that," Jason continued. "But the punishment you intend to deal doesn't fit that singular crime. We aren't like you—we aren't eternal. It is unjust to condemn us for perpetrating the war tens of thousands of years ago. We had no part in it. Our race isn't the same as it was then."

Raena took a step forward. "Jason is right. To destroy us now is to close off any possibility of us becoming better. You gave our ancestors the chance to evolve by setting the treaty. Please, give us that same chance."

"Your ancestors evolved into *you*. And *you* broke their vows to uphold the treaty. Why should it be any different in another hundred thousand years?"

That's a fair question. Jason didn't have an answer. He looked at his parents and Raena.

"We can't offer any guarantees," Wil stated. "I wish we could, but you're right. Information is lost. People change. All that we can control is the here and now. The decision *you* have to make is if you can live for eternity knowing you wiped out trillions of people across a galaxy because a handful of individuals acted selfishly."

The representative stared at him, intense and unwavering. "Your race is in trouble, regardless of the sentence we levy."

"Perhaps. But we adapt and overcome. It is our way."

"That is to say, you would not go quietly."

Wil shook his head. "Not a chance. The question would become, how much hardship could we inflict on you before you destroyed all of us?"

"You no longer have the Gates."

"No, but we have a record of their energy field. You are aware of this ship and its capabilities. There are others like it, and now we know how to use them against you, if needed. The fact that we are still having this conversation suggests you might be open to taking an alternative approach."

"You are bold to threaten us."

"A proportional response to your threat to us. However, we don't seek violence. We stand at a crossroads, and there is a path of peace open to us."

"With all of you? You said it was a rogue faction that used the Gates."

"I can speak for the Taran leaders on that matter," Raena said. "We are striving to improve relations across the Taran worlds. Give us the opportunity to unite."

"Do you share things across these worlds?" the Erebus asked with a curious tilt of its head.

"Of course," Wil replied. "We are one Empire. We offer the tools for prosperity and protection to all."

The Erebus representative evaluated him. "We have considered your words and agree to a stay of your sentence, for now."

Jason breathed a sigh of relief but didn't relax. They still stood on a knife's edge. *That was too easy...*

"We now offer you this... gift," the representative stated.

A device materialized on the deck in front of them. It was no larger than his head and had smooth metal finishes around its cylindrical frame. At first glance, it reminded Jason of a power distribution cell.

Why in the stars are they *giving* us *a gift?* Jason also sensed confusion and wariness from the others in the Command Center.

"Thank you. But... what is it?" Raena asked.

"A power core, constructed using materials easy and plentiful to harvest."

Jason's jaw went slack. *"Do they know about MPS' issues?"* he questioned Raena and his parents.

"They may have surmised the need based on the experience with the Andvari," Saera suggested. *"Rather convenient. Suspiciously so."*

"I know. Something isn't right," Wil agreed. *"But we have to play along."*

"This is quite the gift," Raena said to the Erebus. "You honor us."

"Your previous power source was reaching the end of its supply, correct? This is what you need most across your civilization?"

"How do you know?" She glanced at Jason and their parents. *"This turnaround doesn't make any sense."*

"We have studied you and determined this need," the representative stated.

"I believe you were right about the Andvari *being an experiment, Jason,"* his father said. *"I don't know how they drew that conclusion from the events, but they did."*

"Maybe they studied the salvage contract?" Jason suggested.

"If that's the case, then they might have access to all of the classified information on this ship."

Jason tensed at the thought, but he wasn't about to back down now. *"Is this item even what they claim it is?"*

"If I may conduct an analysis?" Wil asked out loud.

"Yes," the Erebus consented.

Jason looked over the results of the scan in real-time on the viewscreen as the *Conquest*'s onboard AI evaluated the mysterious device. It was, in fact, everything that they needed to replace the current MPS power cores. *Too* perfectly, in fact.

"Why are you helping us?" Wil asked.

"As you stated, Tarans are widespread, and a war now would come at great cost to us. We look toward an alternative future."

Raena smiled sweetly, but Jason could tell it wasn't genuine. "That's very kind."

"To a truce, then?" the representative asked.

Wil and Raena exchanged glances.

"Yes. On behalf of the Taran Empire, we accept your offer of peace," Wil stated.

"Please, enjoy your gift. We look forward to continued

positive relations." The avatar vanished.

Jason blinked several times, staring at the place on the deck where the alien representative had stood. "What just happened?"

"We didn't die," his father replied flippantly. "I'm confused."

"That makes all of us." Saera walked over to the alleged power core and took a closer look. "Is it a bomb?"

"CACI would have picked up on a potential threat," Wil said. "I don't get it. They were ready to kill us all a few minutes ago."

Jason crossed his arms. "It doesn't track."

His father shook his head. "No, it doesn't. *No one* turns around opinion that quickly. They're playing us... I just don't know how yet."

"This *is* everything we need, though," Raena said. "Think about the kind of planetary defense upgrades we could make with a power generator this robust."

Saera nodded. "That's true. And it's not like we're in a position to reject this 'gift'—though I don't actually see it as one."

"I don't trust them one bit. But we don't have a better option at present," Wil stated.

Raena scowled. "I feel like we just sold our souls to alien overlords."

Wil picked up the device. "Not our souls. But maybe our freedom. That remains to be seen."

"Temporary peace is better than getting wiped out on the spot," Saera said. "This at least buys us time."

"I'll smooth over things with the High Council and public relations." Ryan sighed. "They're going to be angry."

Wil scoffed. "They should be thankful—and scared. It

always amazes me how you can save people's lives and they're upset you didn't do it 'their way'."

Jason crossed his arms. "I'm curious to find out what the Aesir think of all this."

"Yes, I'm sure Dahl will have something unhelpfully abstract but wise-sounding to say about the 'gift'. In any case, it's time we reevaluate the technology in the Archive." His father looked very tired.

Raena looked between her parents. "All right, so what do we do now?"

"We graciously accept the Erebus' offer of peace and move forward with our lives."

"They're probably setting us up!" Jason protested. *There's no way this 'gift' doesn't have strings attached.*

His father shrugged. "Right now, that doesn't matter. They can obliterate us with a flick of their wrist we can't even see. This is the smartest decision for our current circumstances."

Raena crossed her arms. "If we acquiesce now, that puts us at a disadvantage."

"It keeps us alive. We don't have much chance if our entire race is wiped out."

Jason shook his head. "They don't have that power. If they did, they would have done it already."

"Perhaps," Wil yielded. "Regardless, this is how we find out what they *can* do and what we can do to coexist—or resist them. Right now, fighting back is beyond even my power."

"You're not alone," Saera said.

"No, but we, the Taran race, are so insignificant." His father shook his head. "This entire universe is part of something so much bigger than any of us can comprehend. The actions we take are simply pulling threads that barely register on the greater cosmic web. Even so, that doesn't mean we should give up. The individual lives are no less important to the people *living* them just because they're a tiny speck in existence. If we can make even one person's life better through our work, then it's our duty to carry on, no matter the odds against us."

"This isn't over. Not even close," Raena said.

Jason let out a long breath. "What is it they say… we live to fight another day?"

Saera smiled. "And then the next."

CHAPTER 32

HAVING NEW ALIEN overlords would take time to get used to. Upon returning to TSS Headquarters, Jason was met by expressions of shock and relief. He tried to assure his students that everything would be okay. Truthfully, he had no idea what the future would bring. *Like Dad said, we're alive. That's what matters.*

Classes were put on hold for two days while the TSS figured out how to monitor the situation with the Erebus in conjunction with the Guard. The landscape of the Taran Empire was changing. Time would tell if it was for the better.

After another long strategy session, Jason was taking a break in his office to catch up on some administrative tasks. His desk lit up with an incoming communication, marked as being from an unidentified caller on Duronis. *I only know one person out that way.*

Sure enough, when he answered, Kira greeted him with a smile.

He smiled back. "Hey! I wasn't expecting to hear from you so soon."

"Well, I saw the news and wanted to check in. Congrats on preventing our horrible demise."

"Yeah, it's been a little crazy around here."

"I can imagine. Aliens, man! Why do they always get up in our business?"

He laughed. "I know, right? Stars, I'm still in a surreal haze about the whole thing!"

"One day at a time."

"So it goes. How are things on your end?"

Her expression turned solemn. "I'll jump to it: you were right to be worried about what's happening out here."

Jason's stomach knotted. "What have you learned?"

"Well, Lexi has offered some interesting insights when I've been able to get her alone to chat. The 'Alliance' she mentioned in her message to the TSS is part of a larger network known as 'the Coalition'. Very cryptic and unhelpful names, I know."

"How widespread is this network?"

"I don't know yet. But the Coalition seems to be made up of different organizations that have started merging and aligning their objectives. I get the impression it has some serious funding behind it—not sure if there could be dynastic ties, but it's possible. From what I can tell so far, this has been building for years."

"And, of course, they pick *now* to ramp up the efforts."

"A prime opportunity to direct people looking for leadership during uncertain times," Kira said. "I saw this kind of thing in my home system. It can turn ugly."

"Propaganda is a dangerous, slippery slope."

"It is. And the people behind this particular messaging are masters."

"What's going on at the ground level?"

"They're crafty," Kira continued. "The messaging is built

around the idea of local governance. Basically, 'trust our local people to know what's best for you, not the Taran leaders on faraway worlds'."

"I can see the appeal," Jason admitted.

"Oh, yeah, so can I. They have the pitch down to a fine art. I've seen a number of variations for different socioeconomic groups in the population here, and the tweaks speak to the needs of each group."

"I'm guessing there's a catch—beyond the obvious issue of wondering whether people really *would* be better off without the oversight of the Central Worlds."

"To your latter point, let me first say that I wouldn't be in the Guard if I didn't believe in the Taran Empire. Just look at what it was like in my home system. I appreciate that the original settlers of the Elvar Trinary tried to go it alone, but there are huge issues on a societal level when a culture is insular. People end up having to take jobs that are needed rather than based on what they want to do with their lives, so morale plummets and social class becomes a serious issue.

"All of that turned around when Elvar rejoined the rest of the Empire. There were instantly opportunities for people unlike anything they'd had before in their lives. Now, only a few years later, the economy and culture are thriving. People are happy because they have *choices*.

"So, while the message of this Coalition to 'think locally' sounds good, there are a few tells that have my gut screaming at me that there's going to be trouble. Namely, that the community representatives were all assigned by the Coalition. The pretense of 'locality' is to get people on board, but it's an obvious means of building a coordinated network between the worlds so leaders can make moves on an interstellar scale. With citizens trusting their community's leader to look out for them, most won't look at the bigger picture."

Jason nodded. "The question is, then, what might the Coalition be trying to achieve by building up this support?"

"I'm not sure, but I can guarantee you that, based on this power structure, they want to be sneaky about it. It's a perfect setup: make people feel valued by convincing them that their individual voices and their community matter so that they begin focusing on local rather than on global or interstellar issues. With everyone fixed on what's right in front of them, they will be far less likely to notice the larger changes outside their immediate sphere. The Coalition could accomplish a lot before anyone notices."

"Well, we've taken notice," Jason said. "Though I'm not sure what to do."

"I have an idea on that front," Kira replied. "I've started to get chummy with that young woman who sent in the tip—Lexi. Interestingly, she's Gifted but doesn't seem to want anyone to know."

"Is she working an angle of her own?"

"I'm not sure yet, beyond wanting to find her friend. But she's entrenched, and she's invited me to a special meeting. I think it might be a sort of vetting session for new recruits into the Coalition ranks. Works out well, since the people she reports to are pissed about their big plans getting messed up—though they don't know it was Lexi that thwarted the deal. Nonetheless, bringing in new recruits, especially a geneticist, will score her points and help her climb the ranks."

"Sounds like a great 'in'."

She nodded. "But, man, there are all sorts of red flags about the Coalition. Beyond their governance agenda and their public call for science specialists, they're also actively recruiting people with military and tactical experience."

"Great." Jason sighed.

"Still not sure what they need with a geneticist, but Leon will find out whatever he can."

"Why does my mind immediately go to a genetically keyed bioweapon?"

"Funny you say that, I thought the same thing." Kira smiled in spite of the grim proposition.

"Fantastic."

"But the bit of good news is that Leon is awesome at his work and is equally curious to find out what these smarmy dudes are up to." She held up her hand. "And before you ask, he's a civilian and can take whatever job he wants. No need to worry about sending him into harm's way. He knows the risks and is on board."

"We appreciate both of your willingness to get your hands dirty. We need answers."

"And I will do my best to get them. I hate this foking shite—people taking advantage of others for their own megalomaniacal power grabs. There are some smart, twisted people behind this, I'm sure of it."

"If anyone can get inside without them suspecting, I know it's you. Just be careful."

"I will. Besides, you know I can take care of myself."

"I do, which is why I endorsed you for this assignment."

She took a long breath. "This could take a while. I'll need to get them to trust me before I expect I'll have direct access to anyone with knowledge of the master plan."

"I figured as much. I think we're going to be in 'wait and see' mode around here when it comes to the Erebus, too."

"Our doom closing in from both sides. Fun times, right?"

"The best."

She laughed. "I'll keep doing what I'm doing until I hear

otherwise. Tell Command I'm their girl to get shite done."

"Stay safe."

"In the meantime, good luck with your alien invasion thing."

"We're calling it a 'compulsory cultural exchange'."

She tilted her head and her nose wrinkled. "Seriously?"

He chuckled. "No. Or not yet, anyway. We'll see how the media spins it."

"This is going to be a wild ride."

—   —   —

Echoes of the Erebus' presence kept catching Raena off-guard. Since the contact, she hadn't broken completely free from it—or that's what it felt like. More likely, it was so profound that it had changed her, in the way a person held onto any great joy or trauma.

She tried to focus on the meeting with her father and Ryan about the rollout of the new power system. With MPS still not being forthcoming in their communications, they'd decided that the best test case for the power cores would be in a new line of ships through DGE. The plan was to test them out with non-sentient AI operators to make sure they were safe and reliable before getting any people involved.

"We'll get on it as soon as possible," Ryan agreed as they wrapped up the discussion of the logistical details for the prototype manufacturing.

"Thank you again for stepping in," Wil said. "I'll feel a lot better about rolling out this tech on a larger scale once I know it's been vetted."

"Where does this leave MPS and Monsari?" Raena asked.

He shrugged. "Remains to be seen. It may be difficult to

hold onto their seat on the High Council if the corporation becomes irrelevant. Once the tech is vetted, we can approach them about scaling the manufacturing of this new power core."

"I'd be freaking out if I were them," Ryan said.

"I'm sure they are." Raena knew they would have to keep a close eye on the Monsari Dynasty. They were rich and powerful, but those resources would dry up if they were no longer able to produce. Desperate people would do anything to survive.

Ryan spread his hands on the table. "At least things have calmed down around Duronis. The arrival of the Erebus has proved to be a wonderful distraction."

Raena cracked a smile. "Reminding people how they aren't so different as soon as aliens are involved—not all that dissimilar from the argument we made about Earth."

"There will be a lot more distraction and disruption to come, I'm sure," Wil said.

"I'll take the breather for now. These last couple of weeks…" Ryan released a long breath as he leaned back in his chair, shaking his head.

"Enjoy the respite. It's well-earned."

"Don't worry, we know it's temporary. We're at the center of this thing, whether we like it or not," Raena said.

Her father gave her a compassionate nod. "I know it was difficult, but it's good you were there to see the Erebus for yourself. I wouldn't wish that danger on anyone, especially you, but it's for the best that someone on the political side talked to them directly."

She knew the meaning behind the words. *Someone needed to see that acquiescing was the only option. We can't fight them, so we need to do whatever they tell us if we want to live.* She'd use much more elegant phrasing when communicating that point to others, but that was the heart of it. It wouldn't be long before she'd need to sell the message, so she realized that finding the right words was a task best undertaken sooner than later.

"Grandpa and Grandma understand," she said.

"Yes, but not like you. It may sometimes be difficult to make your voice heard, but you must be insistent. What they are giving us looks like a gift, but they must have other motives."

Ryan nodded. "I'll do what I can to keep things in perspective on the High Council."

"And I'm working to foster a collaborative relationship with the Guard. We still need to come up with the right branding for it, though," Wil said. "It's critical we present a unified front."

"That's it!" Raena exclaimed.

"Hmm?"

"A little on the nose, but it works. The Taran Unified Front. No, Force. Taran United Force."

Wil smiled. "It's simple, but I love it."

Raena grinned. "And it abbreviates to TUF. It's perfect! 'Taran tough'."

"Putting it like that means you're saying Taran twice," Ryan pointed out.

"Shh, don't over-think it." She patted his arm.

"Thank you, Raena. I'll work with the Guard's public relations team to craft the messaging."

"I can give a heads up to the High Council, if you'd like," Ryan offered.

"That would be wonderful. Thank you both."

"Try to get a break yourself, Dad. Maybe you and Mom can come visit with Jason soon. *No* work."

He smiled. "I'll see what we can do. In the meantime, take care of each other. None of the problems have gone away—just pushed to the background."

Raena took her husband's hand. "Don't worry about us. No matter what comes, we'll face it together."

—   —   —

Jason couldn't help looking at the stars differently during the flight lesson with his students. *The Erebus are out there. What made them go from wanting to destroy us to giving us such a valuable gift?*

He didn't trust them. He knew his parents didn't, either, but they were backed into a corner and everyone knew it. The Erebus knew it.

They could have given us anything and we would've had to agree. It has to be a setup. But for what?

They'd run the power core through every conceivable test, and it had passed. Safety. Reliability. Power output. The answer to all of their hopes and dreams about what could take the civilization to the next level. Yet, something was wrong. He could feel it. The darkness on the horizon was no longer in the distance. It was surrounding them.

He tried to keep the ominous feeling at bay while he doled out instructions to his students. Worrying them wouldn't help matters, and it didn't improve his own state of mind. They were living in a new reality now and he'd need to get used to it.

Still, there was anger and resentment simmering in the back of his mind. The Erebus had killed thousands of people— and a person he loved—for nothing. Why had they opened with an attack rather than offering the 'gift'? He would work with them, but he couldn't forgive them. They'd taken something too precious to get off the hook that easily.

He forced the emotion back, keeping it on reserve. Now was not the time for vengeance. But, at such a time when the Erebus revealed their true intentions, and he had no doubt they would, he would unlock that fury and use it against them.

Jason looked out at the stars, imagining seeing through the dimensional veil to wherever it was the Erebus called their home. *Wrong us again, and you will pay.*

The resolution eased some of the tension he'd been carrying around since the incident. His time to face them would come. Until then, he needed to focus on helping those around him become the best TSS officers they could be.

—

After the flight lesson, he went to his father's office for a check-in. He'd alerted him about hearing from Kira and needed to give his report.

Wil took in the news without giving an outward expression of his feelings on the matter. Only once Jason had finished did he speak. "I'm glad you have a good rapport with her. She's the kind of eyes we need on this."

"The Alliance is just one part, though. What do we do about the Coalition as a whole?" Jason asked.

"As much as I trust your faith in Kira, I'd really like to have one of our own people monitoring the situation from another angle."

"You said before that an Agent—"

"Yes, an Agent would stand out too much. But I've talked with Michael, and we have a candidate. A null in Militia, willing to go deep undercover; as a null, no one will be able to read his mind, so it's the safest option to keep his mission under wraps in the event he comes across a telepath. We'd like him to get close with one of the other organizations we believe is pushing the Coalition behind the scenes."

"Should I let Kira know?"

His father shook his head. "Nothing can get out about our inside man. We've made it clear that he'll be on his own until he's ready for extraction. He knows the risks."

"All right." Jason leaned back into the chair. *Have the odds ever been more against us?*

"It's only going to get more difficult from here, Jason."

He wasn't sure if his father had gleaned the thoughts from the surface of his mind or if his expression was enough. "I know that you've been telling me from the first day I joined the TSS that we train to be ready for anything, but this…"

"Even I didn't see this coming. Well, not *exactly* this."

"A civil war is brewing, too, isn't it?"

"It's looking inevitable, unless this business with the Erebus can somehow bring us together."

"There isn't a choice. I hope people see that."

"At least the TSS and the Guard are united for the first time ever. We're as well-positioned as we can hope to be."

"I'm sure not everyone in the Guard is happy about that."

"They don't need to be. Admiral Mathaen and I are in alignment, and that's the most important thing. We'll be announcing the Taran United Force soon."

"The TUF?" Jason considered it. "A little cheesy, but it works."

"We thought so, too."

"This was Raena's doing, wasn't it?"

"The name, absolutely. The idea was Admiral Mathaen's."

Jason's eye's widened. "Oh, really?"

"I'm glad he's driving the partnership forward and it's not

all on me. It remains to be seen *how* committed he is, but we're moving in the right direction."

"What's the plan for approaching the Erebus now that the Guard is on board?"

"Nothing. We focus on quelling the civil unrest and keeping our people safe."

"We're not fighting back? So that's it, we're giving up?"

Wil shook his head. "No, we didn't achieve freedom from our past would-be oppressors only to have our fate controlled by new overlords."

"Then what's the plan?"

"We wait and observe. It's possible they do have benevolent intentions."

"Hah! Right. From what I've seen, we're just pawns to be manipulated. Lesser beings."

"Yes, it's overly optimistic to think all our indiscretions are forgiven. But, as much as I'd like to stop this invasion now, we have no way to stand up to them at present. So, we must gather information. There's an answer, somewhere, about how we can regain our independence, whether it be through might or wit. Their power is immense, but like us, they have limitations and weaknesses; I'm certain of it."

Jason took a deep breath. "I hope you're right."

"For now, our people aren't in immediate danger. Whatever the Erebus are up to, it's a long game."

"I don't look forward to finding out what it is."

"All part of the process."

"I hope I can eventually be as calm about this as you are."

"It's all age and experience, Jason. Just a matter of perspective."

"I'll watch and learn."

Wil smiled. "You're well on your way."

"Thanks." He did feel he was on the right path. And, more importantly, he knew he was with the right people to help him grow. *The Erebus are going to test us all.*

His father was quiet for a while. "I know it does seem rather bleak right now, but there's something critical you need to believe and remind yourself, especially in the moments when the task at hand seems insurmountable."

"What's that?"

"Whenever the Erebus do make their move, we'll be ready to show them the Taran Empire is here to stay."

THE STORY CONTINUES *EMPIRE UPRISING...*

Ancient secrets may hold the key ...

In the months following formal contact with the Erebus, there's been an unexpected peace. However, that all changes when a series of attacks reveals the Coalition's devious plans for the Outer Colonies.

With the Erebus poised for another assault and rumors that the Coalition is developing an experimental bioweapon, the TSS needs a new defense of their own. The power core 'gift' from the Erebus has opened up new possibilities, but the ancient technology hidden on Earth could be the real game-changer they desperately need.

Unfortunately, the TSS soon learns that the Coalition's influence runs deeper than anyone imagined. Jason and his family are in not only a fight for their lives, but for the very future of the Taran civilization.

ADDITIONAL READING

Cadicle Space Opera Series by A.K. DuBoff
Book 1: Rumors of War (Vol. 1-3)
Book 2: Web of Truth (Vol. 4)
Book 3: Crossroads of Fate (Vol. 5)
Book 4: Path of Justice (Vol. 6)
Book 5: Scions of Change (Vol. 7)

Mindspace Series by A.K. DuBoff
Book 1: Infiltration
Book 2: Conspiracy
Book 3: Offensive
Book 4: Endgame

Verity Chronicles by T.S. Valmond & A.K. DuBoff
Book 1: Exile
Book 2: Divided Loyalties
Book 3: On the Run

Shadowed Space Series by Lucinda Pebre & A.K. DuBoff
Book 1: Shadow Behind the Stars
Book 2: Shadow Rising
Book 3: Shadow Beyond the Reach

In Darkness Dwells by James Fox & A.K. DuBoff

AUTHORS' NOTES

Thank you for reading *Empire Reborn*! Wow, it's great to be back with these characters in the Cadicle Universe. Though this may be your introduction to this story world, it's been a part of my life for more than two decades.

I began building out this universe as a kid—around the time I was ten or eleven years old. The original series was all about Wil's story as the titled 'Cadicle' figure, but I always intended for this universe to be much bigger than that. Every tale in the Cadicle Universe has interpersonal relationships at its core, so characters grow and change and start families of their own. It's only natural that the story now continue with the next generation taking the lead and coming into their own.

In the event you have *not* read anything else in the Cadicle Universe, you may be wondering about how this book connects to others. So, in short:

- To read about the Bakzen War and fall of the Priesthood, check out the original Cadicle series.

- To read about the Gatekeepers incident, read the Verity Chronicles co-authored with T.S. Valmond.

- To find out how Kira got her special nanotech, read the Mindspace series.

- To learn about what happened to the *Andvari* from their point of view, read *In Darkness Dwells* co-authored with James Fox (coming in Q2 2021).

- To learn about what else the Coalition is up to behind the scenes, read the Shadowed Space series with

Lucinda Pebre (this book will connect more with later volumes in the Taran Empire Saga).

Needless to say, *Empire Reborn* had a lot of work to do as a single book—pulling together so many side storylines while (hopefully) also being readable as a universe entry point *and* as a sequel series. No matter what you have read or haven't in the broader universe, I hope you enjoyed this novel!

One of the things I have enjoyed most about the universe is how it's continued to evolve and expand as new authors come on board and readers get more involved. The story is far from over, and I look forward to continuing the journey with you!

Like many people, my 2020 was filled with lots of disruption. I would have had this book to you a year sooner if things had gone differently, but I ultimately landed where I feel I'm meant to be at this point in my life. I owe all of that to James Fox and his family for taking me and my husband in when we were stranded across an ocean from our home after the borders closed for the lockdowns. They gave us refuge, but we ended up calling their family ranch our new home. We'd never met in person before, and I'm still floored by their generosity. The sense of community on the ranch has been so inspiring, and this book wouldn't be the same without that experience. James is an incredible writer, and I'm proud to call him a colleague and a close friend.

Just as well, none of my books would be what they are without my amazing support team behind the scenes. I am once again indebted to my amazing beta readers for their honest feedback and patience as I pester them with questions. Sincere thanks to John Ashmore, Doug Burnham, Kaj Fleischmann, Charles Obert, SJ Schauer, Steve DeBacker, Troy

Mullens, Gil Forbes, Jim Dean, Jeanette Bedard, Louise Bishop, Liz Singleton, David Frydrych, Heather Lewis, Leo Roars, Andrea Fornero, Kurt Schulenburg, Eric Haneberg, Kevin McLaughlin, Lisa Richman, and Brian Busby.

A huge thank-you to my incredible proofreaders, Diane L. Smith, Angel LaVey, and others, who always manage to see things everyone else has missed. Thank you for once again lending me your eagle eyes to help add the final polish!

I'd also like to acknowledge my family for their ongoing support. My parents, Randy and Deborah, for helping me become the person I am today; they have been so supportive of me over the years, and I don't think I would have ever become a writer without their encouragement. Likewise, my husband, Nick, is my biggest cheerleader, and he always makes me feel loved and supported even when I'm doubting myself. I am so fortunate to have a family who always has my back!

Thank you again for reading this first novel in the Taran Empire Saga, and I hope you explore the rest of the Cadicle Universe while you wait for Book 2. Until next time, happy reading!

GLOSSARY

Timeline of Key Events

All dates are adjusted for the standard Earth calendar

~98,000 BC - Ancient war and signing of the peace treaty between Tarans, the Gatekeepers, and the transdimensional aliens

AD ~50 - Priesthood's rise to power as a governing entity on Tararia

AD ~1000 - Taran Revolution period, following the split of the Priesthood when the Aesir left Tararia

AD 1587 - First skirmishes of the Bakzen War

AD 2016 - Invention of the Independent Jump Drive

AD 2025 - Official end of the Bakzen War; destruction of the Bakzen homeworld

AD 2050 - Fall of the Priesthood; transition of Dynasty corporations into public entities

AD 2054 - Reactivation of Gatekeeper tech

AD 2055 - Reopening of the rift/tear and reappearance of the transdimensional aliens

Key Terms

Aesir *(Ay-seer)* - A group of Tarans who broke away from the Empire around 1000 AD (Earth years) to engage in metaphysical pursuits, such as reading cosmic energy patterns. The founders of the Aesir were all former members of the Priesthood and possess strong telepathic and telekinetic abilities. The Aesir are isolationist and long-lived, possessing advanced technology lost to the rest of the Empire during the Priesthood's corrupt reign.

Agent - A class of officer within the TSS reserved for those with telekinetic and telepathic gifts. There are three levels of Agent based on level of ability: Primus, Sacon and Trion.

Ateron *(at-er-on)* - An element that oscillates between normal space and subspace, facilitating high levels of telekinetic energy transfer.

Baellas *(bAy-las)* - A corporation run by the Baellas Dynasty, producing housewares, clothing, furniture, and other textiles for use across the Taran civilization. Additional specialty lines managed by other smaller corporations are licensed to Baellas for distribution.

Bakzen *(Bak-zen)* - A militaristic race that lived beyond the Outer Colonies. All Bakzen were clones and possesses varying levels of telekinetic capabilities.

Bakzen War - A centuries-long conflict waged primarily in a secret spatial rift, with the TSS fighting on behalf of the Taran civilization.

Cadicle *(Kad-i-kl)* - The definition of individual perfection in the Priesthood's founding ideology, with the emergence of the Cadicle heralding the start to the next stage of evolution for the Taran race.

Course Rank (CR) - The official measurement of an Agent's ability level, taken at the end of their training immediately before graduation from Junior Agent to Agent. The Course Rank Test is a multi-phase examination, including direct focusing of telekinetic energy into a testing sphere. The magnitude of energy focused during the exercise is the primary factor dictating the Agent's CR.

Dainetris Dynasty *(Dayn-ee-tris)* – One of the seven High Dynasties, the Dainetris Dynasty was considered lost for nearly two hundred years. After members of the family spoke out against the Priesthood's corruption, the Priesthood destroyed the family and buried the city that served as their seat of power. The Dynasty's status was restored in 2050, and a new seat of power was established on the Priesthood's former administrative island, renamed Morningstar Isle after the flower in the Dainetris crest.

Earth - A planet occupied by humans, a divergent race of Tarans. Considered a "lost colony," Earth is not recognized as part of the Taran government.

Gatekeepers - An ancient alien race with advanced portal tech. Little is known about their native form beyond that they are higher-dimensional beings and create hybrid versions of themselves to interact with spacetime reality, including Taran hybrid vessels.

Generation Cycle - Also known as the Twelve Generation Cycle. A genetic mutation in Tarans where seven generations will express no telepathic or telekinetic abilities, followed by five with those Gifts—the strongest expression being 10th Generation. It is believed that the genetic line descending from the Cadicle may hold the key to developing a genetic patch to fix the mutation. The Aesir left the Empire before the dissemination of the gene therapy that resulted in the Generation Cycle, so they do not suffer from the mutation; they do not intermingle with other Tarans for this reason.

Gifts – The colloquial term used to describe a variety of telepathic and telekinetic abilities, ranging from simple mind-reading, to object levitation, to manipulating energy fields on small or large scales. These Gifts typically emerge between the age of sixteen to eighteen. Before the Priesthood's fall, all but telepathy were illegal; since then, telekinesis has been legalized for non-violent applications. The TSS remains the foremost training institution for those with abilities.

High Commander - The officer responsible for the administration of the TSS. Always an Agent from the Primus class.

High Dynasties - Seven families on Tararia that control the corporations critical to the functioning of Taran society. Each have a designated Region on Tararia, which is the seat of their power. The Dynasties in aggregate form A High Council oligarchical government for the Taran Empire.

Independent Jump Drive - A jump drive that does not rely on the SiNavTech beacon network for navigation, instead using a mathematical formula to calculate jump positions through normal space and the Rift.

Initiate - The second stage of the TSS training program for Agents. A trainee will typically remain at the Initiate stage for two or three years.

Jump Drive - The engine system for travel through subspace. Conventional jump drives require an interface with the SiNavTech navigation system and subspace navigation beacons.

Junior Agent - The third stage of the TSS training program for Agents. A trainee will typically remain at the Junior Agent stage for three to five years.

Lead Agent - The highest-ranking Agent and second-in-command to the High Commander. The Lead Agent is responsible for overseeing the Agent training program and frequently serves as a liaison for TSS business with Taran colonies.

Lower Dynasties - There are 247 recognized Lower Dynasties in Taran society. Many of these families have a presence on Tararia, but some are residents of the other inner colonies.

Makaris Corp *(Mak-ayr-is)* - A corporation run by the Makaris High Dynasty responsible for the distribution of food, water filters, and other necessary supplies to Taran colonies without diverse natural resources.

Monsari Power Solutions (MPS) *(Mon-sayr-ee)* - A corporation run by the Monsari Dynasty, responsible for power generation systems for the Taran worlds, including geothermal generators, portable generators, and reactors to power spacecraft. Their foremost product are the Perpetual Energy Modules (PEMs) that function in the most critical systems.

Rift - A habitable pocket between normal space and subspace. The largest rift—specifically known as *the* Rift—is located at the site of the former Bakzen homeworld, a wound left by the destruction of the planet at the end of the Bakzen War. It is thought to be a place where the veil between dimensions is thinner.

Sacon *(Sak-on)* - The middle tier of TSS Agents. Typically, Sacon Agents will score a CR between 6 and 7.9.

Sietinen Dynasty *(sIgh-tin-en)* - High Dynasty overseeing the Third Region of Tararia, responsible for the SiNavTech navigation network. Considered the most influential of the Taran dynasties due to the family's ties to the TSS and responsibility for the Empire's transportation infrastructure.

SiNavTech - A corporation run by the Sietinen High Dynasty, which controls and maintains the subspace navigation network used by Taran civilians and the TSS.

Spatial Dislocation - The act of physically transitioning from normal space to the brink of subspace, either by means of a jump drive or telekinetic abilities.

TalEx - A corporation run by the Talsari Dynasty, managing mining operations and ore processing across Taran territories.

Tarans *(tayr-ans)* - The general term for all individuals with genetic relation to Tararian ancestry. Several divergent races are recognized by their planet or system. Humans are of Taran descent.

Tararia *(Tayr-ayr-ee-a)* - The home planet for the Taran race and seat of the central government.

Tararian *(Tayr-ayr-ee-an)* - Someone from or residing on the planet Tararia.

Tararian Selective Service (TSS) - A quasi-military organization with two divisions: (1) Agent Class, and (2) Militia Class. Agents possess telekinetic and telepathic abilities; the TSS is the only place where individuals with such gifts can gain official training. The Militia class offers a formal training program for those without telekinetic abilities, providing tactical and administrative support to Agents. TSS Headquarters is located inside the moon of the planet Earth. Additional Militia training facilities are located throughout the Taran worlds and there are numerous TSS bases throughout the Empire. Since the end of the Bakzen War, the TSS has also engaged in more academic pursuits so many Agents can pursue careers related to the sciences rather than being 'soldiers'.

Trainee - The generic term for a student of the TSS, and also the term for first-year Agent students (when capitalized Trainee). Students are not fully "initiated" into the TSS until their second year.

Trion *(Try-on)* - The lowest tier of TSS Agents. Typically, Trion Agents will score a CR below 5.9.

Priesthood of the Cadicle - The institution formerly

responsible for oversight of all governmental affairs and the flow of information throughout the Taran colonies. During its rule until 2050 AD, the Priesthood had jurisdiction over even the High Dynasties and provided a tiebreaking vote on new initiatives. The organization perpetrated many secret experimentations on Taran citizens and was voted out of power by the High Council. All known associates have been arrested or were killed in the fall.

Primus *(Pree-mus)* - The highest of three Agent classes within the TSS, reserved for those with the strongest telekinetic abilities. Typically, Primus Agents will score a CR above 8.

Primus Elite - A special classification of Agent above Primus signifying an exceptional level of ability.

Vaenetri Dynasty *(Vayn-E-tree)* - High Dynasty overseeing the First Region of Tararia. The family operates VComm, a corporation specializing in telecommunications.

VComm - A telecommunications corporation owned and operated by the Vaenetri Dynasty.

ABOUT THE AUTHOR

A.K. (Amy) DuBoff has always loved science fiction in all its forms—books, movies, shows, and games. If it involves outer space, even better! She is a Nebula Award finalist and *USA Today* bestselling author most known for her Cadicle Universe, but she's also written a variety of space fantasy and comedic sci-fi. Now a full-time author, Amy can frequently be found traveling the world. When she's not writing, she enjoys wine tasting, binge-watching TV series, and playing epic strategy board games.

www.amyduboff.com

Made in United States
Troutdale, OR
08/31/2025

34146160R00256